THE GREATEST
# CAT STORIES
EVER TOLD

# THE GREATEST
# CAT STORIES
## EVER TOLD

## 30 INCREDIBLE TALES BY
Mark Twain, Rudyard Kipling, Dorothy L. Sayers, and many others

### EDITED AND WITH AN INTRODUCTION BY
### CHARLES ELLIOTT

GRAMERCY BOOKS
NEW YORK

This 2004 edition is published by Gramercy Books, an imprint of Random House Value Publishing, a division of Random House, Inc., New York, by arrangement with The Lyons Press.

Gramercy is a registered trademark and the colophon is a trademark of Random House, Inc.

Pages 286-288 constitute an extension of this copyright page.

Random House
New York • Toronto • London • Sydney • Auckland
www.randomhouse.com

Printed and bound in the United States

Library of Congress Cataloging-in-Publication Data

The greatest cat stories ever told / edited and with an introduction by Charles Elliott.
    p. cm.
  Originally published: Guilford, Conn. : Lyons Press, c2001.
  ISBN 0-517-22287-6
  1. Cats—Fiction. I. Elliott, Charles, 1930-

PN6120.95.C3G74 2004
808.83'1083629752—dc22

2003049409

10 9 8 7 6 5 4 3 2 1

# Contents

# Introduction

I T IS NECESSARY to approach collecting cat stories in a severely critical mood. The fact is, there are a great many stories available. Next to keeping cats around the house, people apparently enjoy writing about them, and affectionate accounts of dear little pussy tend to run to type. On the other hand, those great writers who have chosen to deal with cats—or at least include cats in their casts of characters—frequently evince less interest in the animals themselves than in the way they affect the human beings around them. This is perhaps wise.

I find that there have been a large number of extremely specialized cat-story collections: detective stories involving cats, science fiction cats, cat joke books, books restricted to Siamese or Persian cats, books of cat adventures. I can well imagine a book of cat surgery, or cat cookbooks (active or passive). Frankly, I wouldn't want to get anywhere near them. While certain themes do constantly crop up in writings about cats—their essential mystery or unearthliness, for example—it may be best not to focus too narrowly. There are, after all, plenty of other things in the world to care about.

So it is with a certain deference that I offer this collection of cat stories. They range from the reasonably esoteric to the homely, from familiar tales to stories that I hope will come as a surprise. Some, though frequently anthologized, are too good to be omitted, while others will not have not been seen in anthologies before (at least they weren't by me). And whether it is entirely true to say that these are the greatest cat stories ever told—"greatest" is a slippery term at best—I can say in all confidence that every one has plenty to recommend it. Exactly what could be said, if you like, about a cat.

# Lillian

BY DAMON RUNYON

I N THE ESTIMATION of his biographer Jimmy Breslin, Damon Runyon (1880–1936) invented Broadway. Hyperbole or not, it's certain that nobody ever saw the place and wrote about it the way he did. With its crew of guys and dolls, amiable drunks and shysters, hoods and gamblers, Runyon's Broadway is now an authentic part of American folklore, and Runyon himself an unlikely ornament to the body of American literature. Not bad for a regular newspaperman.

 "Lillian" first appeared in 1938 in a collection called *Furthermore*. It could be argued that the eponymous heroine lacks perfect reality—Runyon was probably not what you would call a cat person—but there's no doubt that this proto-leopard ("blacker than a yard up a chimney," as the author put it) had some memorable talents. In any case, New York cats *are* different.

   ★  ★  ★  ★  ★

WHAT I ALWAYS SAY is that Wilbur Willard is nothing but a very lucky guy, because what is it but luck that has him teetering along Forty-ninth Street one
cold snowy morning when Lillian is mer-owing around the sidewalk looking
for her mamma?

And what is it but luck that has Wilbur Willard all mulled up to a million, what with him having been sitting out a few glasses of Scotch with a
friend by the name of Haggerty in an apartment over in Fifty-ninth Street?
Because if Wilbur Willard is not mulled up he will see Lillian is nothing but a
little black cat, and give her plenty of room, for everybody knows that black
cats are terribly bad luck, even when they are only kittens.

But being mulled up like I tell you, things look very different to
Wilbur Willard, and he does not see Lillian as a little black kitten scrabbling
around in the snow. He sees a beautiful leopard; because a copper by the name
of O'Hara, who is walking past about then, and who knows Wilbur Willard,
hears him say:

"Oh, you beautiful leopard!"

The copper takes a quick peek himself, because he does not wish any
leopards running around his beat, it being against the law, but all he sees, as he
tells me afterwards, is this rumpot ham, Wilbur Willard, picking up a scrawny
little black kitten and shoving it in his overcoat pocket, and he also hears
Wilbur say:

"Your name is Lillian."

Then Wilbur teeters on up to his room on the top floor of an old
fleabag in Eighth Avenue that is called the Hotel de Brussels, where he lives
quite a while, because the management does not mind actors, the management
of the Hotel de Brussels being very broadminded, indeed.

There is some complaint this same morning from one of Wilbur's
neighbours, an old burlesque doll by the name of Minnie Madigan, who is not
working since Abraham Lincoln is assassinated, because she hears Wilbur going
on in his room about a beautiful leopard, and calls up the clerk to say that a
hotel which allows wild animals is not respectable. But the clerk looks in on
Wilbur and finds him playing with nothing but a harmless-looking little black
kitten, and nothing comes of the old doll's grouse, especially as nobody ever
claims the Hotel de Brussels is respectable anyway, or at least not much.

Of course when Wilbur comes out from under the ether next afternoon he can see Lillian is not a leopard, and in fact Wilbur is quite astonished
to find himself in bed with a little black kitten, because it seems Lillian is sleeping on Wilbur's chest to keep warm. At first Wilbur does not believe what he

sees, and puts it down to Haggerty's Scotch, but finally he is convinced, and so he puts Lillian in his pocket, and takes her over to the Hot Box night club and gives her some milk, of which it seems Lillian is very fond.

Now where Lillian comes from in the first place of course nobody knows. The chances are somebody chucks her out of a window into the snow, because people are always chucking kittens, and one thing and another, out of windows in New York. In fact, if there is one thing this town has plenty of, it is kittens, which finally grow up to be cats, and go snooping around ash cans, and mer-owing on roofs, and keeping people from sleeping well.

Personally, I have no use for cats, including kittens, because I never seen one that has any too much sense, although I know a guy by the name of Pussy McGuire who makes a first-rate living doing nothing but stealing cats, and sometimes dogs, and selling them to old dolls who like such things for company. But Pussy only steals Persian and Angora cats, which are very fine cats, and of course Lillian is no such cat as this. Lillian is nothing but a black cat, and nobody will give you a dime a dozen for black cats in this town, as they are generally regarded as very bad jinxes.

Furthermore, it comes out in a few weeks that Wilbur Willard can just as well name her Herman, or Sidney, as not, but Wilbur sticks to Lillian, because this is the name of his partner when he is in vaudeville years ago. He often tells me about Lillian Withington when he is mulled up, which is more often than somewhat, for Wilbur is a great hand for drinking Scotch, or rye, or bourbon, or gin, or whatever else there is around for drinking, except water. In fact, Wilbur Willard is a high-class drinking man, and it does no good telling him it is against the law to drink in this country, because it only makes him mad, and he says to the dickens with the law, only Wilbur Willard uses a much rougher word than dickens.

"She is like a beautiful leopard," Wilbur says to me about Lillian Withington. "Black-haired, and black-eyed, and all ripply, like a leopard I see in an animal act on the same bill at the Palace with us once. We are headliners then," he says, "Willard and Withington, the best singing and dancing act in the country.

"I pick her up in San Antonio, which is a spot in Texas," Wilbur says. "She is not long out of a convent, and I just lose my old partner, Mary McGee, who ups and dies on me of pneumonia down there. Lillian wishes to go on the stage, and joins out with me. A natural-born actress with a great voice. But like a leopard," Wilbur says, "Like a leopard. There is cat in her, no doubt of this, and cats and women are both ungrateful. I love Lillian Withington. I wish to marry her. But she is cold to me. She says she is not going to follow the stage all her life. She says she wishes money, and luxury, and a fine home, and of course a guy like me cannot give a doll such things.

"I wait on her hand and foot," Wilbur says. "I am her slave. There is nothing I will not do for her. Then one day she walks in on me in Boston very cool and says she is quitting me. She says she is marrying a rich guy there. Well, naturally it busts up the act and I never have the heart to look for another partner, and then I get to belting that old black bottle around, and now what am I but a cabaret performer?"

Then sometimes he will bust out crying, and sometimes I will cry with him, although the way I look at it, Wilbur gets a pretty fair break, at that, in getting rid of a doll who wishes things he cannot give her. Many a guy in this town is tangled up with a doll who wishes things he cannot give her, but who keeps him tangled up just the same and busting himself trying to keep her quiet.

Wilbur makes pretty fair money as an entertainer in the Hot Box, though he spends most of it for Scotch, and he is not a bad entertainer, either. I often go to the Hot Box when I am feeling blue to hear him sing Melancholy Baby, and Moonshine Valley, and other sad songs which break my heart. Personally, I do not see why any doll cannot love Wilbur, especially if they listen to him sing such songs as Melancholy Baby when he is mulled up well, because he is a tall, nice-looking guy with long eyelashes, and sleepy brown eyes, and his voice has a low moaning sound that usually goes very big with the dolls. In fact, many a doll does do some pitching to Wilbur when he is singing in the Hot Box, but somehow Wilbur never gives them a tumble, which I suppose is because he is thinking only of Lillian Withington.

Well, after he gets Lillian, the black kitten, Wilbur seems to find a new interest in life, and Lillian turns out to be right cute, and not bad-looking after Wilbur gets her fed up well. She is blacker than a yard up a chimney, with not a white spot on her, and she grows so fast that by and by Wilbur cannot carry her in his pocket any more, so he puts a collar on her and leads her around. So Lillian becomes very well known on Broadway, what with Wilbur taking her to many places, and finally she does not even have to be led around by Willard, but follows him like a pooch. And in all the Roaring Forties there is no pooch that cares to have any truck with Lillian, for she will leap aboard them quicker than you can say scat, and scratch and bite them until they are very glad indeed to get away from her.

But of course the pooches in the Forties are mainly nothing but Chows, and Pekes, and Poms, or little woolly white poodles, which are led around by blonde dolls, and are not fit to take their own part against a smart cat. In fact, Wilbur Willard is finally not on speaking terms with any doll that owns a pooch between Times Square and Columbus Circle, and they are all hoping that both Wilbur and Lillian will go lay down and die somewhere. Furthermore, Wilbur has a couple of battles with guys who also belong to the dolls, but Wilbur is no boob in a battle if he is not mulled up too much and leg-weary.

After he is through entertaining people in the Hot Box, Wilbur generally goes around to any speakeasies which may still be open, and does a little off-hand drinking on top of what he already drinks down in the Hot Box, which is plenty, and although it is considered very risky in this town to mix Hot Box liquor with any other, it never seems to bother Wilbur. Along toward daylight he takes a couple of bottles of Scotch over to his room in the Hotel de Brussels and uses them for a nightcap, so by the time Wilbur Willard is ready to slide off to sleep he has plenty of liquor of one kind and another inside him, and he sleeps pretty good.

Of course nobody on Broadway blames Wilbur so very much for being such a rumpot, because they know about him loving Lillian Withington, and losing her, and it is considered a reasonable excuse in this town for a guy to do some drinking when he loses a doll, which is why there is so much drinking here, but it is a mystery to one and all how Wilbur stands all this liquor without croaking. The cemeteries are full of guys who do a lot less drinking than Wilbur, but he never even seems to feel extra tough, or if he does he keeps it to himself and does not go around saying it is the kind of liquor you get nowadays.

He costs some of the boys around Mindy's plenty of dough one winter, because he starts in doing most of his drinking after hours in Good Time Charley's speakeasy, and the boys lay a price of four to one against him lasting until spring, never figuring a guy can drink very much of Good Time Charley's liquor and keep on living. But Wilbur Willard does it just the same, so everybody says the guy is just naturally superhuman, and lets it go at that.

Sometimes Wilbur drops into Mindy's with Lillian following him on the look-out for pooches, or riding on his shoulder if the weather is bad, and the two of them will sit with us for hours chewing the rag about one thing and another. At such times Wilbur generally has a bottle on his hip and takes a shot now and then, but of course this does not come under the head of serious drinking with him. When Lillian is with Wilbur she always lies as close to him as she can get and anybody can see that she seems to be very fond of Wilbur, and that he is very fond of her, although he sometimes forgets himself and speaks of her as a beautiful leopard. But of course this is only a slip of the tongue, and anyway if Wilbur gets any pleasure out of thinking Lillian is a leopard, it is nobody's business but his own.

"I suppose she will run away from me some day," Wilbur says, running his hand over Lillian's back until her fur crackles. "Yes, although I give her plenty of liver and catnip, and one thing and another, and all my affection, she will probably give me the go-by. Cats are like women, and women are like cats. They are both very ungrateful."

"They are both generally bad luck," Big Nip, the crap shooter, says. "Especially cats, and most especially black cats."

Many other guys tell Wilbur about black cats being bad luck, and advise him to slip Lillian into the North River some night with a sinker on her, but Wilbur claims he already has all the bad luck in the world when he loses Lillian Withington, and that Lillian, the cat, cannot make it any worse, so he goes on taking extra good care of her, and Lillian goes on getting bigger and bigger until I commence thinking maybe there is some St. Bernard in her.

Finally I commence to notice something funny about Lillian. Sometimes she will be acting very loving towards Wilbur, and then again she will be very unfriendly to him, and will spit at him, and snatch at him with her claws, very hostile. It seems to me that she is all right when Wilbur is mulled up, but is as sad and fretful as he is himself when he is only a little bit mulled. And when Lillian is sad and fretful she makes it very tough indeed on the pooches in the neighbourhood of the Brussels.

In fact, Lillian takes to pooch-hunting, sneaking off when Wilbur is getting his rest, and running pooches bow-legged, especially when she finds one that is not on a leash. A loose pooch is just naturally cherry pie for Lillian.

Well, of course this causes great indignation among the dolls who own the pooches, particularly when Lillian comes home one day carrying a Peke as big as she is herself by the scruff of the neck, and with a very excited blonde doll following her and yelling bloody murder outside Wilbur Willard's door when Lillian pops into Wilbur's room through a hole he cuts in the door for her, still lugging the Peke. But it seems that instead of being mad at Lillian and giving her a pasting for such goings on, Wilbur is somewhat pleased, because he happens to be still in a fog when Lillian arrives with the Peke, and is thinking of Lillian as a beautiful leopard.

"Why," Wilbur says, "this is devotion, indeed. My beautiful leopard goes off into the jungle and fetches me an antelope for dinner."

Now of course there is no sense whatever to this, because a Peke is certainly not anything like an antelope, but the blonde doll outside Wilbur's door hears Wilbur mumble, and gets the idea that he is going to eat her Peke for dinner and the squawk she puts up is very terrible. There is plenty of trouble around the Brussels in cooling the blonde doll's rage over Lillian snagging her Peke, and what is more the blonde doll's ever-loving guy, who turns out to be a tough Ginney bootlegger by the name of Gregorio, shows up at the Hot Box the next night and wishes to put the slug on Wilbur Willard.

But Wilbur rounds him up with a few drinks and by singing Melancholy Baby to him, and before he leaves the Ginney gets very sentimental towards Wilbur, and Lillian, too, and wishes to give Wilbur five bucks to let Lillian grab the Peke again, if Lillian will promise not to bring it back. It seems Gregorio does not really care for the Peke, and is only acting quarrelsome to please the blonde doll and make her think he loves her dearly.

But I can see Lillian is having different moods, and finally I ask Wilbur if he notices it.

"Yes," he says, very sad, "I do not seem to be holding her love. She is getting very fickle. A guy moves on to my floor at the Brussels the other day with a little boy, and Lillian becomes very fond of this kid at once. In fact, they are great friends. Ah, well," Wilbur says, "cats are like women. Their affection does not last."

I happen to go over to the Brussels a few days later to explain to a guy by the name of Crutchy, who lives on the same floor as Wilbur Willard, that some of our citizens do not like his face and that it may be a good idea for him to leave town, especially if he insists on bringing ale into their territory, and I see Lillian out in the hall with a youngster which I judge is the kid Wilbur is talking about. This kid is maybe three years old, and very cute, what with black hair and black eyes, and he is mauling Lillian around the hall in a way that is most surprising, for Lillian is not such a cat as will stand for much mauling around, not even from Wilbur Willard.

I am wondering how anybody comes to take such a kid to a place like the Brussels, but I figure it is some actor's kid, and that maybe there is no mamma for it. Later I am talking to Wilbur about this, and he says:

"Well, if the kid's old man is an actor, he is not working at it. He sticks close to his room all the time, and he does not allow the kid to go anywhere but in the hall, and I feel sorry for the little guy, which is why I allow Lillian to play with him."

Now it comes on a very cold spell, and a bunch of us are sitting in Mindy's along towards five o'clock in the morning when we hear fire engines going past. By and by in comes a guy by the name of Kansas, who is named Kansas because he comes from Kansas, and who is a gambler by trade.

"The old Brussels is on fire," this guy Kansas says.

"She is always on fire," Big Nip says, meaning there is always plenty of hot stuff going on around the Brussels.

About this time who walks in but Wilbur Willard, and anybody can see he is just naturally floating. The chances are he comes from Good Time Charley's, and is certainly carrying plenty of pressure. I never see Wilbur Willard mulled up more. He does not have Lillian with him, but then he never takes Lillian to Good Time Charley's because Charley hates cats.

"Hey, Wilbur," Big Nip says, "your joint, the Brussels, is on fire."

"Well," Wilbur says, "I am a little firefly, and I need a light. Let us go where there is a fire."

The Brussels is only a few blocks from Mindy's and there is nothing else to do just then, so some of us walk over to Eighth Avenue with Wilbur teetering along ahead of us. The old shack is certainly roaring away when we get in sight of it, and the firemen are tossing water into it, and the coppers have the fire lines out to keep the crowd back, although there is not much of a crowd at such an hour in the morning.

"Is it not beautiful?" Wilbur Willard says, looking up at the flames. "Is it not like a fairy palace all lighted up this way?"

You see, Wilbur does not realise the place is on fire, although guys and dolls are running out of it every which way, most of them half dressed, or not dressed at all, and the firemen are getting out the life nets in case anybody wishes to hop out of the windows.

"It is certainly beautiful," Wilbur says, "I must get Lillian so she can see this."

And before anybody has time to think, there is Wilbur Willard walking into the front door of the Brussels as if nothing happens. The firemen and the coppers are so astonished all they can do is holler at Wilbur, but he pays no attention whatever. Well, naturally everybody figures Wilbur is a gone gosling, but in ten minutes he comes walking out of this same door through the fire and smoke as cool as you please, and he has Lillian in his arms.

"You know," Wilbur says, coming over to where we are standing with our eyes popping out, "I have to walk all the way up to my floor because the elevators seem to be out of commission. The service is getting terrible in this hotel. I will certainly make a strong complaint to the management about it as soon as I pay something on my account."

Then what happens but Lillian lets out a big mer-row, and hops out of Wilbur's arms and skips past the coppers and the firemen with her back all humped up, and the next thing anybody knows she is tearing through the front door of the old hotel and making plenty of speed.

"Well, well," Wilbur says, looking much surprised, "there goes Lillian."

And what does this daffy Wilbur Willard do but turn and go marching back into the Brussels again, and by this time the smoke is pouring out of the front door so thick he is out of sight in a second. Naturally he takes the coppers and firemen by surprise, because they are not used to guys walking in and out of fires on them.

This time anybody standing around will lay you plenty of odds—two and a half and maybe three to one that Wilbur never shows up again, because the old Brussels is now just popping with fire and smoke from the lower windows, although there does not seem to be quite so much fire in the upper storey. Everybody seems to be out of the building, and even the firemen are fighting the blaze from the outside because the Brussels is so old and ramshackly there is no sense in them risking the floors.

I mean everybody is out of the place except Wilbur Willard and Lillian, and we figure they are getting a good frying somewhere inside, although Feet Samuels is around offering to take thirteen to five for a few small bets that Lillian comes out okay, because Feet claims that a cat has nine lives and that is a fair bet at the price.

Well, up comes a swell-looking doll all heated up about something and pushing and clawing her way through the crowd up to the ropes and screaming until you can hardly hear yourself think, and about this same minute everybody hears a voice going ai-lee-hi-hee-hoo, like a Swiss yodeller, which comes from the roof of the Brussels, and looking up what do we see but Wilbur Willard standing up there on the edge of the roof, high above the fire and smoke, and yodelling very loud.

Under one arm he has a big bundle of some kind, and under the other he has the little kid I see playing in the hall with Lillian. As he stands up there going ai-lee-hi-hee-hoo, the swell-dressed doll near us begins screaming louder than Wilbur is yodelling, and the firemen rush over under him with a life net.

Wilbur lets go another ai-lee-hi-hee-hoo, and down he comes all spraddled out, with the bundle and the kid, but he hits the net sitting down and bounces up and back again for a couple of minutes before he finally settles. In fact, Wilbur is enjoying the bouncing, and the chances are he will be bouncing yet if the firemen do not drop their hold on the net and let him fall to the ground.

Then Wilbur steps out of the net, and I can see the bundle is a rolled-up blanket with Lillian's eyes peeking out of one end. He still has the kid under the other arm with his head stuck out in front, and his legs stuck out behind and it does not seem to be that Wilbur is handling the kid as careful as he is handling Lillian. He stands there looking at the firemen with a very sneering look, and finally he says:

"Do not think you can catch me in your net unless I wish to be caught. I am a butterfly, and very hard to overtake."

Then all of a sudden the swell-dressed doll who is doing so much hollering, piles on top of Wilbur and grabs the kid from him and begins hugging and kissing it.

"Wilbur," she says, "God bless you, Wilbur, for saving my baby! Oh, thank you, Wilbur, thank you! My wretched husband kidnaps and runs away with him, and it is only a few hours ago that my detectives find out where he is."

Wilbur gives the doll a funny look for about half a minute and starts to walk away, but Lillian comes wiggling out of the blanket, looking and smelling pretty much singed up, and the kid sees Lillian and begins hollering for her, so Wilbur finally hands Lillian over to the kid. And not wishing to leave Lillian, Wilbur stands around somewhat confused, and the doll gets talking to him, and finally they go away together, and as they go Wilbur is carrying the kid, and the kid is carrying Lillian, and Lillian is not feeling so good from her burns.

Furthermore, Wilbur is probably more sober than he ever is before in years at this hour in the morning, but before they go I get a chance to talk some to Wilbur when he is still rambling somewhat, and I make out from what he says that the first time he goes to get Lillian he finds her in his room and does not see hide or hair of the little kid and does not even think of him, because he does not know what room the kid is in, anyway, having never noticed such a thing.

But the second time he goes up, Lillian is sniffing at the crack under the door of a room down the hall from Wilbur's and Wilbur says he seems to remember seeing a trickle of something like water coming out of the crack.

"And," Wilbur says, "as I am looking for a blanket for Lillian, and it will be a bother to go back to my room, I figure I will get one out of this room. I try the knob but the door is locked, so I kick it in, and walk in to find the room is full of smoke, and fire is shooting through the windows very lovely, and when I grab a blanket off the bed for Lillian, what is under the blanket but the kid?

"Well," Wilbur says, "the kid is squawking, and Lillian is mer-owing, and there is so much confusion generally that it makes me nervous, so I figure we better go up on the roof and let the stink blow off us, and look at the fire from there. It seems there is a guy stretched out on the floor of the room alongside an upset table between the door and the bed. He has a bottle in one hand, and he is dead. Well, naturally there is nothing to be gained by lugging a dead guy along, so I take Lillian and the kid and go up on the roof, and we just naturally fly off like humming birds. Now I must get a drink," Wilbur says. "I wonder if anybody has anything on their hip?"

Well, the papers are certainly full of Wilbur and Lillian the next day, especially Lillian, and they are both great heroes.

But Wilbur cannot stand publicity very long, because he never has no time to himself for his drinking, what with the scribes and the photographers hopping on him every few minutes wishing to hear his story, and to take more pictures of him and Lillian, so one night he disappears, and Lillian disappears with him.

About a year later it comes out that he marries his old doll, Lillian Withington-Harmon, and falls into a lot of dough, and what is more he cuts out the liquor and becomes quite a useful citizen one way and another. So everybody has to admit that black cats are not always bad luck, although I say Wilbur's case is a little exceptional because he does not start out knowing Lillian is a black cat, but thinking she is a leopard.

I happen to run into Wilbur one day all dressed up in good clothes and jewellery and cutting quite a swell.

"Wilbur," I say to him, "I often think how remarkable it is the way Lillian suddenly gets such an attachment for the little kid and remembers about him being in the hotel and leads you back there a second time to the right room. If I do not see this come off with my own eyes, I will never believe a cat has brains enough to do such a thing, because I consider cats are extra dumb."

"Brains nothing," Wilbur says. "Lillian does not have brains enough to grease a gimlet. And what is more she has no more attachment for the kid than a jack rabbit. The time has come," Wilbur says, "to expose Lillian. She gets a lot of credit which is never coming to her. I will now tell you about Lillian, and nobody knows this but me.

"You see," Wilbur says, "when Lillian is a little kitten I always put a little Scotch in her milk, partly to help make her good and strong, and partly because I am never no hand to drink alone, unless there is nobody with me. Well, at first Lillian does not care so much for this Scotch in her milk, but finally she takes a liking to it, and I keep making her toddy stronger until in the end she will lap up a good big snort without any milk for a chaser, and yell for more. In fact, I suddenly realize that Lillian becomes a rumpot, just like I am in those days, and simply must have her grog, and it is when she is good and rummed up that Lillian goes off snatching Pekes, and acting tough generally.

"Now," Wilbur says, "the time of the fire is about the time I get home every morning and give Lillian her schnapps. But when I go into the hotel and get her the first time I forget to Scotch her up, and the reason she runs back into the hotel is because she is looking for her shot. And the reason she is sniffing at the kid's door is not because the kid is in there but because the trickle that is coming through the crack under the door is nothing but Scotch running out of the bottle in the dead guy's hand. I never mention this before because I figure it may be a knock to a dead guy's memory," Wilbur says. "Drinking is certainly a disgusting thing, especially secret drinking."

"But how is Lillian getting along these days?" I ask Wilbur Willard.

"I am greatly disappointed in Lillian," he says. "She refuses to reform when I do and the last I hear of her she takes up with Gregorio, the Ginney bootlegger, who keeps her well Scotched up all the time so she will lead his blonde doll's Peke a dog's life."

# Cats' Paradise

BY ÉMILE ZOLA

A S A POWERFUL and prolific novelist of lower-class French life, Émile Zola (1840–1902) occupies an important place in 19th-century literary history. With books like *Nana* and *Thérèse Raquin,* he explored the darker side of society, disdaining any attempts to romanticize or idealize situations sometimes unbearably grim. His frankness often brought him near imprisonment (and in fact led his English translator and publisher Henry Vizetelly to jail). But the clarity and honesty of his fiction won through.

"Cats' Paradise," Zola's best-known animal story, was first published in 1874 in a collection called *Nouveaux Contes á Ninon.* It displays some of the same cynicism to be found in his major works, but it also captures in vivid form the contradictory nature of cats dependent on human keepers—and of those cats of the rooftops who refuse to have keepers at all.

★   ★   ★   ★   ★

AN AUNT LEFT me an Angora cat that is the stupidest beast I know. This is the story he told me one winter evening in front of the fire.

## I

I was then two years old, the fattest and most naïve cat you've ever seen. At that tender age, I presumptuously disdained all the pleasures of the house, and did not even give thanks to Providence for having placed me with your aunt. That wonderful woman adored me! At the bottom of a wardrobe I had a real bedroom, fitted out with a comforter and three blankets. The food was as good as the bed: no bread, no soup, nothing but meat, lovely red meat.

Ah well! In the midst of all this sweetness, I had but one desire, one dream—to slip out of a half-opened window and escape over the rooftops. Caresses seemed insipid, the softness of my bed made me feel ill, I was fat and I disgusted myself. I was bored with being happy all day long.

I must tell you that by stretching my neck I had been able to see a roof just outside the window. On that day, four cats played there on the blue tiles in the warm sun, fur bristling and tails erect, with every appearance of joy. I had never seen anything so extraordinary. From then on, I was fixed in the notion that happiness was to be found on the roofs, beyond that window so carefully closed—closed in fact, just as carefully as the doors of the cupboard where the meat was kept.

I decided to run away. There had to be other things in life besides juicy flesh. Out there was the unknown, the ideal existence. One day, someone forgot to push the kitchen window shut. I escaped onto a small roof that I found just beneath it.

## II

How beautiful were the rooftops! The large gutters along the edge exhaled delicious odors, and I stalked voluptuously down them. My paws were immersed in the fine mud, which had a certain infinite sweetness and warmth. I felt as though I was walking over velvet. The pleasant heat of the sun seemed to be dissolving my fat.

I cannot hide from you the fact that I was trembling in every limb. There was something terrifying in my joy. I remember above all the terrible shock I felt—it actually made me lose my footing on the tiles—when three cats rolled down from the top of a house and came up to me meowing frightfully. I practically fainted, but they simply called me a fat scaredy-cat and explained that all the meowing was just a joke. So I joined in. It was delightful. These bravos weren't as fat as I was, however, and made fun of me when I slipped and rolled like a ball across the tin roof heated by the sun. One old tom was particularly friendly. He offered to educate me, and I accepted the offer eagerly.

Ah, the ease of life with your aunt was now far away. I drank from the gutters, and milk with sugar had never tasted so sweet. Everything struck me as good and beautiful. A cat passed by, a gorgeous cat, and simply the sight of her touched off in me a deep and unfamiliar emotion. Only in my dreams had I ever seen such an exquisite creature, with so adorably supple a back. My three companions and I dashed forward to greet her, and I was actually slightly ahead of the others in offering my compliments to this ravishing creature when one of my comrades gave me a savage bite in the neck. I emitted a howl of pain. "Bah," said the old tom, dragging me away. "You'll see plenty more of those."

### III

After strolling for an hour or so, I developed a ferocious appetite.

"What do you eat up here on the rooftops?" I asked my friend the tom.

"Whatever you can find," he replied wisely.

This reply perplexed me, because hunt as I might I found nothing. Finally, however, I spotted a young workman preparing his lunch in an attic room. On the table, just under the window, was a lovely cutlet, appetizingly red.

"That's the answer," I told myself in all innocence.

At that I leaped on the table and snatched the cutlet. But the workman had seen me first, and gave me a terrific blow on the back with a broom. I dropped the cutlet and scurried away, cursing under my breath.

"What kind of an idiot are you?" the old tom asked. "Food on a table is supposed to be admired only from a distance. What we've got to do is hunt in the gutters."

I have never understood why food in a kitchen is off-limits to cats. My stomach had begun growling seriously. The tom put the finishing touch to my despair by saying that we needed to wait until night, when we could go down into the street and scavenge in the garbage heaps. Wait until night! He said this calmly and philosophically. As for me, I was faint at the very thought of prolonging my fast even a moment more.

### IV

The night came on slowly, a night of fog that made me rigid with cold. Soon it began to rain, a fine, penetrating downpour blown about by brisk gusts of wind. We descended by way of a glassed skylight over a stairway. How shabby the street appeared! Here there was none of that pleasant heat of the sun, the roofs gleaming white where we had languished so deliciously. My paws slipped on the greasy pavement. I thought sadly of my three blankets and my comforter.

No sooner were we in the street than my friend the old tom began to tremble. He crouched down and crept craftily along the house wall, telling me to follow quickly behind him. Arriving at a doorway, he lost no time in hiding himself, simultaneously purring with satisfaction. When I asked him what was going on, he said, "Did you see that man with the basket and the hook?"

"Yes."

"Well, if he had seen us, we would have been caught and roasted on a spit!"

"Roasted on a spit!" I cried. "The street is no place for us. You can't eat, but you can be eaten!"

## V

Meanwhile, rubbish was being put out in front of doors. I rummaged through it hopelessly. Two or three skinny bones that had been dragged through ashes made me realize just how succulent fresh meat can be. My friend the tom pawed through the garbage with enormous artistry and made me do the same all the night long, examining every paving stone without the least sign of hurry. After nearly ten hours of rain I was shivering all over. Damned street! Damned liberty! How I missed my prison!

In the morning the tom, noticing my shaky state, asked in an odd voice, "Have you had enough?"

"Oh, yes," I replied.

"Do you want to go back home?"

"I certainly do. But how can I find it?"

"Come on. The morning I saw you come out I knew that a fat cat like you is not cut out for the joys of liberty. I know where you live, I'll show you to the door."

He said all this with simple dignity. And when we arrived at the house, he bade me adieu without the least show of emotion.

"No," I cried, "we cannot take leave of each other like this. Come with me. We will share the same bed and the same food. My mistress is a wonderful woman ..."

He didn't let me finish.

"Shut up," he said brusquely. "You are a fool. I'd die in your warm soft-ness. Your life of abundance is fine for spoiled cats. Free cats will never buy your ease and your comforter for the price of being imprisoned. . . . Goodbye."

He climbed back onto his rooftops. I saw his great thin shadow shud-der with pleasure at the caresses of the rising sun.

When I went back in, your aunt played the disciplinarian and pun-ished me. I received my punishment with extreme joy. It produced in me a kind of voluptuous pleasure, being warm and being beaten at the same time. And even as I was being struck I could dream about the delicious snacks that would surely follow.

## VI

So you see—thus concluded my cat, stretched out in front of the fire—the true happiness, the paradise, my dear master, is to be locked up and beaten in a place where there is meat.

I speak for cats.

# Tom Quartz

BY MARK TWAIN

THERE ARE PLENTY of wise cats in the world—in fact, from their serious demeanor, cats probably get more credit for wisdom than they deserve—but even among the more sagacious members of the feline community, Tom Quartz was a standout. Of course, as Mark Twain (1835–1910) makes plain in this classic tale from the California mining camps, he learned a few things the hard way. From Tom's point of view, panning for bits of loose gold in a brook made a lot more sense than trying to hack shafts in solid rock anyway. And who can say that he was wrong?

★   ★   ★   ★   ★

ONE OF MY COMRADES there—another of those victims of eighteen years of unrequited toil and blighted hopes—was one of the gentlest spirits that ever bore its patient cross in a weary exile: grave and simple Dick Baker, pocket miner of Dead-House Gulch. He was forty-six, grey as a rat, thoughtful, slenderly educated, slouchily dressed and clay-soiled, but his heart was finer metal than any gold his shovel ever brought to light—than any, indeed, that ever was mined or minted.

Whenever he was out of luck and a little down-hearted, he would fall to mourning over the loss of a wonderful cat he used to own (for where women and children are not, men of kindly impulses take up with pets, for they must love something). And he always spoke of the strange sagacity of that cat with the air of a man who believed in his secret heart that there was something human about it—maybe even supernatural.

I heard him talking about this animal once. He said:

"Gentlemen, I used to have a cat here, by the name of Tom Quartz, which you'd a took an interest in, I reckon—most anybody would. I had him here eight year—and he was the remarkablest cat I ever see. He was a large grey one of the Tom specie, an' he had more hard, natchral sense than any man in this camp—'n' a *power* of dignity—he wouldn't let the Guv'nor of Californy be familiar with him. He never ketched a rat in his life—'peared to be above it. He never cared for nothing but mining. He knowed more about mining, that cat did, than any man I ever, ever see. You couldn't tell *him* noth'n' 'bout placer diggin's—'n' as for pocket mining, why, he was just born for it. He would dig out after me an' Jim when we went over the hills, prospect'n', and he would trot along behind us for as much as five mile, if we went so fur. An' he had the best judgment about mining ground—why, you never see anything like it. When we went to work, he'd scatter a glance around, 'n' if he didn't think much of the indications, he would give a look as much as to say, 'Well, I'll have to get you to excuse *me*,' 'n' without another word he'd hyste his nose into the air 'n' shove for home. But if the ground suited him, he would lay low 'n' keep dark till the first pan was washed, 'n' then he would sidle up 'n' take a look, an' if there was about six or seven grains of gold *he* was satisfied—he didn't want no better prospect 'n' that—'n' then he would lay down on our coats and snore like a steamboat till we'd struck the pocket, an' then get up 'n' superintend. He was nearly lightnin' on superintending.

"Well, by-an'-bye, up comes this yer quartz excitement. Everybody was into it—everybody was pick'n' 'n' blast'n' instead of shovellin' dirt on the hill-side—everybody was put'n' down a shaft instead of scrapin' the surface.

Noth'n' would do Jim but *we* must tackle the ledges, too, 'n' so we did. We commenced put'n' down a shaft, 'n' Tom Quartz he begin to wonder what in the Dickens it was all about. *He* hadn't ever seen any mining like that before, 'n' he was all upset, as you may say—he couldn't come to a right understanding of it no way—it was too many for *him*. He was down on it, too, you bet you— he was down on it powerful—'n' always appeared to consider it the cussedest foolishness out. But that cat, you know, was *always* agin new-fangled arrangements—somehow he never could abide 'em. *You* know how it is with old habits. But by-an'-bye Tom Quartz begin to git sort of reconciled a little, though he never *could* altogether understand that eternal sinkin' of a shaft an' never pannin' out anything. At last he got to comin' down in the shaft, hisself, to try to cipher it out. An' when he'd git the blues, 'n' feel kind of scruffy, 'n' aggravated 'n' disgusted—knowin', as he did, that the bills was runnin' up all the time an' we warn't makin' a cent—he would curl up on a gunny-sack in the corner an' go to sleep. Well, one day when the shaft was down about eight foot, the rock got so hard that we had to put in a blast—the first blast'n' we'd ever done since Tom Quartz was born. An' then we lit the fuse, 'n' climb out 'n' got off 'bout fifty yards—'n' forgot 'n' left Tom Quartz sound asleep on the gunny-sack. In 'bout a minute we seen a puff of smoke bust up out of the hole, 'n' then everything let go with an awful crash, 'n' about four million ton of rocks 'n' dirt 'n' smoke 'n' splinters shot up 'bout a mile an' a half into the air, an' by George, right in the dead centre of it was old Tom Quartz a-goin' end over end, an' a snortin' an' a sneez'n', an' a clawin' an' a reachin' for things like all possessed. But it warn't no use, you know, it warn't no use. An' that was the last we see of *him* for about two minutes 'n' a half, an' then all of a sudden it begin to rain rocks and rubbage, an' directly he come down kerwhop about ten foot off f'm where we stood. Well, I reckon he was p'raps the orneriest-lookin' beast you ever see. One ear was sot back on his neck, 'n' his tail was stove up, 'n' his eye-winkers was swinged off, 'n' he was all blacked up with powder an' smoke, an' all sloppy with mud 'n' slush f'm one end to the other. Well, sir, it warn't no use to try to apologize—we couldn't say a word. He took a sort of a disgusted look at hisself, 'n' then he looked at us—an' it was just exactly the same as if he had said—'Gents, maybe *you* think it's smart to take advantage of a cat that 'ain't had no experience of quartz minin', but *I* think *different*'—an' then he turned on his heel 'n' marched off home without ever saying another word.

"That was jest his style. An' maybe you won't believe it, but after that you never see a cat so prejudiced agin quartz mining as what he was. An' by-an'-bye when he *did* get to goin' down in the shaft agin, you'd a been aston-ished at his sagacity. The minute we'd tetch off a blast 'n' the fuse'd begin to siz-zle, he'd give a look as much as to say, 'Well, I'll have to git you to excuse *me*,' an' it was surpris'n' the way he'd shin out of that hole 'n' go f'r a tree. Sagacity? It ain't no name for it. 'Twas *inspiration!*"

I said, "Well, Mr. Baker, his prejudice against quartz mining *was* re-markable, considering how he came by it. Couldn't you ever cure him of it?"

"*Cure him!* No! When Tom Quartz was sot once, he was *always* sot— and you might a blowed him up as much as three million times 'n' you'd never a broken him of his cussed prejudice agin quartz mining."

The affection and the pride that lit up Baker's face when he delivered this tribute to the firmness of his humble friend of other days will always be a vivid memory with me.

# Ming's Biggest Prey

BY PATRICIA HIGHSMITH

C ATS ARE KILLERS. We have to accept that. No cat would survive long in the wild without a taste for blood, and even the most domesticated tabby has a murderous streak when faced with a mouse or a butterfly. Patricia Highsmith (1921–1995) is exceptional among writers for facing up to this propensity without flinching. *The Animal-Lover's Book of Beastly Murder,* where "Ming's Biggest Prey" first appeared, is entirely devoted to non-human criminal activity.

That animals can involve themselves in murder will come as no surprise to anyone familiar with Highsmith's better-known works, from *Strangers on a Train* (the source of Alfred Hitchcock's classic movie) to *The Talented Mr. Ripley* and its sequels. Her novels and stories seem to inhabit a region of claustrophobia and irrationality which, as Graham Greene once observed, "we enter each time with a sense of personal danger." In "Ming's Biggest Prey" this is no less true—in spite of the fact that the protagonist is a cat.

★　★　★　★　★

MING WAS RESTING comfortably on the foot of his mistress' bunk, when the man picked him up by the back of the neck, stuck him out on the deck and closed the cabin door. Ming's blue eyes widened in shock and brief anger, then nearly closed again because of the brilliant sunlight. It was not the first time Ming had been thrust out of the cabin rudely, and Ming realized that the man did it when his mistress, Elaine, was not looking.

The sailboat now offered no shelter from the sun, but Ming was not yet too warm. He leapt easily to the cabin roof and stepped onto the coil of rope just behind the mast. Ming liked the rope coil as a couch, because he could see everything from the height, the cup shape of the rope protected him from strong breezes, and also minimized the swaying and sudden changes of angle of the *White Lark,* since it was more or less the centre point. But just now the sail had been taken down, because Elaine and the man had eaten lunch, and often they had a siesta afterward, during which time, Ming knew, the man didn't like him in the cabin. Lunchtime was all right. In fact, Ming had just lunched on delicious grilled fish and a bit of lobster. Now, lying in a relaxed curve on the coil of rope, Ming opened his mouth in a great yawn, then with his slant eyes almost closed against the strong sunlight, gazed at the beige hills and the white and pink houses and hotels that circled the bay of Acapulco. Between the *White Lark* and the shore where people plashed inaudibly, the sun twinkled on the water's surface like thousands of tiny electric lights going on and off. A water-skier went by, skimming up white spray behind him. Such activity! Ming half dozed, feeling the heat of the sun sink into his fur. Ming was from New York, and he considered Acapulco a great improvement over his environment in the first weeks of his life. He remembered a sunless box with straw on the bottom, three or four other kittens in with him, and a window behind which giant forms paused for a few moments, tried to catch his attention by tapping, then passed on. He did not remember his mother at all. One day a young woman who smelled of something pleasant came into the place and took him away—away from the ugly, frightening smell of dogs, of medicine and parrot dung. Then they went on what Ming now knew was an aeroplane. He was quite used to aeroplanes now and rather liked them. On aeroplanes he sat on Elaine's lap, or slept on her lap, and there were always tit-bits to eat if he was hungry.

Elaine spent much of the day in a shop in Acapulco, where dresses and slacks and bathing suits hung on all the walls. This place smelled clean and fresh, there were flowers in pots and in boxes out front, and the floor was of cool blue and white tile. Ming had perfect freedom to wander out into the patio behind the shop, or to sleep in his basket in a corner. There was more sunlight in front of the shop, but mischievous boys often tried to grab him if he sat in front, and Ming could never relax there.

Ming liked best lying in the sun with his mistress on one of the long canvas chairs on their terrace at home. What Ming did not like were the people she sometimes invited to their house, people who spent the night, people by the score who stayed up very late eating and drinking, playing the gramophone or the piano—people who separated him from Elaine. People who stepped on his toes, people who sometimes picked him up from behind before he could do anything about it, so that he had to squirm and fight to get free, people who stroked him roughly, people who closed a door somewhere, locking him in. *People!* Ming detested people. In all the world, he liked only Elaine. Elaine loved him and understood him.

Especially this man called Teddie Ming detested now. Teddie was around all the time lately. Ming did not like the way Teddie looked at him, when Elaine was not watching. And sometimes Teddie, when Elaine was not near, muttered something which Ming knew was a threat. Or a command to leave the room. Ming took it calmly. Dignity was to be preserved. Besides, wasn't his mistress on his side? The man was the intruder. When Elaine was watching, the man sometimes pretended a fondness for him, but Ming always moved gracefully but unmistakably in another direction.

Ming's nap was interrupted by the sound of the cabin door opening. He heard Elaine and the man laughing and talking. The big red-orange sun was near the horizon.

"Ming!" Elaine came over to him. "Aren't you getting *cooked,* darling? I thought you were *in!*"

"So did I!" said Teddie.

Ming purred as he always did when he awakened. She picked him up gently, cradled him in her arms, and took him below into the suddenly cool shade of the cabin. She was talking to the man, and not in a gentle tone. She set Ming down in front of his dish of water, and though he was not thirsty, he drank a little to please her. Ming did feel addled by the heat, and he staggered a little.

Elaine took a wet towel and wiped Ming's face, his ears and his four paws. Then she laid him gently on the bunk that smelled of Elaine's perfume but also of the man whom Ming detested.

Now his mistress and the man were quarrelling. Ming could tell from the tone. Elaine was staying with Ming, sitting on the edge of the bunk. Ming at last heard the splash that meant Teddie had dived into the water. Ming hoped he stayed there, hoped he drowned, hoped he never came back. Elaine wet a bathtowel in the aluminum sink, wrung it out, spread it on the bunk, and lifted Ming onto it. She brought water, and now Ming was thirsty, and drank. She left him to sleep again while she washed and put away the dishes. These were comfortable sounds that Ming liked to hear.

But soon there was another *plash* and *plop,* Teddie's wet feet on the deck, and Ming was awake again.

The tone of quarrelling recommenced. Elaine went up the few steps onto the deck. Ming, tense but with his chin still resting on the moist bathtowel, kept his eyes on the cabin door. It was Teddie's feet that he heard descending. Ming lifted his head slightly, aware that there was no exit behind him, that he was trapped in the cabin. The man paused with a towel in his hands, staring at Ming.

Ming relaxed completely, as he might do preparatory to a yawn, and this caused his eyes to cross. Ming then let his tongue slide a little way out of his mouth. The man started to say something, looked as if he wanted to hurl the wadded towel at Ming, but he wavered, whatever he had been going to say never got out of his mouth, and he threw the towel in the sink, then bent to wash his face. It was not the first time Ming had let his tongue slide out at Teddie. Lots of people laughed when Ming did this, if they were people at a party, for instance, and Ming rather enjoyed that. But Ming sensed that Teddie took it as a hostile gesture of some kind, which was why Ming did it deliberately to Teddie, whereas among other people, it was often an accident when Ming's tongue slid out.

The quarrelling continued. Elaine made coffee. Ming began to feel better, and went on deck again, because the sun had now set. Elaine had started the motor, and they were gliding slowly toward the shore. Ming caught the song of birds, the odd screams like shrill phrases of certain birds that cried only at sunset. Ming looked forward to the adobe house on the cliff that was his and his mistress' home. He knew that the reason she did not leave him at home (where he would have been more comfortable) when she went on the boat, was because she was afraid that people might trap him, even kill him. Ming understood. People had tried to grab him from almost under Elaine's eyes. Once he had been all the way in a cloth bag suddenly, and though fighting as hard as he could, he was not sure he would have been able to get out, if Elaine had not hit the boy herself and grabbed the bag from him.

Ming had intended to jump up on the cabin roof again, but after glancing at it, he decided to save his strength, so he crouched on the warm, gently sloping deck with his feet tucked in, and gazed at the approaching shore. Now he could hear guitar music from the beach. The voices of his mistress and the man had come to a halt. For a few moments, the loudest sound was the chug-chug-chug of the boat's motor. Then Ming heard the man's bare feet climbing the cabin steps. Ming did not turn his head to look at him, but his ears twitched back a little, involuntarily. Ming looked at the water just the distance of a short leap in front of him and below him. Strangely, there was no sound from the man behind him. The hair on Ming's neck prickled, and Ming glanced over his right shoulder.

At that instant, the man bent forward and rushed at Ming with his arms outspread.

Ming was on his feet at once, darting straight toward the man which was the only direction of safety on the railless deck, and the man swung his left arm and cuffed Ming in the chest. Ming went flying backward, claws scraping the deck, but his hind legs went over the edge. Ming clung with his front feet to the sleek wood which gave him little hold, while his hind legs worked to heave him up, worked at the side of the boat which sloped to Ming's disadvantage.

The man advanced to shove a foot against Ming's paws, but Elaine came up the cabin steps just then.

"What's happening? *Ming!*"

Ming's strong hind legs were getting him onto the deck little by little. The man had knelt as if to lend a hand. Elaine had fallen onto her knees, also, and had Ming by the back of the neck now.

Ming relaxed, hunched on the deck. His tail was wet.

"He fell overboard!" Teddie said. "It's true he's groggy. Just lurched over and fell when the boat gave a dip."

"It's the sun. Poor *Ming!*" Elaine held the cat.

The man came down into the cabin. Elaine had Ming on the bunk and was talking softly to him. Ming's heart was still beating fast. He was alert against the man at the wheel, even though Elaine was with him. Ming was aware that they had entered the little cove where they always went before getting off the boat.

Here were the friends and allies of Teddie, whom Ming detested by association, although these were merely Mexican boys. Two or three boys in shorts called "Señor Teddie!" and offered a hand to Elaine to climb onto the dock, took the rope attached to the front of the boat, offered to carry "Ming!—Ming!" Ming leapt onto the dock himself and crouched, waiting for Elaine, ready to dart away from any other hand that might reach for him. And there were several brown hands making a rush for him, so that Ming had to keep jumping aside. There were laughs, yelps, stomps of bare feet on wooden boards. But there was also the reassuring voice of Elaine, warning them off. Ming knew she was busy carrying off the plastic satchels, locking the cabin door. Teddie with the aid of one of the Mexican boys was stretching the canvas over the cabin now. And Elaine's sandalled feet were beside Ming. Ming followed her as she walked away. A boy took the things Elaine was carrying, then she picked Ming up.

They got into the big car without a roof that belonged to Teddie, and drove up the winding road toward Elaine's and Ming's house. One of the boys was driving. Now the tone in which Elaine and Teddie were speaking was calmer, softer. The man laughed. Ming sat tensely on his mistress' lap. He could feel her concern for him in the way she stroked him and touched the back of his neck. The man reached out to put his fingers on Ming's back, and Ming gave a low growl that rose and fell and rumbled deep in his throat.

"Well, well," said the man, pretending to be amused and took his hand away.

Elaine's voice had stopped in the middle of something she was saying. Ming was tired, and wanted nothing more than to take a nap on the big bed at home. The bed was covered with a red and white striped blanket of thin wool.

Hardly had Ming thought of this, when he found himself in the cool, fragrant atmosphere of his own home, being lowered gently onto the bed with the soft woollen cover. His mistress kissed his cheek, and said something with the word hungry in it. Ming understood, at any rate. He was to tell her when he was hungry.

Ming dozed, and awakened at the sound of voices on the terrace a couple of yards away, past the open glass doors. Now it was dark. Ming could see one end of the table, and could tell from the quality of the light that there were candles on the table. Concha, the servant who slept in the house, was clearing the table. Ming heard her voice, then the voices of Elaine and the man. Ming smelled cigar smoke. Ming jumped to the floor and sat for a moment looking out the door toward the terrace. He yawned, then arched his back and stretched, and limbered up his muscles by digging his claws into the thick straw carpet. Then he slipped out to the right on the terrace and glided silently down the long stairway of broad stones to the garden below. The garden was like a jungle or a forest. Avocado trees and mango trees grew as high as the terrace itself, there were bougainvilleas against the wall, orchids in the trees, and magnolias and several camellias which Elaine had planted. Ming could hear birds twittering and stirring in their nests. Sometimes he climbed trees to get at their nests, but tonight he was not in the mood, though he was no longer tired. The voices of his mistress and the man disturbed him. His mistress was not a friend of the man's tonight, that was plain.

Concha was probably still in the kitchen, and Ming decided to go in and ask her for something to eat. Concha liked him. One maid who had not liked him had been dismissed by Elaine. Ming thought he fancied barbecued pork. That was what his mistress and the man had eaten tonight. The breeze blew fresh from the ocean, ruffling Ming's fur slightly. Ming felt completely re-covered from the awful experience of nearly falling into the sea.

Now the terrace was empty of people. Ming went left, back into the bedroom, and was at once aware of the man's presence, though there was no light on and Ming could not see him. The man was standing by the dressing-table, opening a box. Again involuntarily Ming gave a low growl which rose and fell, and Ming remained frozen in the position he had been in when he first became aware of the man, his right front paw extended for the next step. Now his ears were back, he was prepared to spring in any direction, although the man had not seen him.

"*Ssss-st!* Damn you!" the man said in a whisper. He stamped his foot, not very hard, to make the cat go away.

Ming did not move at all. Ming heard the soft rattle of the white necklace which belonged to his mistress. The man put it into his pocket, then moved to Ming's right, out the door that went into the big living-room. Ming now heard the clink of a bottle against glass, heard liquid being poured. Ming went through the same door and turned left toward the kitchen.

Here he miaowed, and was greeted by Elaine and Concha. Concha had her radio turned on to music.

"Fish?—Pork. He likes pork," Elaine said, speaking the odd form of words which she used with Concha.

Ming, without much difficulty, conveyed his preference for pork, and got it. He fell to with a good appetite. Concha was exclaiming "Ah-eee-ee!" as his mistress spoke with her, spoke at length. Then Concha bent to stroke him, and Ming put up with it, still looking down at his plate, until she left off and he could finish his meal. Then Elaine left the kitchen. Concha gave him some of the tinned milk, which he loved, in his now empty saucer, and Ming lapped this up. Then he rubbed himself against her bare leg by way of thanks, and went out of the kitchen, made his way cautiously into the living-room en route to the bedroom. But now his mistress and the man were out on the terrace. Ming had just entered the bedroom, when he heard Elaine call:

"Ming? Where are you?"

Ming went to the terrace door and stopped, and sat on the threshold.

Elaine was sitting sideways at the end of the table, and the candlelight was bright on her long fair hair, on the white of her trousers. She slapped her thigh, and Ming jumped onto her lap.

The man said something in a low tone, something not nice.

Elaine replied something in the same tone. But she laughed a little.

Then the telephone rang.

Elaine put Ming down, and went into the living-room toward the telephone.

The man finished what was in his glass, muttered something at Ming, then set the glass on the table. He got up and tried to circle Ming, or to get him toward the edge of the terrace, Ming realized, and Ming also realized that the man was drunk—therefore moving slowly and a little clumsily. The terrace had a parapet about as high as the man's hips, but it was broken by grilles in three places, grilles with bars wide enough for Ming to pass through, though Ming never did, merely looked through the grilles sometimes. It was plain to Ming that the man wanted to drive him through one of the grilles, or grab him and toss him over the terrace parapet. There was nothing easier for Ming than to elude him. Then the man picked up a chair and swung it suddenly, catching Ming on the hip. That had been quick, and it hurt. Ming took the nearest exit, which was down the outside steps that led to the garden.

The man started down the steps after him. Without reflecting, Ming dashed back up the few steps he had come, keeping close to the wall which was in shadow. The man hadn't seen him, Ming knew. Ming leapt to the terrace parapet, sat down and licked a paw once to recover and collect himself. His heart beat fast as if he were in the middle of a fight. And hatred ran in his veins. Hatred burned his eyes as he crouched and listened to the man uncertainly climbing the steps below him. The man came into view.

Ming tensed himself for a jump, then jumped as hard as he could, landing with all four feet on the man's right arm near the shoulder. Ming clung to the cloth of the man's white jacket, but they were both falling. The man groaned. Ming hung on. Branches crackled. Ming could not tell up from down. Ming jumped off the man, became aware of direction and of the earth too late and landed on his side. Almost at the same time, he heard the thud of the man hitting the ground, then of his body rolling a little way, then there was silence. Ming had to breathe fast with his mouth open until his chest stopped hurting. From the direction of the man, he could smell drink, cigar, and the sharp odour that meant fear. But the man was not moving.

Ming could now see quite well. There was even a bit of moonlight. Ming headed for the steps again, had to go a long way through the bush, over stones and sand, to where the steps began. Then he glided up and arrived once more upon the terrace.

Elaine was just coming onto the terrace.

"Teddie?" she called. Then she went back into the bedroom where she turned on a lamp. She went into the kitchen. Ming followed her. Concha had left the light on, but Concha was now in her own room, where the radio played.

Elaine opened the front door.

The man's car was still in the driveway, Ming saw. Now Ming's hip had begun to hurt, or now he had begun to notice it. It caused him to limp a little. Elaine noticed this, touched his back, and asked him what was the matter. Ming only purred.

"Teddie?—Where are you?" Elaine called.

She took a torch and shone it down into the garden, down among the great trunks of the avocado trees, among the orchids and the lavender and pink blossoms of the bougainvilleas. Ming, safe beside her on the terrace parapet, followed the beam of the torch with his eyes and purred with content. The man was not below here, but below and to the right. Elaine went to the terrace steps and carefully, because there was no rail here, only broad steps, pointed the beam of the light downward. Ming did not bother looking. He sat on the terrace where the steps began.

"Teddie!" she said. *"Teddie!"* Then she ran down the steps.

Ming still did not follow her. He heard her draw in her breath. Then she cried:

*"Concha!"*

Elaine ran back up the steps.

Concha had come out of her room. Elaine spoke to Concha. Then Concha became excited. Elaine went to the telephone, and spoke for a short while, then she and Concha went down the steps together. Ming settled himself with his paws tucked under him on the terrace, which was still faintly warm from the day's sun. A car arrived. Elaine came up the steps, and went and opened the front door. Ming kept out of the way on the terrace, in a shadowy corner, as three or four strange men came out on the terrace and tramped down the steps. There was a great deal of talk below, noises of feet, breaking of bushes, and then the smell of all of them mounted the steps, the smell of tobacco, sweat, and the familiar smell of blood. The man's blood. Ming was pleased, as he was pleased when he killed a bird and created this smell of blood under his own teeth. This was big prey. Ming, unnoticed by any of the others, stood up to his full height as the group passed with the corpse, and inhaled the aroma of his victory with a lifted nose.

Then suddenly the house was empty. Everyone had gone, even Concha. Ming drank a little water from his bowl in the kitchen, then went to his mistress' bed, curled against the slope of the pillows, and fell fast asleep. He was awakened by the rr-rr-r of an unfamiliar car. Then the front door opened, and he recognized the step of Elaine and then Concha. Ming stayed where he was. Elaine and Concha talked softly for a few minutes. Then Elaine came into the bedroom. The lamp was still on. Ming watched her slowly open the box on her dressing table, and into it she let fall the white necklace that made a little clatter. Then she closed the box. She began to unbutton her shirt, but before she had finished, she flung herself on the bed and stroked Ming's head, lifted his left paw and pressed it gently so that the claws came forth.

"Oh Ming—Ming," she said.

Ming recognized the tones of love.

# The Cheshire Cat

From *Alice's Adventures in Wonderland*

BY LEWIS CARROLL

DOES A CAT GRIN? Well, stranger things happen in *Alice's Adventures in Wonderland,* but few that have made such a lasting impression as the grin on the face of the Cheshire cat, or the disembodied grin that lingers on after the cat itself has departed. Someone once asked Charles Dodgson (1832–1898, pen name Lewis Carroll) how he managed to think up such bizarre notions, and he replied that they arrived unbidden. "Every such idea and every word of the dialogue, *came of itself* . . . whenever or however it comes, *it comes of itself.*" Perhaps Dodgson was just being modest, but whatever the case we must be grateful. No cat in history is quite as memorable as that toothy creature crouching tentatively in its tree, whether he was an invention or an inspiration.

★　★　★　★　★

THE ONLY THINGS in the kitchen that did not sneeze were the cook, and a large cat which was sitting on the hearth and grinning from ear to ear.

"Please, would you tell me," said Alice a bit timidly, for she was not quite sure whether it was good manners for her to speak first, "why your cat grins like that?"

"It's a Cheshire cat," said the Duchess, "and that's why. Pig!"

She said the last word with such sudden violence that Alice quite jumped; but she saw in another moment that it was addressed to the baby, and not to her, so she took courage and went on again:

"I didn't know that Cheshire cats always grinned; in fact, I didn't know that cats *could* grin."

"They all can," said the Duchess, "and most of 'em do."

'I don't know of any that do,' Alice said very politely, feeling quite pleased to have got into a conversation.

"You don't know much," said the Duchess, "and that's a fact."

Alice did not at all like the tone of this remark, and thought it would be as well to introduce some other subject of conversation. While she was trying to fix on one, the cook took the caldron of soup off the fire, and at once set to work throwing everything within her reach at the Duchess and the baby—the fire-irons came first; then followed a shower of saucepans, plates and dishes. The Duchess took no notice of them even when they hit her; and the baby was howling so much already that it was quite impossible to say whether the blows hurt it or not.

"Oh, *please* mind what you're doing!" cried Alice, jumping up and down in an agony of terror. "Oh, there goes his *precious* nose," as an unusually large saucepan flew close by it, and very nearly carried it off.

"If everybody minded their own business," the Duchess said in a hoarse growl, "the world would go round a deal faster than it does."

"Which would *not* be an advantage," said Alice, who felt very glad to get an opportunity of showing off a little of her knowledge. "Just think what work it would make with the day and night! You see the earth takes twenty-four hours to turn round on its axis—"

"Talking of axes," said the Duchess, "chop off her head!"

Alice glanced rather anxiously at the cook, to see if she meant to take the hint; but the cook was busily engaged in stirring the soup, and did not seem to be listening, so she ventured to go on again: "Twenty-four hours, I *think*; or is it twelve? I—"

"Oh, don't bother *me,*" said the Duchess. "I never could abide figures!" And with that she began nursing her child again, singing a sort of lullaby to it as she did so, and giving it a violent shake at the end of every line:

> Speak roughly to your little boy,
> And beat him when he sneezes:
> He only does it to annoy,
> Because he knows it teases.

Chorus (which the cook and the baby joined):

> Wow! wow! wow!

While the Duchess sang the second verse of the song, she kept tossing the baby violently up and down, and the poor little thing howled so, that Alice could hardly hear the words:

> I speak severely to my boy,
> I beat him when he sneezes;
> For he can thoroughly enjoy
> The pepper when he pleases!

Chorus:

> Wow! wow! wow!

"Here! You may nurse it a bit, if you like!" the Duchess said to Alice, flinging the baby at her as she spoke. "I must go and get ready to play croquet with the Queen," and she hurried out of the room. The cook threw a frying-pan after her as she went out, but it just missed her.

Alice caught the baby with some difficulty, as it was a queer-shaped lit-tle creature and held out its arms and legs in all directions, "just like a star-fish," thought Alice. The poor little thing was snorting like a steam-engine when she caught it, and kept doubling itself up and straightening itself out again, so that altogether, for the first minute or two, it was as much as she could do to hold it.

As soon as she made out the proper way of nursing it (which was to twist it up into a sort of knot, and then keep tight hold of its right ear and left foot, so as to prevent its undoing itself), she carried it out into the open air. "If I don't take this child away with me," thought Alice, "they're sure to kill it in a day or two; wouldn't it be murder to leave it behind?" She said the last words out loud, and the little thing grunted in reply (it had left off sneezing by this time). "Don't grunt," said Alice, "that's not at all a proper way of expressing yourself."

The baby grunted again, and Alice looked very anxiously into its face to see what was the matter with it. There could be no doubt that it had a *very* turn-up nose, much more like a snout than a real nose; also its eyes were getting extremely small for a baby. Altogether, Alice did not like the look of the thing at all. "But perhaps it was only sobbing," she thought, and looked into its eyes again to see if there were any tears.

No, there were no tears. "If you're going to turn into a pig, my dear," said Alice, seriously, "I'll have nothing more to do with you. Mind now!" The poor little thing sobbed again (or grunted, it was impossible to say which), and they went on for some while in silence.

Alice was just beginning to think to herself, "Now, what am I to do with this creature when I get it home?" when it grunted again, so violently, that she looked down into its face in some alarm. This time there could be *no* mistake about it: it was neither more nor less than a pig, and she felt that it would be quite absurd for her to carry it any further.

So she set the little creature down, and felt quite relieved to see it trot away quietly into the wood. "If it had grown up," she said to herself, "it would have made a dreadfully ugly child; but it makes rather a handsome pig, I think." And she began thinking over other children she knew, who might do very well as pigs, and was just saying to herself, "If one only knew the right way to change them—" when she was a little startled by seeing the Cheshire Cat sitting on a bough of a tree a few yards off.

The Cat only grinned when it saw Alice. It looked good-natured, she thought; still, it had *very* long claws and a great many teeth, so she felt that it ought to be treated with respect.

"Cheshire Puss," she began, rather timidly, as she did not at all know whether it would like the name; however, it only grinned a little wider. "Come, it's pleased so far," thought Alice, and she went on: "Would you tell me, please, which way I ought to go from here?"

"That depends a good deal on where you want to get to," said the Cat.

"I don't much care where—" said Alice.

"Then it doesn't matter which way you go," said the Cat.

"—so long as I get *somewhere*," Alice added as an explanation.

"Oh, you're sure to do that," said the Cat, "if you only walk long enough."

Alice felt that this could not be denied so, she tried another question: "What sort of people live about here?"

"In *that* direction," the Cat said, waving its right paw round, "lives a Hatter; and in *that* direction," waving the other paw, "lives a March Hare. Visit either you like; they're both mad."

"But I don't want to go among mad people," Alice remarked.

"Oh, but you can't help that," said the Cat: "We're all mad here. I'm mad. You're mad."

"How do you know I'm mad?" said Alice.

"You must be," said the Cat, "or you wouldn't have come here."

Alice didn't think that proved it at all; however, she went on. "And how do you know that you're mad?"

"To begin with," said the Cat, "a dog's not mad. You grant that?"

"I suppose so," said Alice.

"Well, then," the Cat went on, "you see a dog growls when it's angry, and wags its tail when it's pleased. Now *I* growl when I'm pleased, and wag my tail when I'm angry. Therefore, I'm mad."

"I call it purring, not growling," said Alice.

"Call it what you like," said the Cat. "Do you play croquet with the Queen today?"

"I should like it very much," said Alice, "but I haven't been invited yet."

"You'll see me there," said the Cat, and vanished.

Alice was not much surprised at this, she was getting so used to queer things happening. While she was looking at the place where it had been, it suddenly appeared again.

"By the by, what became of the baby?" said the Cat. "I'd nearly forgotten to ask."

"It turned into a pig," Alice quietly said, just as if it had come back in a natural way.

"I thought it would," said the Cat, and vanished again.

Alice waited a little, half expecting to see it again, but it did not appear, and after a minute or two she walked on in the direction in which the March Hare was said to live. "I've seen hatters before," she said to herself; "the March Hare will be much the most interesting, and perhaps, as this is May, it won't be raving mad—at least not so mad as it was in March." As she said this, she looked up, and there was the Cat again, sitting on a branch of a tree.

"Did you say pig, or fig?" said the Cat.

"I said pig," replied Alice, "and I wish you wouldn't keep appearing and vanishing so suddenly. You make one quite giddy."

"All right," said the Cat; and this time it vanished quite slowly, beginning with the end of the tail and ending with the grin, which remained some time after the rest of it had gone.

"Well! I've often seen a cat without a grin," thought Alice, "but a grin without a cat! It's the most curious thing I ever saw in all my life!"

# The Garden of Stubborn Cats

I TALIAN WRITER ITALO CALVINO (1923–1985) began his career as a realist, with a powerful novel about the Italian anti-fascist resistance during World War II. But he soon turned to fantasy and myth, becoming one of the principal exemplars of what is now known as magic realism. He achieved international fame with such fantasies as *Invisible Cities* and his fascinating (if circular) tale *If on a Winter's Night a Traveler.* "The Garden of Stubborn Cats," from *Marcovaldo, or the Seasons in the City,* is a wonderfully imaginative excursion into a Roman kingdom of cats, not quite real but nonetheless perfectly believable. Italian cats do tend to get their own way.

★　★　★　★　★

THE CITY OF CATS and the city of men exist one inside the other, but they are not the same city. Few cats recall the time when there was no distinction: the streets and squares of men were also streets and squares of cats, and the lawns, courtyards, balconies, and fountains; you lived in a broad and various space. But for several generations now domestic felines have been prisoners of an uninhabitable city; the streets are uninterruptedly overrun by the mortal traffic of cat-crushing automobiles; in every square foot of terrain where once a garden extended or a vacant lot or the ruins of an old demolition, now condominiums loom up, welfare housing, brand-new skyscrapers; every entrance is crammed with parked cars; the courtyards, one by one, have been roofed by reinforced concrete and transformed into garages or movie houses or storerooms or workshops. And where a rolling plateau of low roofs once extended, copings, terraces, water tanks, balconies, skylights, corrugated-iron sheds, now one general superstructure rises wherever structures can rise; the intermediate differences in height, between the low ground of the street and the supernal heaven of the penthouses, disappear; the cat of a recent litter seeks in vain the itinerary of its fathers, the point from which to make the soft leap from balustrade to cornice to drainpipe, or for the quick climb on the roof tiles.

But in this vertical city, in this compressed city where all voids tend to fill up and every block of cement tends to mingle with other blocks of cement, a kind of countercity opens, a negative city, that consists of empty slices between wall and wall, of the minimal distances ordained by the building regulations between two constructions, between the rear of one construction and the rear of the next; it is a city of cavities, wells, air conduits, driveways, inner yards, accesses to basements, like a network of dry canals on a planet of stucco and tar, and it is through this network, grazing the walls, that the ancient cat population still scurries.

On occasion, to pass the time, Marcovaldo would follow a cat. It was during the work break, between noon and three, when all the personnel except Marcovaldo went home to eat, and he—who brought his lunch in his bag—laid his place among the packing cases in the warehouse, chewed his snack, smoked a half cigar, and wandered around, alone and idle, waiting for work to resume. In those hours, a cat that peeped in at a window was always welcome company, and a guide for new explorations. He had made friends with a tabby, well fed, a blue ribbon around its neck, surely living with some well-to-do family. This tabby shared with Marcovaldo the habit of an afternoon stroll right after lunch; and naturally a friendship sprang up.

Following his tabby friend, Marcovaldo had started looking at places as if through the round eyes of a cat and even if these places were the usual environs of his firm he saw them in a different light, as settings for cattish stories, with connections practicable only by light, velvety paws. Though from the outside the neighborhood seemed poor in cats, every day on his rounds Marcovaldo made the acquaintance of some new face, and a meow, a hiss, a stiffening of fur on an arched back was enough for him to sense ties and intrigues and rivalries among them. At those moments he thought he had already penetrated the secrecy of the felines' society; and then he felt himself scrutinized by pupils that became slits, under the surveillance of the antennae of taut whiskers, and all the cats around him sat impassive as sphinxes, the pink triangle of their noses convergent on the black triangles of their lips, and the only things that moved were the tips of the ears, with a vibrant jerk like radar. They reached the end of a narrow passage, between squalid blank walls; and, looking around, Marcovaldo saw that the cats that had led him this far had vanished, all of them together, no telling in which direction, even his tabby friend, and they had left him alone. Their realm had territories, ceremonies, customs that it was not yet granted to him to discover.

On the other hand, from the cat city there opened unsuspected peepholes onto the city of men; and one day the same tabby led him to discover the great Biarritz Restaurant.

Anyone wishing to see the Biarritz Restaurant had only to assume the posture of a cat, that is, proceed on all fours. Cat and man, in this fashion, walked around a kind of dome, at whose foot some low, rectangular little windows opened. Following the tabby's example, Marcovaldo looked down. They were transoms through which the luxurious hall received air and light. To the sound of Gypsy violins, partridges and quails swirled by on silver dishes balanced by the white-gloved fingers of waiters in tailcoats. Or, more precisely, above the partridges and quails the dishes whirled, and above the dishes the white gloves, and poised on the waiters' patent-leather shoes, the gleaming parquet floor, from which hung dwarf potted palms and tablecloths and crystal and buckets like bells with the champagne bottle for their clapper: everything was turned upside down because Marcovaldo, for fear of being seen, wouldn't stick his head inside the window and confined himself to looking at the reversed reflection of the room in the tilted pane.

But it was not so much the windows of the dining room as those of the kitchens that interested the cat: looking through the former you saw, distant and somehow transfigured, what in the kitchens presented itself—quite concrete and within paw's reach—as a plucked bird or a fresh fish. And it was toward the kitchens, in fact, that the tabby wanted to lead Marcovaldo, either through a gesture of altruistic friendship or else because it counted on the man's help for one of its raids. Marcovaldo, however, was reluctant to leave his belvedere over the main room, first as he was fascinated by the luxury of the place, and then because something down there had riveted his attention. To such an extent that, overcoming his fear of being seen, he kept peeking in, with his head in the transom.

In the midst of the room, directly under that pane, there was a little glass fish tank, a kind of aquarium, where some fat trout were swimming. A special customer approached, a man with a shiny bald pate, black suit, black beard. An old waiter in tailcoat followed him, carrying a little net as if he were going to catch butterflies. The gentleman in black looked at the trout with a grave, intent air; then he raised one hand and with a slow, solemn gesture singled out a fish. The waiter dipped the net into the tank, pursued the appointed trout, captured it, headed for the kitchens, holding out in front of him, like a lance, the net in which the fish wriggled. The gentleman in black, solemn as magistrate who has handed down a capital sentence, went to take his seat and wait for the return of the trout, sautéed *à la meunière*.

If I found a way to drop a line from up here and make one of those trout bite, Marcovaldo thought, I couldn't be accused of theft; at worst, of fishing in an unauthorized place. And ignoring the meows that called him toward the kitchens, he went to collect his fishing tackle.

Nobody in the crowded dining room of the Biarritz saw the long, fine line, armed with hook and bait, as it slowly dropped into the tank. The fish saw the bait, and flung themselves on it. In the fray one trout managed to bite the worm, and immediately it began to rise, rise, emerge from the water, a silvery flash, it darted up high, over the laid tables and the trolleys of hors d'oeuvres, over the blue flames of the crêpes Suzette, until it vanished into the heavens of the transom.

Marcovaldo had yanked the rod with the brisk snap of the expert fisherman, so the fish landed behind his back. The trout had barely touched the ground when the cat sprang. What little life the trout still had was lost between the tabby's teeth. Marcovaldo, who had abandoned his line at that moment to run and grab the fish, saw it snatched from under his nose, hook and all. He was quick to put one foot on the rod, but the snatch had been so strong that the rod was all the man had left, while the tabby ran off with the fish, pulling the line after it. Treacherous kitty! It had vanished.

But this time it wouldn't escape him; there was that long line trailing after him and showing the way he had taken. Though he had lost sight of the cat, Marcovaldo followed the end of the line; there it was, running along a wall; it climbed a parapet, wound through a doorway, was swallowed up by a basement. . . . Marcovaldo, venturing into more and more cattish places, climbed roofs, straddled railings, always managed to catch a glimpse—perhaps only a second before it disappeared—of that moving trace that indicated the thief's path.

Now the line played out down a sidewalk, in the midst of the traffic, and Marcovaldo, running after it, almost managed to grab it. He flung himself down on his belly; there, he grabbed it! He managed to seize one end of the line before it slipped between the bars of a gate.

Beyond a half-rusted gate and two bits of wall buried under climbing plants, there was a little rank garden, with a small, abandoned-looking building at the far end of it. A carpet of dry leaves covered the path, and dry leaves lay everywhere under the boughs of the two plane trees, forming actually some little mounds in the yard. A layer of leaves was yellowing in the green water of a pool. Enormous buildings rose all around, skyscrapers with thousands of windows, like so many eyes trained disapprovingly on that little square patch with two trees, a few tiles, and all those yellow leaves, surviving right in the middle of an area of great traffic.

And in this garden, perched on the capitals and balustrades, lying on the dry leaves of the flower beds, climbing on the trunks of the trees or on the drainpipes, motionless on their four paws, their tails making a question mark, seated to wash their faces, there were tiger cats, black cats, white cats, calico cats, tabbies, Angoras, Persians, house cats and stray cats, perfumed cats and mangy cats. Marcovaldo realized he had finally reached the heart of the cats' realm, their secret island. And, in his emotion, he almost forgot his fish.

It had remained, that fish, hanging by the line from the branch of a tree, out of reach of the cats' leaps; it must have dropped from its kidnapper's mouth at some clumsy movement, perhaps as it was defended from the others, or perhaps displayed as an extraordinary prize. The line had got tangled, and Marcovaldo, tug as he would, couldn't manage to yank it loose. A furious battle had meanwhile been joined among the cats, to reach that unreachable fish, or rather, to win the right to try and reach it. Each wanted to prevent the others from leaping; they hurled themselves on one another, they tangled in midair, they rolled around clutching each other, and finally a general war broke out in a whirl of dry, crackling leaves.

After many futile yanks, Marcovaldo now felt the line was free, but he took care not to pull it: the trout would have fallen right in the midst of that infuriated scrimmage of felines.

It was at this moment that, from the top of the walls of the gardens, a strange rain began to fall: fishbones, heads, tails, even bits of lung and lights. Immediately the cats' attention was distracted from the suspended trout and they flung themselves on the new delicacies. To Marcovaldo, this seemed the right moment to pull the line and regain his fish. But, before he had time to act, from a blind of the little villa, two yellow, skinny hands darted out: one was brandishing scissors; the other, a frying pan. The hand with the scissors was raised above the trout, the hand with the frying pan was thrust under it. The scissors cut the line, the trout fell into the pan; hands, scissors, and pan withdrew, the blind closed—all in the space of a second. Marcovaldo was totally bewildered.

"Are you also a cat lover?" A voice at his back made him turn round. He was surrounded by little old women, some of them ancient, wearing old-fashioned hats on their heads; others, younger, but with the look of spinsters; and all were carrying in their hands or their bags packages of leftover meat or fish, and some even had little pans of milk. "Will you help me throw this package over the fence, for those poor creatures?"

All the ladies, cat lovers, gathered at this hour around the garden of dry leaves to take food to their protégés.

"Can you tell me why they are all here, these cats?" Marcovaldo inquired.

"Where else could they go? This garden is all they have left! Cats come here from other neighborhoods, too, from miles and miles around. . . ."

"And birds, as well," another lady added. "They're forced to live by the hundreds and hundreds on these few trees. . . ."

"And the frogs, they're all in that pool, and at night they never stop croaking. . . . You can hear them even on the eighth floor of the buildings around here."

"Who does this villa belong to anyway?" Marcovaldo asked. Now, outside the gate, there weren't just the cat-loving ladies but also other people: the man from the gas pump opposite, the apprentices from a mechanic's shop, the postman, the grocer, some passersby. And none of them, men and women, had to be asked twice; all wanted to have their say, as always when a mysterious and controversial subject comes up.

"It belongs to a marchesa. She lives there, but you never see her. . . ."

"She's been offered millions and millions, by developers, for this little patch of land, but she won't sell. . . ."

"What would she do with millions, an old woman all alone in the world? She wants to hold on to her house, even if it's falling to pieces, rather than be forced to move. . . ." "It's the only undeveloped bit of land in the downtown area. . . . Its value goes up every year. . . . They've made her offers—"

"Offers! That's not all. Threats, intimidation, persecution . . . you don't know the half of it! Those contractors!"

"But she holds out. She's held out for years. . . ."

"She's a saint. Without her, where would those poor animals go?"

"A lot she cares about the animals, the old miser! Have you ever seen her give them anything to eat?"

"How can she feed the cats when she doesn't have food for herself? She's the last descendant of a ruined family!"

"She hates cats. I've seen her chasing them and hitting them with an umbrella!"

"Because they were tearing up her flower beds!"

"What flower beds? I've never seen anything in this garden but a great crop of weeds!"

Marcovaldo realized that with regard to the old marchesa opinions were sharply divided: some saw her as an angelic being, others as an egoist and a miser.

"It's the same with the birds; she never gives them a crumb!"

"She gives them hospitality. Isn't that plenty?"

"Like she gives the mosquitoes, you mean. They all come from here, from that pool. In the summertime the mosquitoes eat us alive, and it's all the fault of that marchesa!"

"And the mice? This villa is a mine of mice. Under the dead leaves they have their burrows, and at night they come out. . . ."

"As far as the mice go, the cats take care of them. . . ."

"Oh, you and your cats! If we had to rely on them. . . ."

"Why? Have you got something to say against cats?"

Here the discussion degenerated into a general quarrel.

"The authorities should do something: confiscate the villa!" one man cried.

"What gives them the right?" another protested.

"In a modern neighborhood like ours, a mouse nest like this . . . it should be forbidden. . . ."

"Why, I picked my apartment precisely because it overlooked this little bit of green. . . ."

"Green, hell! Think of the fine skyscraper they could build here!"

Marcovaldo would have liked to add something of his own, but he couldn't get a word in. Finally, all in one breath, he exclaimed: "The marchesa stole a trout from me!"

The unexpected news supplied fresh ammunition to the old woman's enemies, but her defenders exploited it as proof of the indigence to which the unfortunate noblewoman was reduced. Both sides agreed that Marcovaldo should go and knock at her door to demand an explanation.

It wasn't clear whether the gate was locked or unlocked; in any case, it opened, after a push, with a mournful creak. Marcovaldo picked his way among the leaves and cats, climbed the steps to the porch, knocked hard at the entrance.

At a window (the very one where the frying pan had appeared), the blind was raised slightly and in one corner a round, pale blue eye was seen, and a clump of hair dyed an undefinable color, and a dry skinny hand. A voice was heard, asking: "Who is it? Who's at the door?" the words accompanied by a cloud smelling of fried oil.

"It's me, Marchesa. The trout man," Marcovaldo explained. "I don't mean to trouble you. I only wanted to tell you, in case you didn't know, that the trout was stolen from me, by that cat, and I'm the one who caught it. In fact the line—"

"Those cats! It's always those cats . . . ," the marchesa said from behind the shutter, with a shrill, somewhat nasal voice. "All my troubles come from the cats! Nobody knows what I go through! Prisoner night and day of those horrid beasts! And with all the refuse people throw over the walls, to spite me!"

"But my trout . . ."

"Your trout! What am I supposed to know about your trout!" The marchesa's voice became almost a scream, as if she wanted to drown out the sizzle of the oil in the pan, which came through the window along with the aroma of fried fish. "How can I make sense of anything, with all the stuff that rains into my house?"

"I understand, but did you take the trout or didn't you?"

"When I think of all the damage I suffer because of the cats! Ah, fine state of affairs! I'm not responsible for anything! I can't tell you what I've lost! Thanks to those cats, who've occupied house and garden for years! My life at the mercy of those animals! Go and find the owners! Make them pay damages! Damages? A whole life destroyed! A prisoner here, unable to move a step!"

"Excuse me for asking: but who's forcing you to stay?"

From the crack in the blind there appeared sometimes a round, pale blue eye, sometimes a mouth with two protruding teeth; for a moment the whole face was visible, and to Marcovaldo it seemed, bewilderingly, the face of a cat.

"They keep me prisoner, they do, those cats! Oh, I'd be glad to leave! What wouldn't I give for a little apartment all my own, in a nice clean modern building! But I can't go out. . . . They follow me, they block my path, they trip me up!" The voice became a whisper, as if to confide a secret. "They're afraid I'll sell the lot. . . . They won't leave me. . . . won't allow me. . . . When the builders come to offer me a contract, you should see them, those cats! They get in the way, pull out their claws; they even chased a lawyer off! Once I had the contract right here, I was about to sign it, and they dived in through the window, knocked over the inkwell, tore up all the pages. . . ."

All of a sudden Marcovaldo remembered the time, the shipping department, the boss. He tiptoed off over the dried leaves, as the voice continued to come through the slats of the blind, enfolded in that cloud apparently from the oil of a frying pan. "They even scratched me. . . . I still have the scar. . . . All alone here at the mercy of these demons. . . ."

Winter came. A blossoming of white flakes decked the branches and capitals and the cats' tails. Under the snow, the dry leaves dissolved into mush. The cats were rarely seen, the cat lovers even less; the packages of fishbones were consigned only to cats who came to the door. Nobody, for quite a while, had seen anything of the marchesa. No smoke came now from the chimneypot of the villa.

One snowy day, the garden was again full of cats, who had returned as if it were spring, and they were meowing as if on a moonlight night. The neighbors realized that something had happened; they went and knocked at the marchesa's door. She didn't answer: she was dead.

In the spring, instead of the garden, there was a huge building site that a contractor had set up. The steam shovels dug down to great depths to make room for the foundations, cement poured into the iron armatures, a very high crane passed beams to the workmen who were making the scaffoldings. But how could they go on with their work? Cats walked along all the planks, they made bricks fall and upset buckets of mortar, they fought in the midst of the piles of sand. When you started to raise an armature, you found a cat perched on the top of it, hissing fiercely. More treacherous pusses climbed onto the masons' backs as if to purr, and there was no getting rid of them. And the birds continued making their nests in all the trestles, the cab of the crane looked like an aviary. . . . And you couldn't dip up a bucket of water that wasn't full of frogs, croaking and hopping. . . .

# The Cat That Walked by Himself

BY RUDYARD KIPLING

I N 1902 RUDYARD KIPLING (1865–1936) published a book for children en-titled *Just So Stories*. It was an instant success and has not been out of print since, which is more than can be said for much of the rest of Kipling's huge and widely varied output—poems, ballads, stories, novels and other non-fiction. Among the *Just So Stories,* "The Cat That Walked by Himself" holds a special place in the hearts of cat lovers, because in the guise of fable it spells out perfectly the mixture of aloofness and ingratiating cleverness that is peculiarly feline. Cats are still walking by themselves, but they are also still coming home to a warm spot by the fire—or the radiator.

★  ★  ★  ★  ★

HEAR AND ATTEND and listen; for this befell and behappened and became and was, O my Best Beloved, when the Tame animals were wild. The Dog was wild, and the Horse was wild, and the Cow was wild, and the Sheep was wild, and the Pig was wild—as wild as wild could be—and they walked in the Wet Wild Woods by their wild lones. But the wildest of all the wild animals was the Cat. He walked by himself, and all places were alike to him.

Of course the Man was wild too. He was dreadfully wild. He didn't even begin to be tame till he met the Woman, and she told him that she did not like living in his wild ways. She picked out a nice dry Cave, instead of a heap of wet leaves, to lie down in; and she strewed clean sand on the floor; and she lit a nice fire of wood at the back of the Cave; and she hung a dried wild-horse skin, tail-down, across the opening of the Cave; and she said, "Wipe your feet, dear, when you come in, and now we'll keep house."

That night, Best Beloved, they ate wild sheep roasted on the hot stones, and flavoured with wild garlic and wild pepper; and wild duck stuffed with wild rice and wild fenugreek and wild coriander; and marrow-bones of wild oxen; and wild cherries, and wild grenadillas. Then the Man went to sleep in front of the fire ever so happy; but the Woman sat up, combing her hair. She took the bone of the shoulder of mutton—the big flat blade-bone—and she looked at the wonderful marks on it, and she threw more wood on the fire, and she made a Magic. She made the First Singing Magic in the world.

Out of the Wet Wild Woods all the wild animals gathered together where they could see the light of the fire a long way off, and they wondered what it meant.

Then Wild Horse stamped with his wild foot and said, "O my Friends and O my Enemies, why have the Man and the Woman made that great light in that great Cave, and what harm will it do us?"

Wild Dog lifted up his wild nose and smelled the smell of the roast mutton, and said, "I will go up and see and look, and say; for I think it is good. Cat, come with me."

"Nenni!" said the Cat. "I am the Cat who walks by himself, and all places are alike to me. I will not come."

"Then we can never be friends again," said Wild Dog, and he trotted off to the Cave. But when he had gone a little way the Cat said to himself, "All places are alike to me. Why should I not go too and see and look and come away at my own liking?" So he slipped after Wild Dog softly, very softly, and hid himself where he could hear everything.

When Wild Dog reached the mouth of the Cave he lifted up the dried horse-skin with his nose and sniffed the beautiful smell of the roast mutton, and the Woman, looking at the blade-bone, heard him, and laughed, and said, "Here comes the first. Wild Thing out of the Wild Woods, what do you want?"

Wild Dog said, "O my Enemy and Wife of my Enemy, what is this that smells so good in the Wild Woods?"

Then the Woman picked up a roasted mutton-bone and threw it to Wild Dog and said, "Wild Thing out of the Wild Woods, taste and try." Wild Dog gnawed the bone, and it was more delicious than anything he had ever tasted, and he said, "O my Enemy and Wife of my Enemy, give me another."

The Woman said, "Wild Thing out of the Wild Woods, help my Man to hunt through the day and guard this Cave at night, and I will give you as many roast bones as you need."

"Ah!" said the Cat, listening. "This is a very wise Woman, but she is not so wise as I am."

Wild Dog crawled into the Cave and laid his head on the Woman's lap, and said, "O my Friend and Wife of my Friend, I will help your Man to hunt through the day, and at night I will guard your Cave."

"Ah!" said the Cat, listening. "That is a very foolish Dog." And he went back through the Wet Wild Woods waving his wild tail, and walking by his wild lone. But he never told anybody.

When the Man waked up he said, "What is Wild Dog doing here?" And the Woman said, "His name is not Wild Dog any more, but the First Friend, because he will be our friend for always and always and always. Take him with you when you go hunting."

Next night the Woman cut great green armfuls of fresh grass from the water-meadows, and dried it before the fire, so that it smelt like new-mown hay, and she sat at the mouth of the Cave and plaited a halter out of horse-hide, and she looked at the shoulder-of-mutton bone—at the big broad blade-bone—and she made a Magic. She made the Second Singing Magic in the world.

Out of the Wild Woods all the wild animals wondered what had happened to Wild Dog, and at last Wild Horse stamped with his foot and said, "I will go and see and say why Wild Dog has not returned. Cat, come with me."

"Nenni!" said the Cat. "I am the Cat who walks by himself, and all places are alike to me. I will not come." But all the same he followed Wild Horse softly, very softly, and hid himself where he could hear everything.

When the Woman heard Wild Horse tripping and stumbling on his long mane, she laughed and said, "Here comes the second. Wild Thing out of the Wild Woods, what do you want?"

Wild Horse said, "O my Enemy and Wife of my Enemy, where is Wild Dog?"

The Woman laughed, and picked up the blade-bone and looked at it, and said, "Wild Thing out of the Wild Woods, you did not come here for Wild Dog, but for the sake of this good grass."

And Wild Horse, tripping and stumbling on his long mane, said, "That is true; give it me to eat."

The Woman said, "Wild Thing out of the Wild Woods, bend your wild head and wear what I give you, and you shall eat the wonderful grass three times a day."

"Ah!" said the Cat, listening. "This is a clever Woman, but she is not so clever as I am."

Wild Horse bent his wild head, and the Woman slipped the plaited-hide halter over it, and Wild Horse breathed on the Woman's feet and said, "O my Mistress, and Wife of my Master, I will be your servant for the sake of the wonderful grass."

"Ah!" said the Cat, listening. "That is a very foolish Horse." And he went back through the Wet Wild Woods, waving his wild tail and walking by his wild lone. But he never told anybody.

When the Man and the Dog came back from hunting, the Man said, "What is Wild Horse doing here?" And the Woman said, "His name is not Wild Horse any more, but the First Servant, because he will carry us from place to place for always and always and always. Ride on his back when you go hunting."

Next day, holding her wild head high that her wild horns should not catch in the wild trees, Wild Cow came up to the Cave, and the Cat followed, and hid himself just the same as before; and everything happened just the same as before; and the Cat said the same things as before; and when Wild Cow had promised to give her milk to the Woman every day in exchange for the wonderful grass, the Cat went back through the Wet Wild Woods waving his wild tail and walking by his wild lone, just the same as before. But he never told anybody. And when the Man and the Horse and the Dog came home from hunting and asked the same questions same as before, the Woman said, "Her name is not Wild Cow any more, but the Giver of Good Food. She will give us the warm white milk for always and always and always, and I will take care of her while you and the First Friend and the First Servant go hunting."

Next day the Cat waited to see if any other Wild Thing would go up to the Cave, but no one moved in the Wet Wild Woods, so the Cat walked there by himself; and he saw the Woman milking the Cow, and he saw the light of the fire in the Cave, and he smelt the smell of the warm white milk.

Cat said, "O my Enemy and Wife of my Enemy, where did Wild Cow go?"

The Woman laughed and said, "Wild Thing out of the Wild Woods, go back to the Woods again, for I have braided up my hair, and I have put away the magic blade-bone and we have no more need of either friends or servants in our Cave."

Cat said, "I am not a friend, and I am not a servant. I am the Cat who walks by himself, and I wish to come into your Cave."

Woman said, "Then why did you not come with First Friend on the first night?"

Cat grew very angry and said, "Has Wild Dog told tales of me?"

Then the Woman laughed and said, "You are the Cat who walks by himself, and all places are alike to you. You are neither a friend nor a servant. You have said it yourself. Go away and walk by yourself in all places alike."

Then Cat pretended to be sorry and said, "Must I never come into the Cave? Must I never sit by the warm fire? Must I never drink the warm white milk? You are very wise and very beautiful. You should not be cruel even to a Cat."

Woman said, "I knew I was wise, but I did not know I was beautiful. So I will make a bargain with you. If ever I say one word in your praise, you may come into the Cave."

"And if you say two words in my praise?" said the Cat.

"I never shall," said the Woman, "but if I say two words in your praise, you may sit by the fire in the Cave."

"And if you say three words?" said the Cat.

"I never shall," said the Woman, "but if I say three words in your praise, you may drink the warm white milk three times a day for always and always and always."

Then the Cat arched his back and said, "Now let the Curtain at the mouth of the Cave, and the Fire at the back of the Cave, and the Milkpots that stand beside the Fire, remember what my Enemy and the Wife of my Enemy has said." And he went away through the Wet Wild Woods waving his wild tail and walking by his wild lone.

That night when the Man and the Horse and the Dog came home from hunting, the Woman did not tell them of the bargain that she had made with the Cat, because she was afraid that they might not like it.

Cat went far and far away and hid himself in the Wet Wild Woods by his wild lone for a long time till the Woman forgot all about him. Only the Bat—the little upside-down Bat—that hung inside the Cave knew where Cat hid; and every evening Bat would fly to Cat with news of what was happening.

One evening Bat said, "There is a Baby in the Cave. He is new and pink and fat and small, and the Woman is very fond of him."

"Ah," said the Cat, listening. "But what is the Baby fond of?"

"He is fond of things that are soft and tickle," said the Bat. "He is fond of warm things to hold in his arms when he goes to sleep. He is fond of being played with. He is fond of all those things."

"Ah," said the Cat, listening. "Then my time has come."

Next night Cat walked through the Wet Wild Woods and hid very near the Cave till morning-time, and Man and Dog and Horse went hunting. The Woman was busy cooking that morning, and the Baby cried and inter-rupted. So she carried him outside the Cave and gave him a handful of pebbles to play with. But still the Baby cried.

Then the Cat put out his paddy paw and patted the Baby on the cheek, and it cooed; and the Cat rubbed against its fat knees and tickled it under its fat chin with his tail. And the Baby laughed; and the Woman heard him and smiled.

Then the Bat—the little upside-down Bat—that hung in the mouth of the Cave said, "O my Hostess and Wife of my Host and Mother of my Host's Son, a Wild Thing from the Wild Woods is most beautifully playing with your Baby."

"A blessing on that Wild Thing whoever he may be," said the Woman, straightening her back, "for I was a busy woman this morning and he has done me a service."

That very minute and second, Best Beloved, the dried horse-skin Cur-tain that was stretched tail-down at the mouth of the Cave fell down— *woosh!*—because it remembered the bargain she had made with the Cat; and when the Woman went to pick it up—lo and behold!—the Cat was sitting quite comfy inside the Cave.

"O my Enemy and Wife of my Enemy and Mother of my Enemy," said the Cat, "it is I: for you have spoken a word in my praise, and now I can sit within the Cave for always and always and always. But still I am the Cat who walks by himself, and all places are alike to me."

The Woman was very angry, and shut her lips tight and took up her spinning-wheel and began to spin.

But the Baby cried because the Cat had gone away, and the Woman could not hush it, for it struggled and kicked and grew black in the face.

"O my Enemy and Wife of my Enemy and Mother of my Enemy," said the Cat, "take a strand of the thread that you are spinning and tie it to your spindle-whorl and drag it along the floor, and I will show you a Magic that shall make your Baby laugh as loudly as he is now crying."

"I will do so," said the Woman, "because I am at my wits' end; but I will not thank you for it."

She tied the thread to the little clay spindle-whorl and drew it across the floor, and Cat ran after it and patted it with his paws and rolled head over heels, and tossed it backward over his shoulder and chased it between his hind legs and pretended to lose it, and pounced down upon it again, till the Baby laughed as loudly as it had been crying, and scrambled after the Cat and frolicked all over the Cave till it grew tired and settled down to sleep with the Cat in its arms.

"Now," said Cat, "I will sing the Baby a song that shall keep him asleep for an hour." And he began to purr, loud and low, low and loud, till the Baby fell fast asleep. The Woman smiled as she looked down upon the two of them, and said, "That was wonderfully done. No question but you are very clever, O Cat."

That very minute and second, Best Beloved, the smoke of the Fire at the back of the Cave came down in clouds from the roof—*puff!*—because it remembered the bargain she had made with the Cat; and when it had cleared away—lo and behold!—the Cat was sitting quite comfy close to the fire.

"O my Enemy and Wife of my Enemy and Mother of my Enemy," said the Cat, "it is I: for you have spoken a second word in my praise, and now I can sit by the warm fire at the back of the Cave for always and always and always. But still I am the Cat who walks by himself, and all places are alike to me."

Then the Woman was very very angry, and let down her hair and put more wood on the fire and brought out the broad blade-bone of the shoulder of mutton and began to make a Magic that should prevent her from saying a third word in praise of the Cat. It was not a Singing Magic, Best Beloved, it was a Still Magic; and by and by the Cave grew so still that a little wee-wee mouse crept out of a corner and ran across the floor.

"O my Enemy and Wife of my Enemy and Mother of my Enemy," said the Cat, "is that little mouse part of your Magic?"

"Ouh! Chee! No indeed!" said the Woman, and she dropped the blade-bone and jumped upon the footstool in front of the fire and braided up her hair very quick for fear that the mouse should run up it.

"Ah," said the Cat, watching. "Then the mouse will do me no harm if I eat it?"

"No," said the Woman, braiding up her hair, "eat it quickly and I will ever be grateful to you."

Cat made one jump and caught the little mouse, and the Woman said, "A hundred thanks. Even the First Friend is not quick enough to catch little mice as you have done. You must be very wise."

That very minute and second, O Best Beloved, the Milk-pot that stood by the fire cracked in two pieces—*ffft!*—because it remembered the bargain she had made with the Cat; and when the Woman jumped down from the footstool—lo and behold!—the Cat was lapping up the warm white milk that lay in one of the broken pieces.

"O my Enemy and Wife of my Enemy and Mother of my Enemy," said the Cat, "it is I: for you have spoken three words in my praise, and now I can drink the warm white milk three times a day for always and always and always. But *still* I am the Cat who walks by himself, and all places are alike to me."

Then the Woman laughed and set the Cat a bowl of the warm white milk and said, "O Cat, you are as clever as a man, but remember that your bargain was not made with the Man or the Dog, and I do not know what they will do when they come home."

"What is that to me?" said the Cat. "If I have my place in the Cave by the fire and my warm white milk three times a day I do not care what the Man or the Dog can do."

That evening when the Man and the Dog came into the Cave, the Woman told them all the story of the bargain, while the Cat sat by the fire and smiled. Then the Man said, "Yes, but he has not made a bargain with *me* or with all proper Men after me." Then he took off his two leather boots and he took up his little stone axe (that makes three) and he fetched a piece of wood and a hatchet (that is five altogether), and he set them out in a row and he said, "Now we will make *our* bargain. If you do not catch mice when you are in the Cave for always and always and always, I will throw these five things at you whenever I see you, and so shall all proper Men do after me."

"Ah!" said the Woman, listening. "This is a very clever Cat, but he is not as clever as my Man."

The Cat counted the five things (and they looked very knobby) and he said, "I will catch mice when I am in the Cave for always and always and always; but *still* I am the Cat who walks by himself, and all places are alike to me."

"Not when I am near," said the Man. "If you had not said that last I would have put all these things away for always and always and always; but now I am going to throw my two boots and my little stone axe (that makes three) at you whenever I meet you. And so shall all proper Men do after me!"

Then the Dog said, "Wait a minute. He has not made a bargain with *me* or with all proper Dogs after me." And he showed his teeth and said, "If you are not kind to the Baby while I am in the Cave for always and always and always, I will hunt you till I catch you, and when I catch you I will bite you. And so shall all proper Dogs do after me."

"Ah!" said the Woman, listening. "This is a very clever Cat, but he is not so clever as the Dog."

Cat counted the Dog's teeth (and they looked very pointed) and he said, "I will be kind to the Baby while I am in the cave, as long as he does not pull my tail too hard, for always and always and always. But *still* I am the Cat who walks by himself, and all places are alike to me."

"Not when I am near," said the Dog. "If you had not said that last I would have shut my mouth for always and always and always; but *now* I am going to hunt you up a tree whenever I meet you. And so shall all proper Dogs do after me."

Then the Man threw his two boots and his little stone axe (that makes three) at the Cat, and the Cat ran out of the Cave and the Dog chased him up a tree; and from that day to this, Best Beloved, three proper Men out of five will always throw things at a Cat whenever they meet him, and all proper Dogs will chase him up a tree. But the Cat keeps his side of the bargain too. He will kill mice, and he will be kind to Babies when he is in the house, just as long as they do not pull his tail too hard. But when he has done that, and between times, and when the moon gets up and night comes, he is the Cat that walks by himself, and all places are alike to him. Then he goes out to the Wet Wild Woods or up the Wet Wild Trees or on the Wet Wild Roofs, waving his wild tail and walking by his wild lone.

# Rhubarb

BY H. ALLEN SMITH

C ATS HAVE BEEN the oblivious inheritors of many fortunes of various shapes and sizes, but only Rhubarb has ever inherited a big-league baseball team. According to H. Allen Smith (1906–1976), the chronicler of Rhubarb in three books (from the first of which, *Rhubarb,* this extract is taken), the cat's exceptional fortune was not due to his beauty or charming nature. On the contrary, he was a bad-tempered yellow tom with a penchant for attacking dogs and postmen, and it was this behavior that endeared him to the equally bad-tempered millionaire named Banner who willed him the New York Loons.

H. Allen Smith was a journalist, chili expert, and humorist. He published his first book, *Low Man on a Totem Pole,* in 1939, and seldom thereafter failed to have a book on the best-seller list. *Rhubarb* was made into a movie in 1951.

★   ★   ★   ★   ★

APRIL IN NEW YORK. Weather. Scenery. The first cat-owned big-league baseball team in recorded history was ready to open its season.

Clarissa Wood insisted that she supervise preparation of the owner's field box, situated immediately behind the home team's dugout at Banner Field. She wanted a cat-sized throne done in platinum and black velvet set up in the middle of the box. She wanted to order a cedar tree from Mount Lebanon in Syria and have a scratching post made from it and placed in a conspicuous position. She contended that Rhubarb's jewel-encrusted sanitary tray should be placed in a small enclosure at the back of the box, out of sight of the populace.

One by one her ideas were knocked down.

Len Sickles had a good deal to say about the arrangements. He told Eric that whenever the new owner of the Loons was present at Banner Field for a baseball game, he, the owner, would have to be within easy reach of the Loon players. That, said Len, was a primary consideration.

"These goons of mine," the manager explained, "are playing ball like they were the nine Apostles. They are inspired. They believe that this cat brings them luck. And they insist that Rhubarb's gotta be somewhere close to the dugout, so they can run up and touch him."

Whereupon Eric invented a gadget. Rhubarb's pedestal was built into the structure of the box and against the back wall of the dugout. A small hole was cut into the wall, communicating between dugout and owner's box, a hole just big enough to accommodate a man's hand. Of necessity the hole was down near the floor of the owner's box, and Rhubarb, if placed beside it, where the players could reach through and touch him, would have been out of sight all the time. The gadget solved the problem. It was a cat elevator. Normally Rhubarb's pedestal extended above the roof of the dugout, giving the cat a clear view of the playing field and giving the fans a clear view of the cat. If an emergency arose, a tight spot, a clutch, a situation in which a player felt the need of touching Rhubarb, he turned a crank and the pedestal would sink, with Rhubarb on it. The player who wanted to touch Rhubarb for luck poked his hand through the aperture to do the touching, then withdrew it and cranked the pedestal back into its normal position. This arrangement obviated use of the silver cage, a situation that gave Eric some worry. He decided that some physical restraint would have to be put on the cat, so a strong fishline was hooked to a heavy staple in the wall of the box, with a snap fastener at the other end for Rhubarb's collar.

As for the sanitary tray, Eric vetoed Miss Wood's scheme for hiding it away out of sight.

"Rhubarb owns this ball club," he told her. "That means he owns this ball park—every inch of it. If he wants to go he can walk right out to home plate, or the pitcher's mound, and go. The fans will love it."

Miss Wood was incensed over the very thought of such a thing. "In the first place," she said, "someone would have to go with him and have him on his leash. I assure you, Mr. Yaeger, from the bottom of my heart, that a cat will not do such a thing while on a leash. Furthermore, who is going to take him out there in front of all those rowdy people?"

"I wouldn't mind doing it myself," Eric assured her. "I have my hammy moments."

"You are being most unreasonable," she said. "The very idea of that sweet kitty-cat having to do his business in front of the public horrifies me. What if he does own the park? Mr. Rockefeller owns Rockefeller Center, but *he* doesn't go on the skating rink."

"He would draw a good crowd if he did," said Eric. "He would get more skaters."

St. Louis was to oppose the Loons on opening day, and Eric led Rhubarb's entourage to Banner Field two hours before game time. Doom carried the cat and was flanked by Willy Bodfish and Clarissa Wood. Willy was unhappy, having had to cancel a date at his dentist's. Polly Pinckley accompanied Eric, clutching Ration Book Number Three in her hand. She insisted on carrying it wherever she went in the belief that she would shame Eric into abolishing the Office of Guava Jelly Administration.

The party went first to the executive quarters, and Rhubarb was introduced for the first time to his own private office. He seemed bored by it. Then Eric led the way to the Second Guess Club, a large room where the sports writers gathered before and after games. For this momentous occasion the sports writers were reinforced by a horde of feature writers, all of whom were clamoring for the right to sit in the owner's box. Some of these feature writers tried to pull an old dodge on Eric.

"My city editor," one young woman said to him, "assigned me to sit in the box with Rhubarb. I've simply got to do it. If I don't I lose my job. My city editor said so. And I've simply got to keep my job, Mr. Yaeger. I'm the sole support of my old mother who's dying of heartburn, and—"

"Nuts, sister!" Eric brushed her off. "I used to work on newspapers myself."

A sports columnist came forward escorting the Mayor. His Honor had been preparing for the ceremonial job of throwing out the first ball. He had been preparing for it at the bar, and it showed on him.

"Let me see the beautiful pussy!" boomed the Mayor.

"Shhh!" said Polly.

"I feel deeply honored," the Mayor plowed on. "I might even say I feel *deeply* honored. Indeed I do. Deeply. Rhubarb, my boy, I salute thee! You have become the *second* citizen of our great metropolis. I salute the second citizen! Hello, pussy! You ole pussy, you! I'm your Mayor! Yes sir! Lord Mayor of Dick Whittington! That's me! And I got a piece of advice for you, cat. I quote what that little jerk used to squeak: 'Patience and formaldehyde!' Where's the god-damn ball!"

"Your Honor," said Eric, "why don't you step over to the bar and have yourself a pleasant toddy? It's on Rhubarb. He owns all this, you know, including the toddies. Have a couple of snifters on a cat. It'll strengthen your throwing arm, improve your aim."

"Will it?" bayed the Mayor. "Adoo, adoo, kind friends, adoo! Off weedershine! Hoista mananna!"

The Mayor headed for the bar.

"It looks to me," murmured Polly, "as if His Honor is going to throw up the first ball."

A press photographer called Eric to one side.

"Listen, Mr. Yaeger, I got a marvelous idea. I want to get something unusual in the way of a picture."

"Good God, man!"

"I mean unusualer than the others. Now, I studied up this idea. Instead of having the Mayor throw out a baseball, why don't we let him throw out a meat ball? Leave the cat go after it. You could have him throw it out towards first base, and I'll be waiting out there and I'll get an unusual shot."

"Son, you have a fair sort of idea there, but didn't you just see His Honor? He'd have meat smeared all over Section 18."

The photographer was disappointed and went away grumbling and placed Eric in a prominent position on his son-of-a-bitch list, meaning that someday he'd try to snap a picture of Eric while Eric was picking his nose.

It was time to get down to the field. The stands were already packed as Eric came up through the Loons' dugout with Rhubarb in his arms. A roar of welcome greeted them. Eric walked across the grass toward the St. Louis dugout, stopping near home plate to hold the cat above his head, so all could see. The roar redoubled in volume.

At the visitors' dugout Eric came up against an unpleasant situation which he should have anticipated. St. Louis was the traditional enemy of the Loons, and Eric quickly recognized a strong undercurrent of animosity toward the cat. Several of the players, presumably the more superstitious members of the St. Louis team, ducked into their dugout and disappeared. Eric heard one man growl, "Git that godammn Joner outa here!"

Dick Madison, the St. Louis manager, furnished the tip-off on what to expect. The St. Louis gang was going to use ridicule as its chief weapon against Rhubarb. Madison minced up to Eric, took off his cap, and executed a low sweeping bow. Then he stepped back into the dugout and returned with a mousetrap. It was probably the biggest mousetrap ever manufactured—being about four feet long and two feet wide. It was already set and baited with a wedge of yellow cheese that probably cost around a dollar eighty-five. Madison clowned his way out toward home plate and daintily set the trap down on the grass. Then he stood up and gestured with his right arm, indicating that Rhubarb was to help himself to the cheese, a present from his host of St. Louis admirers. The crowd roared with laughter.

Meanwhile the St. Louis players had quietly gathered at the dugout entrance. Now they formed a conga line and started to dance. Each man was carrying a long cattail, and the fans were highly amused at the line of capering players curved and circled around the field. Eric wasn't greatly amused.

"Cute," he said acidly to Dick Madison. "Very, very cute!"

"Ah, shuddup!" said Madison. "Go scratch yourself a hole in the ground, you cat nurse, and crawl in it and cover yourself up!"

Eric felt like popping him one, but he had his arms full of cat. He chose the course of discretion and hurried back across the grass to the Loons' dugout. Here he encountered an explosive situation. Len Sickles was having difficulty keeping the Loons in hand. They wanted to open proceedings by swarming onto the field and beating the brains out of their opponents for making fun of their owner.

They gathered excitedly around Eric, and some of them talked reassuring baby talk to Rhubarb.

"Yes, Rhubarb!" crooned Benny Seymour, the coach. "You sweet liddle Rhubarb you! You sweet thing! Pay no attention to them filthy bastards, honey! We'll fix 'em for you! Yes sir, we will!"

Others expressed similar sentiments. Eric was somehow pleased with it all. The boys were one hundred percent back of Rhubarb. Old Thad had never commanded such loyalty.

The others were already in the owner's box, and Eric took Rhubarb to his pedestal. The cat was behaving like a gentleman. He sat on the pedestal for a while, looking around at all the color and activity and noise, and then he hopped over into Eric's lap and went to sleep.

Eric had to wake him up when the time came for the game to start. The line-ups were being announced over the loud-speaker system. The announcer called attention to the presence of the new owner of the Loons. Eric put the cat back on the pedestal, and Rhubarb stretched himself and yawned for the edification of the crowd.

Across the way two men held the Mayor up, pointed him in the direction of the field, and told him to throw. He threw, and the ball went into Section 5 behind the Mayor and hit a woman in the eye. Almost everyone in the park was watching Rhubarb, so the Mayor's inadequate performance attracted little attention and he was given no opportunity to repeat it.

Rhubarb now appeared to take an interest in the proceedings. He sat up and watched the Loons take the field. Goff was pitching, and the St. Louis center fielder, Peterson, was the first man to face him. Peterson connected with the first ball thrown to him.

A split second after the bat cracked against the ball something cracked in the owner's box. Rhubarb shot forward, the fishline snapped, and the yellow cat streaked into right field.

It was the fastest Eric had ever seen Rhubarb move. The ball went to the right of the first baseman, and Rhubarb was on it before the right fielder could reach it. The fielder ran up, then stopped in bewilderment. Rhubarb was trying to seize the baseball in his teeth, and the fielder's perplexity was so great that he could do nothing but stand there helplessly. Meanwhile Peterson was quickly circling the bases.

Then a new element of confusion entered the picture. Someone in the St. Louis dugout played the visitors' trump card. They turned loose a bulldog. At the same moment someone in the right-field bleachers tossed a terrier over the fence.

Both dogs went for Rhubarb full tilt.

The stands, the dugouts, the players on the field, the game officials—everyone was in an uproar.

Rhubarb looked up from the ball and saw the bulldog coming at him. He feinted, pretending that he was about to flee in the direction of his box.

The bulldog was lost. He swerved, and as he swerved Rhubarb hit him, clawing and biting. The dog let forth a scream of anguish just as the terrier arrived on the scene. That shriek did something to the terrier. He put on the brakes, skidded to an amazed halt, took another quick look just to make sure, then wheeled around and started for what he hoped would be some secluded spot fifty miles away. But Rhubarb was after him like a bullet, leaving the bulldog lying on the field, yelping and bleeding. Now came the terrier's turn. The cat ripped and whipsawed him up one side and down the other.

People were beginning to pour onto the field, and the din was deafening, yet above it all sounded a howl of pain that came from no dog. The High Commissioner had jumped over the wall of his box; he had taken about five quick steps with his eyes fixed on the distant ruckus. He had stepped squarely into the big mousetrap, and the thing had almost torn his leg off.

Willy Bodfish was the first occupant of the owner's box to reach the scene of combat, and he succeeded in prying Rhubarb loose from the terrier. The fallen dogs were removed from the arena, and back in the box Eric got Rhubarb into his cage while police were herding the more excited fans off the field. There was an immediate and acrimonious conference in front of the Loons' dugout involving the umpires, the High Commissioner (free of the trap but sorely wounded), officials of the league, managers of both teams, and most of the players.

Dick Madison was hot with fury—so enraged that he simply jumped up and down on the ground.

"That's my kid's dog!" he screamed in anger. "That cat's killed him! Leave me at him!"

They finally had to seize and restrain Madison. Len Sickles, too, had his dander up and was howling that he was going to punch Dick Madison's head off.

"I saw it!" yelled Sickles. "Everybody saw it! You turned that dog loose outa your own dugout!"

There was a prolonged and angry consideration of ground rules. The High Commissioner stood by, glaring at Dick Madison, for he had seen where that damned trap came from. The umpires, after a whispered conference with the High Commissioner, announced that Peterson was not entitled to a home run. He was not entitled to anything. Madison went into a new tantrum bordering on epilepsy over this fresh manifestation of man's inhumanity to man. His players milled around with fists clenched, eager to start a fight. Madison wanted to take his team and leave, go back to St. Louis, and never again have any relations with the Loons.

The argument over Peterson's status—whether or not he was entitled to at least a hit—went on for fifteen minutes.

"It was an act of God," said the High Commissioner.

"Then, by God, we get a home run out of it!" bellowed Madison.

"You'll get a bust in the nose out of it," yelled the High Commissioner. "What the hell do you mean by leaving that trap out there for me to fall into? Look what it did! Ripped my pants leg clear off! I oughta kill you and then bar you from baseball for the rest of your lousy life! Peterson gets no hit. I rule that Peterson must return to the plate and we start all over again. And"—he gave Eric an ominous glance—"if that cat gets onto the field again, I'll outlaw you and the cat and your whole damn team so you won't even be able to get into the Piedmont League!"

"That cat won't get onto the field again," said a stranger, stepping forward. "I seize this cat in the name of the law."

The stranger looked around for a cat to seize in the name of the law, but Rhubarb was some thirty feet away in his cage.

"Now what?" said Eric.

"Hand over that cat," said the stranger. He pulled back his coat and exhibited a shield. "I happen to be the sheriff of this county. Judge Loudermilk of Surrogate Court commands the appearance of one Rhubarb Banner forthwith, for examination before trial, in the case of Tatlock versus Banner."

"You're crazy!" cried Eric. "You can't examine a cat before trial! What'll you examine him for, fleas?"

"All I know is I got my orders," said the sheriff. "The cat goes, and he goes right now."

"Furthermore," Eric argued, "this doesn't look legally proper to me. Maybe you've got a subpoena. But you can't come out here and seize Rhubarb like this."

"I've got a subpoena," said the sheriff, "and if that cat was a human I'd serve it on him and be done with my duty. But this cat ain't a human. It's a case where I got to make up my own rules as I go along. Judge Loudermilk wants Rhubarb Banner, and Rhubarb Banner he gets. Let's get going."

And so Rhubarb and Eric and Polly and Doom and Clarissa and Willy trooped out of the stands and got into automobiles and drove to downtown Manhattan. Back at Banner Field the opening game of the season was started anew, and the Loons, deprived of a cat to touch, lost it by a score of 12–0.

# The Cyprian Cat

BY DOROTHY L. SAYERS

W HAT IS IT about cats that suggests the mysterious, even the bizarre? Unlike the open candor of a dog, a cat always seems to be hiding something, presumably something a mere man or woman wouldn't be able to understand anyway. Few stories better catch this essential scariness of cathood (to susceptible humans, at least) than Dorothy Sayers' elegant "The Cyprian Cat," or links it so clearly with evil. With sex, too—the term "Cyprian" is traditionally associated with Aphrodite, the Greek goddess of love.

Dorothy Leigh Sayers (1893–1957) was in her day the *grande dame* of mystery novelists, famed for such classics as *The Nine Tailors* and other stories dealing with her detective hero Lord Peter Wimsey. "The Cyprian Cat" first appeared in a short story collection titled *In the Teeth of the Evidence,* in 1940.

★   ★   ★   ★   ★

IT'S EXTRAORDINARILY DECENT of you to come along and see me like this, Harringay. Believe me, I do appreciate it. It isn't every busy K.C. who'd do as much for such a hopeless sort of client. I only wish I could spin you a more workable kind of story, but honestly I can only tell you exactly what I told Peabody. Of course, I can see he doesn't believe a word of it, and I don't blame him. He thinks I ought to be able to make up a more plausible tale than that, and I suppose I could, but where's the use? One's almost bound to fall down somewhere if one tries to swear to a lie. What I'm going to tell you is the absolute truth. I fired one shot and one shot only, and that was at the cat. It's funny that one should be hanged for shooting at a cat.

Merridew and I were always the best of friends, school and college and all that sort of thing. We didn't see very much of each other after the war, because we were living at opposite ends of the country; but we met in town from time to time and wrote occasionally, and each of us knew that the other was there in the background, so to speak. Two years ago he wrote and told me he was getting married. He was just turned forty and the girl was fifteen years younger, and he was tremendously in love. It gave me a bit of a jolt. You know how it is when your friends marry. You feel they will never be quite the same again, and I'd got used to the idea that Merridew and I were cut out to be old bachelors. But of course I congratulated him and sent him a wedding present, and I did sincerely hope he'd be happy. He was obviously over head and ears, almost dangerously so, I thought, considering all things. Though except for the difference of age, it seemed suitable enough. He told me he had met her at—of all places—a rectory garden party down in Norfolk, and that she had actually never been out of her native village. I mean literally—not so much as a trip to the nearest town. I'm not trying to convey that she wasn't pukka, or anything like that. Her father was some queer sort of recluse—a medievalist or something—desperately poor. He died shortly after their marriage.

I didn't see anything of them for the first year or so. Merridew is a civil engineer, you know, and he took his wife away after the honeymoon to Liverpool, where he was doing something in connection with the harbor. It must have been a big change for her from the wilds of Norfolk. I was in Birmingham, with my nose kept pretty close to the grindstone, so we only exchanged occasional letters. His were what I can only call deliriously happy, especially at first. Later on, he seemed a little worried about his wife's health. She was restless; town life didn't suit her; he'd be glad when he could finish up his Liverpool job and get her away into the country. There wasn't any doubt about their happiness, you understand. She'd got him body and soul as they say, and as far as I could make out it was mutual. I want to make that perfectly clear.

Well, to cut a long story short, Merridew wrote to me at the beginning of last month and said he was just off to a new job, a waterworks extension scheme down in Somerset, and he asked if I could possibly cut loose and join them there for a few weeks. He wanted to have a yarn with me, and Felice was longing to make my acquaintance. They had got rooms at the village inn. It was rather a remote spot, but there was fishing and scenery and so forth, and I should be able to keep Felice company while he was working up at the dam. I was about fed up with Birmingham, what with the heat and one thing and another, and it looked pretty good to me, and I was due for a holiday anyhow, so I fixed up to go. I had a bit of business to do in town, which I calculated would take me about a week, so I said I'd go down to Little Hexham on June 20.

As it happened, my business in London finished itself off unexpectedly soon, and on the sixteenth I found myself absolutely free and stuck in a hotel with road drills working just under the windows and a tar-spraying machine to make things livelier. You remember what a hot month it was—flaming June and no mistake about it. I didn't see any point in waiting, so I sent off a wire to Merridew, packed my bag, and took the train for Somerset the same evening. I couldn't get a compartment to myself, but I found a first-class smoker with only three seats occupied and stowed myself thankfully into the fourth corner. There was a military-looking old boy, an elderly female with a lot of bags and baskets, and a girl. I thought I should have a nice peaceful journey.

So I should have, if it hadn't been for the unfortunate way I'm built. It was quite all right at first. As a matter of fact, I think I was half asleep, and I only woke up properly at seven o'clock, when the waiter came to say that dinner was on. The other people weren't taking it, and when I came back from the restaurant car I found that the old boy had gone, and there were only the two women left. I settled down in my corner again, and gradually, as we went along, I found a horrible feeling creeping over me that there was a cat in the compartment somewhere. I'm one of those wretched people who can't stand cats. I don't mean just that I prefer dogs. I mean that the presence of a cat in the same room with me makes me feel like nothing on earth. I can't describe it, but I believe quite a lot of people are affected that way. Something to do with electricity, or so they tell me. I've read that very often the dislike is mutual, but it isn't so with me. The brutes seem to find me abominably fascinating, make a beeline for my legs every time. It's a funny sort of complaint, and it doesn't make me at all popular with dear old ladies.

Anyway, I began to feel more and more awful, and I realized that the old girl at the other end of the seat must have a cat in one of her innumerable baskets. I thought of asking her to put it out in the corridor or calling the guard and having it removed, but I knew how silly it would sound and made up my mind to try and stick it. I couldn't say the animal was misbehaving itself or anything, and she looked a pleasant old lady; it wasn't her fault that I was a freak. I tried to distract my mind by looking at the girl.

She was worth looking at, too—very slim and dark with one of those dead-white skins that make you think of magnolia blossom. She had the most astonishing eyes, too—I've never seen eyes quite like them—a very pale brown, almost amber, set wide apart and a little slanting, and they seemed to have a kind of luminosity of their own, if you get what I mean. I don't know if this sounds—I don't want you to think I was bowled over or anything. As a matter of fact, she held no sort of attraction for me, though I could imagine a different type of man going potty about her. She was just unusual, that was all. But however much I tried to think of other things I couldn't get rid of the uncomfortable feeling, and eventually I gave it up and went out into the corridor. I just mention this because it will help you to understand the rest of the story. If you can only realize how perfectly awful I feel when there's a cat about—even when it's shut up in a basket—you'll understand better how I came to buy the revolver.

Well, we got to Hexham Junction, which was the nearest station to Little Hexham, and there was old Merridew waiting on the platform. The girl was getting out too—but not the old lady with the cat, thank goodness—and I was just handing her traps out after her when he came galloping up and hailed us.

"Hullo," he said, "why that's splendid! Have you introduced yourselves?" So I tumbled to it then that the girl was Mrs. Merridew, who'd been up to Town on a shopping expedition, and I explained to her about my change of plans, and she said how jolly it was that I could come—the usual things. I noticed what an attractive low voice she had and how graceful her movements were, and I understood—though, mind you, I didn't share—Merridew's infatuation.

We got into his car; Mrs. Merridew sat in the back, and I got up beside Merridew and was very glad to feel the air and to get rid of the oppressive electric feeling I'd had in the train. He told me the place suited them wonderfully and had given Felice an absolutely new lease on life, so to speak. He said he was very fit, too, but I thought myself that he looked rather fagged and nervy.

You'd have liked that inn, Harringay. The real, old-fashioned stuff, as quaint as you make 'em, and everything genuine—none of your Tottenham Court Road antiques. We'd all had our grub, and Mrs. Merridew said she was tired; so she went up to bed early, and Merridew and I had a drink and went for a stroll around the village. It's a tiny hamlet quite at the other end of nowhere; lights out at ten, little thatched houses with pinched-up attic windows like furry ears. The place purred in its sleep. Merridew's working gang didn't sleep there, of course; they'd put up huts for them at the dams, a mile beyond the village.

The landlord was just locking up the bar when we came in, a block of a man with an absolutely expressionless face. His wife was a thin, sandy-haired woman who looked as though she was too downtrodden to open her mouth. But I found out afterward that was a mistake, for one evening when he'd taken one or two over the eight and showed signs of wanting to make a night of it, his wife sent him off upstairs with a gesture and a look that took the heart out of him. That first night she was sitting on the porch and hardly glanced at us as we passed her. I always thought her an uncomfortable kind of woman, but she certainly kept her house most exquisitely neat and clean.

They'd given me a noble bedroom, close under the eaves with a long, low casement window overlooking the garden. The sheets smelled of lavender, and I was between them and asleep almost before you could count ten. I was tired, you see. But later in the night I woke up. I was too hot, so took off some of the blankets and then strolled across to the window to get a breath of air. The garden was bathed in moonshine, and on the lawn I could see something twisting and turning oddly. I stared a bit before I made it out to be two cats. They didn't worry me at that distance, and I watched them for a bit before I turned in again. They were rolling over one another and jumping away again and chasing their own shadows on the grass, intent on their own mysterious business, taking themselves seriously, the way cats always do. It looked like a kind of ritual dance. Then something seemed to startle them, and they scampered away.

I went back to bed, but I couldn't get to sleep again. My nerves seemed to be all on edge. I lay watching the window and listening to a kind of soft rustling noise that seemed to be going on in the big wisteria that ran along my side of the house. And then something landed with a soft thud on the sill— a great Cyprian cat.

What did you say? Well, one of those striped gray-and-black cats. Tabby, that's right. In my part of the country they call them Cyprus cats, or

Cyprian cats. I'd never seen such a monster. It stood with its head cocked sideways, staring into the room and rubbing its ears very softly against the upright bar of the casement.

Of course, I couldn't do with that. I shooed the brute away, and it made off without a sound. Heat or no heat, I shut and fastened the window. Far out in the shrubbery I thought I heard a faint meowing, then silence. After that, I went straight off to sleep again and lay like a log till the girl came in to call me.

The next day Merridew ran us up in his car to see the place where they were making the dam, and that was the first time I realized that Felice's nerviness had not been altogether cured. He showed us where they had diverted part of the river into a swift little stream that was to be used for working the dynamo of an electrical plant. There were a couple of planks laid across the stream, and he wanted to take us over to show us the engine. It wasn't extraordinarily wide or dangerous, but Mrs. Merridew peremptorily refused to cross it and got quite hysterical when he tried to insist. Eventually he and I went over and inspected the machinery by ourselves. When we got back, she had recovered her temper and apologized for being so silly. Merridew abased himself, of course, and I began to feel a little *de trop*. She told me afterward that she had once fallen into the river as a child and been nearly drowned, and it had left her with a what d'ye call it—a complex about running water. And but for this one trifling episode, I never heard a single sharp word pass between them all the time I was there; nor, for a whole week, did I notice anything else to suggest a flaw in Mrs. Merridew's radiant health. Indeed, as the days wore on to midsummer and the heat grew more intense, her whole body seemed to glow with vitality. It was as though she was lit up from within.

Merridew was out all day and working very hard. I thought he was overdoing it and asked him if he was sleeping badly. He told me that, on the contrary, he fell asleep every night the moment his head touched the pillow and—what was most unusual with him—had no dreams of any kind. I myself felt well enough, but the hot weather made me languid and disinclined for exertion. Mrs. Merridew took me out for long drives in the car. I would sit for hours, lulled into a half slumber by the rush of warm air and the purring of the engine and gazing at my driver, upright at the wheel, her eyes fixed unwaveringly upon the spinning road. We explored the whole of the country to the south and east of Little Hexham, and once or twice went as far north as Bath. Once I suggested that we should turn eastward over the bridge and run down into what looked like rather beautiful wooded country, but Mrs. Merridew didn't care for the idea; she said it was a bad road and that the scenery on that side was disappointing.

Altogether I spent a pleasant week at Little Hexham, and if it had not been for the cats I should have been perfectly comfortable. Every night the garden seemed to be haunted by them—the Cyprian cat that I had seen the first night of my stay, a little ginger one, and a horrible stinking black tom were especially tiresome. And one night there was a terrified white kitten that mewed for an hour on end under my window. I flung boots and books at my visitors till I was heartily weary, but they seemed determined to make the inn garden their rendezvous. The nuisance grew worse from night to night; on one occasion I counted fifteen of them, sitting on their hinder ends in a circle, while the Cyprian cat danced her shadow dance among them, working in and out like a weaver's shuttle. I had to keep my window shut, for the Cyprian cat evidently made a habit of climbing up by the wisteria. The door, too, for once when I had gone down to fetch something from the sitting room, I found her on my bed, kneading the coverlet with her paws—*pr'rp, pr'rp, pr'rp*—with her eyes closed in a sensuous ecstasy. I beat her off, and she spat at me as she fled into the dark passage.

I asked the landlady about her, but she replied rather curtly that they kept no cat at the inn, and it is true that I never saw any of the beasts in the daytime. One evening, however, about dusk I caught the landlord in one of the outhouses. He had the ginger cat on his shoulder and was feeding her with something that looked like strips of liver. I remonstrated with him for encouraging the cats about the place and asked whether I could have a different room, explaining that the nightly caterwauling disturbed me. He half opened his slits of eyes and murmured that he would ask his wife about it, but nothing was done, and in fact I believe there was no other bedroom in the house.

And all this time the weather got hotter and heavier, working up for thunder, with the sky like brass and the earth like iron, and the air quivering over it so that it hurt your eyes to look at it.

All right, Harringay, I am trying to keep to the point. And I'm not concealing anything from you. I say that my relations with Mrs. Merridew were perfectly ordinary. Of course, I saw a good deal of her, because as I explained Merridew was out all day. We went up to the dam with him in the morning and brought the car back, and naturally we had to amuse one another as best we could till the evening. She seemed quite pleased to be in my company, and I couldn't dislike her. I can't tell you what we talked about—nothing in particular. She was not a talkative woman. She would sit or lie for hours in the sunshine, hardly speaking, only stretching out her body to the light and heat. Sometimes she would spend a whole afternoon playing with a twig or a pebble, while I sat and smoked. Restful! No. No, I shouldn't call her a restful personality exactly. Not to me, at any rate. In the evening she would liven up and talk a little more, but she generally went up to bed early and left Merridew and me to yarn together in the garden.

Oh, about the revolver! Yes. I bought that in Bath, when I had been at Little Hexham exactly a week. We drove over in the morning, and while Mrs. Merridew got some things for her husband, I prowled around the secondhand shops. I had intended to get an air gun or a peashooter or something of that kind, when I saw this. You've seen it, of course. It's very tiny—what people in books describe as "little more than a toy"—but deadly enough. The old boy who sold it to me didn't seem to know much about firearms. He'd taken it in pawn sometime back, he told me, and there were ten rounds of ammunition with it. He made no bones about a license or anything, glad enough to make a sale, no doubt, without putting difficulties in a customer's way. I told him I knew how to handle it and mentioned by way of a joke that I meant to take a potshot or two at the cats. That seemed to wake him up a bit. He was a dried-up little fellow, with a scrawny gray beard and a stringy neck. He asked me where I was staying. I told him at Little Hexham.

"You better be careful, sir," he said. "They think a heap of their cats down there, and it's reckoned unlucky to kill them." And then he added something I couldn't quite catch, about a silver bullet. He was a doddering old fellow, and he seemed to have some sort of scruple about letting me take the parcel away, but I assured him that I was perfectly capable of looking after it and myself. I left him standing in the door of his shop, pulling at his beard and staring after me.

That night the thunder came. The sky had turned to lead before evening, but the dull heat was more oppressive than the sunshine. Both the Merridews seemed to be in a state of nerves—he sulking and swearing at the weather and the flies, and she wrought up to a queer kind of vivid excitement. Thunder affects some people that way. I wasn't much better, and to make things worse I got the feeling that the house was full of cats. I couldn't see them, but I knew they were there, lurking behind the cupboards and flitting noiselessly about the corridors. I could scarcely sit in the parlor and was thankful to escape to my room.

Cats or no cats I had to open the window, and I sat there with my pajama jacket unbuttoned, trying to get a breath of air. But the place was like the inside of a copper furnace. And pitch-dark. I could scarcely see from my window where the bushes ended and the lawn began. But I could hear and feel the cats. There were little scrapings in the wisteria and scufflings among the leaves, and about eleven o'clock one of them started the concert with a loud and hideous wail. Then another and another joined in—I'll swear there were fifty of them. And presently I got that foul sensation of nausea, and the flesh crawled on my bones, and I knew that one of them was slinking close to me in the darkness.

I looked around quickly, and there she stood, the great Cyprian, right against my shoulder, her eyes glowing like green lamps. I yelled and struck out at her, and she snarled as she leaped out and down. I heard her thump the gravel, and the yowling burst out all over the garden with renewed vehemence. And then all in a moment there was utter silence, and in the far distance there came a flickering blue flash and then another. In the first of them I saw the far garden wall, topped along all its length with cats, like a nursery frieze. When the second flash came the wall was empty.

At two o'clock the rain came. For three hours before that I had sat there, watching the lightning as it spat across the sky and exulting in the crash of the thunder. The storm seemed to carry off all the electrical disturbance in my body; I could have shouted with excitement and relief. Then the first heavy drops fell, then a steady downpour, then a deluge. It struck the iron-baked garden with a noise like steel rods falling. The smell of the ground came up intoxicatingly, and the wind rose and flung the rain in against my face. At the other end of the passage I heard a window thrown to and fastened, but I leaned out into the tumult and let the water drench my head and shoulders. The thunder still rumbled intermittently, but with less noise and farther off, and in an occasional flash I saw the white grille of falling water drawn between me and the garden.

It was after one of these thunderpeals that I became aware of a knocking at my door. I opened it, and there was Merridew. He had a candle in his hand, and his face was terrified.

"Felice!" he said abruptly. "She's ill. I can't wake her. For God's sake, come and give me a hand."

I hurried down the passage after him. There were two beds in his room—a great four-poster, hung with crimson damask, and a small camp bedstead drawn up near to the window. The small bed was empty, the bedclothes tossed aside; evidently he had just risen from it. In the four-poster lay Mrs. Merridew, naked, with only a sheet upon her. She was stretched flat upon her back, her long black hair in two plaits over her shoulders. Her face was waxen and shrunk, like the face of a corpse, and her pulse, when I felt it, was so faint that at first I could scarcely feel it. Her breathing was very slow and shallow and her flesh cold. I shook her, but there was no response at all. I lifted her eyelids and noticed how the eyeballs were turned up under the upper lid, so that only the whites were visible. The touch of my fingertip upon the sensitive ball evoked no reaction. I immediately wondered whether she took drugs.

Merridew seemed to think it necessary to make some explanation. He was babbling about the heat—she couldn't bear so much as a silk nightgown—she had suggested that he should occupy the other bed—he had slept heavily—right through the thunder. The rain blowing in on his face had aroused him. He had got up and shut the window. Then he had called to Felice to know if she was all right; he thought the storm might have frightened her. There was no answer. He had struck a light. Her condition had alarmed him, and so on.

I told him to pull himself together and to try whether, by chafing his wife's hands and feet, we could restore the circulation. I had it firmly in my mind that she was under the influence of some opiate. We set to work, rubbing and pinching and slapping her with wet towels and shouting her name in her ear. It was like handling a dead woman, except for the very slight but perfectly regular rise and fall of her bosom, on which—with a kind of surprise that there should be any flaw on its magnolia whiteness—I noticed a large brown mole, just over the heart. To my perturbed fancy it suggested a wound and a menace. We had been at it for some time, with the sweat pouring off us, when we became aware of something going on outside the window—a stealthy bumping and scraping against the panes. I snatched up the candle and looked out.

On the sill, the Cyprian cat sat and clawed at the casement. Her drenched fur clung limply to her body; her eyes glared into mine; her mouth was opened in protest. She scrabbled furiously at the latch, her hind claws slipping and scratching on the woodwork. I hammered on the pane and bawled at her, and she struck back at the glass as though possessed. As I cursed her and turned away she set up a long, despairing wail.

Merridew called to me to bring back the candle and leave the brute alone. I returned to the bed, but the dismal crying went on and on incessantly. I suggested to Merridew that he should wake the landlord and get hot-water bottles and some brandy from the bar and see if a messenger could not be sent for a doctor. He departed on this errand, while I went on with my massage. It seemed to me that the pulse was growing still fainter. Then I suddenly recol-

DOROTHY L. SAYERS . **79**

lected that I had a small brandy flask in my bag. I ran out to fetch it, and as I did so the cat suddenly stopped its howling.

As I entered my own room the air blowing through the open window struck gratefully upon me. I found my bag in the dark and was rummaging for the flask among my shirts and socks when I heard a loud, triumphant mew and turned around in time to see the Cyprian cat crouched for a moment on the sill, before it sprang in past me and out at the door. I found the flask and hastened back with it, just as Merridew and the landlord came running up the stairs.

We all went into the room together. As we did so, Mrs. Merridew stirred, sat up, and asked us what in the world was the matter.

I have seldom felt quite such a fool.

Next day the weather was cooler; the storm had cleared the air. What Merridew had said to his wife I do not know. None of us made any public allusion to the night's disturbance, and to all appearance Mrs. Merridew was in the best of health and spirits. Merridew took a day off from the waterworks, and we all went for a long drive and picnic together. We were on the best of terms with one another. Ask Merridew. He will tell you the same thing. He would not—he could not, surely—say otherwise. I can't believe, Harringay, I simply cannot believe that he could imagine or suspect me. I say, there was nothing to suspect. Nothing.

Yes—this is the important date—the twenty-fourth of June. I can't tell you any more details; there is nothing to tell. We came back and had dinner just as usual. All three of us were together all day, till bedtime. On my honor I had no private interview of any kind that day, either with him or with her. I was the first to go to bed, and I heard the others come upstairs about half an hour later. They were talking cheerfully.

It was a moonlight night. For once, no caterwauling came to trouble me. I didn't even bother to shut the window or the door. I put the revolver on the chair beside me before I lay down. Yes, it was loaded. I had no special object in putting it there, except that I meant to have a go at the cats if they started their games again.

I was desperately tired and thought I should drop off to sleep at once, but I didn't. I must have been overtired, I suppose. I lay and looked at the moonlight. And then, about midnight, I heard what I had been half expecting: a stealthy scrabbling in the wisteria and a faint meowing sound.

I sat up in bed and reached for the revolver. I heard the *plop* as the big cat sprang up onto the window ledge; I saw her black-and-silver flanks and the outline of her round head, pricked ears, and upright tail. I aimed and fired, and the beast let out one frightful cry and sprang down into the room.

I jumped out of bed. The crack of the shot had sounded terrific in the silent house, and somewhere I heard a distant voice call out. I pursued the cat into the passage, revolver in hand, with some idea of finishing it off, I suppose. And then, at the door of the Merridews' room, I saw Mrs. Merridew. She stood with one hand on each doorpost, swaying to and fro. Then she fell down at my feet. Her bare breast was all stained with blood. And as I stood staring at her, clutching the revolver, Merridew came out and found us—like that.

Well, Harringay, that's my story, exactly as I told it to Peabody. I'm afraid it won't sound very well in court, but what can I say? The trail of blood led from my room to hers; the cat must have run that way; I *know* it was the cat I shot. I can't offer any explanation. I don't know who shot Mrs. Merridew, or why. I can't help it if the people at the inn say they never saw the Cyprian cat; Merridew saw it that other night, and I know he wouldn't lie about it. Search the house, Harringay. That's the only thing to do. Pull the place to pieces, till you find the body of the Cyprian cat. It will have my bullet in it.

# A Cat, a Man, and Two Women

BY JUNICHIRŌ TANIZAKI

*A* CAT, *A* MAN, *and Two Women,* a novella from which this extract is taken, is a story of cat-obsession. Shozo has been recently divorced from Shinako, and has remarried Fukuko. The problem is that Shozo has a greater love than either of the two women: his cat, Lily. She is an exquisite tortoiseshell with a seductive personality and a way of wrapping Shozo around her little paw. Another problem is that Shinako has managed to claim Lily for herself.

Junichirō Tanizaki (1886–1965) is widely regarded as the leading modern Japanese novelist. Most of his major works have been translated into English and other languages, and several have been filmed. Tanizaki was a great cat-fancier, yet one with a twist: during the last years of his life he always kept two cats, loving one but hating the other. A suitable state of affairs, perhaps, for a man who could create the winsome but duplicitous Lily.

★   ★   ★   ★   ★

SHOZO VIVIDLY RECALLED that time long ago when Lily had returned from Amagasaki. It was at dawn one day around the middle of autumn that the slumbering Shozo was awakened by a familiar "meow, meow. . . ." He was single at the time, and slept upstairs while his mother slept on the ground floor. The shutters were still closed at this hour of the morning; but somewhere nearby a cat was mewing, and as Shozo listened, half asleep, it sounded uncannily like Lily. They had sent her off to Amagasaki a whole month ago, so how could she be here now? Yet the more he listened, the more it sounded like her. He heard the scratch and patter of paws on the tin roof outside his room at the back. . . . Now it was just outside his window. . . . He *had* to know. Leaping up from his quilts, he pushed open the shutters. There on the roof just in front of him, restlessly moving back and forth, was an extremely weary-looking but unquestionably identifiable Lily!

Shozo, hardly trusting his own eyes, called hesitantly: "Lily. . . ."

"Meow," she replied, looking up, her large, lovely eyes wide with happiness. She came to a point just below the bay window where he was standing; but when he reached out to lift her up, she slipped away, darting two or three feet in the opposite direction. She didn't go far, though, and at the sound of "Lily!" would give a "meow" and reapproach. Again Shozo would reach for her, and again she would slip from his grasp. It was precisely this aspect of a cat's character that Shozo loved. She *must* care for him, since she went to so much trouble to return. Yet, when she was safely back at her old familiar home and gazing up at the face of the master she hadn't seen for so many weeks, what did she do if he reached out for her? Run away. Perhaps, knowing his love for her, she enjoyed playing upon it like this; or perhaps she felt a bit awkward at their first meeting after such a long separation, and her shyness took this form. In any case, Lily kept on moving back and forth across the roof, replying with a "meow" each time Shozo called her name. Right away he noticed how thin she'd become, and as he looked more carefully he saw too that her fur had lost its sheen of a month before. Her head and tail were covered with mud, and bits of pampas grass stuck to her here and there. The grocer who had taken her in was known to be a cat lover, so it was unlikely he would have mistreated her in any way. No, Lily's pitiful state was obviously due to the "hardships of the road" she had suffered on her lonely journey back from Amagasaki. She must have walked all night to have arrived home at such an early hour—but it was certainly more than one night's journey. Night after night she must have walked, after fleeing from the strange house some days before. Losing her way, wandering down dark byways without knowing where they led, until at last she reached home. . . . The tufts of pampas grass proved that she hadn't come straight back along the highway, which was lined with houses and other buildings. How piercing the winds at dawn and dusk would have felt to a cat that, typically, disliked the cold. Besides, showers were common at that time of year, and she must have sometimes crept into thickets to escape the rain, or hidden in fields to evade pursuing dogs. She had been lucky to survive the journey.

Imagining all this, Shozo wanted to hold Lily and gently stroke her, and so he kept reaching out to catch hold of her. Gradually Lily, though seeming still a bit shy, began to brush her body against Shozo's outstretched hands, until at last she let her master have his wish.

Later Shozo learned that Lily had disappeared from the place in Amagasaki about one week before. Even now, years afterward, he couldn't forget the sound of her voice and the look on her face that morning. And there were many other memories: there was, for example, the day he first brought the cat home from Kobe. He'd just quit his last job as apprentice cook at the Shinkoken and returned to Ashiya. He was twenty that year; his father had died not long before, and the forty-ninth day memorial service was about to be held. Shozo had already kept a *miké* or "three-colored" cat in the kitchen of the restaurant and, when that died, a jet-black tom called "Blacky." Then one day the man from the butcher shop told him about a cute little female cat of a European breed, about three months old, that was available; it was Lily. When he quit the restaurant, Shozo left Blacky behind but couldn't bring himself to give up the new kitten. So he took her back to his house in Ashiya, carefully stowing her in a corner of a cart he had borrowed, together with his wicker trunk.

According to the owner of the butcher shop, the English called this particular type of cat a "tortoiseshell," and indeed the distinct black spots spreading with a lustrous sheen over the brown coat did resemble the polished surface of a turtle's shell. Certainly Shozo had never had such a lovely cat before, with such a magnificent coat. European cats are generally free from the stiff, square-shouldered look of Japanese cats; they have clean, chic-looking lines, like a beautiful woman with gently sloping shoulders. Japanese cats also usually have long, narrow heads, with slight hollows beneath the eyes and prominent cheekbones, but Lily's head was small and compact. Her wonderfully large and beautiful gold-colored eyes and nervously twitching nose were set within the well-defined contours of a face shaped exactly like a clam shell placed upside down. But it was not her coat or face or body that so attracted Shozo to this kitten. If it were only a matter of outward form, he himself had seen Persian and Siamese cats that were even more beautiful. It was Lily's personality that was so appealing. When first brought to Ashiya, she was still terribly small, small enough to be held in the palm of one hand, but her wild tomboyish ways were just like those of a seven- or eight-year-old girl, a primary-school student at her most mischievous. She was much lighter than now and could jump to a height of three or four feet when her master held some food above her head during dinner. If he were seated, she could reach it so easily that he often had to stand up in the middle of his meal to make the game interesting. He began training her in such acrobatics from the moment she arrived. The morsel of food held at the end of his chopsticks would be raised little by little—three feet, four feet, then five feet—and each time Lily successfully made the jump. Finally she would leap onto Shozo's kimono at about knee height and nimbly crawl up his chest to his shoulder, then traverse his outstretched arm like a rat crossing a rafter, till she could reach the very tip of the chopsticks. Sometimes she would leap onto the curtains in the shop window and climb quickly up to just below ceiling level, cross from one side to the other, and then crawl down, again clinging to the curtains. Again and again she did it, revolving like a waterwheel.

From her kitten days she had a charming, lively expression; her eyes and mouth, the movements of her nostrils, and her breathing all showed the shifts of her emotions, exactly like a human being. Her large, bright eyes in particular, were always roving about; whether she was being affectionate, or mischievous, or acquisitive, there was always something lovable about her. When she got angry, Shozo found her quite funny: small as she was, she would round her back and bristle her fur as cats do; her tail would rise straight up and, prancing and pawing the ground with her little feet, she would glare fiercely at her foe. It was like a child imitating an adult, and no one who saw her could keep from smiling.

Nor could Shozo forget Lily's gentle, appealing gaze when she first had kittens. One morning about six months after arriving at Ashiya, she started following Shozo around the house, mewing plaintively—she sensed she was about to give birth. He spread an old cushion in the bottom of an empty soft-drink carton and placed it at the back of the closet. Then he picked her up and carried her to her bed. She stayed in the box only briefly, soon opening the closet door and emerging to follow him about again, mewing all the while. Her voice was not the one he was used to hearing. It was still "meow," of course, but this "meow" had another, peculiar meaning to it. It sounded as if she were saying "Oh, what shall I do? I don't feel well, suddenly. . . . I'm afraid something very odd is about to happen to me. . . . I've never felt anything like this before! What do you think it could be? Am I going to be all right? . . . *Am* I?"

When Shozo stroked her head and said, "There's nothing to worry about. You're going to be a mother, that's all," she placed her forepaws on his knee as if to cling to him, uttered one "meeoww," and looked at him as though trying her best to understand what he was telling her. Shozo carried her back to the closet and placed her in her box. "Now you stay right here, okay? You're not to come out. Okay? You understand?" Having made this little speech, he closed the door and started to stand up, when there was another plaintive "meeeoow." It seemed to be saying "Wait a moment. Don't go away." Shozo melted at the sound and opened the door just a crack to peek in. There in the farthest corner of the closet, which was filled with a jumble of trunks and cloth-wrapped bundles, was the box with Lily's head sticking out. "Meeooow," she cried, gazing at him. "She may be just an animal," thought Shozo, "but what a loving look she has in those eyes of hers!" It was strange, but Lily's eyes shining in the closet's dim recesses were no longer those of a mischievous little kitten. In that instant they had become truly feminine, full of an inexpressible sadness and seduction. Shozo had never seen a woman in childbirth; but he was sure that if she were young and beautiful, she would call to her husband with just the same pained, reproachful look as this. Any number of times he closed the closet door and began to walk away, only to go back for another look; and each time Lily would poke her head out of the box and peer at him, like a child playing peekaboo.

All this had happened as much as ten years ago, and Shinako had only appeared on the scene six years later. So, in the intervening period, Shozo had lived on the second floor of the Ashiya house with only this cat for company (apart, of course, from his mother). When he heard people with no knowledge of a cat's character saying that cats were not as loving as dogs, that they were cold and selfish, he always thought to himself how impossible it was to understand the charm and lovableness of a cat if one had not, like him, spent many years living alone with one. The reason was that all cats are to some extent shy creatures: they won't show affection or seek it from their owners in front of a third person but tend rather to be oddly standoffish. Lily too would ignore Shozo or run off when he called her, if his mother was present. But when the two of them were alone, she would climb up on his lap without being called and devote the most flattering attention to him. She often put her forehead against Shozo's face and then pushed as hard as she could; at the same time, with the tip of her rough little tongue she licked away at him—cheeks, chin, the tip of his nose, around his mouth—everywhere.

At night she always slept beside him and would wake him up in the morning. This too was done by licking his face all over. In cold weather she would insert herself under the top quilt near Shozo's pillow and then work her way down into the bedding. She nestled against Shozo's chest, or crawled toward his groin, or lay against his back, wherever, until she found a place where she could sleep comfortably. Even after finally settling down in one spot, she often changed her position if it became the least bit uncomfortable. Her favorite posture seemed to be to lie facing Shozo, with her head on his arm and her face against his chest; but if he moved even a fraction her rest was disturbed, and she would burrow off in another direction, looking for a better spot. Accordingly, whenever she got into his bed, Shozo had to extend one arm as a pillow and then try to sleep in an obliging way, moving as little as possible. So positioned, he would use his other hand to stroke that area of the neck which cats most love to have fondled; and Lily would immediately respond with a satisfied purring. She might begin to bite at his finger, or gently claw him, or drool a bit—all were signs that she was excited.

Once when Shozo broke wind under the quilts, Lily, who was sleeping on top, toward the far end of the bed, awoke with a start and, thinking perhaps that some dubious creature with a very odd sort of voice was hiding there, began searching through the quilts in a great flurry, her eyes full of suspicion.

Then there was the time when Shozo tried to pick up an unwilling Lily: as she broke from his grasp and clambered down, she let fly with an evil-smelling fart which caught him full in the face. Admittedly, Shozo had by mischance clutched with both hands at Lily's belly, full to the bursting point with the meal she had just eaten. And unfortunately her anus at that point was situated just below his face, so that the "breath from her bowels" blew straight up at him. The stench was so bad that even a cat lover like Shozo was forced to toss her to the floor with an "Ugh!" The proverbial "weasel's last fart" must smell something like that. At any rate, it was an extremely stubborn smell which, once it clung to your nose, was not to be dislodged for the rest of the day, no matter how often you rubbed or washed or scrubbed away with soap.

Whenever Shozo had an argument with Shinako over the cat, he was apt to say sarcastically, "After all, Lily and I are so close we've smelled each other's farts!" But when you've spent ten years together, you do develop exceptionally strong ties, even with a cat. The odds were, in fact, that he really did feel closer to Lily than to either of his wives. As it happened, he had only been married to Shinako for a total of two and a half years, spread over four calendar years. And Fukuko had been in the household barely a month. Naturally, then, it was Lily, with whom he'd lived so long, who was more intimately bound up with many memories of his; who formed, in fact, an important part of Shozo's past. Wasn't it only normal to find the thought of giving her up after all those years painful? There was no reason for people to call him eccentric or cat-crazy, as if he'd completely lost his head. He felt ashamed of himself for having knuckled under so easily, for being so weak and helpless as to hand his dear friend over to someone else as if she meant nothing to him, just because of Fukuko's bullying and his mother's preachings. Why hadn't he tried to make them see reason, boldly and directly, like a real man? Why hadn't he been firmer, much more firmer, with both his wife and his mother? He might still have lost, and seen the same result, but by not having put up even that much of a fight, he had certainly failed in his duty to Lily.

Suppose for a moment that Lily had not come back after being sent off to Amagasaki. . . . That time, he had himself agreed to her being given to the other family, so he would have been resigned to it. Yet when he'd finally managed to catch Lily as she stood meowing on the tin roof that morning, and held her in his arms, rubbing his cheek against her, he'd thought, "What a terrible thing I did! It was downright cruel. From now on I'll never give her away to anyone, no matter what. . . . I'll keep her here to the end." He had not only vowed this to himself but felt that he'd made a firm promise to Lily as well. And now, when he considered how he had driven her out a second time, he was appalled at his own callousness.

What made it sadder still was that Lily had in the past two or three years clearly begun to age, the signs of decrepitude appearing in the way she carried herself, the look in her eyes, the color and condition of her coat. And no wonder: when Shozo first brought her home in that cart, he was still a youth of twenty; next year he would be almost thirty. In terms of a cat's life, ten years would probably be equivalent to fifty or sixty. So it was only natural that Lily should have lost her old vitality; and yet when Shozo—recalling as if it were only yesterday how the kitten would climb up to the top of the curtains and perform her tightrope act—looked at Lily now, scrawny-flanked, walking with head drooping and wobbling from side to side, he felt an indescribable sadness. It was as if he were being given a personal demonstration of the Buddhist truth that "all things pass away."

There were many signs of Lily's rapid decline: one of them, for example, was her no longer being able to jump up with ease to Shozo's height and snatch a bite to eat. It didn't have to be food at mealtimes, either; any time she was shown something, she would make a leap for it. But each year the number of leaps grew fewer, and the height she reached lower. Recently, if she were shown a bit of food when she was hungry, she would first check to see if it was something she liked or not, and then jump; and, even so, it had to be held no higher than a foot or so above her head. If it were any higher she would give up the idea of jumping and either climb up Shozo's body or, when even that seemed too much for her, simply look up at him with those soulful eyes, her nose twitching hungrily. "Be kind to me. I'm starving, and I really do want to jump up and take that food. But at my age I just can't do it any more. So please, don't be mean; just toss it down to me—now." She made her wordless appeal as if knowing exactly how weak her master's character was. When Shinako got that sad look in her eyes, it didn't bother Shozo very much; but for some reason, when it was Lily, he was strangely overcome with pity.

She'd been such a charming and lively kitten—so when did her eyes begin to take on that mournful look? It must have been at the time she was about to give birth to her first litter, when she poked her head out of the carton in the corner of the closet and looked out helplessly at him. From that day on, her eyes were shadowed with a sadness which gradually deepened as she grew older. Looking into Lily's eyes, Shozo sometimes found himself wondering how it was that a little animal, no matter how clever, could have a gaze that seemed so full of meaning: was she really thinking sad thoughts at such moments? The cats he'd kept before, the three-colored one and Blacky, had never once had this sort of poignant expression—perhaps they were too stupid for that. Yet it wasn't that Lily had a particularly gloomy or melancholy temperament. When she was a kitten she was very tomboyish, and even after becoming a mother she could hold her own in a fight; she was a spirited cat, even a bit wild sometimes. But when she approached her master to be stroked, or lay basking in the sun with a bored look on her face, her eyes seemed full of a profound sadness. Sometimes they even became moist, as if with tears. When she was younger, that mistiness in her gaze seemed to have something voluptuous about it. But as she grew older, her bright eyes became cloudy, and mucus formed in their corners. Her sadness was so evident it was painful to see.

Perhaps this wasn't the way her eyes would naturally have looked, but was rather the result of the environment in which she'd been raised. After all, people's faces and characters often change when they've suffered a lot, and why shouldn't it be the same with cats? The more Shozo thought about it, the more guilty he felt toward Lily. For a period of ten long years he'd made her lead a lonely, dismal existence with only himself for company. Of course he had loved and cared for her; but when he had brought her home, it was just he and his mother living there, a far cry from the lively bustle of the Shinkoken's kitchen. And then, since his mother disliked her, Lily and he had had to share the lonely intimacy of a room upstairs. After six years had passed in this fashion, Shinako entered the household as his bride; and this intruder began to treat Lily merely as a nuisance, making her position still more uncomfortable and humiliating.

Shozo felt even guiltier about something else he had done. He should at least have let Lily keep and raise her kittens, but he'd adopted a policy of finding homes for them as soon as possible after their birth, so that not one remained in the Ishii house. Despite this, Lily kept on having kittens. She had three litters for every two of the average cat. Shozo had no way of knowing who her partner was, but the kittens were of mixed breed, and since they retained something of the look of a tortoiseshell, there were quite a few willing takers. Still, at times Shozo had to spirit some of them off to the seashore, or leave them under the pine trees on the Ashiya River embankment. It goes without saying that this was done out of concern for his mother's feelings; but Shozo himself believed that Lily's rapid aging might be due in part to her giving birth so often. If he couldn't prevent her from becoming pregnant, he could at least keep her from nursing so many kittens. It was from this point of view that he dealt with the matter. And, truly, Lily grew visibly older each time she had a litter. When Shozo saw her with her belly bulging like a kangaroo's and that mournful look in her eyes, he would say in a miserable voice, "You stupid cat. If you keep getting pregnant all the time, you'll be an old granny before you know it." If it had been a tomcat, he would have had it neutered, but the vet warned him that the same sort of operation was difficult with females. "Well, then, how about doing it with X rays?" The man just laughed at this suggestion. Everything Shozo had done was for Lily's sake; he'd had no intention of treating her unkindly. Yet it was undeniable that taking all of her offspring from her like that had turned her into a lonely, unfortunate cat.

Looking back, Shozo realized that he had put Lily through a lot. She had been a comfort to him over the years but had not had a pleasant life herself. Particularly in the last year or two, with quarrels between Shozo and his wife, and money troubles often creating household problems into which Lily was somehow always drawn, the cat had become demoralized, confused about her place in the family and uncertain what to do.

When his mother used to send for Shozo to come and take her home from Fukuko's house in Imazu, it was Lily rather than Shinako who tried to keep him from going, clinging to the skirts of his kimono with a pleading look. And when he shook her off and set out anyway, she followed along after him for a block or two, as a dog would. Shozo, in turn, would try to come back from Imazu as quickly as possible out of concern for the feelings, not of Shinako, but of Lily. If he had to stay away for two or three days, it seemed to him on his return that she looked even more forlorn than usual—or was it only his imagination?

Perhaps Lily was not long for this world. . . . The ominous thought had often bothered him recently—he'd even seen her death in several dreams. Shozo himself appeared in them, sunk in grief as if he'd lost a parent, brother, or sister, his face wet with tears; and it occurred to him that, if he really did lose Lily, he would be just as heartbroken as in those dreams. And as one thought led to another, he felt frustration, shame, and anger all over again: how could he have handed her over so tamely? Sometimes he was sure he felt her reproachful gaze fixed on him from some corner or other. It was too late now for regrets, of course, but how *could* he have been so cruel as to drive that sad old creature away? Why didn't he let her die here at home, in peace? . . .

"Do you know *why* Shinako wanted the cat so badly?" asked Fukuko with an air of embarrassment, as she looked at her husband across the dinner table that evening. Shozo sat dejectedly sipping at his saké in the now strangely silent, desolate room.

"Hmmm. . . . I don't know . . . ," he replied, his face masked with incomprehension.

"She thinks if she has Lily, you'll come over to see her. That's it, don't you think?"

"Of course not. What a stupid idea. . . ."

"I'm sure that's it. It hit me today, for the first time. . . . And don't you be taken in by her tricks!"

"No, no, don't worry, I won't be."

"You're sure about that now?"

"There's no need to make such a fuss about it," said Shozo, giving a complacent little laugh and taking another sip of saké.

# Puss-in-Boots

BY ANGELA CARTER

A NGELA CARTER'S slam-bang version of this fairy tale isn't for children, but in its energy and wild humor it may come closer to the original than the one most of us know. It is certainly more fun to read. Carter (1940–1992) was an English writer, journalist, and translator who before her tragically early death had developed a wide following for her fiction and her powerful feminist essays. She was fascinated by fairy stories, which in her hands frequently took on surprising forms despite her famous definition: "A fairy tale is the kind of story in which one king goes to borrow a cup of sugar from another king."

★　★　★　★　★

FIGARO HERE; FIGARO, THERE, I tell you! Figaro upstairs, Figaro downstairs and—oh, my goodness me, this little Figaro can slip into my lady's chamber smart as you like at any time whatsoever that he takes the fancy for, don't you know, he's a cat of the world, cosmopolitan, sophisticated; he can tell when a furry friend is the Missus' best company. For what lady in all the world could say "no" to the passionate yet toujours discret advances of a fine marmalade cat? (Unless it be her eyes incontinently overflow at the slightest whiff of fur, which happened once, as you shall hear.)

A tom, sirs, a ginger tom and proud of it. Proud of his fine, white shirt-front that dazzles harmoniously against his orange and tangerine tessellations (oh! what a fiery suit of lights have I); proud of his bird-entrancing eye and more than military whiskers; proud, to a fault, some say, of his fine, musical voice. All the windows in the square fly open when I break into impromptu song at the spectacle of the moon above Bergamo. If the poor players in the square, the sullen rout of ragged trash that haunts the provinces, are rewarded with a hail of pennies when they set up their makeshift stage and start their raucous choruses, then how much more liberally do the citizens deluge me with pails of the freshest water, vegetables hardly spoiled and, occasionally, slippers, shoes and boots.

Do you see these fine, high, shining leather boots of mine? A young cavalry officer made me the tribute of, first, one; then, after I celebrate his generosity with a fresh obbligato, the moon no fuller than my heart—whoops! I nimbly spring aside—down comes the other. Their high heels will click like castanets when Puss takes his promenade upon the tiles, for my song recalls flamenco, all cats have a Spanish tinge although Puss himself elegantly lubricates his virile, muscular, native Bergamasque with French, since this is the only language in which you can purr.

"Merrrrrrrrrrrci!"

Instanter I draw my new boots on over the natty white stockings that terminate my hinder legs. That young man, observing with curiosity by moonlight the use to which I put his footwear, calls out: "Hey, Puss! Puss, there!"

"At your service, sir!"

"Up to my balcony, young Puss!"

He leans out, in his nightshirt, offering encouragement as I swing succinctly up the façade, forepaws on a curly cherub's pate, hindpaws on a stucco wreath, bring them up to meet your forepaws while, first paw forward, hup! on to the stone nymph's tit; left paw down a bit, the satyr's bum should do the trick. Nothing to it, once you know how, rococo's no problem. Acrobatics?

Born to them; Puss can perform a back somersault whilst holding aloft a glass of vino in his right paw and *never spill a drop.*

But, to my shame, the famous death-defying triple somersault en plein air, that is, in middle air, that is, unsupported and without a safety net, I, Puss, have never yet attempted though often I have dashingly brought off the double tour, to the applause of all.

"You strike me as a cat of parts," says this young man when I'm arrived at his window-sill. I made him a handsome genuflection, rump out, tail up, head down, to facilitate his friendly chuck under my chin; and, as involuntary free gift, my natural, my habitual smile.

For all cats have this particularity, each and every one, from the meanest alley sneaker to the proudest, whitest she that ever graced a pontiff's pillow—we have our smiles, as it were, painted on. Those small, cool, quiet Mona Lisa smiles that smile we must, no matter whether it's been fun or it's been not. So all cats have a politician's air; we smile and smile and so they think we're villains. But, I note, this young man is something of a smiler hisself.

"A sandwich," he offers. "And, perhaps, a snifter of brandy."

His lodgings are poor, though he's handsome enough and even en déshabillé, nightcap and all, there's a neat, smart, dandified air about him. Here is one who knows what's what, thinks I; a man who keeps up appearances in the bedchamber can never embarrass you out of it. And excellent beef sandwiches; I relish a lean slice of roast beef and early learned a taste for spirits, since I started life as a wine-shop cat, hunting cellar rats for my keep, before the world sharpened my wits enough to let me live by them.

And the upshot of this midnight interview? I'm engaged, on the spot, as Sir's valet: valet de chambre and, from time to time, his body servant, for, when funds are running low, as they must do for every gallant officer when the pickings fall off, he pawns the quilt, doesn't he. Then faithful Puss curls up on his chest to keep him warm at nights. And if he don't like me to knead his nipples, which, out of the purest affection and the desire—ouch! he says—to test the retractability of my claws, I do in moments of absence of mind, then what other valet could slip into a young girl's sacred privacy and deliver her a billet-doux at the very moment when she's reading her prayerbook with her sainted mother? A task I once or twice perform for him, to his infinite gratitude.

And, as you will hear, brought him at last to the best of fortunes for us all.

So Puss got his post at the same time as his boots and I dare say the Master and I have much in common for he's proud as the devil, touchy as tin-tacks, lecherous as liquorice and, though I say it as loves him, as quick-witted a rascal as ever put on clean linen.

When times were hard, I'd pilfer the market for breakfast—a herring, an orange, a loaf; we never went hungry. Puss served him well in the gaming salons, too, for a cat may move from lap to lap with impunity and cast his eye over any hand of cards. A cat can jump on the dice—he can't resist to see it roll! poor thing, mistook it for a bird; and, after I've been, limp-spined, stiff-legged, playing the silly buggers, scooped up to be chastised, who can remember how the dice fell in the first place?

And we had, besides, less . . . gentlemanly means of maintenance when they closed the tables to us, as churlishly, they sometimes did. I'd perform my little Spanish dance while he went round with his hat: *olé!* But he only put my loyalty and affection to the test of this humiliation when the cupboard was as bare as his backside; after, in fact, he'd sunk so low as to pawn his drawers.

So all went right as ninepence and you never saw such boon companions as Puss and his master; until the man must needs go fall in love.

"Head over heels, Puss."

I went about my ablutions, tonguing my arsehole with the impeccable hygienic integrity of cats, one leg stuck in the air like a ham bone; I choose to remain silent. Love? What has my rakish master, for whom I've jumped through the window of every brothel in the city, besides haunting the virginal back garden of the convent and god knows what other goatish errands, to do with the tender passion?

"And she. A princess in a tower. Remote and shining as Aldebaran. Chained to a dolt and dragon-guarded."

I withdrew my head from my privates and fixed him with my most satiric smile; I dare him warble on in *that* strain.

"All cats are cynics," he opines, quailing beneath my yellow glare.

It is the hazard of it draws him, see.

There is a lady sits in a window for one hour and one hour only, at the tenderest time of dusk. You can scarcely see her features, the curtains almost hide her; shrouded like a holy image, she looks out at the piazza as the shops shut up, the stalls go down, the night comes on. And that is all the world she ever sees. Never a girl in all Bergamo so secluded except, on Sundays, they let her go to Mass, bundled up in black, with a veil on. And then she is in the company of an aged hag, her keeper, who grumps along grim as a prison dinner.

How did he see that secret face? Who else but Puss revealed it?

Back we come from the tables so late, so very late at night we found, to our emergent surprise, that all at once it was early in the morning. His pockets were heavy with silver and both our guts sweetly a-gurgle with champagne; Lady Luck had sat with us, what fine spirits were we in! Winter and cold weather. The pious trot to church already with little lanterns through the chill fog as we go ungodly rolling home.

See, a black barque, like a state funeral; and Puss takes it into his bubbly-addled brain to board her. Tacking obliquely to her side, I rub my marmalade pate against her shin; how could any duenna, be she never so stern, take offence at such attentions to her chargeling from a little cat? (As it turns out, this one: *at-tishooo!* does.) A white hand fragrant as Arabia descends from the black cloak and reciprocally rubs behind his ears at just the ecstatic spot. Puss lets rip a roaring purr, rears briefly on his high-heeled boots; jig with joy and pirouette with glee—she laughs to see and draws her veil aside. Puss glimpses high above, as it were, an alabaster lamp lit behind by dawn's first flush: her face.

And she smiling.

For a moment, just that moment, you would have thought it was May morning.

"Come along! Come! Don't dawdle over the nasty beast!" snaps the old hag, with the one tooth in her mouth, and warts; she sneezes.

The veil comes down; so cold it is, and dark, again.

It was not I alone who saw her; with that smile he swears she stole his heart.

Love.

I've sat inscrutably by and washed my face and sparkling dicky with my clever paw while he made the beast with two backs with every harlot in the city, besides a number of good wives, dutiful daughters, rosy country girls come to sell celery and endive on the corner, and the chambermaid who strips the bed, what's more. The Mayor's wife, even, shed her diamond earrings for him and the wife of the notary unshuffled her petticoats and, if I could, I would blush to remember how her daughter shook out her flaxen plaits and jumped in bed between them and she not sixteen years old. But never the word, "love", has fallen from his lips, nor in nor out of any of these transports, until my master saw the wife of Signor Panteleone as she went walking out to Mass, and she lifted up her veil though not for him.

And now he is half sick with it and will go to the tables no more for lack of heart and never even pats the bustling rump of the chambermaid in his new-found, maudlin celibacy, so we get our slops left festering for days and the sheets filthy and the wench goes banging about bad-temperedly with her broom enough to fetch the plaster off the walls.

I'll swear he lives for Sunday morning, though never before was he a religious man. Saturday nights, he bathes himself punctiliously, even, I'm glad to see, washes behind his ears, perfumes himself, presses his uniform so you'd think he had a right to wear it. So much in love he very rarely panders to the pleasures, even of Onan, as he lies tossing on his couch, for he cannot sleep for fear he miss the summoning bell. Then out into the cold morning, harking after that black, vague shape, hapless fisherman for this sealed oyster with such a pearl in it. He creeps behind her across the square; how can so amorous bear to be so inconspicuous? And yet, he must; though, sometimes, the old hag sneezes and says she swears there is a cat about.

He will insinuate himself into the pew behind milady and sometimes contrive to touch the hem of her garment, when they all kneel, and never a thought to his orisons; she is the divinity he's come to worship. Then sits silent, in a dream, till bed-time; what pleasure is his company for me?

He won't eat, either. I brought him a fine pigeon from the inn kitchen, fresh off the spit, parfumé avec tarragon, but he wouldn't touch it so I crunched it up, bones and all. Performing, as ever after meals, my meditative toilette, I pondered, thus: one, he is in a fair way to ruining us both by neglecting his business; two, love is desire sustained by unfulfilment. If I lead him to her bedchamber and there he takes his fill of her lily-white, he'll be right as rain in two shakes and next day tricks as usual.

Then Master and his Puss will soon be solvent once again.

Which, at the moment, very much not, sir.

This Signor Panteleone employs, his only servant but the hag, a kitchen cat, a sleek, spry tabby whom I accost. Grasping the slack of her neck firmly between my teeth, I gave her the customary tribute of a few firm thrusts of my striped loins and, when she got her breath back, she assured me in the friendliest fashion the old man was a fool and a miser who kept herself on short commons for the sake of the mousing and the young lady a soft-hearted creature who smuggled breast of chicken and sometimes, when the hag-dragon-governess napped at midday, snatched this pretty kitty out of the hearth and into her bedroom to play with reels of silk and run after trailed handkerchiefs, when she and she had as much fun together as two Cinderellas at an all-girls' ball.

Poor, lonely lady, married so young to an old dodderer with his bald pate and his goggle eyes and his limp, his avarice, his gore belly, his rheumaticks, and his flag hangs all the time at half-mast indeed; and jealous as he is impotent, tabby declares—he'd put a stop to all the rutting in the world, if he had his way, just to certify his young wife don't get from another what she can't get from him.

"Then shall we hatch a plot to antler him, my precious?"

Nothing loath, she tells me the best time for this accomplishment should be the one day in all the week he forsakes his wife and his counting-house to ride off into the country to extort most grasping rents from starveling tenant farmers. And she's left all alone, then, behind so many bolts and bars you wouldn't believe; all alone—but for the hag!

Aha! This hag turns out to be the biggest snag; an iron-plated, copper-bottomed, sworn man-hater of some sixty bitter winters who—as ill luck would have it—shatters, clatters, erupts into paroxysms of the *sneeze* at the very glimpse of a cat's whisker. No chance of Puss worming his winsome way into *that* one's affections, nor for my tabby, neither! But, oh my dear, I say; see how my ingenuity rises to this challenge. . . . So we resume the sweetest part of our conversation in the dusty convenience of the coalhole and she promises me, least she can do, to see the fair, hitherto-inaccessible one gets a letter safe if I slip it to her and slip it to her forthwith I do, though somewhat discommoded by my boots.

He spent three hours over his letter, did my master, as long as it takes me to lick the coaldust off my dicky. He tears up half a quire of paper, splays five pen-nibs with the force of his adoration: "Look not for any peace, my heart; having become a slave to this beauty's tyranny, dazzled am I by this sun's rays and my torments cannot be assuaged." *That's* not the high road to the rumpling of the bedcovers; she's got *one* ninny between them already!

"Speak from the heart," I finally exhort. "And all good women have a missionary streak, sir; convince her her orifice will be your salvation and she's yours."

"When I want your advice, Puss, I'll ask for it," he says, all at once hoity-toity. But at last he manages to pen ten pages; a rake, a profligate, a card-sharper, a cashiered officer well on the way to rack and ruin when first he saw, as if it were a glimpse of grace, her face . . . his angel, his good angel, who will lead him from perdition.

Oh, what a masterpiece he penned!

"Such tears she wept at his addresses!" says my tabby friend. "Oh, Tabs, she sobs—for she calls me 'Tabs'—I never meant to wreak such havoc with a pure heart when I smiled to see a booted cat! And put his paper next to her heart and swore, it was a good soul that sent her his vows and she was too much in love with virtue to withstand him. If, she adds, for she's a sensible girl, he's neither old as the hills nor ugly as sin, that is."

An admirable little note the lady's sent him in return, per Figaro here and there; she adopts a responsive yet uncompromising tone. For, says she, how can she usefully discuss his passion further without a glimpse of his person?

He kisses her letter once, twice, a thousand times; she must and will see me! I shall serenade her this very evening!

So, when dusk falls, off we trot to the piazza, he with an old guitar he pawned his sword to buy and most, if I may say so, outlandishly rigged out in some kind of vagabond mountebank's outfit he bartered his gold-braided waistcoat with poor Pierrot braying in the square for, moonstruck zany, lovelorn loon he was himself and even plastered his face with flour to make it white, poor fool, and so ram home his heartsick state.

There she is, the evening star with the clouds around her; but such a creaking of carts in the square, such a clatter and crash as they dismantle the stalls, such an ululation of ballad-singers and oration of nostrum-peddlers and perturbation of errand boys that though he wails out his heart to her: "Oh, my beloved!", why she, all in a dream, sits with her gaze in the middle distance, where there's a crescent moon stuck on the sky behind the cathedral pretty as a painted stage, and so is she.

Does she hear him?

Not a grace-note.

Does she see him?

Never a glance.

"Up you go, Puss; tell her to look my way!"

If rococo's a piece of cake, that chaste, tasteful, early Palladian stumped many a better cat than I in its time. Agility's not in it, when it comes to Palladian; daring alone will carry the day and, though the first storey's graced with a hefty caryatid whose bulbous loincloth and tremendous pects facilitate the first ascent, the Doric column on her head proves a horse of a different colour, I can tell you. Had I not seen my precious Tabby crouched in the gutter above me keening encouragement, I, even I, might never have braved that flying, upward leap that brought me, as if Harlequin himself on wires, in one bound to her window-sill.

"Dear god!" the lady says, and jumps. I see she, too, ah, sentimental thing! clutches a well-thumbed letter. "Puss in boots!"

I bow her with a courtly flourish. What luck to hear no sniff or sneeze; where's hag? A sudden flux sped her to the privy—not a moment to lose.

"Cast your eye below," I hiss. "Him you know of lurks below, in white with the big hat, ready to sing you an evening ditty."

The bedroom door creaks open, then, and: whee! through the air Puss goes, discretion is the better part. And, for both their sweet sakes I did it, the sight of both their bright eyes inspired me to the never-before-attempted, by me or any other cat, in boots or out of them—the death-defying triple somersault!

And a three-story drop to ground, what's more; a grand descent.

Only the merest trifle winded, I'm proud to say, I neatly land on all my fours and Tabs goes wild, huzzah! But has my master witnessed my triumph? Has he, my arse. He's tuning up that old mandolin and breaks, as down I come, again into his song.

I would never have said, in the normal course of things, his voice would charm the birds out of the trees, like mine; and yet the bustle died for him, the homeward-turning costers paused in their tracks to hearken, the preening street girls forgot their hard-edged smiles as they turned to him and some of the old ones wept, they did.

Tabs, up on the roof there, prick up your ears! For by its power I know my heart is in his voice.

And now the lady lowers her eyes to him and smiles, as once she smiled at me.

Then, bang! a stern hand pulls the shutters to. And it was as if all the violets in all the baskets of all the flower-sellers drooped and faded at once; and spring stopped dead in its tracks and might, this time, not come at all; and the bustle and the business of the square, that had so magically quieted for his song, now rose up again with the harsh clamour of the loss of love.

And we trudge drearily off to dirty sheets and a mean supper of bread and cheese, all I can steal him, but at least the poor soul manifests a hearty appetite now she knows he's in the world and not the ugliest of mortals; for the first time since that fateful morning, sleeps sound. But sleep comes hard to Puss tonight. He takes a midnight stroll across the square, soon comfortably discusses a choice morsel of salt cod his tabby friend found among the ashes on the hearth before our converse turns to other matters.

"Rats!" she says. "And take your boots off, you uncouth bugger; those three-inch heels wreak havoc with the soft flesh of my underbelly!"

When we'd recovered ourselves a little, I ask her what she means by those "rats" of hers and she proposes her scheme to me. How my master must pose as a *rat-catcher* and I, his ambulant marmalade rat-trap. How we will then go kill the rats that ravage milady's bedchamber, the day the old fool goes to fetch his rents, and she can have her will of the lad at leisure for, if there is one thing the hag fears more than a cat, it is a rat and she'll cower in a cupboard till the last rat is off the premises before she comes out. Oh, this tabby one, sharp as a tack is she! I congratulate her ingenuity with a few affectionate cuffs round the head and home again, for breakfast, ubiquitous Puss, here, there and everywhere, who's your Figaro?

Master applauds the rat ploy; but, as to the rats themselves, how are they to arrive in the house in the first place? he queries.

"Nothing easier, sir; my accomplice, a witty soubrette who lives among the cinders, dedicated as she is to the young lady's happiness, will personally strew a large number of dead and dying rats she has herself collected about the bedroom of the said ingénue's duenna, and, most particularly, that of the said ingénue herself. This is to be done tomorrow morning, as soon as Sir Pantaloon rides out to fetch his rents. By good fortune, down in the square, plying for hire, a rat-catcher! Since our hag cannot abide either a rat or a cat, it falls to milady to escort the rat-catcher, none other than yourself, sir, and his intrepid hunter, myself, to the site of the infestation.

"Once you're in her bedroom, sir, if *you* don't know what to do, then I can't help you."

"Keep your foul thoughts to yourself, Puss."

Some things, I see, are sacrosanct from humour.

Sure enough, prompt at five in the bleak next morning, I observe with my own eyes the lovely lady's lubberly husband hump off on his horse like a sack of potatoes to rake in his dues. We're ready with our sign: SIGNOR FURIOSO, THE LIVING DEATH OF RATS; and in the leathers he's borrowed from the porter, I hardly recognize him myself, not with the false moustache. He coaxes the chambermaid with a few kisses—poor, deceived girl! love knows no shame—and so we install ourselves under a certain shuttered window with the great pile of traps she's lent us, the sign of our profession, Puss perched atop them bearing the humble yet determined look of a sworn enemy of vermin.

We've not waited more than fifteen minutes—and just as well, so many rat-plagued Bergamots approach us already and are not easily dissuaded from employing us—when the front door flies open on a lusty scream. The hag, aghast, flings her arms round flinching Furioso; how fortuitous to find him! But, at the whiff of me, she's sneezing so valiantly, her eyes awash, the vertical gutters of her nostrils aswill with snot, she barely can depict the scenes inside, rattus domesticus dead in her bed and all; and worse! in the Missus' room.

So Signor Furioso and his questing Puss are ushered into the very sanctuary of the goddess, our presence announced by a fanfare from her keeper on the noseharp. *Attishhoooo!!!*

Sweet and pleasant in a morning gown of loose linen, our ingénue jumps at the tattoo of my boot heels but recovers instantly and the wheezing, hawking hag is in no state to sniffle more than: "Ain't I seen that cat before?"

"Not a chance," says my master. "Why, he's come but yesterday with me from Milano."

So she has to make do with that.

My Tabs has lined the very stairs with rats; she's made a morgue of the hag's room but something more lively of the lady's. For some of her prey she's very cleverly not killed but crippled; a big black beastie weaves its way towards us over the turkey carpet, Puss, pounce! Between screaming and sneezing, the hag's in a fine state, I can tell you, though milady exhibits a most praiseworthy and collected presence of mind, being, I guess, a young woman of no small grasp so, perhaps, she has a sniff of the plot, already.

My master goes down hands and knees under the bed.

"My god!" he cries. "There's the biggest hole, here in the wainscoting, I ever saw in all my professional career! And there's an army of black rats gathering behind it, ready to storm through! To arms!"

But, for all her terror, the hag's loath to leave the Master and me alone to deal with the rats; she casts her eye on a silver-backed hairbrush, a coral rosary, twitters, hovers, screeches, mutters until milady assures her, amidst scenes of rising pandemonium:

"I shall stay here myself and see that Signor Furioso doesn't make off with my trinkets. You go and recover yourself with an infusion of friar's balsam and don't come back until I call."

The hag departs; quick as a flash, la belle turns the key in the door on her and softly laughs, the naughty one.

Dusting the slut-fluff from his knees, Signor Furioso now stands slowly upright; swiftly, he removes his false moustache, for no element of the farcical must mar this first, delirious encounter of these lovers, must it. (Poor soul, how his hands tremble!)

Accustomed as I am to the splendid, feline nakedness of my kind, that offers no concealment of that soul made manifest in the flesh of lovers, I am always a little moved by the poignant reticence with which humanity shyly hesitates to divest itself of its clutter of concealing rags in the presence of desire. So, first, these two smile, a little, as if to say: "How strange to meet you here!", uncertain of a loving welcome, still. And do I deceive myself, or do I see a tear a-twinkle in the corner of his eye? But who is it steps towards the other first? Why, she; women, I think, are, of the two sexes, the more keenly tuned to the sweet music of their bodies. (A penny for my foul thoughts, indeed! Does she, that wise, grave personage in the négligé, think you've staged this grand charade merely in order to kiss her hand?) But, then—oh, what a pretty blush! steps back; now it's his turn to take two steps forward in the saraband of Eros.

I could wish, though, they'd dance a little faster; the hag will soon recover from her spasms and shall she find them in flagrante?

His hand, then, trembling, upon her bosom; hers, initially more hesitant, sequentially more purposeful, upon his breeches. Then their strange trance breaks; that sentimental havering done, I never saw two fall to it with such appetite. As if the whirlwind got into their fingers, they strip each other bare in a twinkling and she falls back on the bed, shows him the target, he displays the dart, scores an instant bullseye. Bravo! Never can that old bed have shook with such a storm before. And their sweet, choked mutterings, poor things: "I never . . ." "My darling . . ." "More . . ." And etc. etc. Enough to melt the thorniest heart.

He rises up on his elbows once and gasps at me: "Mimic the murder of the rats, Puss! Mask the music of Venus with the clamour of Diana!"

A-hunting we shall go! Loyal to the last, I play catch as catch can with Tab's dead rats, giving the dying the coup de grâce and baying with resonant vigour to drown the extravagant screeches that break forth from that (who would have suspected?) more passionate young woman as she comes off in fine style. (Full marks, Master.)

At that, the old hag comes battering at the door. What's going on? Whyfor the racket? And the door rattles on its hinges.

"Peace!" cries Signor Furioso. "Haven't I just now blocked the great hole?"

But milady's in no hurry to don her smock again, she takes her lovely time about it; so full of pleasure gratified her languorous limbs you'd think her very navel smiled. She pecks my master prettily thank-you on the cheek, wets the gum on his false moustache with the tip of her strawberry tongue and sticks it back on his upper lip for him, then lets her wardress into the scene of the faux carnage with the most modest and irreproachable air in the world.

"See! Puss has slaughtered all the rats."

I rush, purring proud, to greet the hag; instantly, her eyes o'erflow.

"Why the bedclothes so disordered?" she squeaks, not quite blinded, yet, by phlegm and chosen for her post from all the other applicants on account of her suspicious mind, even (oh, dutiful) when in grande peur des rats.

"Puss had a mighty battle with the biggest beast you ever saw upon this very bed; can't you see the bloodstains on the sheets? And now, what do we owe you, Signor Furioso, for this singular service?"

"A hundred ducats," says I, quick as a flash, for I know my master, left to himself, would, like an honourable fool, take nothing.

"That's the entire household expenses for a month!" wails avarice's well-chosen accomplice.

"And worth every penny! For those rats would have eaten us out of house and home." I see the glimmerings of sturdy backbone in this little lady. "Go, pay them from your private savings that I know of, that you've skimmed off the housekeeping."

Muttering and moaning but nothing for it except do as she is bid; and the furious Sir and I take off a laundry basket full of dead rats as souvenir—we drop it, plop! in the nearest sewer. And sit down to one dinner honestly paid for, for a wonder.

But the young fool is off his feed again. Pushes his plate aside, laughs, weeps, buries his head in his hands and, time and time again, goes to the window to stare at the shutters behind which his sweetheart scrubs the blood away and my dear Tabs rests from her supreme exertions. He sits, for a while, and scribbles; rips the page in four, hurls it aside. I spear a falling fragment with a claw. Dear God, he's took to writing poetry.

"I must and will have her for ever," he exclaims.

I see my plan has come to nothing. Satisfaction has not satisfied him; that soul they both saw in one another's bodies has such insatiable hunger no single meal could ever appease it. I fall to the toilette of my hinder parts, my favourite stance when contemplating the ways of the world.

"How can I live without her?"

You did so for twenty-seven years, sir, and never missed her for a moment.

"I'm burning with the fever of love!"

Then we're spared the expenses of fires.

"I shall steal her away from her husband to live with me."

"What do you propose to live on, sir?"

"Kisses," he said distractedly. "Embraces."

"Well, you won't grow fat on that, sir; though *she* will. And then, more mouths to feed."

"I'm sick and tired of your foul-mouthed barbs, Puss," he snaps. And yet my heart is moved, for now he speaks the plain, clear, foolish rhetoric of love and who is there cunning enough to help him to happiness but I? Scheme, loyal Puss, scheme!

My wash completed, I step out across the square to visit that charming she who's wormed her way directly into my own hitherto-untrammelled heart with her sharp wits and her pretty ways. She exhibits warm emotion to see me; and, oh! what news she has to tell me! News of a rapt and personal nature, that turns my mind to thoughts of the future, and, yes, domestic plans of most familial nature. She's saved me a pig's trotter, a whole, entire pig's trotter the Missus smuggled to her with a wink. A feast! Masticating, I muse.

"Recapitulate," I suggest, "the daily motions of Sir Pantaloon when he's at home."

They set the cathedral clock by him, so rigid and so regular his habits. Up at the crack, he meagrely breakfasts off yesterday's crusts and a cup of cold water, to spare the expense of heating it up. Down to his counting-house, counting out his money, until a bowl of well-watered gruel at midday. The afternoon he devotes to usury, bankrupting, here, a small tradesman, there, a weeping widow, for fun and profit. Dinner's luxurious, at four; soup, with a bit of rancid beef or a tough bird in it—he's an arrangement with the butcher, takes unsold stock off his hands in return for a shut mouth about a pie that had a finger in it. From four-thirty until five-thirty, he unlocks the shutters and lets his wife look out, oh, don't I know! while hag sits beside her to make sure she doesn't smile. (Oh, that blessed flux, those precious loose minutes that set the game in motion!)

And while she breathes the air of evening, why, he checks up on his chest of gems, his bales of silk, all those treasures he loves too much to share with daylight and if he wastes a candle when he so indulges himself, why, any man is entitled to one little extravagance. Another draught of Adam's ale healthfully concludes the day; up he tucks besides Missus and, since she is his prize possession, consents to finger her a little. He palpates her hide and slaps her flanks: "What a good bargain!" Alack, can do no more, not wishing to profligate his natural essence. And so drifts off to sinless slumber amid the prospects of tomorrow's gold.

"How rich is he?"

"Croesus."

"Enough to keep two loving couples?"

"Sumptuous."

Early in the uncandled morning, groping to the privy bleared with sleep, were the old man to place his foot upon the subfusc yet volatile fur of a shadow-camouflaged young tabby cat—

"You read my thoughts, my love."

I say to my master: "Now, you get yourself a doctor's gown, impedimenta all complete or I'm done with you."

"What's this, Puss?"

"Do as I say and never mind the reason! The less you know of why, the better."

So he expends a few of the hag's ducats on a black gown with a white collar and his skull cap and his black bag and, under my direction, makes himself another sign that announces, with all due pomposity, how he is Il Famed Dottore: *Aches cured, pains prevented, bones set, graduate of Bologna, physician extraordinary.* He demands to know, is she to play the invalid to give him further access to her bedroom?

"I'll clasp her in my arms and jump out of the window; we too shall both perform the triple somersault of love."

"You just mind your own business, sir, and let me mind it for you after my own fashion."

Another raw and misty morning! Here in the hills, will the weather ever change? So bleak it is, and dreary; but there he stands, grave as a sermon in his black gown and half the market people come with coughs and boils and broken heads and I dispense the plasters and the vials of coloured water I'd forethoughtfully stowed in his bag, he too agitato to sell for himself. (And, who knows, might we not have stumbled on a profitable profession for future pursuit, if my present plans miscarry?)

Until dawn shoots his little yet how flaming arrow past the cathedral on which the clock strikes six. At the last stroke, that famous door flies open once again and—*eeeeeeeeeeeeech!* the hag lets rip.

"Oh, Doctor, oh, Doctor, come quick as you can; our good man's taken a sorry tumble!"

And weeping fit to float a smack, she is, so doesn't see the doctor's apprentice is most colourfully and completely furred and whiskered.

The old booby's flat out at the foot of the stair, his head at an acute angle that might turn chronic and a big bunch of keys, still, gripped in his right hand as if they were the keys to heaven marked: *Wanted on voyage*. And Missus, in her wrap, bends over him with a pretty air of concern.

"A fall—" she begins when she sees the doctor but stops short when she sees your servant, Puss, looking as suitably down-in-the-mouth as his chronic smile will let him, humping his master's stock-in-trade and hawing like a sawbones. "You, again," she says, and can't forbear to giggle. But the dragon's too blubbered to hear.

My master puts his ear to the old man's chest and shakes his head dolefully; then takes the mirror from his pocket and puts it to the old man's mouth. Not a breath clouds it. Oh, sad! Oh, sorrowful!

"Dead, is he?" sobs the hag. "Broke his neck, has he?"

And she slyly makes a little grab for the keys, in spite of her well-orchestrated distress; but Missus slaps her hand and she gives over.

"Let's get him to a softer bed," says Master.

He ups the corpse, carries it aloft to the room we know full well, bumps Pantaloon down, twitches an eyelid, taps a kneecap, feels a pulse.

"Dead as a doornail," he pronounces. "It's not a doctor you want, it's an undertaker."

Missus has a handkerchief very dutifully and correctly to her eyes.

"You just run along and get one," she says to hag. "And then I'll read the will. Because don't think he's forgotten you, thou faithful servant. Oh, my goodness, no."

So off goes hag; you never saw a woman of her accumulated Christmases sprint so fast. As soon as they are left alone, no trifling, this time; they're at it, hammer and tongs, down on the carpet since the bed is occupé. Up and down, up and down his arse; in and out, in and out her legs. Then she heaves him up and throws him on his back, her turn at the grind, now, and you'd think she'll never stop.

Toujours discret, Puss occupies himself in unfastening the shutters and throwing the windows open to the beautiful beginnings of morning in whose lively yet fragrant air his sensitive nostrils catch the first and vernal hint of spring. In a few moments, my dear friend joins me. I notice already—or is it only my fond imagination?—a charming new *portliness* in her gait, hitherto so elastic, so spring-heeled. And there we sit upon the window-sill, like the two genii and protectors of the house; ah, Puss, your rambling days are over. I shall become a hearthrug cat, a fat and cosy cushion cat, sing to the moon no more, settle at last amid the sedentary joys of a domesticity we two, she and I, have so richly earned.

Their cries of rapture rouse me from this pleasant revery.

The hag chooses, naturellement, this tender if outrageous moment to return with the undertaker in his chiffoned topper, plus a brace of mutes black as beetles, glum as bailiffs, bearing the elm box between them to take the corpse away in. But they cheer up something wonderful at the unexpected spectacle before them and he and she conclude their amorous interlude amidst roars of approbation and torrents of applause.

But what a racket the hag makes! Police, murder, thieves! Until the Master chucks her purseful of gold back again, for a gratuity. (Meanwhile, I note that sensible young woman, mother-naked as she is, has yet the presence of mind to catch hold of her husband's keyring and sharply tug it from his sere, cold grip. Once she's got the keys secure, she's in charge of all.)

"Now, no more of your nonsense!" she snaps to hag. "If I hereby give you the sack, you'll get a handsome gift to go along with you for now"— flourishing the keys—"I am a rich widow and here"—indicating to all my bare yet blissful master—"is the young man who'll be my second husband."

When the governess found Signor Panteleone had indeed remembered her in his will, left her a keepsake of the cup he drank his morning water from, she made not a squeak more, pocketed a fat sum with thanks and, sneezing, took herself off with no more cries of "murder", neither. The old buffoon briskly bundled in his coffin and buried; Master comes into a great fortune and Missus rounding out already and they as happy as pigs in plunk.

But my Tabs beat her to it, since cats don't take much time about engendering; three fine, new-minted ginger kittens, all complete with snowy socks and shirtfronts, tumble in the cream and tangle Missus's knitting and put a smile on every face, not just their mother's and proud father's for Tabs and I smile all day long and, these days, we put our hearts in it.

So may all your wives, if you need them, be rich and pretty; and all your husbands, if you want them, be young and virile; and all your cats as wily, perspicacious and resourceful as:

PUSS-IN-BOOTS.

# Mehitabel and Her Kittens

BY DON MARQUIS

YOU MIGHT CALL IT poetry—at least it's printed that way—but no book of cat prose would be complete without a chunk of Don Marquis's classic story of Mehitabel the Cat, as chronicled in lower-case letters by the cockroach Archy. (Archy, being a cockroach, is unable to hit the shift button of the typewriter, so capitals are out.) Marquis (1878–1937) was a newspaperman born in the Midwest, who made his name as a columnist for the old *New York Sun*. His tales of Archy and Mehitabel began appearing in the 1920s, eventually filling several volumes. Mehitabel is a splendidly memorable cat but, you have to admit, not much of a mother.

★　★　★　★　★

well boss
mehitabel the cat
has reappeared in her old
haunts with a
flock of kittens
three of them this time

archy she said to me
yesterday
the life of a female
artist is continually
hampered what in hell
have i done to deserve
all these kittens

i look back on my life
and it seems to me to be
just one damned kitten
after another
i am a dancer archy
and my only prayer
is to be allowed
to give my best to my art
but just as i feel
that i am succeeding
in my life work
along comes another batch
of these damned kittens
it is not archy
that i am shy on mother love
god knows i care for
the sweet little things
curse them
but am i never to be allowed
to live my own life
i have purposefully avoided
matrimony in the interests
of the higher life

but i might just
as well have been a domestic
slave for all the freedom
i have gained
i hope none of them
gets run over by
an automobile
my heart would bleed
if anything happened
to them and i found it out
but it isn t fair archy
it isn t fair
these damned tom cats have all
the fun and freedom
if i was like some of these
green eyed feline vamps i know
i would simply walk out on the
bunch of them and
let them shift for themselves
but i am not that kind
archy i am full of mother love
my kindness has always
been my curse
a tender heart is the cross i bear
self sacrifice always and forever
is my motto damn them
i will make a home
for the sweet innocent
little things
unless of course providence
in his wisdom should remove
them they are living
just now in an abandoned
garbage can just behind
a made over stable in greenwich
village and if it rained
into the can before i could
get back and rescue them

i am afraid the little
dears might drown
it makes me shudder just
to think of it
of course if i were a family cat
they would probably
be drowned anyhow
sometimes i think
the kinder thing would be
for me to carry the
sweet little things
over to the river
and drop them in myself
but a mother s love archy
is so unreasonable
something always prevents me
these terrible
conflicts are always
presenting themselves
to the artist
the eternal struggle
between art and life archy
is something fierce
yes something fierce
my what a dramatic
life i have lived
one moment up the next
moment down again
but always gay archy always gay
and always the lady too
in spite of hell
well boss it will
be interesting to note
just how mehitabel
works out her present problem
a dark mystery still broods
over the manner
in which the former

family of three kittens
disappeared
one day she was talking to me
of the kittens
and the next day when i asked
her about them
she said innocently
what kittens
interrogation point
and that was all
i could ever get out
of her on the subject
we had a heavy rain
right after she spoke to me
but probably that garbage can
leaks and so the kittens
have not yet
been drowned

                        archy

# Calvin: A Study of Character

BY CHARLES DUDLEY WARNER

O N THE WHOLE," writes Charles Dudley Warner (1829–1900) of Calvin, "his life was not only a successful one, but a happy one." The same might be said of Warner's account of that life. Written with delicacy and scarcely suppressed humor, it tells the story of a cat which, except for its unusual poise and slightly mysterious history, will be absolutely familiar to most cat owners, a sort of Everycat. At the same time, of course, Calvin is bursting with personality—like all cats.

Warner was a journalist and newspaper editor in Hartford when "Calvin" was first published in *Scribner's Monthly* in 1877. He later became a regular magazine essayist, writing novels (including *The Gilded Age* with Mark Twain) and travel books on the side. Possibly his most successful book was *My Summer in a Garden,* which like "Calvin" displays his easy wit and charm, skirting sentimentality without ever succumbing to it. In fact, Warner is the ideal chronicler for someone as fastidious as Calvin. It's obvious why they were friends.

★    ★    ★    ★    ★

CALVIN IS DEAD. His life, long to him, but short for the rest of us, was not marked by startling adventures, but his character was so uncommon and his qualities were so worthy of imitation, that I have been asked by those who personally knew him to set down my recollections of his career.

His origin and ancestry were shrouded in mystery; even his age was a matter of pure conjecture. Although he was of the Maltese race, I have reason to suppose that he was American by birth as he certainly was in sympathy. Calvin was given to me eight years ago by Mrs. Stowe, but she knew nothing of his age or origin. He walked into her house one day out of the great unknown and became at once at home, as if he had been always a friend of the family. He appeared to have artistic and literary tastes, and it was as if he had inquired at the door, if that was the residence of the author of "Uncle Tom's Cabin," and, upon being assured that it was, had decided to dwell there. This is, of course, fanciful, for his antecedents were wholly unknown, but in his time he could hardly have been in any household where he would not have heard "Uncle Tom's Cabin" talked about. When he came to Mrs. Stowe, he was as large as he ever was, and apparently as old as he ever became. Yet there was in him no appearance of age; he was in the happy maturity of all his powers, and you would rather have said that in that maturity he had found the secret of perpetual youth. And it was as difficult to believe that he would ever be aged as it was to imagine that he had ever been in immature youth. There was in him a mysterious perpetuity.

After some years, when Mrs. Stowe made her winter home in Florida, Calvin came to live with us. From the first moment, he fell into the ways of the house and assumed a recognized position in the family,—I say recognized, because after he became known he was always inquired for by visitors, and in the letters to the other members of the family he always received a message. Although the least obtrusive of beings, his individuality always made itself felt.

His personal appearance had much to do with this, for he was of royal mold, and had an air of high breeding. He was large, but he had nothing of the fat grossness of the celebrated Angora family; though powerful, he was exquisitely proportioned, and as graceful in every movement as a young leopard. When he stood up to open a door—he opened all the doors with old-fashioned latches—he was portentously tall, and when stretched on the rug before the fire he seemed too long for this world—as indeed he was. His coat was the finest and softest I have ever seen, a shade of quiet Maltese; and from his throat downward, underneath, to the white tips of his feet, he wore the whitest and most delicate ermine; and no person was ever more fastidiously neat. In his finely formed head you saw something of his aristocratic character; the ears were small and cleanly cut, there was a tinge of pink in the nostrils, his face was handsome and the expression of his countenance exceedingly intelligent—I should call it even a sweet expression if the term were not inconsistent with his look of alertness and sagacity.

It is difficult to convey a just idea of his gayety in connection with his dignity and gravity, which his name expressed. As we know nothing of his family, of course it will be understood that Calvin was his Christian name. He had times of relaxation into utter playfulness, delighting in a ball of yarn, catching sportively at stray ribbons when his mistress was at her toilet, and pursuing his own tail, with hilarity, for lack of anything better. He could amuse himself by the hour, and he did not care for children; perhaps something in his past was present to his memory. He had absolutely no bad habits, and his disposition was perfect. I never saw him exactly angry, though I have seen his tail grow to an enormous size when a strange cat appeared upon his lawn. He disliked cats, evidently regarding them as feline and treacherous, and he had no association with them. Occasionally there would be heard a night concert in the shrubbery. Calvin would ask to have the door opened, and then you would hear a rush and a "pestzt," and the concert would explode, and Calvin would quietly come in and resume his seat on the hearth. There was no trace of anger in his manner, but he wouldn't have any of that about the house. He had the rare virtue of magnanimity. Although he had fixed notions about his own rights, and extraordinary persistency in getting them, he never showed temper at a repulse; he simply and firmly persisted till he had what he wanted. His diet was one point; his idea was that of the scholars about dictionaries,—to "get the best." He knew as well as any one what was in the house, and would refuse beef if turkey was to be had; and if there were oysters, he would wait over the turkey to see if the oysters would not be forthcoming. And yet he was not a gross gourmand; he would eat bread if he saw me eating it, and thought he was not being imposed on. His habits of feeding, also, were refined; he never used a knife, and he would put up his hand and draw the fork down to his mouth as gracefully as a grown person. Unless necessity compelled, he would not eat in the kitchen, but insisted upon his meals in the dining-room, and would wait patiently, unless a stranger were present; and then he was sure to importune the visitor, hoping that the latter was ignorant of the rule of the house, and would give him something. They used to say that he preferred as his table-cloth on the floor a certain well-known church journal; but this was said by an Episcopalian. So far as I know, he had no religious prejudices, except that he did not like the association with Romanists. He tolerated the servants, because they belonged to the house, and would sometimes linger by the kitchen stove; but the moment visitors came in he arose, opened the door, and marched into the drawing-room. Yet he enjoyed the company of his equals, and never withdrew, no matter how many callers—whom he recognized as of his society,—might come into the drawing-room. Calvin was fond of company, but he wanted to choose it; and I have no doubt that his was an aristocratic fastidiousness, rather than one of faith. It is so with most people.

The intelligence of Calvin was something phenomenal, in his rank of life. He established a method of communicating his wants, and even some of his sentiments; and he could help himself in many things. There was a furnace register in a retired room, where he used to go when he wished to be alone, that he always opened when he desired more heat; but never shut it, any more than he shut the door after himself. He could do almost everything but speak; and you would declare sometimes that you could see a pathetic longing to do that in his intelligent face. I have no desire to overdraw his qualities, but if there was one thing in him more noticeable than another, it was his fondness for nature. He could content himself for hours at a low window, looking into the ravine and at the great trees, noting the smallest stir there; he delighted, above all things, to accompany me walking about the garden, hearing the birds, getting the smell of the fresh earth, and rejoicing in the sunshine. He followed me and gamboled like a dog, rolling over on the turf and exhibiting his delight in a hundred ways. If I worked, he sat and watched me, or looked off over the bank, and kept his ear open to the twitter in the cherry-trees. When it stormed, he was sure to sit at the window, keenly watching the rain or the snow, glancing up and down at its falling; and a winter tempest always delighted him. I think he was genuinely fond of birds, but, so far as I know, he usually confined himself to one a day; he never killed, as some sportsmen do, for the sake of killing, but only as civilized people do,—from necessity. He was intimate with the flying-squirrels who dwell in the chestnut-trees,—too intimate, for almost every day in the summer he would bring in one, until he nearly discouraged them. He was, indeed, a superb hunter, and would have been a devastating one, if his bump of destructiveness had not been offset by a bump of moderation. There was very little of the brutality of the lower animals about him; I don't think he enjoyed rats for themselves, but he knew his business, and for the first few months of his residence with us he waged an awful campaign against the horde, and after that his simple presence was sufficient to deter them from coming on the premises. Mice amused him, but he usually considered them too small game to be taken seriously; I have seen him play for an hour with a mouse, and then let him go with a royal condescension. In this whole matter of "getting a living," Calvin was a great contrast to the rapacity of the age in which he lived.

I hesitate a little to speak of his capacity for friendship and the affectionateness of his nature, for I know from his own reserve that he would not care to have it much talked about. We understood each other perfectly, but we never made any fuss about it; when I spoke his name and snapped my fingers, he came to me; when I returned home at night, he was pretty sure to be waiting for me near the gate, and would rise and saunter along the walk, as if his being there were purely accidental,—so shy was he commonly of showing feeling; and when I opened the door he never rushed in, like a cat, but loitered, and lounged, as if he had had no intention of going in, but would condescend to. And yet, the fact was, he knew dinner was ready, and he was bound to be there. He kept the run of dinner-time. It happened sometimes, during our absence in the summer, that dinner would be early, and Calvin, walking about the grounds, missed it and came in late. But he never made a mistake the second day. There was one thing he never did,—he never rushed through an open door-way. He never forgot his dignity. If he had asked to have the door opened, and was eager to go out, he always went deliberately; I can see him now, standing on the sill, looking about at the sky as if he was thinking whether it were worth while to take an umbrella, until he was near having his tail shut in.

His friendship was rather constant than demonstrative. When we returned from an absence of nearly two years, Calvin welcomed us with evident pleasure, but showed his satisfaction rather by tranquil happiness than by fuming about. He had the faculty of making us glad to get home. It was his constancy that was so attractive. He liked companionship, but he wouldn't be petted, or fussed over, or sit in any one's lap a moment; he always extricated himself from such familiarity with dignity and with no show of temper. If there was any petting to be done, however, he chose to do it. Often he would sit looking at me, and then, moved by a delicate affection, come and pull at my coat and sleeve until he could touch my face with his nose, and then go away contented. He had a habit of coming to my study in the morning, sitting quietly by my side or on the table for hours, watching the pen run over the paper, occasionally swinging his tail round for a blotter, and then going to sleep among the papers by the inkstand. Or, more rarely, he would watch the writing from a perch on my shoulder. Writing always interested him, and, until he understood it, he wanted to hold the pen.

He always held himself in a kind of reserve with his friend, as if he had said, "Let us respect our personality, and not make a 'mess' of friendship." He saw, with Emerson, the risk of degrading it to trivial conveniency. "Why insist on rash personal relations with your friend?" "Leave this touching and clawing." Yet I would not give an unfair notion of his aloofness, his fine sense of the sacredness of the me and the not-me. And, at the risk of not being believed, I will relate an incident, which was often repeated. Calvin had the practice of passing a portion of the night in the contemplation of its beauties, and would come into our chamber over the roof of the conservatory through the open window, summer and winter, and go to sleep on the foot of my bed. He would do this always exactly in this way; he never was content to stay in the chamber if we compelled him to go upstairs and through the door. He had the obstinacy of General Grant. But this is by the way. In the morning, he performed his toilet and went down to breakfast with the rest of the family. Now, when the mistress was absent from home, and at no other time, Calvin would come in the morning, when the bell rang, to the head of the bed, put up his feet and look into my face, follow me about when I rose, "assist" at the dressing, and in many purring ways show his fondness, as if he had plainly said, "I know that she has gone away, but I am here." Such was Calvin in rare moments.

He had his limitations. Whatever passion he had for nature, he had no conception of art. There was sent to him once a fine and very expressive cat's head in bronze, by Frémiet. I placed it on the floor. He regarded it intently, approached it cautiously and crouchingly, touched it with his nose, perceived the fraud, turned away abruptly, and never would notice it afterward. On the whole, his life was not only a successful one, but a happy one. He never had but one fear, so far as I know: he had a mortal and a reasonable terror of plumbers. He would never stay in the house when they were here. No coaxing could quiet him. Of course he didn't share our fear about their charges, but he must have had some dreadful experience with them in that portion of his life which is unknown to us. A plumber was to him the devil, and I have no doubt that, in his scheme, plumbers were foreordained to do him mischief.

In speaking of his worth, it has never occurred to me to estimate Calvin by the worldly standard. I know that it is customary now, when anyone dies, to ask how much he was worth, and that no obituary in the newspapers is considered complete without such an estimate. The plumbers in our house were one day overheard to say that, "They say that *she* says that *he* says that he wouldn't take a hundred dollars for him." It is unnecessary to say that I never made such a remark, and that, so far as Calvin was concerned, there was no purchase in money.

As I look back upon it, Calvin's life seems to me a fortunate one, for it was natural and unforced. He ate when he was hungry, slept when he was sleepy, and enjoyed existence to the very tips of his toes and the end of his expressive and slow-moving tail. He delighted to roam about the garden, and stroll among the trees, and to lie on the green grass and luxuriate in all the sweet influences of summer. You could never accuse him of idleness, and yet he knew the secret of repose. The poet who wrote so prettily of him that his little life was rounded with a sleep, understated his felicity; it was rounded with a good many. His conscience never seemed to interfere with his slumbers. In fact, he had good habits and a contented mind. I can see him now walk in at the study door, sit down by my chair, bring his tail artistically about his feet, and look up at me with unspeakable happiness in his handsome face. I often thought that he felt the dumb limitation which denied him the power of language. But since he was denied speech, he scorned the inarticulate mouthings of the lower animals. The vulgar mewing and yowling of the cat species was beneath him; he sometimes uttered a sort of articulate and well-bred ejaculation, when he wished to call attention to something that he considered remarkable, or to some want of his, but he never went whining about. He would sit for hours at a closed window, when he desired to enter, without a murmur, and when it was opened he never admitted that he had been impatient by "bolting" in. Though speech he had not, and the unpleasant kind of utterance given to his race he would not use, he had a mighty power of purr to express his measureless content with congenial society. There was in him a musical organ with stops of varied power and expression, upon which I have no doubt he could have performed Sebastian Bach's celebrated cat's-fugue.

Whether Calvin died of old age, or was carried off by one of the diseases incident to youth, it is impossible to say; for his departure was as quiet as his advent was mysterious. I only know that he appeared to us in this world in his perfect stature and beauty, and that after a time, like Lohengrin, he withdrew. In his illness, there was nothing more to be regretted than in all his blameless life. I suppose there never was an illness that had more of dignity, and sweetness, and resignation in it. It came on gradually, in a kind of listlessness and want of appetite. An alarming symptom was his preference for the warmth of a furnace-register to the lively sparkle of the open wood-fire. Whatever pain he suffered, he bore it in silence, and seemed only anxious not to obtrude his malady. We tempted him with the delicacies of the season, but it soon became impossible for him to eat, and for two weeks he ate or drank scarcely anything. Sometimes he made an effort to take something, but it was evident that he made the effort to please us. The neighbors—and I am convinced that the advice of neighbors is never good for anything—suggested catnip. He wouldn't even smell it. We had the attendance of an amateur practitioner of medicine, whose real office was the cure of souls, but nothing touched his case. He took what was offered, but it was with the air of one to whom the time for pellets was passed. He sat or lay day after day almost motionless, never once making a display of those vulgar convulsions or contortions of pain which are so disagreeable to society. His favorite place was on the brightest spot of a Smyrna rug by the conservatory, where the sunlight fell and he could hear the fountain play. If we went to him and exhibited our interest in his condition, he always purred in recognition of our sympathy. And when I spoke his name, he looked up with an expression that said, "I understand it, old fellow, but it's no use." He was to all who came to visit him a model of calmness and patience in affliction.

I was absent from home at the last, but heard by daily postal-card of his failing condition; and never again saw him alive. One sunny morning, he rose from his rug, went into the conservatory (he was very thin then), walked around it deliberately, looking at all the plants he knew, and then went to the bay-window in the dining-room, and stood a long time looking out upon the little field, now brown and sere, and toward the garden, where perhaps the happiest hours of his life had been spent. It was a last look. He turned and walked away, laid himself down upon the bright spot in the rug, and quietly died.

It is not too much to say that a little shock went through the neighborhood when it was known that Calvin was dead, so marked was his individuality; and his friends, one after another, came in to see him. There was no sentimental nonsense about his obsequies; it was felt that any parade would have been distasteful to him. John, who acted as undertaker, prepared a candle-box for him, and I believe assumed a professional decorum; but there may have been the usual levity underneath, for I heard that he remarked in the kitchen that it was the "dryest wake he ever attended." Everybody, however, felt a fondness for Calvin, and regarded him with a certain respect. Between him and Bertha there existed a great friendship, and she apprehended his nature; she used to say that sometimes she was afraid of him, he looked at her so intelligently; she was never certain that he was what he appeared to be.

When I returned, they had laid Calvin on a table in an upper chamber by an open window. It was February. He reposed in a candle-box, lined about the edge with evergreen, and at his head stood a little wine-glass with flowers. He lay with his head tucked down in his arms,—a favorite position of his before the fire,—as if asleep in the comfort of his soft and exquisite fur. It was the involuntary exclamation of those who saw him, "How natural he looks!" As for myself, I said nothing. John buried him under the twin hawthorn-trees,—one white and the other pink,—in a spot where Calvin was fond of lying and listening to the hum of summer insects and the twitter of birds.

Perhaps I have failed to make appear the individuality of character that was so evident to those who knew him. At any rate, I have set down nothing concerning him but the literal truth. He was always a mystery. I did not know whence he came; I do not know whither he has gone. I would not weave one spray of falsehood in the wreath I lay upon his grave.

# The Immortal Cat

From *I Had a Dog and a Cat*

BY KAREL ČAPEK

I N THE YEARS between the two world wars, Karel Čapek (1890–1938) was probably Czechoslovakia's most famous writer, internationally known for such plays as *R. U. R.: Rossum's Universal Robots* (which introduced the word "robot" into the English language) and novels like *The War with the Newts.* He was also a short story writer, and an essayist of enormous charm and delicacy. It was in this latter capacity that he wrote about his dogs and cats and his garden, in his Prague newspaper columns and in numerous books. Along with his brother Josef, Čapek was a lucid and powerful voice on behalf of Czech democracy at a time when Hitler's threat was growing. Yet in the end he was beaten—he died at the age of only 48 in 1938, just after the Nazi takeover of his country. His brother died in Auschwitz.

Čapek's account of Pudlenka[s] will strike a chord with anyone who has been, at one time or another, overprovided with kittens.

★　★　★　★　★

THIS STORY ABOUT A CAT (with the inconsequence which is the very characteristic of reality) is at the beginning about a tomcat, in fact, about a tomcat which was presented to me. Every gift has about it something supernatural; each comes, so to speak, from another world, it drops from heaven, is sent upon us, invades our lives independently of its own and with some kind of exuberance, especially if it happens to be a particular tomcat with a blue ribbon round his neck. And he was called Philip, Percy, Scamp, and Rogue, in accordance with his various moral qualities; he was an Angora kitten, but dishevelled and carrotty like any other Christian scamp. One day on a tour of exploration he fell from the balcony onto the head of some female person; on the one hand she was scratched by it, on the other deeply offended, and she brought out a charge against my cat as a dangerous animal which springs from balconies onto peoples' heads. As a matter of fact I established the innocence of this Seraphic little beast; but three days later the little animal breathed his last, poisoned with arsenic and human malice. Just as through a strange mist I saw how with his last tremor his hips had sunken in, there was a mew at my doorstep; a stray brindled kitten was trembling there, as scraggy as a ridge-tile, and as frightened as a wandering child. Well, come here, Pussy; perhaps it is the finger of God, the will of Fate, a mysterious sign or whatever it is called; most probably the departed has sent you in his place; unfathomable is the continuity of life.

Such then was the first arrival of a cat which for her modesty was given the name of Pudlenka; as you see, she came from the Unknown, but I bear witness that she in no way puffed herself up on account of her mysterious and perhaps even supernatural origin. On the contrary, she behaved like every normal cat: she drank milk and stole the meat, she slept in one's lap and roamed in the night; and when her time had come, she gave birth to five kittens of which one was red, one black, one mixed, one brindled, and one Angora. And I began to accost all the people I knew. "Listen," I began magnanimously, "I've got a marvellous kitten for you." Some of them (out of extreme modesty, very likely) managed to extricate themselves, saying that they would love to, but that unfortunately they couldn't, and so on; but others were so taken by surprise that before they would utter a word I had pressed their hand, and declared that it was settled then, they needn't worry, I was going to send them that kitten in due course; and already I was off after the next. Nothing is more charming than such a cat's maternal happiness; you ought to. have a cat for yourself, if for nothing else but for those kittens. After six weeks Pudlenka let the kittens be kittens, and went to listen at first hand to the heroic baritone of the tomcat from the adjoining street. In fifty-three days she delivered six young ones. In a year and a day they added up to seventeen. Most probably that miraculous fertility was a legacy and post-mortem mission of the deceased bachelor little cat.

I always used to be of the opinion, may the deuce take them, that I had heaps of acquaintances, but from the time that Pudlenka threw herself into producing kittens, I found that in this life of ours I was terribly alone; for instance, I had no one to present with the twenty-sixth kitten. When I had to make myself known to someone I mumbled my name, and said: "Don't you want a kitten?" "What kitten?" they enquired dubiously. "I don't know yet," was my general answer; "but I think that I shall be having some kittens again." Soon I began to have the feeling that people were avoiding me; perhaps it was out of envy because I had such luck with kittens. According to Brehm cats bear young twice a year; Pudlenka had them three to four times a year without any regard to the seasons; she was a supernatural cat—apparently she had a higher mission, to revenge and replace a hundredfold the life of that tomcat which was done to death.

After three years of fertile vigour Pudlenka suddenly perished; some caretaker broke her back on the undignified pretext that according to him she had eaten a goose in his larder. The very same day that Pudlenka disappeared, her youngest daughter came back to us, a cat which I had pressed onto the people next door; and she lived with us under the name of Pudlenka II as a direct continuation of her deceased mother. She continued her to perfection; she was still a girlish adolescent when she began to swell, and then brought into the world four kittens. One was black, and had a noble, carrotty colour of the Vršovice race, one the elongated nose of the Strašnice cats, while the fourth was spotty like a bean, as the cats of Malâ Strana are. Pudlenka II produced kittens three times a year with the regularity of a law of Nature; in two and a quarter years she enriched the world with one and twenty kittens, of all colours and breeds, except that of the cats of the Isle of Man which are born without tails. For the twenty-first kitten I really had no market. I was just making up my mind that I ought to join the Free Thought or the Rosary Brotherhood, to gain a new circle of acquaintances when our neighbour's Rolf bit to death Pudlenka II. We carried her home and laid her on the bed; her chin still was trembling. Then the chin stopped shaking and from her dense coat fleas rapidly crawled away; this is the unmistakable sign of death with a cat. So then her surviving kitten for whom there was no market remained with us as Pudlenka III. In four months' time Pudlenka III gave birth to five kittens; from that time on she has conscientiously fulfilled her task of this life at regular intervals of fifteen weeks; only during those great frosts of this year did she miss one term.

You might not perhaps say of her that she had such a big and immortal mission; to look at, she seems an ordinary, many-coloured democratic puss, who spends the whole day long dozing on the family patriarch's lap, or on the bed. She has a highly-developed sense for her personal comfort, maintains a healthy distrust of men and animals, and when it comes to it she can defend her interests *dente unguibusque*. But when her fifteen weeks are over she begins to be excited and restless, and she sits nervously by the door giving one to understand: "Man, let me out quickly, I have got the tummy ache." After this, she dashes out like an arrow into the evening darkness, and doesn't return till morning, with a drawn face and rings round her eyes. At such times a huge black tomcat comes from the North, where the Olšany Cemeteries are; from the South, where Vršovice is, appears a carrotty and one-eyed fighter; from the West, the seat of civilization, arrives an Angora cat, with a bush of ostrich feathers; from the East, where there is nothing, a mysterious white animal appears with a curved-up tail. In their midst sits the simple many-coloured Pudlenka III, and with burning fascinated eyes she listens to their howling, stifled exclamations, screams as of murdered children, roar of drunken mariners, saxophones, roll of drums and other instruments in the Cats' Symphony. To put it clearly, not only are strength and courage necessary for a tomcat, but also perseverance; sometimes for a week at a time these four tomcats of the Apocalypse besiege Pudlenka's home, blockade the gate, make their way through the windows into the house, and leave behind them merely a hellish stench. At last the night arrives when Pudlenka III no longer has any desire to go out. "Let me sleep," she says. "Let me sleep, sleep for ever. Sleep, dream. . . . Ah, I'm so unhappy!" After this, at the proper time, she delivers five kittens. On this question I have already had a certain amount of experience: there will be five of them. I already see them, those dear, sweet little lumps, stumping, and padding about over the house, pulling over electric lamps, making little puddles in slippers, crawling up my legs, onto my lap (my legs are scratched by them, like Lazarus's), I see myself finding a kitten in the sleeve when I'm putting on my coat, and my tie under the bed when I want to put it on—Children are worrying, everybody will tell you that. It isn't enough just to bring them up; you have to ensure their future.

In the editorial office everybody now has got a kitten from me; very well, I shall have to get taken on at another place. I am ready to put my name down for any society, or organization, if they will assure me of the disposal of at least twenty-one kittens. While I shall be struggling along in a hostile world to find room for more generations, Pudlenka III, or Pudlenka IV, will be purring, her paws folded up beneath her, and spinning the immortal thread of cat life. She will dream of the cats' world, of the hosts of cats, of cats, when there will be enough of them, seizing power to rule over the universe. For it is a Great Task which was imposed upon her by the little Angora tomcat, innocently done to death.

Seriously, now, wouldn't you like a kitten?

# Tobermory

BY SAKI

T
OBERMORY" MUST BE among the most popular cat stories ever written. (One indication: whenever the editor of this collection mentioned to friends that he was looking for cat stories, the first question was usually "Do you have 'Tobermory?' ") Hector Hugo Munro (1870–1916), who wrote under the pen name Saki and was killed on the Western Front during the First World War, published the story in 1912, in a collection called *The Chronicles of Clovis.* Its subject is a cat who is taught to speak. Tobermory, however, turns out to be altogether too outspoken for the good of his teacher—to say nothing of himself.

★　★　★　★　★

IT WAS A CHILL, rain-washed afternoon of a late August day, that indefinite season when partridges are still in the security of cold storage, and there is nothing to hunt—unless one is bounded on the north by the Bristol Channel, in which case one may lawfully gallop after fat red stags. Lady Blemley's house-party was not bounded on the north by the Bristol Channel, hence there was a full gathering of her guests round the tea-table on this particular afternoon. And, in spite of the blankness of the season and the triteness of the occasion, there was no trace in the company of that fatigued restlessness which means a dread of the pianola and a subdued hankering for auction bridge. The undisguised, open-mouthed attention of the entire party was fixed on the homely, negative personality of Mr Cornelius Appin. Of all her guests, he was the one who had come to Lady Blemley with the vaguest reputation. Someone had said he was "clever", and he had got his invitation in the moderate expectation, on the part of his hostess, that some portion at least of his cleverness would be contributed to the general entertainment. Until tea-time that day she had been unable to discover in what direction, if any, his cleverness lay. He was neither a wit nor a croquet champion, a hypnotic force nor a begetter of amateur theatricals. Neither did his exterior suggest the sort of man in whom women are willing to pardon a generous measure of mental deficiency. He had subsided into mere Mr Appin, and the Cornelius seemed a piece of transparent baptismal bluff. And now he was claiming to have launched on the world a discovery beside which the invention of gun powder, of the printing-press, and of steam locomotion were inconsiderable trifles. Science had made bewildering strides in many directions during recent decades, but this thing seemed to belong to the domain of miracle rather than to scientific achievement.

"And do you really ask us to believe," Sir Wilfrid was saying, "that you have discovered a means for instructing animals in the art of human speech and that dear old Tobermory has proved your first successful pupil?"

"It is a problem at which I have worked for the past seventeen years," said Mr Appin, "but only during the last eight or nine months have I been rewarded with glimmerings of success. Of course I have experimented with thousands of animals, but latterly only with cats, those wonderful creatures which have assimilated themselves so marvellously with our civilization while retaining all their highly developed feral instincts. Here and there among cats one comes across an outstanding superior intellect, just as one does among the ruck of human beings, and when I made the acquaintance of Tobermory a week ago I saw at once that I was in contact with a "Beyond-cat" of extraordinary intelligence. I had gone far along the road to success in recent experiments; with Tobermory, as you call him, I have reached the goal."

Mr Appin concluded his remarkable statement in a voice which he strove to divest of a triumphant inflexion. No one said "Rats," though Clovis's lips moved in a monosyllabic contortion which probably invoked those rodents of disbelief.

"And do you mean to say," asked Miss Resker, after a slight pause, "that you have taught Tobermory to say and understand easy sentences of one syllable?"

"My dear Miss Resker," said the wonder-worker patiently, "one teaches little children and savages and backward adults in that piecemeal fashion; when one has once solved the problem of making a beginning with an animal of highly developed intelligence one has no need for those halting methods. Tobermory can speak our language with perfect correctness."

This time Clovis very distinctly said, "Beyond-rats!" Sir Wilfrid was more polite, but equally sceptical.

"Hadn't we better have the cat in and judge for ourselves?" suggested Lady Blemley.

Sir Wilfrid went in search of the animal, and the company settled themselves down to the languid expectation of witnessing some more or less adroit drawing-room ventriloquism.

In a minute Sir Wilfrid was back in the room, his face white beneath its tan and his eyes dilated with excitement.

"By Gad, it's true!"

His agitation was unmistakably genuine, and his hearers started forward in a thrill of awakened interest.

Collapsing into an armchair he continued breathlessly; "I found him dozing in the smoking-room, and called after him to come for his tea. He blinked at me in his usual way, and I said, "Come on, Toby; don't keep us waiting;" and, by Gad! he drawled out in a most horribly natural voice, that he'd come when he dashed well pleased! I nearly jumped out of my skin!"

Appin had preached to absolutely incredulous hearers; Sir Wilfrid's statement carried instant conviction. A Babel-like chorus of startled exclamation arose, amid which the scientist sat mutely enjoying the first fruit of his stupendous discovery.

In the midst of the clamour Tobermory entered the room and made his way with velvet tread and studied unconcern across to the group seated round the tea-table.

A sudden hush of awkwardness and constraint fell on the company. Somehow there seemed an element of embarrassment in addressing on equal terms a domestic cat of acknowledged mental ability.

"Will you have some milk, Tobermory?" asked Lady Blemley in a rather strained voice.

"I don't mind if I do," was the response, couched in a tone of even indifference. A shiver of suppressed excitement went through the listeners, and Lady Blemley might be excused for pouring out the saucerful of milk rather unsteadily.

"I am afraid I have spilled a good deal of it," she said apologetically.

"After all, it's not my Axminster," was Tobermory's rejoinder.

Another silence fell on the group, and then Miss Resker, in her best district-visitor manner, asked if the human language had been difficult to learn. Tobermory looked squarely at her for a moment and then fixed his gaze serenely on the middle distance. It was obvious that boring questions lay outside his scheme of life.

"What do you think of human intelligence?" asked Mavis Pellington lamely.

"Of whose intelligence in particular?" asked Tobermory coldly.

"Oh, well, mine for instance," said Mavis, with a feeble laugh.

"You put me in an embarrassing position," said Tobermory, whose tone and attitude certainly did not suggest a shred of embarrassment. "When your inclusion in this house party was suggested, Sir Wilfrid protested that you were the most brainless woman of his acquaintance, and that there was a wide distinction between hospitality and the care of the feeble-minded. Lady Blemley replied that your lack of brain-power was the precise quality which had earned you your invitation, as you were the only person she could think of who might be idiotic enough to buy their old car. You know, the one they call "The Envy of Sisyphus", because it goes quite nicely uphill if you push it."

Lady Blemley's protestations would have had greater effect if she had not casually suggested to Mavis only that morning that the car in question would be just the thing for her down at her Devonshire home.

Major Barfield plunged in heavily to effect a diversion.

"How about your carryings-on with the tortoiseshell puss up at the stables, eh?"

The moment he had said it everyone realized the blunder.

"One does not usually discuss these matters in public," said Tobermory frigidly. "From a slight observation of your ways since you've been in this house I should imagine you'd find it inconvenient if I were to shift the conversation on to your own little affairs."

The panic which ensued was not confined to the Major.

"Would you like to go and see if cook has got your dinner ready?" suggested Lady Blemley hurriedly, affecting to ignore the fact that it wanted at least two hours to Tobermory's dinner-time.

"Thanks," said Tobermory, "not quite so soon after my tea. I don't want to die of indigestion."

"Cats have nine lives, you know," said Sir Wilfrid heartily.

"Possibly," answered Tobermory; "but only one liver."

"Adelaide!" said Mrs. Cornett, "do you mean to encourage that cat to go out and gossip about us in the servants' hall?"

The panic had indeed become general. A narrow ornamental balustrade ran in front of most of the bedroom windows at the Towers, and it was recalled with dismay that this had formed a favourite promenade for Tobermory at all hours, whence he could watch the pigeons—and heaven knew what else besides. If he intended to become reminiscent in his present outspoken strain the effect would be something more than disconcerting. Mrs. Cornett, who spent much time at her toilet table, and whose complexion was reputed to be of a nomadic though punctual disposition, looked as ill at ease as the Major. Miss Scrawen, who wrote fiercely sensuous poetry and led a blameless life, merely displayed irritation; if you are methodical and virtuous in private you don't necessarily want everyone to know it. Bertie van Tahn, who was so depraved at seventeen that he had long ago given up trying to be any worse, turned a dull shade of gardenia white, but he did not commit the error of dashing out of the room like Odo Finsberry, a young gentleman who was understood to be reading for the Church and who was possibly disturbed at the thought of scandals he might hear concerning other people. Clovis had the presence of mind to maintain a composed exterior; privately he was calculating how long it would take to procure a box of fancy mice through the agency of the *Exchange and Mart* as a species of hush-money.

Even in a delicate situation like the present, Agnes Resker could not endure to remain too long in the background.

"Why did I ever come down here?" she asked dramatically. Tobermory immediately accepted the opening.

"Judging by what you said to Mrs Cornett on the croquet lawn yesterday, you were out for food. You described the Blemleys as the dullest people to stay with that you knew, but said they were clever enough to employ a first-rate cook; otherwise they'd find it difficult to get anyone to come down a second time."

"There's not a word of truth in it! I appeal to Mrs Cornett—" exclaimed the discomfitted Agnes.

"Mrs Cornett repeated your remark afterwards to Bertie van Tahn," continued Tobermory, "and said, 'That woman is a regular Hunger Marcher; she'd go anywhere for four square meals a day' and Bertie van Tahn said—"

At this point the chronicle mercifully ceased. Tobermory had caught a glimpse of the big yellow Tom from the Rectory working his way through the shrubbery towards the stable wing. In a flash he had vanished through the open French window.

With the disappearance of his too brilliant pupil Cornelius Appin found himself beset by a hurricane of bitter upbraiding, anxious inquiry, and frightened entreaty. The responsibility for the situation lay with him, and he must prevent matters from becoming worse. Could Tobermory impart his dangerous gift to other cats? was the first question he had to answer. It was possible, he replied, that he might have initiated his intimate friend the stable puss into his new accomplishment, but it was unlikely that his teaching could have taken a wider range as yet.

"Then," said Mrs Cornett, "Tobermory may be a valuable cat and a great pet; but I'm sure you'll agree, Adelaide, that both he and the stable cat must be done away with without delay."

"You don't suppose I've enjoyed the last quarter of an hour, do you?" said Lady Blemley bitterly. "My husband and I are very fond of Tobermory— at least, we were before this horrible accomplishment was infused into him; but now, of course, the only thing is to have him destroyed as soon as possible."

"We can put some strychnine in the scraps he always gets at dinner-time," said Sir Wilfrid, "and I will go and drown the stable cat myself. The coachman will be very sore at losing his pet, but I'll say a very catching form of mange has broken out in both cats and we're afraid of it spreading to the kennels."

"But my great discovery!" expostulated Mr Appin; "after all my years of research and experiment—"

"You can go and experiment on the short-horns at the farm, who are under proper control," said Mrs Cornett, "or the elephants at the Zoological Gardens. They're said to be highly intelligent, and they have this recommendation, that they don't come creeping about our bedrooms and under chairs, and so forth."

An archangel ecstatically proclaiming the Millennium, and then finding that it clashed with Henley and would have to be indefinitely postponed, could hardly have felt more crestfallen than Cornelius Appin at the reception of his wonderful achievements. Public opinion, however, was against him—in fact, had the general voice been consulted on the subject it is probable that a strong minority vote would have been in favour of including him in the strychnine diet.

Defective train arrangements and a nervous desire to see matters brought to a finish prevented an immediate dispersal of the party, but dinner that evening was not a social success. Sir Wilfrid had had rather a trying time with the stable cat and subsequently with the coachman. Agnes Resker ostentatiously limited her repast to a morsel of dry toast, which she bit as though it were a personal enemy, while Mavis Pellington maintained a vindictive silence throughout the meal. Lady Blemley kept up a flow of what she hoped was conversation, but her attention was fixed on the doorway. A plateful of carefully dosed fish scraps was in readiness on the sideboard, but sweets and savoury and dessert went their way, and no Tobermory appeared either in the dining-room or kitchen.

The sepulchral dinner was cheerful compared with the subsequent vigil in the smoking-room. Eating and drinking had at least supplied a distraction and cloak to the prevailing embarrassment. Bridge was out of the question in the general tension of nerves and tempers, and after Odo Finsberry had given a lugubrious rendering of "Melisande in the Wood" to a frigid audience, music was tacitly avoided. At eleven the servants went to bed, announcing that the small window in the pantry had been left open as usual for Tobermory's private use. The guests read steadily through the current batch of magazines, and fell back gradually on the "Badminton Library" and bound volumes of *Punch*. Lady Blemley made periodic visits to the pantry, returning each time with an expression of listless depression which forestalled questioning.

At two o'clock Clovis broke the dominating silence.

"He won't turn up to-night. He's probably in the local newspaper office at the present moment, dictating the first instalment of his reminiscences. Lady What's-her-name's book won't be in it. It will be the event of the day."

Having made this contribution to the general cheerfulness, Clovis went to bed. At long intervals the various members of the house party followed his example.

The servants taking round the early tea made a uniform announcement in reply to a uniform question. Tobermory had not returned.

Breakfast was, if anything, a more unpleasant function than dinner had been, but before its conclusion the situation was relieved. Tobermory's corpse was brought in from the shrubbery, where a gardener had just discovered it. From the bites on his throat and the yellow fur which coated his claws it was evident that he had fallen in unequal combat with the big Tom from the Rectory.

By midday most of the guests had quitted the Towers, and after lunch Lady Blemley had sufficiently recovered her spirits to write an extremely nasty letter to the Rectory about the loss of her valuable pet.

Tobermory had been Appin's one successful pupil, and he was destined to have no successor. A few weeks later an elephant in the Dresden Zoological Garden, which had shown no previous signs of irritability, broke loose and killed an Englishman who had apparently been teasing it. The victim's name was variously reported in the papers as Oppin and Eppelin, but his front name was faithfully rendered Cornelius.

"If he was trying German irregular verbs on the poor beast," said Clovis, "he deserved all he got."

# George Eliot: A Medical Study

BY JEAN STAFFORD

T HIS MAY NOT be the greatest cat story ever told, but it is surely one of the funniest, mainly because Jean Stafford (1915–1979) was a dazzling writer who happened to be, against her evident better judgment, a sucker for cats. Best-known as a novelist (*Boston Adventure, The Mountain Lion*) and many short stories published in *The New Yorker* (her *Collected Stories* won the Pulitzer Prize), she may have been happiest writing about cats, as in this story and the children's book *Elphi, the Cat with High IQ*. Which is not to say that her own experience with cats was necessarily always happy—or cheap—as "George Eliot" goes some way to prove.

★   ★   ★   ★   ★

THE SUBJECT OF THIS MONOLOGUE was not born Mary Ann Evans nor was she united, without legal form, to George Henry Lewes; she did not, furthermore, die Mrs. John Walter Cross. She was born, I regret to say, "Stripey," and she had a long and fertile (*highly* fertile) relationship with a country fellow named Robert until she was obliged (indeed, commanded) to have a hysterectomy. She is still alive, thanks to the miracles of modern medicine, and is, as a matter of fact, staring at me right now with the big grape eyes she inherited from her Persian mother. It has been proposed by a good many perceptive people that she is probably the most beautiful cat in the Western Hemisphere; she has a silvery coat and ebony necklaces and ebony bracelets and ebony rings around her tail and her purr, to those attuned, is the music of the spheres.

George Eliot was given to me as a Christmas present by a Norwegian friend of mine who, cribbing a line from an I. J. Fox ad, observed that "a small fur piece is a joy forever." When I first saw her, on a sparkling, cold Connecticut day, she was lying with her sleeping siblings, one black and one white (Blackie and Whitey) in a baby's playpen along with a sleeping blond baby (Nils; the Norwegians were better at naming specimens of *homo sapiens* than they were at naming those of *felis domestica*). A great big Norwegian explorer, a guest in the house en route from the Galapagos to Lapland, was playing sweet folk tunes on a fiddle and silver tabby kitten, Stripey, was looking up at him with an expression of wonder, showing, even at this early age, a sensitivity to the finer things of life. We established an immediate rapport and while we have had our ups and downs, we have, on the whole, been much contented with each other for seven years.

I have never had so expensive a Christmas present and by expensive, I don't mean what it cost the Norwegians, I mean what it has cost me. When I go away, I store the silver in the bank for fifty cents a month and I store *her* in posh cat-houses for a dollar a day. It pleases her to remove parts of her silken coat to, preferably, black surfaces, ideally, black velvet; my cleaning bills and those of my friends (the few I have left) are staggering. She would rather starve than eat anything so non-U as Puss 'n Boots; she despises horsemeat; she is fond of boiled chicken lightly salted, and of cantaloupe; for daily fare she puts up with baby food at 26 cents a jar. Her hospital and medical bills have run into four figures and mine, after getting the bills, have not been inconsiderable—when I am not insomniac, I am in a dead faint.

We lived, she and I, at first in New York, but she was so bored and woebegone, so homesick for the trees of her infancy, that after a few months we moved to Connecticut so that this prominent cat would not perish of inanition. She was immediately transformed by the country air and one would never have guessed that she had ever suffered depression. She patrolled the grounds, routing great oafish English setters whose only goal in life was to overturn my garbage pail and strew my lawn with things I did not want to know existed; she brought me presents of vivisected shrews and deer mice; she climbed the trees and smelled the flowers and chased the butterflies and she purred the livelong day. Robert, an outside cat came with the house and at first George Eliot disdained him. And no wonder, for no cat in the world ever cared less for his personal appearance than Robert, unless it was Pegleg, George Eliot's father, a randy old boy who had fathered thousands. Robert was scarred from fights without number, there were burns as old as himself attached to his dusty, uncombed coat; he had the shoulders of a bull and the manners of a hired man. I'd invite him to come into the kitchen but he would never accept—he said, in effect, "No thanks, ma'am. I'd like my handout right here on the welcome mat." George Eliot, looking at him through the screen door, said, in effect, "Bumpkin!"

And then, when the peonies were blooming and the weigela was out and the roses were beginning, when the air was heady with all the perfumes and the mysterious noises of spring, George Eliot, nubile and ready to fall in love, fell in love with dirty old Robert. She, so dignified and so fastidious, behaved like the most shameless of tarts and the pair of them made the kind of racket in the picking garden that causes me to blush when I recall it. The results of their rendezvous were Daniel Deronda, Silas Marner, Milly and Flossie (subsequently renamed by the illiterate children to whom they went to live "Blackie," "Whitey," "Stripey," and "Baby"). The delivery, in a coat closet, was difficult, but recovery was uneventful and was far too rapid for my taste; she was only just getting her figure back when she encountered Robert again, and so sprang to life Middlemarch, Adam Bede, Romola—the Spanish Gypsy died soon after birth. George Eliot's pathological philoprogeneity knew no season and no sooner than Stripey, Pinky and Blackie, as they came to be called, had been indentured to the homes of ailurophiliac children, than she hotfooted it out to the barn to wake up Robert. I had run out of easy targets—the children were duck soup but their parents had begun to snub me—and I had also run out of names. The third group were called Mr. Gilfil, Felix Holt and Scenes of Clerical Life. (They exist today as Stripey, Blackie and Roger.) I refused to let her see Robert again after this confinement because I would not, I could not be confronted with more kittens, one of whom would have to be called Essence of Christianity. I kept her under lock and key until a well-known surgeon of the community could schedule her for an operation. This doctor, whom I will call Dr. Catwalder, had an excellent reputation for his bedside manner with ailing animals, especially cats; cats, I was told, hated to leave his hospital. George Eliot loathed him on sight.

On that day of the operation, he telephoned me to say that she had worms and that he could not perform the hysterectomy until he had cured her of them. Five days later he called again to say that she refused to eat or drink, that she was dying, that it would be a kindness to let her die at home. Sobbing a lot, I went to get her, but before I left the house, I prepared a dainty invalid's meal just in case: some breast of chicken, some heavy cream, some chopped bacon. When I opened the top of her carrier in the kitchen, she leaped out of it with a trilling mew of pleasure, ate everything in sight and asked for more. She washed, checked the house to make sure everything was still there and then pretended that she had never been away at all. Her act had been nothing more nor less than a suicide threat and Dr. Catwalder, when I called to make another appointment, refused to take her on. "There was no transference," he said.

Next we went to a Dr. Catlett whom she loved, or rather, she loved the Mexican burro belonging to Dr. Catlett's children which she could see through the window in his consulting room. He operated successfully and recovery was uneventful. Thereafter she treated Robert like scum.

Dr. Catlett saw her through a kidney ailment (at first he diagnosed it as tubercular in origin but to our relief he found that it was streptococcic—there is, so far as I know, no cat equivalent of Saranac), for tonsilitis and virus pneumonia, for hepatitis, for the common cold. The only disease she didn't have was Asiatic flu and she didn't have that simply because it hadn't yet been introduced to this country by *Life* magazine.

After a few years, George Eliot and I moved from the outskirts into the village itself to a house on a heavily traveled street and for some time I did not allow her to go outdoors since she had had no experience with traffic. But she sneaked out one evening in the early spring and made the acquaintance of a neighboring castrate named Balzac, and she had such a good romp with him, she was so happy to be in charge of the wine-glass elm trees and being in the grass that I began to let her out for a few hours each day. She was sensible about the cars and never went into the road and she took enormous pleasure in climbing a tree outside my second-storey study and peering in at me, winking sometimes. Only once that summer was she ill. She was treated for worms by a Dr. Cattell who happened to be nearer than Dr. Catlett and she liked him and she adored his kennel-boy who was probably a substitute figure for Dr. Catlett's burro.

And then an altogether awful thing happened. One evening at dusk, I went out to call my pretty cat and I found a gathering of people gazing down at something in the road. It was my poor George Eliot and I was told by the outraged witnesses that she had been hit by a car that had not slowed down but had sped straight on. The kind people told me to go and call for help and they promised to watch her and reroute cars. I called the ASPCA for an ambulance and they sent it immediately with an interne who carried a net. Sensing this, with the last bit of strength she had left, she leaped into the bushes in front of the house across the road from mine and when he followed her, she streaked away under the porch. The ASPCA man asked leave of the owner of the house to tear down some of the steps and she, a benevolent old Irishwoman who had one time been a belly dancer, said, "Tear down the whole house, but rescue that dear kitty!" The ASPCA man sought her in the darkness with his flashlight and then he turned to me with a sigh and said, "Won't do any good now. She's dying." Hours later my dead cat came home. I heard the faintest of mews at the front door and opened it to find George Eliot limping and reeling, blood-stained and begrimed; she managed to get up the stairs and onto my bed and there she lay motionless, waiting to die on a familiar counterpane. Drs. Catlett and Cattell were both away fishing in Canada and I had no choice but to call her enemy, Dr. Catwalder, rousing him out of a sound sleep. She spent the night in his hospital and in the morning he telephoned to say that he thought her skull was fractured and that she apparently had internal injuries and that she could not possibly live. So again I brought her home for her final rites. For the next forty-eight hours she lay under my bed, refusing to eat, refusing to drink, but trying, stalwart cat, to purr. At last I could bear the spectacle no longer and I called a psychiatrist friend of mine who was a cat lover and told him that I was going to have a nervous breakdown. He did not doubt me for a moment and he suggested that I call a Dr. Catto, a cat specialist with offices on Park Avenue.

Dr. Catto, who drove a Mercedes, paid only house calls. Once he had had a hospital, but he had so many casualties from homesickness that he had abandoned it. He treated patients in New Jersey, in upstate New York, Pennsylvania and Connecticut and he was consulted over long distance by cat fanciers with unwell cats in Hollywood. For eight nights, he called on George Eliot; he injected her with caffein and with penicillin; he swabbed her perforated paw; he massaged her, prescribed infant glycerine suppositories and he put her on a diet of Junior beef. He left me a handful of oral antibiotics which I took later on myself when I had flu. He saved my cat all right and when his bill came I lay right down on the floor and screamed.

Now she has asthma. Dr. Cattell (the one with the nice kennel-boy) has examined her. Originally he said that possibly she had an allergy to house dust or to the fumes from aluminum cooking vessels. But after keeping her for some time in his surgery he said to me, "There is nothing *physical* to explain it," and giving me a hard look, he added, "she doesn't have asthma when she's here with us." And the truth is that no one has ever seen her have an attack except when I have been around; last summer I was away for four months and her hostess reported that she did not cough or gasp once. What have I deprived her of? That old bum, Robert, I suppose, who reminded her of her father. Right this minute she is wheezing; she has stopped staring at me and is sitting on the typewriter paper with her back to me, wheezing, and every now and again she glances over her shoulder at me to make sure she's giving me a rough time. Well, she's going to be rid of me for a while. I am going to London and while I'm gone, she is going to be in residence at 10 Downing Street. The fact that it isn't the real 10 Downing Street but is in New York City doesn't matter because she isn't the real George Eliot either and quite possibly she won't know the difference.

# The Black Cat

BY EDGAR ALLAN POE

THIS IS, to put it bluntly, a horror story. No cat jokes, no fluffy kittens, no sentimentality of the sort cats tend to accumulate around themselves even in the most cynical households. But if it is true to say of Edgar Allan Poe (1809–1849), as the American poet James Russell Lowell once did, that he was "three fifths of him genius and two fifths sheer fudge," "The Black Cat" is a highly satisfactory mixture of the two—thoroughly hokey, yet at the same time spine-chilling in the over-the-top manner that was Poe's specialty. Its moral, if it has one, is that you shouldn't mistreat cats (or wives), but if you do, be careful about walling up bodies in cellars. Cats, like elephants, don't forget.

★ ★ ★ ★ ★

FOR THE MOST WILD yet most homely narrative which I am about to pen, I neither expect nor solicit belief. Mad indeed would I be to expect it, in a case where my very senses reject their own evidence. Yet, mad am I not—and very surely do I not dream. But to-morrow I die, and to-day I would unburthen my soul. My immediate purpose is to place before the world, plainly, succinctly, and without comment, a series of mere household events. In their consequences, these events have terrified—have tortured—have destroyed me. Yet I will not attempt to expound them. To me, they have presented little but horror—to many they will seem less terrible than *barroques*. Hereafter, perhaps, some intellect may be found which will reduce my phantasm to the commonplace—some intellect more calm, more logical, and far less excitable than my own, which will perceive, in the circumstances I detail with awe, nothing more than an ordinary succession of very natural causes and effects.

From my infancy I was noted for the docility and humanity of my disposition. My tenderness of heart was even so conspicuous as to make me the jest of my companions. I was especially fond of animals, and was indulged by my parents with a great variety of pets. With these I spent most of my time, and never was so happy as when feeding and caressing them. This peculiarity of character grew with my growth, and, in my manhood, I derived from it one of my principal sources of pleasure. To those who have cherished an affection for a faithful and sagacious dog, I need hardly be at the trouble of explaining the nature or the intensity of the gratification thus derivable. There is something in the unselfish and self-sacrificing love of a brute, which goes directly to the heart of him who has had frequent occasion to test the paltry friendship and gossamer fidelity of mere *Man*.

I married early, and was happy to find in my wife a disposition not uncongenial with my own. Observing my partiality for domestic pets, she lost no opportunity of procuring those of the most agreeable kind. We had birds, goldfish, a fine dog, rabbits, a small monkey, and a *cat*.

This latter was a remarkably large and beautiful animal, entirely black, and sagacious to an astonishing degree. In speaking of his intelligence, my wife, who at heart was not a little tinctured with superstition, made frequent allusions to the ancient popular notion, which regarded all black cats as witches in disguise. Not that she was ever *serious* upon this point—and I mention the matter at all for no better reason than that it happens, just now, to be remembered.

Pluto—this was the cat's name—was my favorite pet and playmate. I alone fed him, and he attended me wherever I went about the house. It was even with difficulty that I could prevent him from following me through the streets.

Our friendship lasted, in this manner, for several years, during which my general temperament and character—through the instrumentality of the Fiend Intemperance—had (I blush to confess it) experienced a radical alteration for the worse. I grew, day by day, more moody, more irritable, more regardless of the feelings of others. I suffered myself to use intemperate language to my wife. At length, I even offered her personal violence. My pets, of course, were made to feel the change in my disposition. I not only neglected, but illused them. For Pluto, however, I still retained sufficient regard to restrain me from maltreating him, as I made no scruple of maltreating the rabbits, the monkey, or even the dog, when, by accident, or through affection, they came in my way. But my disease grew upon me—for what disease is like Alcohol!—and at length even Pluto, who was now becoming old, and consequently somewhat peevish—even Pluto began to experience the effects of my ill temper.

One night, returning home, much intoxicated, from one of my haunts about town, I fancied that the cat avoided my presence. I seized him; when, in his fright at my violence, he inflicted a slight wound upon my hand with his teeth. The fury of a demon instantly possessed me. I knew myself no longer. My original soul seemed, at once, to take its flight from my body; and a more than fiendish malevolence, gin-nurtured, thrilled every fibre of my frame. I took from my waistcoat-pocket a penknife, opened it, grasped the poor beast by the throat, and deliberately cut one of its eyes from the socket! I blush, I burn, I shudder, while I pen the damnable atrocity.

When reason returned with the morning—when I had slept off the fumes of the night's debauch—I experienced a sentiment half of horror, half of remorse, for the crime of which I had been guilty; but it was, at best, a feeble and equivocal feeling, and the soul remained untouched. I again plunged into excess, and soon drowned in wine all memory of the deed.

In the meantime the cat slowly recovered. The socket of the lost eye presented, it is true, a frightful appearance, but he no longer appeared to suffer any pain. He went about the house as usual, but, as might be expected, fled in extreme terror at my approach. I had so much of my old heart left, as to be at first grieved by this evident dislike on the part of a creature which had once so loved me. But this feeling soon gave place to irritation. And then came, as if to my final and irrevocable overthrow, the spirit of PERVERSENESS. Of this spirit philosophy takes no account. Yet I am not more sure that my soul lives, than I am that perverseness is one of the primitive impulses of the human heart—one of the indivisible primary faculties, or sentiments, which give direction to the character of Man. Who has not, a hundred times, found himself committing a vile or a silly action, for no other reason than because he knows he should *not?* Have we not a perpetual inclination, in the teeth of our best judgment, to violate that which is *Law,* merely because we understand it to be such? This spirit of perverseness, I say, came to my final overthrow. It was this unfathomable longing of the soul to *vex itself*—to offer violence to its own nature—to do wrong for the wrong's sake only—that urged me to continue and finally to consummate the injury I had inflicted upon the offending brute. One morning, in cool blood, I slipped a noose about its neck and hung it to the limb of a tree—hung it with the tears streaming from my eyes, and with the bitterest remorse at my heart—hung it *because* I knew that it had loved me, and *because* I felt it had given me no reason of offence;—hung it *because* I knew that in so doing I was committing a sin—a deadly sin that would so jeopardize my immortal soul as to place it—if such a thing were possible—even beyond the reach of the infinite mercy of the Most Merciful and Most Terrible God.

On the night of the day on which this cruel deed was done, I was aroused from sleep by the cry of fire. The curtains of my bed were in flames. The whole house was blazing. It was with great difficulty that my wife, a servant, and myself, made our escape from the conflagration. The destruction was complete. My entire worldly wealth was swallowed up, and I resigned myself thenceforward to despair.

I am above the weakness of seeking to establish a sequence of cause and effect, between the disaster and the atrocity. But I am detailing a chain of facts—and wish not to leave even a possible link imperfect. On the day succeeding the fire, I visited the ruins. The walls, with one exception, had fallen in. This exception was found in a compartment wall, not very thick, which stood about the middle of the house, and against which had rested the head of my bed. The plastering had here, in great measure, resisted the action of the fire—a fact which I attributed to its having been recently spread. About this wall a dense crowd were collected, and many persons seemed to be examining a particular portion of it with very minute and eager attention. The words "strange!" "singular!" and other similar expressions, excited my curiosity. I approached and saw, as if graven in *bas-relief* upon the white surface, the figure of a gigantic *cat*. The impression was given with an accuracy truly marvellous. There was a rope about the animal's neck.

When I first beheld this apparition—for I could scarcely regard it as less—my wonder and my terror were extreme. But at length reflection came to my aid. The cat, I remembered, had been hung in a garden adjacent to the house. Upon the alarm of fire, this garden had been immediately filled by the crowd—by some one of whom the animal must have been cut from the tree and thrown, through an open window, into my chamber. This had probably been done with the view of arousing me from sleep. The falling of other walls had compressed the victim of my cruelty into the substance of the freshly-spread plaster; the lime of which, with the flames, and the *ammonia* from the carcass, had then accomplished the portraiture as I saw it.

Although I thus readily accounted to my reason, if not altogether to my conscience, for the startling fact just detailed, it did not the less fail to make a deep impression upon my fancy. For months I could not rid myself of the phantasm of the cat; and, during this period, there came back into my spirit a half-sentiment that seemed, but was not, remorse. I went so far as to regret the loss of the animal, and to look about me, among the vile haunts which I now habitually frequented, for another pet of the same species, and of somewhat similar appearance, with which to supply its place.

One night as I sat, half stupefied, in a den of more than infamy, my attention was suddenly drawn to some black object, reposing upon the head of one of the immense hogsheads of Gin, or of Rum, which constituted the chief furniture of the apartment. I had been looking steadily at the top of this hogshead for some minutes, and what now caused me surprise was the fact that I had not sooner perceived the object thereupon. I approached it, and touched it with my hand. It was a black cat—a very large one—fully as large as Pluto, and closely resembling him in every respect but one. Pluto had not a white hair upon any portion of his body; but this cat had a large, although indefinite splotch of white, covering nearly the whole region of the breast.

Upon my touching him, he immediately arose, purred loudly, rubbed against my hand, and appeared delighted with my notice. This, then, was the very creature of which I was in search. I at once offered to purchase it of the landlord; but this person made no claim to it—knew nothing of it—had never seen it before.

I continued my caresses, and when I prepared to go home, the animal evinced a disposition to accompany me. I permitted it to do so; occasionally stooping and patting it as I proceeded. When it reached the house it domesticated itself at once, and became immediately a great favorite with my wife.

For my own part, I soon found a dislike to it arising within me. This was just the reverse of what I had anticipated; but—I know not how or why it was—its evident fondness for myself rather disgusted and annoyed. By slow degrees these feelings of disgust and annoyance rose into the bitterness of hatred. I avoided the creature; a certain sense of shame, and the remembrance of my former deed of cruelty, prevented me from physically abusing it. I did not, for some weeks, strike, or otherwise violently ill use it; but gradually—very gradually—I came to look upon it with unutterable loathing, and to flee silently from its odious presence, as from the breath of a pestilence.

What added, no doubt, to my hatred of the beast, was the discovery, on the morning after I brought it home, that, like Pluto, it also had been deprived of one of its eyes. This circumstance, however, only endeared it to my wife, who, as I have already said, possessed, in a high degree, that humanity of feeling which had once been my distinguishing trait, and the source of many of my simplest and purest pleasures.

With my aversion to this cat, however, its partiality for myself seemed to increase. It followed my footsteps with a pertinacity which it would be difficult to make the reader comprehend. Wherever I sat, it would crouch beneath my chair, or spring upon my knees, covering me with its loathsome caresses. If I arose to walk it would get between my feet and thus nearly throw me down, or, fastening its long and sharp claws in my dress, clamber, in this manner, to my breast. At such times, although I longed to destroy it with a blow, I was yet withheld from so doing, partly by a memory of my former crime, but chiefly—let me confess it at once—by absolute *dread* of the beast.

This dread was not exactly a dread of physical evil—and yet I should be at a loss how otherwise to define it. I am almost ashamed to own—yes, even in this felon's cell, I am almost ashamed to own—that the terror and horror with which the animal inspired me, had been heightened by one of the merest chimeras it would be possible to conceive. My wife had called my attention, more than once, to the character of the mark of white hair, of which I have spoken, and which constituted the sole visible difference between the strange beast and the one I had destroyed. The reader will remember that this mark, although large, had been originally very indefinite; but, by slow degrees—degrees nearly imperceptible, and which for a long time my reason struggled to reject as fanciful—it had, at length, assumed a rigorous distinctness of outline. It was now the representation of an object that I shudder to name—and for this, above all, I loathed, and dreaded, and would have rid myself of the monster *had I dared*—it was now, I say, the image of a hideous—of a ghastly thing—of the GALLOWS!—oh, mournful and terrible engine of Horror and Crime—of Agony and of Death!

And now I was indeed wretched beyond the wretchedness of mere Humanity. And *a brute beast*—whose fellow I had contemptuously destroyed—*a brute beast* to work out for *me*—for me, a man fashioned in the image of the High God—so much of insufferable wo! Alas! neither by day nor by night knew I the blessing of Rest any more! During the former the creature left me no moment alone, and in the latter I started hourly from dreams of unutterable fear to find the hot breath of *the thing* upon my face, and its vast weight—an incarnate Night-Mare that I had no power to shake off—incumbent eternally upon my *heart!*

Beneath the pressure of torments such as these the feeble remnant of the good within me succumbed. Evil thoughts became my sole intimates—the darkest and most evil of thoughts. The moodiness of my usual temper increased to hatred of all things and of all mankind; while from the sudden, frequent, and ungovernable outbursts of a fury to which I now blindly abandoned myself, my uncomplaining wife, alas! was the most usual and the most patient of sufferers.

One day she accompanied me, upon some household errand, into the cellar of the old building which our poverty compelled us to inhabit. The cat followed me down the steep stairs, and, nearly throwing me headlong, exasperated me to madness. Uplifting an axe, and forgetting in my wrath the childish dread which had hitherto stayed my hand, I aimed a blow at the animal, which, of course, would have proved instantly fatal had it descended as I wished. But this blow was arrested by the hand of my wife. Goaded by the interference into a rage more than demoniacal, I withdrew my arm from her grasp and buried the axe in her brain. She fell dead upon the spot without a groan.

This hideous murder accomplished, I set myself forthwith, and with entire deliberation, to the task of concealing the body. I knew that I could not remove it from the house, either by day or night, without the risk of being observed by the neighbors. Many projects entered my mind. At one period I thought of cutting the corpse into minute fragments, and destroying them by fire. At another, I resolved to dig a grave for it in the floor of the cellar. Again, I deliberated about casting it in the well in the yard—about packing it in a box, as if merchandise, with the usual arrangements, and so getting a porter to take it from the house. Finally I hit upon what I considered a far better expedient than either of these. I determined to wall it up in the cellar—as the monks of the Middle Ages are recorded to have walled up their victims.

For a purpose such as this the cellar was well adapted. Its walls were loosely constructed, and had lately been plastered throughout with a rough plaster, which the dampness of the atmosphere had prevented from hardening. Moreover, in one of the walls was a projection, caused by a false chimney, or fire-place, that had been filled up and made to resemble the rest of the cellar. I made no doubt that I could readily displace the bricks at this point, insert the corpse, and wall the whole up as before, so that no eye could detect any thing suspicious.

And in this calculation I was not deceived. By means of a crow-bar I easily dislodged the bricks, and, having carefully deposited the body against the inner wall, I propped it in that position, while with little trouble I relaid the whole structure as it originally stood. Having procured mortar, sand, and hair, with every possible precaution, I prepared a plaster which could not be distinguished from the old, and with this I very carefully went over the new brickwork. When I had finished, I felt satisfied that all was right. The wall did not present the slightest appearance of having been disturbed. The rubbish on the floor was picked up with the minutest care. I looked around triumphantly, and said to myself—"Here at least, then, my labor has not been in vain."

My next step was to look for the beast which had been the cause of so much wickedness; for I had, at length, firmly resolved to put it to death. Had I been able to meet with it at the moment, there could have been no doubt of its fate; but it appeared that the crafty animal had been alarmed at the violence of my previous anger, and forebore to present itself in my present mood. It is impossible to describe or to imagine the deep, the blissful sense of relief which the absence of the detested creature occasioned in my bosom. It did not make its appearance during the night—and thus for one night, at least, since its introduction into the house, I soundly and tranquilly slept; aye, *slept* even with the burden of murder upon my soul.

The second and the third day passed, and still my tormentor came not. Once again I breathed as a free man. The monster, in terror, had fled the premises for ever! I should behold it no more! My happiness was supreme! The guilt of my dark deed disturbed me but little. Some few inquiries had been made, but these had been readily answered. Even a search had been instituted—but of course nothing was to be discovered. I looked upon my future felicity as secured.

Upon the fourth day of the assassination, a party of the police came, very unexpectedly, into the house, and proceeded again to make rigorous investigation of the premises. Secure, however, in the inscrutability of my place of concealment, I felt no embarrassment whatever. The officers bade me accompany them in their search. They left no nook or corner unexplored. At length, for the third or fourth time, they descended into the cellar. I quivered not in a muscle. My heart beat calmly as that of one who slumbers in innocence. I walked the cellar from end to end. I folded my arms upon my bosom, and roamed easily to and fro. The police were thoroughly satisfied and prepared to depart. The glee at my heart was too strong to be restrained. I burned to say if but one word, by way of triumph, and to render doubly sure their assurance of my guiltlessness.

"Gentlemen," I said at last, as the party ascended the steps, "I delight to have allayed your suspicions. I wish you all health and a little more courtesy. By the bye, gentlemen, this—this is a very well-constructed house," (in the rabid desire to say something easily, I scarcely knew what I uttered at all),—"I may say an *excellently* well-constructed house. These walls—are you going, gentlemen?—these walls are solidly put together"; and here, through the mere frenzy of bravado, I rapped heavily with a cane which I held in my hand, upon that very portion of the brick-work behind which stood the corpse of the wife of my bosom.

But may God shield and deliver me from the fangs of the Arch-Fiend! No sooner had the reverberation of my blows sunk into silence, than I was answered by a voice from within the tomb!—by a cry, at first muffled and broken, like the sobbing of a child, and then quickly swelling into one long, loud and continuous scream, utterly anomalous and inhuman—a howl—a wailing shriek, half of horror and half of triumph, such as might have arisen only out of hell, conjointly from the throats of the damned in their agony and of the demons that exult in the damnation.

Of my own thoughts it is folly to speak. Swooning, I staggered to the opposite wall. For one instant the party on the stairs remained motionless through extremity of terror and awe. In the next a dozen stout arms were toiling at the wall. It fell bodily. The corpse, already greatly decayed and clotted with gore, stood erect before the eyes of the spectators. Upon its head, with red extended mouth and solitary eye of fire, sat the hideous beast whose craft had seduced me into murder, and whose informing voice had consigned me to the hangman. I had walled the monster up within the tomb.

# The Black and White Dynasties

BY THÉOPHILE GAUTIER

T HERE IS AN ARGUMENT to be made for 19th-century France as the true home of cat lovers. Certainly some of the best cat stories and essays were written by French authors of the period, and there are plenty of indications that poets from Baudelaire to Paul Valéry were obsessed by the creatures. Théophile Gautier, poet, critic, novelist, and journalist, is a case in point. He kept cats, and wrote about them with elegance and evident fascination. His account of the black and white dynasties that shared his life strikes an absolutely authentic note. In these more enlightened times, of course, we might object to his treatment of poor Eponine, who could teach our own offspring a thing or two about table manners.

★　★　★　★　★

A CAT BROUGHT FROM Havana by Mademoiselle Aïta de la Penuela, a young Spanish artist whose studies of white angoras may still be seen gracing the printsellers' windows, produced the daintiest little kitten imaginable. It was just like a swan's-down powder-puff, and on account of its immaculate whiteness it received the name of Pierrot. When it grew big this was lengthened to Don Pierrot de Navarre as being more grandiose and majestic.

Don Pierrot, like all animals which are spoilt and made much of, developed a charming amiability of character. He shared the life of the household with all the pleasure which cats find in the intimacy of the domestic hearth. Seated in his usual place near the fire, he really appeared to understand what was being said, and to take an interest in it.

His eyes followed the speakers, and from time to time he would utter little sounds, as though he too wanted to make remarks and give his opinion on literature, which was our usual topic of conversation. He was very fond of books, and when he found one open on a table he would lie on it, look at the page attentively, and turn over the leaves with his paw; then he would end by going to sleep, for all the world as if he were reading a fashionable novel.

Directly I took up a pen he would jump on my writing-desk and with deep attention watch the steel nib tracing black spider-legs on the expanse of white paper, and his head would turn each time I began a new line. Sometimes he tried to take part in the work, and would attempt to pull the pen out of my hand, no doubt in order to write himself, for he was an aesthetic cat, like Hoffman's Murr, and I strongly suspect him of having scribbled his memoirs at night on some house-top by the light of his phosphorescent eyes. Unfortunately these lucubrations have been lost.

Don Pierrot never went to bed until I came in. He waited for me inside the door, and as I entered the hall he would rub himself against my legs and arch his back, purring joyfully all the time. Then he proceeded to walk in front of me like a page, and if I had asked him, he would certainly have carried the candle for me. In this fashion he escorted me to my room and waited while I undressed; then he would jump on the bed, put his paws round my neck, rub noses with me, and lick me with his rasping little pink tongue, while giving vent to soft inarticulate cries, which clearly expressed how pleased he was to see me again. Then when his transports of affection had subsided, and the hour for repose had come, he would balance himself on the rail of the bedstead and sleep there like a bird perched on a bough. When I woke in the morning he would come and lie near me until it was time to get up. Twelve o'clock was the hour at which I was supposed to come in. On this subject Pierrot had all the notions of a concierge.

At that time we had instituted little evening gatherings among a few friends, and had formed a small society, which we called the Four Candles club, the room in which we met being, as it happened, lit by four candles in silver candlesticks, which were placed at the corners of the table.

Sometimes the conversation became so lively that I forgot the time, at the risk of finding, like Cinderella, my carriage turned into a pumpkin and my coachman into a rat.

Pierrot waited for me several times until two o'clock in the morning, but in the end my conduct displeased him, and he went to bed without me. This mute protest against my innocent dissipation touched me so much that ever after I came home regularly at midnight. But it was a long time before Pierrot forgave me. He wanted to be sure that it was not a sham repentance; but when he was convinced of the sincerity of my conversion, he deigned to take me into favour again, and he resumed his nightly post in the entrance-hall.

To gain the friendship of a cat is not an easy thing. It is a philosophic, well-regulated, tranquil animal, a creature of habit and a lover of order and cleanliness. It does not give its affections indiscriminately. It will consent to be your friend if you are worthy of the honour, but it will not be your slave. With all its affection, it preserves its freedom of judgment, and it will not do anything for you which it considers unreasonable; but once it has given its love, what absolute confidence, what fidelity of affection! It will make itself the companion of your hours of work, of loneliness, or of sadness. It will lie the whole evening on your knee, purring and happy in your society, and leaving the company of creatures of its own kind to be with you. In vain the sound of caterwauling reverberates from the house-tops, inviting it to one of those cats' evening parties where essence of red-herring takes the place of tea. It will not be tempted, but continues to keep its vigil with you. If you put it down it climbs up again quickly, with a sort of crooning noise, which is like a gentle reproach. Sometimes, when seated in front of you, it gazes at you with such soft, melting eyes, such a human and caressing look, that you are almost awed, for it seems impossible that reason can be absent from it.

Don Pierrot had a companion of the same race as himself, and no less white. All the imaginable snowy comparisons it were possible to pile up would not suffice to give an idea of that immaculate fur, which would have made ermine look yellow.

I called her Seraphita, in memory of Balzac's Swedenborgian romance. The heroine of that wonderful story, when she climbed the snow peaks of the Falberg with Minna, never shone with a more pure white radiance. Seraphita had a dreamy and pensive character. She would lie motionless on a cushion for hours, not asleep, but with eyes fixed in rapt attention on scenes invisible to ordinary mortals.

Caresses were agreeable to her, but she responded to them with great reserve, and only to those of people whom she favoured with her esteem, which it was not easy to gain. She liked luxury, and it was always in the newest armchair or on the piece of furniture best calculated to show off her swan-like beauty, that she was to be found. Her toilette took an immense time. She would carefully smooth her entire coat every morning, and wash her face with her paw, and every hair on her body shone like new silver when brushed by her pink tongue. If anyone touched her she would immediately efface all traces of the contact, for she could not endure being ruffled. Her elegance and distinction gave one an idea of aristocratic birth, and among her own kind she must have been at least a duchess. She had a passion for scents. She would plunge her nose into bouquets, and nibble a perfumed handkerchief with little paroxysms of delight. She would walk about on the dressing-table sniffling the stoppers of the scent-bottles, and she would have loved to use the violet powder if she had been allowed.

Such was Seraphita, and never was a cat more worthy of a poetic name.

Don Pierrot de Navarre, being a native of Havana, needed a hot-house temperature. This he found indoors, but the house was surrounded by large gardens, divided up by palings through which a cat could easily slip, and planted with big trees in which hosts of birds twittered and sang; and sometimes Pierrot, taking advantage of an open door, would go out hunting of an evening and run over the dewy grass and flowers. He would then have to wait till morning to be let in again, for although he might come mewing under the windows, his appeal did not always wake the sleepers inside.

He had a delicate chest, and one colder night than usual he took a chill which soon developed into consumption. Poor Pierrot, after a year of coughing, became wasted and thin, and his coat, which formerly boasted such a snowy glass, now put one in mind of the lustreless white of a shroud. His great limpid eyes looked enormous in his attenuated face. His pink nose had grown pale, and he would walk sadly along the sunny wall with slow steps, and watch the yellow autumn leaves whirling up in spirals. He looked as though he were reciting Millevoy's elegy.

There is nothing more touching than a sick animal; it submits to suffering with such gentle, pathetic resignation.

Everything possible was done to try and save Pierrot. He had a very clever doctor who sounded him and felt his pulse. He ordered him asses' milk, which the poor creature drank willingly enough out of his little china saucer. He lay for hours on my knee like the ghost of a sphinx, and I could feel the bones of his spine like the beads of a rosary under my fingers. He tried to respond to my caresses with a feeble purr which was like a death rattle.

When he was dying he lay panting on his side, but with a supreme effort he raised himself and came to me with dilated eyes in which there was a look of intense supplication. This look seemed to say: "Cannot you save me, you who are a man?" Then he staggered a short way with eyes already glazing, and fell down with such a lamentable cry, so full of despair and anguish, that I was pierced with silent horror.

He was buried at the bottom of the garden under a white rosebush which still marks his grave.

Seraphita died two or three years later of diphtheria, against which no science could prevail.

She rests not far from Pierrot. With her the white dynasty became extinct, but not the family. To this snow-white pair were born three kittens as black as ink.

Let him explain this mystery who can.

Just at that time Victor Hugo's *Misérables* was in great vogue, and the names of the characters in the novel were on everyone's lips. I called the two male kittens Enjolras and Gavroche, while the little female received the name of Eponine.

They were perfectly charming in their youth. I trained them like dogs to fetch and carry a bit of paper crumpled into a ball, which I threw for them. In time they learnt to fetch it from the tops of cupboards, from behind chests or from the bottom of tall vases, out of which they would pull it very cleverly with their paws. When they grew up they disdained such frivolous games, and acquired that calm philosophic temperament which is the true nature of cats.

To people landing in America in a slave colony all negroes are negroes, and indistinguishable from one another. In the same way, to careless eyes, three black cats are three black cats; but attentive observers make no such mistake. Animal physiognomy varies as much as that of men, and I could distinguish perfectly between those faces, all three as black as Harlequin's mask, and illuminated by emerald disks shot with gold.

Enjolras was by far the handsomest of the three. He was remarkable for his great leonine head and big ruff, his powerful shoulders, long back and splendid feathery tail. There was something theatrical about him, and he seemed to be always posing like a popular actor who knows he is being admired. His movements were slow, undulating and majestic. He put each foot down with as much circumspection as if he were walking on a table covered with Chinese bric-à-brac or Venetian glass. As to his character, he was by no means a stoic, and he showed a love of eating which that virtuous and sober young man, his namesake, would certainly have disapproved. Enjolras would undoubtedly have said to him, like the angel to Swedenborg: "You eat too much."

I humoured this gluttony, which was as amusing as a gastronomic monkey's, and Enjolras attained a size and weight seldom reached by the domestic cat. It occurred to me to have him shaved poodle-fashion, so as to give the finishing touch to his resemblance to a lion.

We left him his mane and a big tuft at the end of his tail, and I would not swear that we did not give him mutton-chop whiskers on his haunches like those Munito wore. Thus tricked out, it must be confessed he was much more like a Japanese monster than an African lion. Never was a more fantastic whim carved out of a living animal. His shaven skin took odd blue tints, which contrasted strangely with his black mane.

Gavroche, as though desirous of calling to mind his namesake in the novel, was a cat with an arch and crafty expression of countenance. He was smaller than Enjolras, and his movements were comically quick and brusque. In him absurd capers and ludicrous postures took the place of the banter and slang of the Parisian gamin. It must be confessed that Gavroche had vulgar tastes. He seized every possible occasion to leave the drawing-room in order to go and make up parties in the backyard, or even in the street, with stray cats,

"De naissance quelconque et de sang peu prouvé,"

in which doubtful company he completely forgot his dignity as cat of Havana, son of Don Pierrot de Navarre, grandee of Spain of the first order, and of the aristocratic and haughty Doña Seraphita. Sometimes in his truant wanderings he picked up emaciated comrades, lean with hunger, and brought them to his plate of food to give them a treat in his good-natured, lordly way. The poor creatures, with ears laid back and watchful side-glances, in fear of being interrupted in their free meal by the broom of the housemaid, swallowed double, triple, and quadruple mouthfuls, and, like the famous dog, Siete-Aguas (seven waters) of Spanish *posadas* (inns), they licked the plate as clean as if it had been washed and polished by one of Gerard Dow's or Mieris's Dutch housewives.

Seeing Gavroche's friends reminded me of a phrase which illustrates one of Gavarni's drawings, "Ils son jolis les amis dont vous êtes susceptible d'aller avec!" ("Pretty kind of friends you like to associate with!")

But that only proved what a good heart Gavroche had, for he could easily have eaten all the food himself.

The cat named after the interesting Eponine was more delicate and slender than her brothers. Her nose was rather long, and her eyes slightly oblique, and green as those of Pallas Athene, to whom Homer always applied the epithet of γλαυχωπιζ. Her nose was of velvety black, with the grain of a fine Périgord truffle; her whiskers were in a perpetual state of agitation, all of which gave her a peculiarly expressive countenance. Her superb black coat was always in motion, and was watered and shot with shadowy markings. Never was there a more sensitive, nervous, electric animal. If one stroked her two or three times in the dark, blue sparks would fly crackling out of her fur.

Eponine attached herself particularly to me, like the Eponine of the novel to Marius, but I, being less taken up with Cosette than that handsome young man, could accept the affection of this gentle and devoted cat, who still shares the pleasure of my suburban retreat and is the inseparable companion of my hours of work.

She comes running up when she hears the front-door bell, receives the visitors, conducts them to the drawing-room, talks to them—yes, talks to them—with little chirruping sounds, that do not in the least resemble the language cats use in taking to their own kind, but which simulate the articulate speech of man. What does she say? She says in the clearest way, "Will you be good enough to wait till monsieur comes down? Please look at the pictures, or chat with me in the meantime, if that will amuse you." Then when I come in she discreetly retires to an armchair or a corner of the piano, like a well-bred animal who knows what is correct in good society. Pretty little Eponine gave so many proofs of intelligence, good disposition and sociability, that by common consent she was raised to the dignity of a *person,* for it was quite evident that she was possessed of higher reasoning power than mere instinct. This dignity conferred on her the privilege of eating at table like a person instead of out of a saucer in a corner of the room like an animal.

So Eponine had a chair next to me at breakfast and dinner, but on account of her small size she was allowed to rest her two front paws on the edge of the table. Her place was laid, without spoon or fork, but she had her glass.

She went right through dinner dish by dish, from soup to dessert, waiting for her turn to be helped, and behaving with such propriety and nice manners as one would like to see in many children. She made her appearance at the first sound of the bell, and on gong into the dining-room one found her already in her place, sitting up in her chair with her paws resting on the edge of the table-cloth, and seeming to offer you her little face to kiss, like a well-brought-up little girl who is affectionately polite towards her parents and elders.

As one finds flaws in diamonds, spots on the sun, and shadows on perfection itself, so Eponine, it must be confessed, had a passion for fish. She shared this in common with all other cats. Contrary to the Latin proverb,

"*Catus amat pisces, sed non vult tingere plantas,*"

she would willingly have dipped her paw into the water if by so doing she could have pulled out a trout or a young carp. She became nearly frantic over fish, and, like a child who is filled with the expectation of dessert, she sometimes rebelled at her soup when she knew (from previous investigations in the kitchen) that fish was coming. When this happened she was not helped, and I would say to her coldly: "Mademoiselle, a person who is not hungry for soup cannot be hungry for fish," and the dish would be pitilessly carried away from under her nose. Convinced that matters were serious, greedy Eponine would swallow her soup in all haste, down to the last drop, polishing off the last crumb of bread or bit of macaroni, and would then turn round and look at me with pride, like someone who has conscientiously done his duty. She was then given her portion, which she consumed with great satisfaction, and after tasting of every dish in turn, she would finish up by drinking a third of a glass of water.

When I am expecting friends to dinner Eponine knows there is going to be a party before she sees the guests. She looks at her place, and if she sees a knife and fork by her plate she decamps at once and seats herself on a music-stool, which is her refuge on these occasions.

Let those who deny reasoning powers to animals explain if they can this little fact, apparently so simple, but which contains a whole serious of in-ductions. From the presence near her plate of those implements which man alone can use, this observant and reflective cat concludes that she will have to give up her place for that day to a guest, and promptly proceeds to do so. She never makes a mistake; but when she knows the visitor well she climbs on his knee and tries to coax a tid-bit out of him by her pretty caressing ways.

# Piazza Vittorio

From *Rome and a Villa*

BY ELEANOR CLARK

**M**OST CATS ARE PETS, but these most decidedly are not. Here are cats in vast abundance, cats who are their own masters, cats wholesale. In this passage from her splendid book *Rome and a Villa,* Eleanor Clark offers an unforgettable description of what she calls "the greatest cat concentration of present-day Rome and possibly of Western civilization." Piazza Vittorio has fish stalls, butcher shops, and vegetable sellers. Most notably, however, it has cats.

Eleanor Clark (1913–1996) went to Rome shortly after the end of World War II intending to write a novel, but was soon caught up in the city and its ways. Her eye for detail is uncanny—see, for example, her account of Roman cats in a sudden shower—and it is apparent that she has a true cat-lover's take on the feline sensibility. As she suggests, it may be no accident that the cats of the Piazza Vittorio have chosen ancient ruins for their home: "Even the stupidest cat seems to know more than any dog or horse; it knows history."

★　★　★　★　★

THOUSANDS OF CATS; a city of cats, as of fountains and churches, and as natu-rally. Most of them are not even roaming but in definite asylums, which were never planned any more than the piazzas were, or seem to have been, for human use. They just come about. The cats are drawn for some reason to one place or another, which may remain the haunt of their descendants for cen-turies, and people come there to feed them. It is not that Romans really con-sider them a sacred or even superior animal, or think about them much at all, yet some ancient habit of respect seems to apply to them, giving them a unique position among the public cats of the world. There are not many private ones—a Siamese in the house is apt to be a sign of neurosis or international marriage; normal Roman life has no more need or use for pets than for similar attachments within its own species. The cats, like people, are mostly strays, and after their great number the striking fact about them is that very few are thin.

In the old days their most famous spot was Trajan's Forum, this of course before Mussolini and the Via dell' Impero, when the forum was not the propped-up showpiece it is now but a weedy ruin-strewn pit sunk among ten-ements, with the triumphal column bolt upright in its old-style grandeur at the end; the cats looked natural there. Sometimes the government saw to feed-ing them, other times just the neighborhood; at night there were the usual back-yard screechings multiplied by a hundred or so but when the fascist au-thorities, before the final overhauling of the area, tried to remove the nuisance there was such protest from the people it had to back down. But then the ten-ements went, the excavations began; the jig was up; Empire Street could not be desecrated by cats; anyway the garbage supply had been cut off. Another place, until recently, used to be around the pyramid of Caius Cestius, beside the Protestant cemetery, but that district finally became too unresidential too.

One of the smaller ancestral centers that remains is in back of the Pan-theon where there is a colony of twenty or thirty, most likely of Renaissance origin. Another is an alley running from the Via Giulia to the rear of the Palazzo Spada, which some people consider rather sinister, probably because the alley is narrow and barred and usually in shadow and the Council of the State meets in the palace. The cats have a barricaded look; the council sits beside the sinister statue of Pompey that Caesar clutched when he fell. But by far the greatest cat congregation of present-day Rome and possibly of Western civilization is in the huge market square on the other side of town from these two—Piazza Vit-torio so-called, really Vittorio Emanuele, for the unifier of Italy.

The name happens to suit the architecture. It is of the early House of Savoy period, airy, sensible and bourgeois; the colonnades around the square

are not of any Roman style that survives though in the ancient city there were miles of them; the quarter around has a solid and quite pleasant middle-class look of eighty years ago. It is all most un-Roman, except as Rome like an insectivorous plant can take in anything, even Turin, and make it Rome. Pines and palms grow in the large parklike center of the square, inside the roaring double ring of the market, and from the middle there is a long lyrical view, from Santa Maria Maggiore to Santa Croce in Gerusalemme and way beyond that, clear as angels and snowy sometimes in winter, the peak of Monte Cavo. There is a high jumble of ruins back of the fish stalls; a set of cabalistic carvings on a door nearby from nobody knows what or when, said to contain a formula for making gold; a baroque fountain of stone corroded to an even wilder appeal than usual; and about a hundred and fifty cats.

They are of course at the fish end, and the ruins, of 3rd Century brick, are their backdrop. They never go far from there, or not for long; it is not necessary; an invisible line around that corner of the square marks their precinct, they have made their own atmosphere there, and prefer it.

The ruins have a connection with water, which the cats in their own way keep vivid. The building, big enough to have been a three-story villa or public library, was a monumental fountain or show-off point for the water of one of the big aqueducts coming in through the quarter, and a gaudy show it must have been, from that height. Now it is a craggy rambling mass with a suggestion of enchantment though of the wrong color for a fairy tale, and the cats, who cannot get inside where the keeper of the garden lives, in their idle hours wander and drape themselves over all its levels and sketchy escarpments and juttings, all the way to the top—unhurried, unchased, wonderfully at home and regal in all their motions, not having to play up to anybody. The choreography is excellent.

In a little window at the very top, opening on to nothing, a cat framed in vines lies like a princess drying her hair; another is oddly reclined below on top of a cluster of sharp posts which are end up; somehow in the mercurial way of cats she has made herself comfortable. Others are stretched or curled in the flower beds and on the chunks of fallen marble cornice and Corinthian capitals lying around, or in favorite dents like couches under the bushes. This will be early in the afternoon when they are not hungry any more, although the market has not yet folded up. They are more or less sated; not groggy, and not really sleeping, because there is still a sense of opportunity in the air at this time of day but they have only half an eye open for it. A calico tom with a black neckline like a court decoration decides to investigate a bloody scrap of paper in which there are still a few scraps from one of the meat stalls, pulls his paw across it languidly a couple of times and saunters back to rest among the zinnias. On the first shelf of the ruin two kittens, one white as a sacred calf, box a moment, not having learned to gage their desires, then in disillusion move apart. Here and there older cats take a swipe or two at washing themselves or each other, and are not too drowsy to have their feelings hurt; obscure episodes of pride and disgrace are taking place all through the happy scene, but that is not the fault of Rome.

Nobody is even watching especially. The cats are taken for granted, as many holier things are; besides in the pace and gusto of its own life, in extent too, this is the Saint Peter's among markets. The fascination is general.

You can buy almost anything there—live fowl and any other foodstuff, leather goods, clothes, toys, stolen bicycle parts, and everybody is head over heels in the business not so much for the sake of the business as the life. An aged woman with two teeth, selling carrots, detects you smiling a little at her bellow of publicity, the same tremendous voice as the others but sharper from age, thinks for a second you wanted to buy, then perceiving that you were only laughing at her goes off in a fit of gaiety herself: "Ah, old age! . . . . CARROTS!" People go out of their way to touch a midget for good luck, and down a side street a man keeping up a brilliant monologue tells fortunes with dolls that rise in a jar of water that he carries on a peg and white mice running up a string outside. Several of the young girls selling vegetables are of typical Roman beauty and aware of it. There is much too much going on for the cats to be a center of attraction.

Nevertheless they do have a special part in the show, more than if anyone were paying attention to them, and not only through the spectacle they provide. There is something else, something in the apparently offhand human treatment of them that takes you way outside of commerce and common sense, not to religion, not to charity. It puts a bargain in another perspective.

Perhaps in the Roman feeling about the species there is some dim recollection from the days of popular Egyptiana in the city, around the time the present ruin was going up in all its water-glory; or it may be only that cats are a mysterious animal as everyone admits, and Romans are alert to mysteries outside their own nature and fall easily into ways of propitiating them. Or perhaps they came into honor as a check to rats carrying plague in the Middle Ages and after—a kind of honor that only the Roman mind would perpetuate, because if they were of any use in that way it would have been the same anywhere in Europe, and no other city has such sanctuaries or would take them as such a matter of course: there would be societies for preservation, committees for extermination, propaganda for equal treatment of dogs or birds, Malthusian editorials etc., or somebody would decide they ought to be somewhere else.

Not in Rome. The regard they are held in is general and careless; the problem, if there is one, solves itself. No doubt there is some element of primitive religious sense, or call it superstition, at the root of the matter, there usually is in tigerology, but it would be hard to trace. There is no particular emphasis on the animal anywhere in Roman culture ancient or Christian, either as good or as evil; they were never deified, nor the familiars of witches, although at one time there were plenty of witches; they are not even liked for their company; you never read of Roman old maids being found dead in a house with seventeen cats, and nobody goes pussy-pussy, meesha-meesha in Italian, indiscriminately.

But there they are, not worshiped or pampered or feared or in any way consciously honored, but honored just the same, rather as the fountains are; with which after all they do have one function in common. They are a link with the past, that is with all time, having kept a clearer set of original instincts together with more various personality than any other tamed animal. There is nothing transitory about a cat, aside from the individual knack of survival; it is the most ancient of our animals. A dead cat never has the look of finality that a dead dog does; neither does a dead Roman, which is why you never see many people bothering to follow funerals there. The eye of a cat is an eye in the forest and in all time and so even the stupidest cat seems to *know* more than any dog or horse; it knows history; you do not have to believe in the transmigration of souls to feel that a living knowledge of Agrippa continues in back of the Pantheon just as it does in the fountain in front of it.

In any case, what with the view and their numbers and the strange beauty of their dwelling, the cats of Piazzo Vittorio have all the look of a sacred colony even if not officially sanctioned like cows or monkeys in other parts of the world. It is not as if they were scavenging all over the market, or in captivity like the wolf on the Capitoline or creatures in a zoo. There is an air of pleasant natural concord all around, a credit to man and beast and not very characteristic of either party in the case. Romans are not notably kind to other animals nor of any Franciscan spirit in general, and cats are not a usual symbol of the earthly paradise. They simply happen to hit it off; they understand one another; consequently the cats are the most civilized in the world.

They are also of the most extraordinary colors. It is a botanical garden of exotic furs, in every combination; marmalades shading to bronze, orange in trout specklings on grey or black, a single contrasting or striped forearm on a monotone coat, every kind of bib and dashing including the common chest triangle, often only one perky ear of solid color like an insistent strain of nobility through the conglomerate birth; but they are all aristocrats though of dead-end breed, even the ones with backsides and front sides of two utterly incompatible schemes, blue-grey and white in front and black with orange behind, like a blue-faced mandrill or a polychrome bust from the late empire; or say a pansy bed took to sprouting mammals, some plain white with only the golden circles of the eyes or all black as pansies can be, which now stalk or rest among the other furless flowers that they would never permit themselves to break any more than if they were of rare porcelain on a mantelpiece.

They have neither the hyper-dependence of house cats nor the fears of alley ones. They are free of the two greatest sufferings of the species, hunger and loneliness, also from the ravages of human temperament pro or con, not to mention surgical abominations. It is much as humans have imagined heaven, only the cats run no danger of spinelessness; in fact the spine, their most distinctive piece of anatomy, and muscular development in general are spectacular in these cats. Among domestic felines only purebred Siamese leap to such marvelous heights and distances, and they have become a race of neurasthenics. In Piazza Vittorio you are seeing cat life at its healthiest, at least the healthiest possible in such a millennium as ours, but for that matter there can never have been such a sight in the wilderness either. The cats have reverted to true tiger prowess and beauty of form in action, but without ferocity. The ancient jungle-gym they have taken over is ideal for all the play that cats must have, watching, stalking, springing etc., and at any hour there will be a few engaged in it, acting as usual on primeval urgencies but with a look more of Greek athletes, especially in the prowl and the slow gallop, two of their most becoming sports. They have lost the jitters of wild life.

They seem to have lost some of their vices too, though not at any cost to individuality; if you hang around awhile you will see them of every character, from pussy willow to the sphinx. But there is not much stealing or fighting. They would not risk approaching the tubs of squid and other heavenly slobber that lie around them on two sides, but they are unusually well-mannered among themselves as well; you see hardly any chewed ears and bloody noses. When a passer-by or one of the fish vendors comes over with a package a dozen or two will bound for it, like planes bouncing in to a landing, from their various marble roosts or solitary promenades, but if they are too late they leave quietly; there will be more later, and not only refuse. The big scene is when the government feeder comes, a woman usually, and familiar with cats; otherwise she could be terrified.

They come streaking from the lower branches of the trees and all the heights of the ruin and everywhere around, leaping over the flower beds and fallen fluted columns, and champ and mew and race scratching up to other branches to leap down on her shoulders; in a few seconds there will be seventy or eighty with their crazy coats all in a roil so you would think they would come out of it with somebody else's markings, and their whiskers aquiver like telegraph wires, but there is no real frenzy; they all get something in the end. A high-strung bronze-and-black, leaner than most, stays on her shoulder trying to snatch at the basket from above; she lets him stay, and in fact though fierce of eye he is all humility in his claws—one of the grieving type, who are more anxious to be grabbed from than to grab and will stay thin all their lives; a more politic black one waits alert with neck stretched from a tree trunk; off on the other side a small white baffled Persian that has somehow joined the flock or perhaps was left there and is not yet used to its ways, tries different approaches, then stands at the rim anxiously lifting one forepaw after the other, his eyes following the whole course of every morsel from basket to the final dash for privacy; he was fed alone by a butler until recently. When it is over they nearly all follow the woman as far as the gravel path which nothing prevents them from crossing but they stop there, and little by little disperse, only to be shot into action ten minutes later by another event: rain.

A cloudburst; there is a human rush for the colonnades; with a subtle shuddering motion the market folds in on itself like a bird into its feathers; tarpaulins appear from nowhere over the destructibles, certain tender points are whisked in altogether, the vendors pull back under their awnings meant for protection from the sun.

This time the motion of the cats is not centripetal. The lines they trace are as fast and straight as before but all in a criss-cross as of night projectiles over a battlefield. It is each not to the nearest cover but the predetermined one, which may be halfway round the ruin or all the way across the lawn, one way to some nook in the structure, another to the sheltering brown pantalettes of a pygmy palm, so for a few seconds the whole ground is a contradiction of flying cat-furs, which resolves itself in a moment without collision or argument or even a swerve of line unless a particular place were taken, when the late-comer shoots off by the same mystic geometry to the nearest alternative. Then there is no further move. Only nursing mothers have stayed where they were, having already chosen some fairly safe location, from which they view the sky's performance with gentle sorrow as others will when all of it comes down.

The rest are watching too, in a different way. There is really no inside room for them at all; they would rather drown in a place fit for guarding than follow the humans into the exposure of the colonnades. They are crouched under every little brick-eave and in clusters under the low-branching pines, all in the same waiting posture and perfectly still, hind paws invisible, the front ones in a plumb line with their noses and shoulder blades, not to spring, only to guard. They will not begin to lick themselves dry until it is over, which is in a couple of minutes.

The sun bursts out; the market is bustling again though not for long— it is nearly packing-up time. Greenery and every kind of impedimenta around the northwest corner begin slowly discharging cats, which revert to their individual natures and ways of doing things and soon are all over the place again with their sinewy purposeful activities and delicate affections: a hundred and fifty personalities, although sooner or later all must dry themselves, at once and thoroughly like fussy housewives or in wayward licks and spinal doublings after racing back to some lone preeminence. Meanwhile they take stock of the damage. Many of their beds are puddles, certain surfaces untrustworthy; even the flowers have become inimical; there are many little new arrangements to be made.

They have another job in common, more than to look after themselves. They are about to be in charge of the empty square, as one cat may be of a grocery store but here it is not so much a question of mice. There is nothing left to attract a mouse. It is astonishing how fast and utterly the enormous market takes itself away; the fantasia of human commodities, wearable, edible, combustible, aesthetic, hygienic and vehicular, the gamut of man's utensils, and all the push and pleasure of life that went into their changing hands, are suddenly gone; booths turn into carts and men into cart horses and everything vanishes. Piazza Vittorio at first glance is a big undistinguished place of northern design, with a park in the middle, where you would imagine little scenes of provincial longing and escape to the movie house. But there is something more.

One cat may be dying. Some will be conceived tonight around the fountain-ruin with horrible shriekings as from the victims of emperors or emperors meeting their own ends, which the people who live above the colonnades will scarcely hear; if they do hear they will turn over and sleep again like children. A more fearful continuity has sprung up where theirs left off; a hundred and fifty charms are working for that neighborhood alone. The cats are not idle at all now, and not playing. Among the vines in the highest window of the jungle palace an eye burns that no human ever saw; between screams a furry figure was caught a second in the streetlight's gleam, in mid-spring, with claws bared to the root sharper than any doctor's tool, plunging to silence and the dark. No troop of Swiss could guard these mysteries.

The market will be back in the morning; for another day Rome is safe; if all were quiet, then you would stay awake.

# An Incident

BY ANTON CHEKHOV

CATS TURN UP in a number of stories by Anton Chekhov (1860–1904), the great Russian dramatist and short story writer, although they are never as important as the human characters. Trained as a doctor in Moscow, Chekhov began writing humorous sketches for magazines when he was still a young man, and gradually developed a more serious approach to literature. But he never lost his taste for black humor, or for satire. This tale nicely blends a sympathetic understanding of childhood with an unexpected solution to the problem of too many cats.

★ ★ ★ ★ ★ ★

MORNING. BRILLIANT SUNSHINE is piercing through the frozen lacework on the window-panes into the nursery. Vanya, a boy of six, with a cropped head and a nose like a button, and his sister Nina, a short, chubby, curly-headed girl of four, wake up and look crossly at each other through the bars of their cots.

"Oo-oo-oo! naughty children!" grumbles their nurse. "Good people have had their breakfast already, while you can't get your eyes open."

The sunbeams frolic over the rugs, the walls, and nurse's skirts, and seem inviting the children to join in their play, but they take no notice. They have woken up in a bad humour. Nina pouts, makes a grimace, and begins to whine:

"Brea-eakfast, nurse, breakfast!"

Vanya knits his brows and ponders what to pitch upon to howl over. He has already begun screwing up his eyes and opening his mouth, but at that instant the voice of mamma reaches them from the drawing-room, saying: "Don't forget to give the cat her milk, she has a family now!"

The children's puckered countenances grow smooth again as they look at each other in astonishment. Then both at once begin shouting, jump out of their cots, and filling the air with piercing shrieks, run barefoot, in their nightgowns, to the kitchen.

"The cat has puppies!" they cry. "The cat has got puppies!"

Under the bench in the kitchen there stands a small box, the one in which Stepan brings coal when he lights the fire. The cat is peeping out of the box. There is an expression of extreme exhaustion on her grey face; her green eyes, with their narrow black pupils, have a languid, sentimental look. . . . From her face it is clear that the only thing lacking to complete her happiness is the presence in the box of "him", the father of her children, to whom she had abandoned herself so recklessly! She wants to mew, and opens her mouth wide, but nothing but a hiss comes from her throat; the squealing of the kittens is audible.

The children squat on their heels before the box, and, motionless, holding their breath, gaze at the cat. . . . They are surprised, impressed, and do not hear nurse grumbling as she pursues them. The most genuine delight shines in the eyes of both.

Domestic animals play a scarcely noticed but undoubtedly beneficial part in the education and life of children. Which of us does not remember powerful but magnanimous dogs, lazy lapdogs, birds dying in captivity, dull-witted but haughty turkeys, mild old tabby cats, who forgave us when we trod on their tails for fun and caused them agonizing pain? I even fancy, sometimes, that the patience, the fidelity, the readiness to forgive, and the sincerity which are characteristic of our domestic animals have a far stronger and more definite effect on the mind of a child than the long exhortations of some dry, pale Karl Karlovitch, or the misty expositions of a governess, trying to prove to children that water is made up of hydrogen and oxygen.

"What little things!" says Nina, opening her eyes wide and going off into a joyous laugh. "They are like mice!"

"One, two three," Vanya counts. "Three kittens. So there is one for you, one for me, and one for somebody else, too."

"Murrm . . . murrm . . ." purrs the mother, flattered by their attention. "Murrm."

After gazing at the kittens, the children take them from under the cat, and begin squeezing them in their hands, then, not satisfied with this, they put them in the skirts of their nightgowns, and run into the other rooms.

"Mamma, the cat has got pups!" they shout.

Mamma is sitting in the drawing-room with some unknown gentleman. Seeing the children unwashed, undressed, with their nightgowns held up high, she is embarrassed, and looks at them severely.

"Let your nightgowns down, disgraceful children," she says. "Go out of the room, or I will punish you."

But the children do not notice either mamma's threats or the presence of a stranger. They put the kittens down on the carpet, and go off into deafening squeals. The mother walks round them, mewing imploringly. When, a little afterwards, the children are dragged off to the nursery, dressed, made to say their prayers, and given their breakfast, they are full of a passionate desire to get away from these prosaic duties as quickly as possible, and to run to the kitchen again.

Their habitual pursuits and games are thrown completely into the background.

The kittens throw everything into the shade by making their appearance in the world, and supply the great sensation of the day. If Nina or Vanya had been offered forty pounds of sweets or ten thousand kopecks for each kitten, they would have rejected such a barter without the slightest hesitation. In spite of the heated protests of the nurse and the cook, the children persist in sitting by the cat's box in the kitchen, busy with the kittens till dinner-time. Their faces are earnest and concentrated and express anxiety. They are worried not so much by the present as by the future of the kittens. They decide that one kitten shall remain at home with the old cat to be a comfort to her mother, while the second shall go to their summer villa, and the third shall live in the cellar, where there are ever so many rats.

"But why don't they look at us?" Nina wondered. "Their eyes are blind like the beggars'."

Vanya, too, is perturbed by this question. He tries to open one kitten's eyes, and spends a long time puffing and breathing hard over it, but his operation is unsuccessful. They are a good deal troubled, too, by the circumstances that the kittens obstinately refuse the milk and the meat that is offered to them. Everything that is put before their little noses is eaten by their grey mamma.

"Let's build the kittens little houses," Vanya suggests. "They shall live in different houses, and the cat shall come and pay them visits. . . ."

Cardboard hat-boxes are put in the different corners of the kitchen and the kittens are installed in them. But this division turns out to be premature: the cat, still wearing an imploring and sentimental expression on her face, goes the round of all the hat-boxes, and carries off her children to their original position.

"The cat's their mother," observed Vanya, "but who is their father?"

"Yes, who is their father?" repeats Nina.

"They must have a father."

Vanya and Nina are a long time deciding who is to be the kittens' father, and, in the end, their choice falls on a big dark-red horse without a tail, which is lying in the store-cupboard under the stairs, together with other relics of toys that have outlived their day. They drag him up out of the store-cupboard and stand him by the box.

"Mind now!" they admonish him, "stand here and see they behave themselves properly."

All this is said and done in the gravest way, with an expression of anxiety on their faces. Vanya and Nina refuse to recognize the existence of any world but the box of kittens. Their joy knows no bounds. But they have to pass through bitter, agonizing moments, too.

Just before dinner, Vanya is sitting in his father's study, gazing dreamily at the table. A kitten is moving about by the lamp, on stamped note paper. Vanya is watching its movements, and thrusting first a pencil, then a match into its little mouth. . . . All at once, as though he has sprung out of the floor, his father is beside the table.

"What's this?" Vanya hears, in an angry voice.

"It's . . . it's the kitty, papa. . . ."

"I'll give it you; look what you have done, you naughty boy! You've dirtied all my paper!"

To Vanya's great surprise his papa does not share his partiality for the kittens, and, instead of being moved to enthusiasm and delight, he pulls Vanya's ear and shouts:

"Stepan, take away this horrid thing."

At dinner, too, there is a scene. . . . During the second course there is suddenly the sound of a shrill mew. They begin to investigate its origin, and discover a kitten under Nina's pinafore.

"Nina, leave the table!" cries her father angrily. "Throw the kittens in the cesspool! I won't have the nasty things in the house! . . ."

Vanya and Nina are horrified. Death in the cesspool, apart from its cruelty, threatens to rob the cat and the wooden horse of their children, to lay waste the cat's box, to destroy their plans for the future, that fair future in which one cat will be a comfort to its old mother, another will live in the country, while the third will catch rats in the cellar. The children begin to cry and entreat that the kittens may be spared. Their father consents, but on the condition that the children do not go into the kitchen and touch the kittens.

After dinner, Vanya and Nina slouch about the rooms, feeling depressed. The prohibition of visits to the kitchen has reduced them to dejection. They refuse sweets, are naughty, and are rude to their mother. When their uncle Petrusha comes in the evening, they draw him aside, and complain to him of their father, who wanted to throw the kittens into the cesspool.

"Uncle Petrusha, tell mamma to have the kittens taken to the nursery," the children beg their uncle, "do-o tell her."

"There, there . . . very well," says their uncle, waving them off. "All right."

Uncle Petrusha does not usually come alone. He is accompanied by Nero, a big black dog of Danish breed, with drooping ears, and a tail as hard as a stick. The dog is silent, morose, and full of a sense of his own dignity. He takes not the slightest notice of the children, and when he passes them hits them with his tail as though they were chairs. The children hate him from the bottom of their hearts, but on this occasion, practical considerations override sentiment.

"I say, Nina," says Vanya, opening his eyes wide. "Let Nero be their father, instead of the horse! The horse is dead and he is alive, you see."

They are waiting the whole evening for the moment when papa will sit down to his cards and it will be possible to take Nero to the kitchen without being observed. . . . At last, papa sits down to cards, mamma is busy with the samovar and not noticing the children. . . .

The happy moment arrives.

"Come along!" Vanya whispers to his sister.

But, at that moment, Stepan comes in and, with a snigger, announces: "Nero has eaten the kittens, madam."

Nina and Vanya turn pale and look at Stepan with horror.

"He really has . . ." laughs the footman, "he went to the box and gobbled them up."

The children expect that all the people in the house will be aghast and fall upon the miscreant Nero. But they all sit calmly in their seats, and only express surprise at the appetite of the huge dog. Papa and mamma laugh. Nero walks about by the table, wags his tail, and licks his lips complacently . . . the cat is the only one who is uneasy. With her tail in the air she walks about the rooms, looking suspiciously at people and mewing plaintively.

"Children, it's past nine," cries mamma, "it's bedtime."

Vanya and Nina go to bed, shed tears, and spend a long time thinking about the injured cat, and the cruel, insolent, and unpunished Nero.

# A Black Affair

BY W. W. JACOBS

W. W. JACOBS (1863–1943) specialized in two kinds of short stories—tales of the macabre like "The Monkey's Paw," his best-known work, and humorous stories dealing with sailors and country folk. "A Black Affair" is a fine example of the latter. Although it deals only incidentally with a cat—two cats, to be precise, one of them slightly ghostly—its energy and high spirits have found it a place in many cat anthologies. Don't be put off by the dialect.

★　★　★　★　★

"I DIDN'T WANT to bring it," said Captain Gubson, regarding somewhat unfavorably a gray parrot whose cage was hanging against the mainmast, "but my old uncle was so set on it I had to. He said a sea voyage would set its 'elth up."

"It seems to be all right at present," said the mate, who was tenderly sucking his forefinger. "Best of spirits, I should say."

"It's playful," assented the skipper. "The old man thinks a rare lot of it. I think I shall have a little bit in that quarter, so keep your eye on the beggar."

"Scratch Poll!" said the parrot, giving its bill a preliminary strop on its perch. "Scratch poor Polly!"

It bent its head against the bars, and waited patiently to play off what it had always regarded as the most consummate practical joke in existence. The first doubt it had ever had about it occurred when the mate came forward and obligingly scratched it with the stem of his pipe. It was a wholly unforeseen development, and the parrot ruffling its feathers, edged along its perch and brooded darkly at the other end of it.

Opinion before the mast was also against the new arrival, the general view being that the wild jealousy which raged in the bosom of the ship's cat would sooner or later lead to mischief.

"Old Satan don't like it," said the cook, shaking his head. "The blessed bird hadn't been aboard ten minutes before Satan was prowling around. The blooming image waited till he was about a foot off the cage, and then he did the perlite and asked him whether he'd like a glass o' beer. *I* never see a cat so took aback in all my life. Never."

"There'll be trouble between 'em," said old Sam, who was the cat's special protector, "mark my words."

"I'd put my money on the parrot," said one of the men confidently. "It's 'ad a crool bit out of the mate's finger. Where 'ud the cat be agin that beak?"

"Well, you'd lose your money," said Sam. "If you want to do the cat a kindness, every time you see him near that cage cuff his 'ed."

The crew being much attached to the cat, which had been presented to them when a kitten by the mate's wife, acted upon the advice with so much zest that for the next two days the indignant animal was like to have been killed with kindness. On the third day, however, the parrot's cage being on the cabin table, the cat stole furtively down, and, at the pressing request of the occupant itself, scratched its head for it.

The skipper was the first to discover the mischief, and he came on deck and published the news in a voice which struck a chill to all hearts.

"Where's that black devil got to!" he yelled.

"Anything wrong, sir?" asked Sam anxiously.

"Come and look here," said the skipper. He led the way to the cabin, where the mate and one of the crew were already standing, shaking their heads over the parrot.

"What do you make of that?" demanded the skipper fiercely.

"Too much dry food," repeated Sam firmly. "A parrot—a gray parrot—wants plenty o' sop. If it don't get it, it molts."

"It's had too much *cat*," the skipper said fiercely, and you know it, and overboard it goes."

"I don't believe it was the cat, sir," interposed the other man. "It's too softhearted to do a thing like that."

"You can shut your jaw," said the skipper, reddening. "Who asked you to come down here at all?"

"Nobody saw the cat do it," urged the mate.

The skipper said nothing, but, stooping down, picked up a tail feather from the floor, and laid it on the table. He then went on deck, followed by the others, and began calling, in seductive tones, for the cat. No reply forthcoming from the sagacious animal, which had gone into hiding, he turned to Sam, and bade him call it.

"No, sir, I won't 'ave no 'and in it," said the old man. "Putting aside my liking for the animal, *I'm* not going to 'ave anything to do with the killing of a black cat."

"Rubbish!" said the skipper.

"Very good, sir," said Sam, shrugging his shoulders. "You know best, best o' course. You're educated and I'm not, an' p'r'aps you can afford to make a laugh o' such things. I knew one man who killed a black cat an' he went mad. There's something very pecooliar about that cat o' ours."

"It knows more than we do," said one of the crew, shaking his head. "That time you—I mean we—ran the smack down, that cat was expecting of it 'ours before. It was like a wild thing."

"Look at the weather we've 'ad—look at the trips we've made since he's been aboard," said the old man. "Tell me it's chance if you like, but I *know* better."

The skipper hesitated. He was a superstitious man even for a sailor, and his weakness was so well known that he had become a sympathetic receptacle for every ghost story which, by reason if its crudeness or lack of corroboration, had been rejected by other experts. He was a perfect reference library for omens, and his interpretations of dreams had gained for him a widespread reputation.

"That's all nonsense," he said, pausing uneasily. "Still, I only want to be just. There's nothing vindictive about me, and I'll have no hand in it myself. Joe, just tie a lump of coal to that cat and heave it overboard."

"Not me," said the cook, following Sam's lead, and working up a shudder. "Not for fifty pun in gold. I don't want to be haunted."

"The parrot's a little better now, sir," said one of the men, taking advantage of his hesitation. "He's opened one eye."

"Well, I only want to be just," repeated the skipper. "I won't do anything in a hurry, but, mark my words, if the parrot dies that cat goes overboard."

Contrary to expectations, the bird was still alive when London was reached, though the cook, who from his connection with the cabin had suddenly reached a position of unusual importance, reported great loss of strength and irritability of temper. It was still alive, but failing fast on the day they were put to sea again; and the fo'c'sle, in preparation for the worst, stowed their pet away in the paint locker, and discussed the situation.

Their council was interrupted by the mysterious behavior of the cook, who, having gone out to lay in a stock of bread, suddenly broke in upon them more in the manner of a member of a secret society than a humble but useful unit of a ship's company.

"Where's the cap'n?" he asked in a hoarse whisper, as he took a seat on the locker with the sack of bread between his knees.

"In the cabin," said Sam, regarding his antics with some disfavor. "What's wrong, cookie?"

"What d' yer think I've got in here?" asked the cook, patting the bag.

The obvious reply to this question was, of course, bread; but as it was known that the cook had departed specially to buy some, and that he could hardly ask a question involving such a simple answer, nobody gave it.

"It come to me all of a sudden," said the cook, in a thrilling whisper. "I'd just bought the bread and left the shop, when I see a big black cat, the very image of ours, sitting on a doorstep. I just stooped down to stroke its 'ed, when it come to me."

"They will sometimes," said one of the seamen.

"I don't mean that," said the cook, with the contempt of genius. "I mean the idea did. Says I to myself, 'You might be old Satan's brother by the look of you; an' if the cap'n wants to kill a cat, let it be you,' I says. And with that, before it could say Jack Robinson, I picked it up by the scruff o' the neck and shoved it in the bag."

"What, all in along of our bread?" said the previous interrupter, in a pained voice.

"Some of yer are 'ard ter please," said the cook, deeply offended.

"Don't mind him, cook," said the admiring Sam. "You're a master-piece, that's what you are."

"Of course, if any of you've got a better plan—" said the cook generously.

"Don't talk rubbish, cook," said Sam. "Fetch the two cats out and put 'em together."

"Don't mix 'em," said the cook warningly, "for you'll never know which is which agin if you do."

He cautiously opened the top of the sack and produced his captive, and Satan having been relieved from his prison, the two animals were carefully compared.

"They're as like as two lumps o' coal," said Sam slowly. "Lord, what a joke on the old man. I must tell the mate o' this; he'll enjoy it."

"It'll be all right if the parrot don't die," said the dainty pessimist, still harping on his pet theme. "All that bread spoilt, and two cats aboard."

"Don't mind what he says," said Sam; "you're a brick, that's what you are. I'll just make a few holes on the lid o' the boy's chest, and pop old Satan in. You don't mind, do you, Billy?"

"Of course he don't," said the other men indignantly.

Matters being thus agreeably arranged, Sam got a gimlet, and prepared the chest for the reception of its tenant, who, convinced that he was being put out of the way to make room for a rival, made a frantic fight for freedom.

"Now get something 'eavy and put on the top of it," said Sam, having convinced himself that the lock was broken; "and, Billy, put the new cat in the paint locker till we start; it's homesick."

The boy obeyed, and the understudy was kept in durance vile until they were off Limehouse, when he came on deck and nearly ended his career there and then by attempting to jump over the bulwark into the next garden. For some time he paced the deck in a perturbed fashion, and then, leaping on the stern, mewed plaintively as his native city receded farther and farther from his view.

"What's the matter with old Satan?" said the mate, who had been let into the secret. "He seems to have something on his mind."

"He'll have something round his neck presently," said the skipper grimly.

The prophecy was fulfilled some three hours later, when he came up on deck ruefully regarding the remains of a bird whose vocabulary had once been the pride of its native town. He threw it on board without a word, and then, seizing the innocent cat, who had followed him under the impression that it was about to lunch, produced half a brick attached to a string, and tied it round his neck. The crew, who were enjoying the joke immensely, raised a howl of protest.

"The *Skylark*'ll never have another like it, sir," said Sam solemnly. "That cat was the luck of the ship."

"I don't want any of your old woman's yarns," said the skipper brutally. "If you want the cat, go and fetch it."

He stepped aft as he spoke, and sent the gentle stranger hurtling through the air. There was a "plomp" as it reached the water, a bubble or two came to the surface, and all was over.

"That's the last o' that," he said, turning away.

The old man shook his head. "You can't kill a black cat for nothing," said he, "mark my words!"

The skipper, who was in a temper at the time, thought little of them, but they recurred to him vividly the next day. The wind had freshened during the night, and rain was falling heavily. On deck the crew stood about in oilskins, while below, the boy, in his new capacity of gaoler, was ministering to the wants of an ungrateful prisoner, when the cook, happening to glance that way, was horrified to see the animal emerge from the fo'c'sle. It eluded easily the frantic clutch of the boy as he sprang up the ladder after it, and walked leisurely along the deck in the direction of the cabin. Just as the crew had given it up for lost it encountered Sam, and the next moment, despite its cries, was caught up and huddled away beneath his stiff clammy oilskins. At the noise the skipper, who was talking to the mate, turned as though he had been shot, and gazed wildly round him.

"Dick," said he, "can you hear a cat?"

"Cat!" said the mate, in accents of great astonishment.

"I thought I heard it," said the puzzled skipper.

"Fancy sir," said Dick firmly, as a mewing, appalling in its wrath, came from beneath Sam's coat.

"Did you hear it, Sam?" called the skipper, as the old man was moving off.

"Hear what, sir?" inquired Sam respectfully, without turning round.

"Nothing," said the skipper, collecting himself. "Nothing. All right."

The old man, hardly able to believe in his good fortune, made his way forward, and, seizing a favorable opportunity, handed his ungrateful burden back to the boy.

"Fancy you heard a cat just now?" inquired the mate casually.

"Well, between you an' me, Dick," said the skipper, in a mysterious voice, "I did, and it wasn't fancy neither. I heard that cat as plain as if it was alive."

"Well, I've heard of such things," said the other, "but I don't believe 'em. What a lark if the old cat comes back climbing up over the side out of the sea tonight, with the brick hanging round its neck."

The skipper stared at him for some time without speaking. "If that's your idea of a lark," he said at length, in a voice which betrayed traces of some emotion. "It ain't mine."

"Well, if you hear it again," said the mate cordially, "you might let me know. I'm rather interested in such things."

The skipper, hearing no more of it that day, tried hard to persuade himself that he was the victim of imagination, but, in spite of this, he was pleased at night, as he stood at the wheel, to reflect on the sense of companionship afforded by the lookout in the bows. On his part the lookout was quite charmed with the unwonted affability of the skipper, as he yelled out to him two or three times on matters only faintly connected with the progress of the schooner.

The night, which had been dirty, cleared somewhat, and the bright crescent of the moon appeared above a heavy bank of clouds as the cat, which had by dint of using its back as a lever at length got free from that cursed chest, licked its shapely limbs, and came up on deck. After its stifling prison, the air was simply delicious.

"Bob!" yelled the skipper suddenly.

"Ay, ay, sir!" said the lookout, in a startled voice.

"Did you mew?" inquired the skipper.

"Did I *wot*, sir?" cried the astonished Bob.

"Mew," said the skipper sharply, "like a cat?"

"No, sir," said the offended seaman. "What 'ud I want to do that for?"

"I don't know what you want to for," said the skipper, looking round him uneasily. "There's some more rain coming, Bob."

"Ay, ay, sir," said Bob.

"Lot o' rain we've had this summer," said the skipper, in a meditative bawl.

"Ay, ay, sir," said Bob. "Sailing ship on the port bow, sir."

The conversation dropped, the skipper, anxious to divert his thoughts, watching the dark mass of sail as it came plunging out of the darkness into the moonlight until it was abreast of his own craft. His eyes followed it as it passed his quarter, so that he saw not the stealthy approach of the cat which came from behind the companion, and sat down close by him. For over thirty hours the animal had been subjected to the grossest indignities at the hands of every man on board the ship except one. That one was the skipper, and there is no doubt but that its subsequent behavior was a direct recognition of that fact. It rose to its feet, and crossing over to the unconscious skipper, rubbed its head affectionately and vigorously against his leg.

From simple causes great events do spring. The skipper sprang four yards, and let off a screech which was the subject of much comment on the bark which had just passed. When Bob, who came shuffling up at the double, reached him he was leaning against the side, incapable of speech, and shaking all over.

"Anything wrong, sir?" inquired the seaman anxiously, as he ran to the wheel.

The skipper pulled himself together a bit, and got closer to his companion.

"Believe me or not, Bob," he said at length, in trembling accents, "just as you please, but the ghost of that—cat, I mean the ghost of that poor affectionate animal which I drowned, and which I wish I hadn't, came and rubbed itself up against my leg."

"Which leg?" inquired Bob, who was ever careful about details.

"What the blazes does it matter which leg?" demanded the skipper, whose nerves were in a terrible state. "Ah, look—look there!"

The seaman followed his outstretched finger, and his heart failed him as he saw the cat, with its back arched, gingerly picking its way along the side of the vessel.

"I can't see nothing," he said doggedly.

"I don't suppose you can, Bob," said the skipper in a melancholy voice, as the cat vanished in the bows. "It's evidently only meant for me to see. What it means I don't know. I'm going down to turn in. I ain't fit for duty. You don't mind being left alone till the mate comes up, do you?"

"I ain't afraid," said Bob.

His superior officer disappeared below, and, shaking the sleepy mate, who protested strongly against the proceedings, narrated in trembling tones his horrible experiences.

"If I were you—" said the mate.

"Yes?" said the skipper, waiting a bit. Then he shook him again, roughly.

"What were you going to say?" he inquired.

"Say?" said the mate, rubbing his eyes. "Nothing."

"About the cat?" suggested the skipper.

"Cat?" said the mate, nestling lovingly down in the blankets again. "What— ca'—goo'ni'—"

Then the skipper drew the blankets from the mate's sleepy clutches, and, rolling him backward and forward in the bunk, patiently explained to him that he was very unwell, that he was going to have a drop of whiskey neat, and turn in, and that he, the mate, was to take the watch. From this moment the joke lost much of its savor for the mate.

"You can have a nip too, Dick," said the skipper, proffering him the whiskey, as the other sullenly dressed himself.

"It's all rot," said the mate, tossing the spirits down his throat, "and it's no use either; you can't run away from a ghost; it's just as likely to be in your bed as anywhere else. Good night."

He left the skipper pondering over his last words, and dubiously eyeing the piece of furniture in question. Nor did he retire until he had subjected it to an analysis of the most searching description, and then, leaving the lamp burning, he sprang hastily in, and forgot his troubles in sleep.

It was day when he awoke, and went on deck to find a heavy sea running, and just sufficient sail set to keep the schooner's head before the wind as she bobbed about on the waters. An exclamation from the skipper, as a wave broke against the side and flung a cloud of spray over him, brought the mate's head round.

"Why, you ain't going to get up?" he said, in tones of insincere surprise.

"Why not?" inquired the other gruffly.

"You go and lay down agin," said the mate, "and have a cup o' nice hot tea an' some toast."

"Clear out," said the skipper, making a dash for the wheel, and reaching it as the wet deck suddenly changed his angle. "I know you didn't like being woke up, Dick; but I got the horrors last night. Go below and turn in."

"All right," said the mollified mate.

"You didn't see anything?" inquired the skipper, as he took the wheel from him.

"Nothing at all," said the other.

The skipper shook his head thoughtfully, then shook it again vigorously, as another shower bath put its head over the side and saluted him.

"I wish I hadn't drowned that cat, Dick," he said.

"You won't see it agin," said Dick, with the confidence of a man who had taken every possible precaution to render the prophecy a safe one.

He went below, leaving the skipper at the wheel idly watching the cook as he performed marvelous feats of jugglery, between the galley and the fo'c'sle, with the men's breakfast.

A little while later, leaving the wheel to Sam, he went below himself and had his own, talking freely, to the discomfort of the conscience-stricken cook, about his weird experiences of the night before.

"You won't see it no more, sir, I don't expect," he said faintly. "I believe it come and rubbed itself up agin your leg to show it forgave you."

"Well, I hope it knows it's understood," said the other. "I don't want it to take any more trouble."

He finished the breakfast in silence, and then went on deck again. It was still blowing hard, and he went over to superintend the men who were attempting to lash together some empties which were rolling about in all directions amidships. A violent roll set them free again, and at the same time separated two chests in the fo'c'sle, which were standing one on top of the other. This enabled Satan, who was crouching in the lower one, half crazed with terror, to come flying madly up on deck and give his feelings full vent. Three times in full view of the horrified skipper he circled the deck at racing speed, and had just started on the fourth when a heavy packing case, which had been temporarily set on end and abandoned by the men at his sudden appearance, fell over and caught him by the tail. Sam rushed to the rescue.

"Stop!" yelled the skipper.

"Won't I put it up, sir?" inquired Sam.

"Do you see what's beneath it?" said the skipper, in a husky voice.

"Beneath it, sir?" said Sam, whose ideas were in a whirl.

"The cat, can't you see the cat?" said the skipper, whose eyes had been riveted on the animal since its first appearance on deck.

Sam hesitated a moment, and then shook his head.

"The case has fallen on the cat," said the skipper, "I can see it distinctly."

He might have said "heard it," too, for Satan was making frenzied appeals to his sympathetic friends for assistance.

"Let me put the case back, sir," said one of the men, "then p'r'aps the wision'll disappear."

"No, stop where you are," said the skipper. "I can stand it better by daylight. It's the most wonderful and extraordinary thing I've ever seen. Do you mean to say you can't see anything, Sam?"

"I can see a case, sir," said Sam, speaking slowly and carefully, "with a bit of rusty iron band sticking out from it. That's what you're mistaking for the cat, p'r'aps, sir."

"Can't you see anything, cook?" demanded the skipper.

"It may be fancy, sir," faltered the cook, lowering his eyes, "but it does seem to me as though I can see a little misty sort o' thing there. Ah, now it's gone."

"No, it ain't," said the skipper. "The ghost of Satan's sitting there. The case seems to have fallen on its tail. It appears to be howling something dreadful."

The men made a desperate effort to display the astonishment suitable to such a marvel, while Satan, who was trying all he knew to get his tail out, cursed freely. How long the superstitious captain of the *Skylark* would have let him remain there will never be known for just then the mate came on deck and caught sight of it before he was quite aware of the part he was expected to play.

"Why the devil don't you lift the thing off the poor brute," he yelled, hurrying up toward the case.

"What, can *you* see it, Dick?" said the skipper impressively, laying his hand on his arm.

"*See* it?" retorted the mate. "D'ye think I'm blind? Listen to the poor brute. I should—oh!"

He became conscious of the concentrated significant gaze of the crew. Five pairs of eyes speaking as one, all saying "idiot" plainly, the boy's eyes conveying an expression too great to be translated.

Turning, the skipper saw the byplay, and a light slowly dawned upon him. But he wanted more, and he wheeled suddenly to the cook for the required illumination.

The cook said it was a lark. Then he corrected himself and said it wasn't a lark, then he corrected himself again and became incoherent. Meantime the skipper eyed him stonily, while the mate released the cat and good-naturedly helped to straighten its tail.

It took fully five minutes of unwilling explanation before the skipper could grasp the situation. He did not appear to fairly understand it until he was shown the chest with the ventilated lid; then his countenance cleared, and, taking the unhappy Billy by the collar, he called sternly for a piece of rope.

By this statesmanlike handling of the subject a question of much delicacy and difficulty was solved, discipline was preserved, and a practical illustration of the perils of deceit afforded to a youngster who was at an age best suited to receive such impressions. That he should exhaust the resources of a youthful but powerful vocabulary upon the crew in general, and Sam in particular, was only to be expected. They bore him no malice for it, but, when he showed signs of going beyond his years, held a hasty consultation, and then stopped his mouth with sixpence-halfpenny and a broken jacknife.

# Schrödinger's Cat

BY URSULA K. LE GUIN

I F THERE IS ANY such thing as the essential modern cat, a cat for this era of particle physics, string theory, and black holes, it must be physicist Erwin Schrödinger's imaginary cat, here celebrated by one of our most engaging (if weird) modern writers of science fiction. For those of you not quite up to speed on the original paradox, it has to do with the contradiction between quantum physics—in which, theoretically, a sub-microscopic particle can exist in two states simultaneously—and our experience of the everyday world, in which an object (such as a cat) has to be in one state or another—either alive, say, or dead. Schrödinger proposed an experiment in which a cat would be closed in a box with a vial of cyanide and a single radioactive atom. The atom would have a 50 percent probability of decaying within one hour, in which case the vial would break and the cat be poisoned. Therefore, during that hour while the box was closed, the atom could be said to be existing in two states simultaneously, both decayed and undecayed. But what about the cat? At the end of the hour, on the same principle, it should be both dead and alive. That's the paradox.

Schrödinger called it a "thought-experiment"; after all, you can't just go around murdering (or semi-murdering) cats. Ursula Le Guin (1929– ) gets slightly closer, but only in the name of entertainment. She obviously likes cats too much to play lethal games with them.

★   ★   ★   ★   ★

AS THINGS APPEAR to be coming to some sort of climax, I have withdrawn to this place. It is cooler here, and nothing moves fast.

On the way here I met a married couple who were coming apart. She had pretty well gone to pieces, but he seemed, at first glance, quite hearty. While he was telling me that he had no hormones of any kind, she pulled herself together and, by supporting her head in the crook of her right knee and hopping on the toes of the right foot, approached us shouting, "Well what's *wrong* with a person trying to express themselves?" The left leg, the arms, and the trunk, which had remained lying in the heap, twitched and jerked in sympathy. "Great legs," the husband pointed out, looking at the slim ankle. 'My wife has great legs."

A cat has arrived, interrupting my narrative. It is a striped yellow tom with white chest and paws. He has long whiskers and yellow eyes. I never noticed before that cats had whiskers above their eyes; is that normal? There is no way to tell. As he has gone to sleep on my knee, I shall proceed.

Where?

Nowhere, evidently. Yet the impulse to narrate remains. Many things are not worth doing, but almost anything is worth telling. In any case, I have a severe congenital case of *Ethica laboris puritanica,* or Adam's Disease. It is incurable except by total decapitation. I even like to dream when asleep, and to try and recall my dreams: it assures me that I haven't wasted seven or eight hours just lying there. Now here I am, lying, here. Hard at it.

Well, the couple I was telling you about finally broke up. The pieces of him trotted around bouncing and cheeping, like little chicks, but she was finally reduced to nothing but a mass of nerves: rather like fine chicken wire, in fact, but hopelessly tangled.

So I came on, placing one foot carefully in front of the other, and grieving. This grief is with me still. I fear it is part of me, like foot or loin or eye, or may even be myself: for I seem to have no other self, nothing further, nothing that lies outside the borders of grief.

Yet I don't know what I grieve for: my wife? my husband? my children, or myself? I can't remember. Most dreams are forgotten, try as one will to remember. Yet later music strikes the note, and the harmonic rings along the mandolin strings of the mind, and we find tears in our eyes. Some note keeps playing that makes me want to cry; but what for? I am not certain.

The yellow cat, who may have belonged to the couple that broke up, is dreaming. His paws twitch now and then, and once he makes a small, suppressed remark with his mouth shut. I wonder what a cat dreams of, and to whom he was speaking just then. Cats seldom waste words. They are quiet beasts. They keep their counsel, they reflect. They reflect all day, and at night their eyes reflect. Overbred Siamese cats may be as noisy as little dogs, and then people say, "They're talking," but the noise is farther from speech than is the deep silence of the hound or the tabby. All this cat can say is meow, but maybe in his silences he will suggest to me what it is that I have lost, what I am grieving for. I have a feeling that he knows. That's why he came here. Cats look out for Number One.

It was getting awfully hot. I mean, you could touch less and less. The stove burners, for instance. Now I know that stove burners always used to get hot; that was their final cause, they existed in order to get hot. But they began to get hot without having been turned on. Electric units or gas rings, there they'd be when you came into the kitchen for breakfast, all four of them glaring away, the air above them shaking like clear jelly with the heat waves. It did no good to turn them off, because they weren't on in the first place. Besides, the knobs and dials were also hot, uncomfortable to the touch.

Some people tried hard to cool them off. The favorite technique was to turn them on. It worked sometimes, but you could not count on it. Others investigated the phenomenon, tried to get at the root of it, the cause. They were probably the most frightened ones, but man is most human at his most frightened. In the face of the hot stove burners they acted with exemplary coolness. They studied, they observed. They were like the fellow in Michelangelo's *Last Judgment,* who has clapped his hands over his face in horror as the devils drag him down to Hell—but only over one eye. The other eye is busy looking. It's all he can do, but he does it. He observes. Indeed, one wonders if Hell would exist, if he did not look at it. However, neither he, nor the people I am talking about, had enough time left to do much about it. And then finally of course there were the people who did not try to do or think anything about it at all.

When the water came out of the cold-water taps hot one morning, however, even people who had blamed it all on the Democrats began to feel a more profound unease. Before long, forks and pencils and wrenches were too hot to handle without gloves; and cars were really terrible. It was like opening the door of an oven going full blast, to open the door of your car. And by then, other people almost scorched your fingers off. A kiss was like a branding iron. Your child's hair flowed along your hand like fire.

Here, as I said, it is cooler; and, as a matter of fact, this animal is cool. A real cool cat. No wonder it's pleasant to pet his fur. Also he moves slowly, at least for the most part, which is all the slowness one can reasonably expect of a cat. He hasn't that frenetic quality most creatures acquired—all they did was ZAP and gone. They lacked presence. I suppose birds always tended to be that way, but even the hummingbird used to halt for a second in the very center of his metabolic frenzy, and hang, still as a hub, present, above the fuchsias—then gone again, but you knew something was there besides the blurring brightness. But it got so that even robins and pigeons, the heavy impudent birds, were a blur; and as for swallows, they cracked the sound barrier. You knew of swallows only by the small, curved sonic booms that looped about the eaves of old houses in the evening.

Worms shot like subway trains through the dirt of gardens, among the writhing roots of roses.

You could scarcely lay a hand on children, by then: too fast to catch, too hot to hold. They grew up before your eyes.

But then, maybe that's always been true.

I was interrupted by the cat, who woke and said meow once, then jumped down from my lap and leaned against my legs diligently. This is a cat who knows how to get fed. He also knows how to jump. There was a lazy fluidity to his leap, as if gravity affected him less than it does other creatures. As a matter of fact there were some localised cases, just before I left, of the failure of gravity; but this quality in the cat's leap was something quite else. I am not yet in such a state of confusion that I can be alarmed by grace. Indeed, I found it reassuring. While I was opening a can of sardines, a person arrived.

Hearing the knock, I thought it might be the mailman. I miss mail very much, so I hurried to the door and said, "Is it the mail?"

A voice replied, "Yah!" I opened the door. He came in, almost pushing me aside in his haste. He dumped down an enormous knapsack he had been carrying, straightened up, massaged his shoulders, and said, "Wow!"

"How did you get here?"

He stared at me and repeated, "How?"

At this my thoughts concerning human and animal speech recurred to me, and I decided that this was probably not a man, but a small dog. (Large dogs seldom go yah, wow, how, unless it is appropriate to do so.)

"Come on, fella," I coaxed him. "Come, come on, that's a boy, good doggie!" I opened a can of pork and beans for him at once, for he looked half starved. He ate voraciously, gulping and lapping. When it was gone he said "Wow!" several times. I was just about to scratch him behind the ears when he stiffened, his hackles bristling, and growled deep in his throat. He had noticed the cat.

The cat had noticed him some time before, without interest, and was now sitting on a copy of *The Well-Tempered Clavier* washing sardine oil off its whiskers.

"Wow!" the dog, whom I had thought of calling Rover, barked. "Wow! Do you know what that is? *That's Schrödinger's cat!*"

"No it's not, not any more; it's my cat," I said, unreasonably offended.

"Oh, well, Schrödinger's dead, of course, but it's his cat. I've seen hundreds of pictures of it. Erwin Schrödinger, the great physicist, you know. Oh, wow! To think of finding it here!"

The cat looked coldly at him for a moment, and began to wash its left shoulder with negligent energy. An almost religious expression had come into Rover's face. "It was meant," he said in a low, impressive tone. "Yah. It was *meant*. It can't be a mere coincidence. It's too improbable. Me, with the box; you, with the cat; to meet—here—now." He looked up at me, his eyes shining with happy fervor. "Isn't it wonderful?" he said. "I'll get the box set up right away." And he started to tear open his huge knapsack.

While the cat washed its front paws, Rover unpacked. While the cat washed its tail and belly, regions hard to reach gracefully, Rover put together what he had unpacked, a complex task. When he and the cat finished their operations simultaneously and looked at me, I was impressed. They had come out even, to the very second. Indeed it seemed that something more than chance was involved. I hoped it was not myself.

"What's that?" I asked, pointing to a protuberance on the outside of the box. I did not ask what the box was as it was quite clearly a box.

"The gun," Rover said with excited pride.

"The gun?"

"To shoot the cat."

"To shoot the cat?"

"Or to *not shoot* the cat. Depending on the photon."

"The photon?"

"Yah! It's Schrödinger's great Gedankenexperiment. You see, there's a little emitter here. At Zero Time, five seconds after the lid of the box is closed, it will emit one photon. The photon will strike a half-silvered mirror. The quantum mechanical probability of the photon passing through the mirror is exactly one half, isn't it? So! If the photon passes through, the trigger will be activated and the gun will fire. If the photon is deflected, the trigger will not be activated and the gun will not fire. Now, you put the cat in. The cat is in the box. You close the lid. You go away! You stay away! What happens?" Rover's eyes were bright.

"The cat gets hungry?"

"The cat gets shot—or not shot," he said, seizing my arm, though not, fortunately, in his teeth. "But the gun is silent, perfectly silent. The box is soundproof. There is no way to know whether or not the cat has been shot, until you lift the lid of the box. There is *no* way! Do you see how central this is to the whole of quantum theory? Before Zero Time the whole system, on the quantum level or on our level, is nice and simple. But after Zero Time the whole system can be represented only by a linear combination of two waves. We cannot predict the behavior of the photon, and thus, once it has behaved, we cannot predict the state of the system it has determined. We cannot predict it! God plays dice with the world! So it is beautifully demonstrated that if you desire certainty, any certainty, you must create it yourself!"

"How?"

"By lifting the lid of the box, of course," Rover said, looking at me with sudden disappointment, perhaps a touch of suspicion, like a Baptist who finds he has been talking church matters not to another Baptist as he thought, but a Methodist, or even, God forbid, an Episcopalian. "To find out whether the cat is dead or not."

"Do you mean," I said carefully, "that until you lift the lid of the box, the cat has neither been shot nor not been shot?"

"Yah!" Rover said, radiant with relief, welcoming me back to the fold. "Or maybe, you know, both."

"But why does opening the box and looking reduce the system back to one probability, either live cat or dead cat? Why don't we get included in the system when we lift the lid of the box?"

There was a pause. "How?" Rover barked, distrustfully.

"Well, we would involve ourselves in the system, you see, the superposition of two waves. There's no reason why it should only exist *inside* an open box, is there? So when we came to look, there we would be, you and I, both looking at a live cat, and both looking at a dead cat. You see?"

A dark cloud lowered on Rover's eyes and brow. He barked twice in a subdued, harsh voice, and walked away. With his back turned to me he said in a firm, sad tone, "You must not complicate the issue. It is complicated enough."

"Are you sure?"

He nodded. Turning, he spoke pleadingly. "Listen. It's all we have—the box. Truly it is. The box. And the cat. And they're here. The box, the cat, at last. Put the cat in the box. Will you? Will you let me put the cat in the box?"

"No," I said, shocked.

"Please. Please. Just for a minute. Just for half a minute! Please let me put the cat in the box!"

"Why?"

"I can't stand this terrible uncertainty," he said, and burst into tears.

I stood some while indecisive. Though I felt sorry for the poor son of a bitch, I was about to tell him, gently, No; when a curious thing happened. The cat walked over to the box, sniffed around it, lifted his tail and sprayed a corner to mark his territory, and then lightly, with that marvelous fluid ease, leapt into it. His yellow tail just flicked the edge of the lid as he jumped, and it closed, falling into place with a soft, decisive click.

"The cat is in the box," I said.

"The cat is in the box," Rover repeated in a whisper, falling to his knees. "Oh, wow. Oh, wow. Oh, wow."

There was silence: deep silence. We both gazed, I afoot, Rover kneeling, at the box. No sound. Nothing happened. Nothing would happen. Nothing would ever happen, until we lifted the lid of the box.

"Like Pandora," I said in a weak whisper. I could not quite recall Pandora's legend. She had let all the plagues and evils out of the box, of course, but there had been something else, too. After all the devils were let loose, something quite different, quite unexpected, had been left. What had it been? Hope? A dead cat? I could not remember.

Impatience welled up in me. I turned on Rover, glaring. He returned the look with expressive brown eyes. You can't tell me dogs haven't got souls.

"Just exactly what are you trying to prove?" I demanded.

"That the cat will be dead, or not dead," he murmured submissively. "Certainty. All I want is certainty. To know for *sure* that God *does* play dice with the world."

I looked at him for a while with fascinated incredulity. "Whether he does, or doesn't," I said, "do you think he's going to leave you a note about it in the box?" I went to the box, and with a rather dramatic gesture, flung the lid back. Rover staggered up from his knees, gasping, to look. The cat was, of course, not there.

Rover neither barked, nor fainted, nor cursed, nor wept. He really took it very well.

"Where is the cat?" he asked at last.

"Where is the box?"

"Here."

"Where's here?"

"Here is now."

"We used to think so," I said, "but really we should use larger boxes."

He gazed about him in mute bewilderment, and did not flinch even when the roof of the house was lifted off just like the lid of a box, letting in the unconscionable, inordinate light of the stars. He had just time to breathe, "Oh, wow!"

I have identified the note that keeps sounding. I checked it on the mandolin before the glue melted. It is the note A, the one that drove the composer Schumann mad. It is a beautiful, clear tone, much clearer now that the stars are visible. I shall miss the cat. I wonder if he found what it was we lost?

# I Am a Cat

BY SOSEKI NATSUME

S OSEKI NATSUME (1867–1916) studied English literature at a time when Japan was first opening to the West, and became one of the country's first and most important writers to be influenced by Western culture. *I Am a Cat,* his first book and the novel from which this extract is taken, is still enormously popular, and it is easy to see why. Natsume's ability to grasp the cat's state of mind and write in his voice with complete conviction almost—but not quite—masks the book's deeper purpose: to satirize his fellow Japanese for their foibles and confusions.

★ ★ ★ ★ ★

I AM A CAT but as yet I have no name.

I haven't the faintest idea of where I was born. The first thing I do remember is that I was crying "meow, meow," somewhere in a gloomy damp place. It was there that I met a human being for the first time in my life. Though I found this all out at a later date, I learned that this human being was called a Student, one of the most ferocious of the human race. I also understand that these Students sometimes catch us, cook us and then take to eating us. But at that time, I did not have the slightest idea of all this so I wasn't frightened a bit. When this Student placed me on the palm of his hand and lifted me up lightly, I only had the feeling of floating around. After a while, I got used to this position and looked around. This was probably the first time I had a good look at a so-called "human being." What impressed me as being most strange still remains deeply imbedded in my mind: the face which should have been covered with hair was a slippery thing similar to what I now know to be a teakettle. I have since come across many other cats but none of them are such freaks. Moreover, the center of the Student's face protruded to a great extent, and from the two holes located there, he would often emit smoke. I was extremely annoyed by being choked by this. That this was what they term as tobacco, I came to know only recently.

I was snuggled up comfortably in the palm of this Student's hand when, after a while, I started to travel around at a terrific speed. I was unable to find out if the Student was moving or if it was just myself that was in motion, but in any case I became terribly dizzy and a little sick. Just as I was thinking that I couldn't last much longer at this rate, I heard a thud and saw sparks. I remember everything up till that moment but think as hard as I can, I can't recall what took place immediately after this.

When I came to, I could not find the Student anywhere. Nor could I find the many cats that had been with me either. Moreover, my dear mother had also disappeared. And the extraordinary thing was that this place, when compared to where I had been before, was extremely bright—ever so bright. I could hardly keep my eyes open. This was because I had been removed from my straw bed and thrown into a bamboo bush.

Finally, mustering up my strength, I crawled out from this bamboo grove and found myself before a large pond. I sat on my haunches and tried to take in the situation. I didn't know what to do but suddenly I had an idea. If I could attract some attention by meowing, the Student might come back for me. I commenced but this was to no avail; nobody came.

By this time, the wind had picked up and came blowing across the pond. Night was falling. I sensed terrible pangs of hunger. Try as I would, my voice failed me and I felt as if all hope were lost. In any case, I resolved to get myself to a place where there was food and so, with this decision in mind, I commenced to circle the water by going around to the left.

This was very difficult but at any rate, I forced myself along and eventually came to a locality where I sensed Man. Finding a hole in a broken bamboo fence, I crawled through, having confidence that it was worth the try, and lo! I found myself within somebody's estate. Fate is strange; if that hole had not been there, I might have starved to death by the roadside. It is well said that every tree may offer shelter. For a long time afterwards, I often used this hole for my trips to call on Mi-ke, the tomcat living next door.

Having sneaked into the estate, I was at a loss as to what the next step should be. Darkness had come and my belly cried for food. The cold was bitter and it started to rain. I had no time to fool around any longer so I went in to a room that looked bright and cozy. Coming to think of it now, I had entered somebody's home for the first time. It was there that I was to confront other humans.

The first person I met was the maid Osan. This was a human much worse than the Student. As soon as she saw me, she grabbed me by the neck and threw me outdoors. I sensed I had no chance against her sudden action so I shut my eyes and let things take their course. But I couldn't endure the hunger and the cold any longer. I don't know how many times I was thrown out but because of this, I came to dislike Osan all through. That's one reason why I stole the fish the other day and why I felt so proud of myself.

When the maid was about to throw me out for the last time, the master of the house made his appearance and asked what all the row was about. The maid turned to him with me hanging limp from her hand, and told him that she had repeatedly tried throwing this stray cat out but that it always kept sneaking into the kitchen again—and that she didn't like it at all. The master, twisting his moustache, looked at me for a while and then told the maid to let me in. He then left the room. I took it that the master was a man of few words. The maid, still mad at me, threw me down on the kitchen floor. In such a way, I was able to establish this place as my home. . . .

At one time, I went in for sports. Some of you, upon hearing this, will surely laugh at me because even some of you humans don't enjoy them. Many of you think that your only mission in life is to eat and sleep. There was once a time when noblemen, with their hands folded at their bosoms and their buttocks rotting on cushions, claimed that they were in a state of ecstasy; they felt they were assuming the honors and the wealth of their superiors. Only recently have we heard that we should take exercise, drink milk, dash cold water over ourselves, dive into the sea, seclude ourselves in the mountains, and eat mist for the good of our health. These are all recent maladies which have infected this divine land from Western countries, and these suggestions should be classified as being as dangerous as the pest, tuberculosis, and neurasthenia. I myself was born only last year so I am only one year old now. Therefore, I did not witness the time that men were first infected by this sickness but it must have been before I began floating around in the wind of this world. But we may say that a year of a cat's life is equal to ten years of a man's. The span of my life is only a fraction of a human's, but during that short interval, I will manage to accomplish what all cats should do. It would be wrong to calculate the days of cats as the same as the days of humans. . . .

I myself thought up many games. One was trying to leap from the edge of the kitchen eaves to the roof of the main house; another was to stand on all four legs on the plum-blossom-shaped tile ends of the roof. I also tried to walk along the bamboo laundry pole (this I could not do because it is so slippery), and to jump suddenly up on a child's back from behind. This last-mentioned game was more fun than any other sport but I usually received a terrible scolding so I try it only about three times a month at the most. At times, a paper bag is put over my head but this game is only agonizing for me. Moreover, as it requires human participation, it isn't much of a success.

Ranking next as my favorite sport is to claw at book covers. This has the disadvantage of being too risky, because when my master catches me in the act he beats me unmercifully. Besides, it only offers exercise for my paws and does not benefit the rest of my body. I like to classify such a sport as old-fashioned.

Of my new sports, the first on the list is to hunt praying mantises. Mantis hunting is not as strenuous as rat hunting, but neither does it involve so many hazards. The best season for this game is from middle summer till early autumn.

As to the method of this game, first of all I go out to the yard and find a mantis. Although it depends on the weather, it's generally quite simple to find one or two. After seeing one, I rush it as fast as the wind. The mantis, sensing danger, will raise its head and get ready to protect itself. Mantises are rather bold, even when they don't know the strength of their foe. They're harmless but they put up a good fight so it's great fun.

The wings of a mantis are like its neck in that they are extremely narrow. According to my understanding, the wings are only there for ornamental purposes—in other words, like the study of English, French, and German for humans. They are not at all practical. When a mantis spreads its good-for-nothing wings, it is doing no good as far as its escape is concerned. Having wings sounds wonderful but actually those of the mantis only drag the owner along the ground as it walks. I often feel sorry for my prey but as it is essential for my exercise, I simply beg its pardon and run after it all the more.

The mantis cannot turn around easily so it usually keeps going straight ahead in its attempt to escape. I give it a tap on its nose, and the mantis spreads its wings and lies prostrate. Then I hold it flat against the ground with my forepaws and take a little rest. Suddenly I let go again, but not for long. I'm quick to press it flat once more. This is the strategy employed by the Chinese warlord K'ungming, who let his foe escape seven times but then captured his adversary seven times.

After about thirty minutes of this, the mantis is exhausted so I pick it up in my mouth and shake it. After I let go, it lies on the ground unable to move. I give it a shove with my paw, and as it again tries to fly, I pounce on it once more. Being a little bored by the game by now, I simply commence to eat it. For those of you who haven't eaten mantises yet, I may as well admit that they're not very tasty. Nor are they especially nutritious, either.

Beside mantises, there are also cicadas to hunt. Not all the cicadas are the same. Just as there are the greasy, the arrogant, and the loud types among humans, you find the same peculiarities among cicadas. The greasy cicadas are literally very rich in oil. The arrogant cicadas are too proud and haughty, and are therefore a nuisance. The species that's most fun to catch is the *oshii-tsuku-tsuku* cicadas, the noisy kind.

I have to wait until late summer before they arrive. When the autumn wind begins to steal through your kimono sleeves and makes you start sneezing, that is the time these insects commence to sing by moving their tails up and down. And when it comes to singing, they really make a lot of noise! They seem to have no other object in life than to sing and to be caught by cats.

So in early autumn, I go about catching cicadas. It is here that I should explain that you won't find cicadas lying around on the ground. The only ones not in trees are those that ants have attacked. But the cicada that is the object of my game is certainly not the kind lying within the jurisdiction of ants! My prey is the cicada that clings to a branch of a high tree, singing out for all it is worth *"Oshii-tsuku-tsuku!"* By the way, I would like to ask you learned humans this question: how do cicadas really sing? Is it *"Oshii-tsuku-tsuku"* or *"tsuku-tsuku-oshii"?* I believe there is still much research to be done on this insect. The reason humans consider themselves so superior to cats may lie in the fact that man supposedly knows all about such matters. But if you can give no immediate reply to this question, you'd better begin worrying more about your superiority. Considering cicadas as insects to be hunted, however, it really doesn't make much difference how they happen to sing. The trick is to climb a tree, track the cicada down by its song, and to catch one when it is in the middle of a shrill chorus. This may sound easy but actually it's quite difficult to accomplish.

I use all my four feet when traversing the good earth, so I do not feel inferior to any other animal. Considering the number of legs I possess, I know that I'm better off than humans—they have only two. But when it comes to climbing trees, there are many animals better equipped than I am. Monkeys are professional tree climbers but there are many descendants of monkeys and apes—humans—who still retain this skill. As climbing is against the law of gravity, not to be able to accomplish it should not cause anyone shame. But cicada hunting, even considered as an exercise, does have its inconveniences.

Fortunately, I have been given those sharp implements called claws so I can climb trees, one way or the other. But frankly speaking, it's not as easy as it may look and, besides, cicadas can fly. Different from mantises, once cicadas take wing, they make it impossible for me to follow. I often find myself in a sad plight, thinking that it would have been better if I hadn't bothered to climb the tree in the first place. Then, last but not least, there is the danger of being urinated on, and it almost seems that cicadas aim at my eyes. Of course, I understand their wanting to fly away, but I'd like to ask them not to make water when doing so. What is the psychological factor that affects a cicada's physiological organs and induces it to urinate when flying away? It is, most probably, caused by some pain. Or is it a way of gaining time, surprising its foes before its flight? If that is so, it would be the same as a squid which squirts black ink when in danger, or as a quick-tempered bully showing off his tattoos before coming to blows, or the same as my master who speaks in Latin when angered. This again, is another problem for researchers to deal with when studying the cicada. It might even win somebody a doctor's degree. But now let's get back to the main subject.

Cicadas concentrate—if you think my use of the word "concentrate" sounds funny, I could say "gather" but "gather" doesn't seem right so I'll stick to my first term—cicadas concentrate mostly on green paulownia trees. This might be a little technical but the green paulownia tree is called *wu t'ung* in Chinese. Its many leaves are as large as fans. When the leaves are thick, it's impossible to see the branches of the tree. This is naturally a great obstacle in cicada hunting. There's a song now popular that goes "though the voice is heard, the figure doesn't appear." It is as if this had been especially written for cicadas, I'm afraid. Therefore, I can only track the insect by listening to its song.

All paulownia trees have a crotch in the main trunk, about six feet above the ground. After climbing this far, I generally rest and then commence searching. I must be careful because if one cicada takes flight, I am out of luck. The rest also fly away.

When it comes to imitating others, cicadas are not inferior to humans—they love to play "follow the leader." Sometimes when I've established myself in the crotch of a tree, I often find the entire paulownia enveloped in silence; and hard as I may look and listen, I don't find a single cicada around. I hardly ever feel like going down to repeat the whole performance after climbing this far, so I generally decide to stay where I am and wait for a second chance. Eventually I become sleepy and take a nap then and there. But, upon waking up, I usually find myself on a stepping stone at the base of the tree.

Yet I must average at least one cicada to each climb. The reason I prefer mantis hunting is that I have to grasp a cicada between my teeth in the tree, so by the time I reach the ground to play with the insect, it is dead.

But cicada hunting is not without its exciting moments. I stealthily creep up to one as it feverishly sings by drawing its tail in and out, and just as I pounce on it, the *tsuku-tsuku* cicada lets out a squeal and flutters its thin transparent wings in all directions. The speed at which all this happens is incredible, something that must be experienced to appreciate. The moribund flutter is indeed the most beautiful sight in the cicada world; and every time I trap one of these *tsuku-tsuku* cicadas, I thrill at this aesthetic performance. After witnessing this spectacle, I ask forgiveness and throw the insect into my mouth. At times, some of them continue to perform this aesthetic act even after they are inside.

The game that I like best next to cicada hunting is pine sliding. There's no need to make a lengthy explanation of this so I'll make it as simple as possible. When I say "pine sliding," you'll naturally presume I take slides down a pine tree, but actually it's more like tree "climbing." In cicada hunting, I climb trees mainly to catch insects but in pine sliding I climb trees with no other purpose beyond the ascent. This is the main difference between the two sports. It is said that Genzaemon Tsuneyo Sano once prepared a meal for a lay priest by the name of Saimyoji in the days of Tokiyori Hojo (1226–1263). He cooked it using a treasured pine tree as fuel so it is said that this evergreen tree became extremely knotty. There's no tree that is so rough surfaced as a pine, and, therefore, there's no tree that's more clawable. In other words, there's no tree easier to climb.

In this game, I dash straight up the trunk and then come dashing down again. In descending, there are two methods. One is to return headfirst, facing the ground; the other is to go down in the same position as climbing up, or backwards.

Now I'd like to ask you humans another question: which do you think would be the more difficult of the two? Like most shallow-brained humans, you will probably say that it would be much easier to descend headfirst. Well, that's where you're wrong. You're probably thinking of Yoshitsune instead of cats. Yoshitsune was the famous warrior who drove his horse over Hiyodorigoe Cliff to win a battle. Do you really think that it would be proper for cats to go headfirst, too? Nothing could be more insulting!

You may already know how the claws of a cat grow, but I'll tell you anyway; they grow with the points curving backwards. That's why we can pull objects towards us so easily, like using a fireman's hook; but when it comes to pushing, we are often quite clumsy.

Let's imagine now that I've just dashed up the trunk of a pine tree. As a cat is an animal born to walk on the ground, it is only natural that I cannot maintain my perch long. If I don't take any action, I will begin to slide down. If I didn't try to break the fall, I would be sure to get hurt. Therefore I must do something to reach the ground safely.

There is a great difference between falling down and going down, but not always as great as it may sound at first. If the descent is slow, it's "going down," but if the "going down" is too fast, it's "falling." The difference lies in a wee bit of reasoning. As I don't like falling down from a pine tree, I try to descend by slackening my speed. In other words, I try to do something to check the downward motion.

As I have already mentioned, all of my claws turn backwards so when I place my paws skyward and stick the claws out, I can slacken the speed. And thus "falling" becomes "going down." This is comprehensive reasoning.

But if I took the opposite position and tried going down the trunk in the Yoshitsune style, or headfirst, the claws would be useless. I'd slip with nothing to check the speed of my heavy body. In any case, I sometimes go down

headfirst intentionally so therefore I am literally falling down. It is quite difficult to go down headfirst, as Yoshitsune must have found out on Hiyodorigoe
Cliff. I believe that of all cats, I'm the only one that can accomplish this feat. I
have therefore named this sport as I please: pine sliding.

I'd also like to say a few words about "going around the fence," one
more form of taking exercise. The fence all around my master's house is made
of bamboo and it forms a rectangle. The sides parallel to the veranda are probably between forty-eight and fifty-four feet long, while the other sides only
measure about twenty-one feet. What I term as the "going-around-the-fence"
sport is to circle the whole fence without falling off. It is true that I often fall
off, but when I'm able to make a complete trek, I feel satisfied to the utmost.

There are several cryptomeria stakes supporting the bamboo lattice
work of the fence. The lower halves of the poles have been burnt so as to prevent their rotting, but on top they are convenient places to take rests.

The other day I was in exceptionally good form so I was able to repeat
my trek three times before noon. The more I practiced, the better I became.
And the better I got, the more interesting I found the sport. I was halfway
around on my fourth trip when three crows came flying from the roof of the
neighboring house and settled in a neat row about three yards ahead of me.

Rather unexpected visitors, and great obstacles to my game! They had
no right to come perching on somebody else's fence, so I hissed at them: "I'm
coming. You'd better get out of my way."

The crow nearest me just looked my way and grinned; the one in the
middle simply stared into my master's yard; and the third bird only continued
to sharpen its beak on the bamboo fence. It most probably had some food in its
mouth.

I gave them three minutes to leave and stood there waiting. I have always known that crows possess very bad memories, but this was the first time
to find this theory true. They had no memory at all! I waited for a long time
but the crows didn't speak to me or fly away. So I started walking ahead again.

The crow right in front of me spread its wings just a little. "Haa! Now
he's afraid and is going to fly!" Or so I thought. Instead, it just hopped up and
round-about-faced itself.

Stupid! If this had happened on the ground, I wouldn't have let it get
away with such impudence. Unfortunately, however, just plain walking on a
fence is difficult enough—chasing birds would be almost impossible. Still, I
didn't feel like waiting until the three crows decided to take flight. In the first
place, my legs wouldn't have lasted much longer. The three creatures in front of

me, however, had wings so they are used to perching on such places and can stay put as long as they want.

As this was my fourth trip around the fence I felt pretty nearly all in. I was doing something similar to tightrope walking besides exercising. It was difficult to stay on the fence even with nothing hindering me, so having these three black-cloaked feathered idiots come to obstruct my path was too much. I was afraid I'd have to quit exercising and get down from the fence.

To avoid trouble, I wondered if it might be better to simply give up. The enemy had me outnumbered and, moreover, they do not come here often. The beak of a crow is rather pointed so these birds seemed as if they had been sent by Tengu, the goblin with a long nose. They would naturally be dangerous in a fight.

Retreat was the wisest action to take. To start a fight and then accidentally fall off would be terribly embarrassing. While I was pondering on what I should do, the one nearest me burst out: "Aho!"* The next one imitated the first, repeating, "Aho!" The other crow even took the trouble to shriek two times: "Aho, aho!"

Even a gentle cat such as I could not stand this! To be insulted by these crows in my own yard was unforgivable and it affected my very honor. You might say that this couldn't hurt me since I don't have any other name in the first place. But my honor and dignity were involved. Now I would never retreat!

When my master talks about "a flock of crows," he is referring to "a disorderly crowd" or "mere rabble," so I decided these three birds might be less dangerous than I had thought. Determined to protect my good name, I commenced walking slowly forward. It seemed as if the crows were talking among themselves because they didn't even glance at me. It was extremely irritating. If the fence had only been five or six inches wider, I'd have been able to give them a good fight. Unfortunately, however, I could only creep along at a slow pace no matter how angry I was. When I was about five or six inches from them, all the crows suddenly flapped their wings and flew up one or two feet in the air, as if by previous arrangement.

The force of the wind from their wings suddenly caught me in the face and a moment later I lost my foothold and fell to the ground. Looking up from the foot of the fence, I saw the three crows still on their perch looking down at me with their beaks in a neat row.

---

*Aho, the cry of a crow, means "fool" in Japanese.

The brutes! I glared at them but it did not have any effect. I bristled my back and snarled, but that didn't work either. Just as symbolical poems are not understood by laymen, neither were my gestures of anger understood by the crows—they showed no reaction.

Well, perhaps it was my own fault. I had been thinking of them as cats but that was wrong. If they had been cats, the crows would have naturally understood—but they were only crows. It was like a businessman trying to impress my master, Mr. Kushami, or like Shogun Yoritomo presenting Bonze Saigyo with a silver cat. It was also like crows letting their droppings fall on the statue of Takamori Saigo. I at last realized that it was to my disadvantage to persist so without more ado, I retreated to the veranda.

It was almost suppertime. Exercise is good but it shouldn't be over- done. I now felt weak and anxious to rest. Besides, my encounter with the crows took place in early autumn and, as I had been in the sun for a long time, my fur coat had absorbed too much heat from the westbound sun. It was un- bearably hot. I kept wishing that the sweat that came out of my pores would run, but no! It only stuck to the roots of my fur like grease. My back felt itchy. This itchiness is quite different from the irritation I have when fleas are crawl- ing around. I can bite at the parts that can be reached with my mouth and I can scratch the places I can reach with my paws, but when the center of my spine becomes itchy, it is beyond the limits of my power to do much about it myself. When it becomes unbearable, I seek out a human and furiously rub myself against him, or I go to a pine tree and give myself a good rubdown; if I don't find relief, I feel uncomfortable and cannot sleep.

Humans are fools. When I purr—now wait, this is the expression hu- mans use. I prefer to say that they are being purred at. In any case, humans are such fools that when they are purred at by me, they mistakenly think that I love them dearly and they do whatever I want them to do. At times, they stroke my head.

But last summer, those little pests called fleas began to inhabit me. They multiplied in my fur so much that when I went close to a human, I was generally grabbed by the neck and flung away. I was avoided only because of these fleas, so little that they can hardly be seen. By this, it would not be alto- gether wrong to say that the sentiments of humans are only skin deep and tend to change abruptly according to the circumstances. Though there were just a measly one or two thousand of these fleas on my back, it was amazing how cal- culating humans acted. The first article in the law of love as practiced by them is: love others only when it brings personal benefit. . . .

# The Cat That Went to Trinity

BY ROBERTSON DAVIES

T HE CAT THAT WENT to Trinity" appears in a book subtitled *A Collection of Ghost Stories,* but you'd have to be pretty timid to be frightened by it. Call it a tall tale instead. Robertson Davies (1913–1995) was regarded by many as the leading Canadian novelist of his time, responsible for dozens of works of fiction as well as many essays, plays, and short stories. For 18 years he was also the first master of Massey College, a graduate college of the University of Toronto, which explains the setting of this story and the author's expressions of annoyance with rival Trinity. In a preface, Davies explains that Mary Shelley's *Frankenstein* was the first ghost story he read, at age 10, and it terrified him "unforgettably and gloriously." No such claims could—or should—be made for this story, but it is still great fun.

★　★　★　★　★

EVERY AUTUMN when I meet my new classes, I look them over to see if there are any pretty girls in them. This is not a custom peculiar to me: all professors do it: I also count the number of young men who are wearing Chairman Mao coats, or horseshoe moustaches. A pretty girl is something on which I can rest my eyes with pleasure while another student is reading a carefully researched but uninspiring paper.

This year, in my seminar on the Gothic Novel, there was an exceptionally pretty girl, whose name was Elizabeth Lavenza. I thought it a coincidence that this should also be the name of the heroine of one of the novels we were about to study—no less a work than Mary Shelley's celebrated romance *Franken-stein*. When I mentioned it to her she brushed it aside as of no significance.

"I was born in Geneva," said she, "where lots of people are called Lavenza."

Nevertheless, it lingered in my mind, and I mentioned it to one of my colleagues, who is a celebrated literary critic.

"You have coincidence on the brain," he said. "Ever since you wrote that book—*Fourth Dimension* or whatever it was called—you've talked about nothing else. Forget it."

I tried, but I couldn't forget it. It troubled me even more after I had met the new group of Junior Fellows in this College, for one of them was young Einstein, who was studying Medical Biophysics. He was a brilliant young man, who came to us with glowing recommendations; some mention was made of a great-uncle of his, an Albert Einstein, whose name meant nothing to me, though it appeared to have special significance in the scientific world. It was young Mr. Einstein's given names that roused an echo in my consciousness, for he was called Victor Frank.

For those among you who have not been reading Gothic Novels lately, I may explain that in Mrs. Shelley's book *Frankenstein, or The Modern Prometheus,* the hero's name is also Victor, and the girl he loved was Elizabeth Lavenza. This richness of coincidence might trouble a mind less disposed to such reflection than mine. I held my peace, for I had been cowed by what my friend the literary critic had said. But I was dogged by apprehension, for I know the disposition of the atmosphere of Massey College to constellate extraordinary elements. Thus, cowed and dogged, I kept my eyes open for what might happen.

It was no more than a matter of days when Fate added another figure to this coincidental pattern, and Fate's instrument was none other than my wife. It is our custom to entertain the men of the College to dinner, in small groups, and my wife invites a few girls to each of these occasions to lighten what might otherwise be a too exclusively academic atmosphere. The night that Frank Einstein appeared in our drawing-room he maintained his usual re-served—not to say morose—demeanour until Elizabeth Lavenza entered the room. Their meeting was, in one sense, a melodramatic cliché. But we must re-member that things become clichés because they are of frequent occurrence, and powerful impact. Everything fell out as a thoroughly bad writer might de-scribe it. Their eyes met across the room. His glance was electric; hers ecstatic. The rest of the company seemed to part before them as he moved to her side. He never left it all evening. She had eyes for no other. From time to time his eyes rose in ardour, while hers fell in modest transport. This rising and falling of eyes was so portentously and swooningly apparent that one or two of our se-nior guests felt positively unwell, as though aboard ship. My heart sank. My wife's on the contrary, was uplifted. As I passed her during the serving of the meal I hissed, "This is Fate." "There is no armour against Fate," she hissed in re-turn. It is a combination of words not easily hissed, but she hissed it.

We had an unusually fine Autumn, as you will recall, and there was hardly a day that I did not see Frank and Elizabeth sitting on one of the benches in the quad, sometimes talking, but usually looking deep into each other's eyes, their foreheads touching. They did it so much that they both be-came slightly cross-eyed, and my dismay mounted. I determined if humanly possible to avert some disastrous outcome (for I assure you that my intuition and my knowledge of the curious atmosphere of this College both oppressed me with boding) and I did all that lay in my power. I heaped work on Eliza-beth Lavenza; I demanded the ultimate from her in reading of the Gothic novel, both as a means of keeping her from Frank, and straightening her vision.

Alas, how puny are our best efforts to avert a foreordained event! One day I saw Frank in the quad, sitting on the bench alone, reading a book. Pre-tending nonchalance, I sat beside him. "And what are you reading, Mr. Ein-stein?" I said in honeyed tones.

Taciturn as always, he held out the book for me to see. It was *Franken-stein*. "Liz said I ought to read it," he said.

"And what do you make of it?" said I, for I am always interested in the puny efforts of art to penetrate the thoroughly scientific mind. His answer as-tonished me.

"Not bad at all," said he. "The Medical Biophysics aspects of the plot is very old-fashioned, of course. I mean when the hero makes that synthetic human being out of scraps from slaughter-houses. We could do better than that now. A lot better," he added, and I thought he seemed to be brooding on nameless possibilities. I decided to change the line of our conversation. I began to talk about the College, and some of the successes and failures we had met with in the past.

Among the failures I mentioned our inability to keep a College Cat. In the ten years of our existence we have had several cats here, but not one of them has remained with us. They all run away, and there is strong evidence that they all go to Trinity. I thought at one time that they must be Anglican cats, and they objected to our oecumenical chapel. I went to the length of getting a Persian cat, raised in the Zoroastrian faith, but it only lasted two days. There is a fine Persian rug in Trinity Chapel. Our most recent cat had been christened Episcopuss, in the hope that this thoroughly Anglican title would content it; furthermore, the Lionel Massey Fund provided money to treat the cat to a surgical operation which is generally thought to lift a cat's mind above purely sectarian considerations. But it, too, left us for Trinity. Rationalists in the College suggested that Trinity has more, and richer, garbage than we have, but I still believe our cats acted on religious impulse.

As I spoke of these things Frank Einstein became more animated than I had ever known him. "I get it," he said; "you want a cat that has been specifically programmed for Massey. An oecumenical cat, highly intelligent so that it prefers graduates to undergraduates, and incapable of making messes in the Round Room. With a few hours of computer time it oughtn't to be too difficult."

I looked into his eyes—though from a greater distance than was usual to Elizabeth Lavenza—and what I saw there caused a familiar shudder to convulse my entire being. It is the shudder I feel when I know, for a certainty, that Massey College is about to be the scene of yet another macabre event.

Nevertheless, in the pressure of examinations and lectures, I forgot my uneasiness, and might perhaps have dismissed the matter from my mind if two further inter-related circumstances—I dare not use the word coincidence in this case—had not aroused my fears again. One autumn morning, reading *The Globe and Mail,* my eye was caught by an item, almost lost at the bottom of a column, which bore the heading "Outrage at Pound"; it appeared that two masked bandits, a man and a woman, had held up the keeper of the pound at gunpoint, while seizing no less than twelve stray cats. Later that same day I saw Frank and Elizabeth coming through the College gate, carrying a large and heavy sack. From the sack dripped a substance which I recognized, with horror, as blood. I picked up a little of it on the tip of my finger; a hasty corpuscle count confirmed my suspicion that the blood was not human.

Night after night in the weeks that followed, I crept down to my study to look across the quad and see if a light was burning in Frank Einstein's room. Invariably it was so. And one morning, when I had wakened early and was standing on my balcony, apostrophizing the dawn, Elizabeth Lavenza stole past me from the College's main gate, her face marked, not by those lineaments of slaked desire so common among our visitors at such an hour, but by the pallor and fatigue of one well-nigh exhausted by intellectual work of the most demanding sort.

The following night I awoke from sleep at around two o'clock with a terrifying apprehension that something was happening in the College which I should investigate. Shouts, the sound of loud music, the riot of late revellers—these things do not particularly disturb me, but there is a quality of deep silence which I know to be the accompaniment of evil. Wearily and reluctantly I rose, wrapped myself in a heavy dressing-gown and made my way into the quadrangle and there—yes, it was as I had feared—the eerie gleam from Frank Einstein's room was the only light to guide me. For there was a thick fog hanging over the University, and even the cruel light through the arrow-slits of the Robarts Library, and the faery radiance from OISE were hidden.

Up to his room I climbed, and tapped on the door. It had not been locked, and my light knock caused it to swing open and there—never can I forget my shock and revulsion at what I saw!—there were Frank and Elizabeth crouched over a table upon which lay an ensanguined form. I burst upon them.

"What bloody feast is this?" I shouted. "Monsters, fiends, cannibals, what do I behold?"

"Shhh," said Elizabeth; "Frank's busy."

"I'm making your cat," said Frank.

"Cat," I shrieked, almost beside myself; "that is no cat. It's as big as a donkey. What cat are you talking about?"

"The Massey College cat," said Frank. "And it is going to be the greatest cat you have ever seen."

I shall not trouble you with a detailed report of the conversation that followed. What emerged was this: Frank, beneath the uncommunicative exterior of a scientist, had a kindly heart, and he had been touched by the unlucky history of Massey College and its cats. "What you said was," said he to me, "that the College never seemed to get the right cat. To you, with your simple, emotional, literary approach to the problem, this was an insuperable difficulty: to my finely-organized biophysical sensibility, it was simply a matter of discovering what kind of cat was wanted, and producing it. Not by the outmoded method of selective breeding, but by the direct creation of the Ideal College Cat, or ICC as I came to think of it. Do you remember that when you talked to me about it I was reading that crazy book Liz was studying with you, about the fellow who made a man? Do you remember what he said? "Whence did the principle of life proceed? It was a bold question, and one which has ever been considered as a mystery; yet with how many things are we upon the brink of becoming acquainted, if cowardice or carelessness did not restrain our enquiries." That was written in 1818. Since then the principle of life has become quite well known, but most scientists are afraid to work on the knowledge they have. You remember that the fellow in the book decided to make a man, but he found that work too fiddly if he made a man of ordinary size, so he decided to make a giant. Me too. A cat of ordinary size is a nuisance, so I decided to multiply the dimensions by twelve. And like the fellow in the book I got my materials and went to work. Here is your cat, about three-quarters finished."

The fatal weakness, the tragic flaw in my character is foolish good-nature, and that, combined with an uninformed but lively scientific curiosity led me into what was, I now perceive, a terrible mistake. I was so interested in what Frank was doing that I allowed him to go ahead, and instead of sleeping at nights I crept up to his room, where Frank and Elizabeth allowed me, after I had given my promise not to interfere or touch anything, to sit in a corner and watch them. Those weeks were perhaps the most intensely lived that I have ever known. Beneath my eyes the ICC grew and took form. By day the carcass was kept in the freezer at Rochdale, where Elizabeth had a room; each night Frank warmed it up and set to work.

The ICC had many novel features which distinguished it from the ordinary domestic cat. Not only was it as big as twelve ordinary cats; it had twelve times the musculature. Frank said proudly that when it was finished it would be able to jump right over the College buildings. Another of its beauties was that it possessed a novel means of elimination. The trouble with all cats is that they seem to be housebroken, but in moments of stress or laziness they relapse into an intolerable bohemianism which creates problems for the cleaning staff. In a twelve-power cat this could be a serious defect. But Frank's cat was made with a small shovel on the end of its tail with which it could, once a week, remove its own ashes and deposit them behind the College in the parking-space occupied by *The Varsity,* where, it was assumed, they would never be noticed. I must hasten to add that the cat was made to sustain itself on a diet of waste-paper, of which we have plenty, and that what it produced in the manner I have described was not unlike confetti.

But the special beauty of the ICC was that it could talk. This, in the minds of Frank and Elizabeth, was its great feature as a College pet. Instead of mewing monotonously when stroked, it would be able to enter into conversation with the College men, and as we pride ourselves on being a community of scholars, it was to be provided with a class of conversation, and a vocabulary, infinitely superior to that of, for instance, a parrot.

This was Elizabeth's special care, and because she was by this time deep in my course on the Gothic Novel she decided, as a compliment to me, to so program the cat that it would speak in the language appropriate to that *genre* of literature. I was not so confident about this refinement as were Frank and Elizabeth, for I knew more about Gothic Novels than they, and have sometimes admitted to myself that they can be wordy. But as I have told you, I was a party to this great adventure only in the character of a spectator, and I was not to interfere. So I held my peace, hoping that the cat would, in the fulness of time, do the same.

At last the great night came, when the cat was to be invested with life. I sat in my corner, my eyes fixed upon the form which Frank was gradually melting out with Elizabeth's electric hair-dryer. It was a sight to strike awe into the boldest heart.

I never dared to make my doubts about the great experiment known to Frank and Elizabeth, but I may tell you that my misgivings were many and acute. I am a creature of my time in that I fully understand that persons of merely aesthetic bias and training, like myself, should be silent in the presence of men of science, who know best about everything. But it was plain to me that the ICC was hideous. Not only was it the size of twelve cats, but the skins of twelve cats had been made to serve as its outer envelope. Four of these cats had been black, four were white, and four were of a marmalade colour. Frank, who liked things to be orderly, had arranged them so that the cat was piebald in mathematically exact squares. Because no ordinary cat's eyes would fit into the huge skull the eyes of a goat had been obtained—I dared not ask how—and as everyone knows, a goat's eyes are flat and have an uncanny oblong pupil. The teeth had been secured at a bargain rate from a denturist, and as I looked at them I knew why dentists say that these people must be kept in check. The tail, with the shovel at the end of it, was disagreeably naked. Its whiskers were like knitting needles. Indeed, the whole appearance of the cat was monstrous and diabolical. In the most exact sense of the words, it was the damnedest thing you ever saw. But Frank had a mind above appearances and to Elizabeth, so beautiful herself, whatever Frank did was right.

The moment had arrived when this marvel of science was to be set going. I know that Frank was entirely scientific, but to my old-fashioned eye he looked like an alchemist as, with his dressing-gown floating around him, he began to read formulae out of a notebook, and Elizabeth worked switches and levers at his command. Suddenly there was a flash, of lightning it seemed to me, and I knew that we had launched the ICC upon its great adventure.

"Come here and look," said Frank. I crept forward, half-afraid yet half-elated that I should be witness to such a triumph of medical biophysics. I leaned over the frightful creature, restraining my revulsion. Slowly, dreamily, the goat's eyes opened and focussed upon me.

"My Creator!" screamed the cat in a very loud voice, that agreed perfectly with the hideousness of its outward person. "A thousand, thousand blessings be upon Thee. Hallowed be Thy name! Thy kingdom come! O rapture, rapture thus to behold the golden dawn!" With which words the cat leapt upon an electric lamp and ate the bulb.

To say that I recoiled is to trifle with words. I leapt backward into a chair and cringed against the wall. The cat pursued me, shrieking Gothic praise and endearment. It put out its monstrous tongue and licked my hand. Imagine, if you can, the tongue of a cat which is twelve cats rolled into one. It was weeks before the skin-graft made necessary by this single caress was completed. But I am ahead of my story.

"No, no," I cried; "my dear animal, listen to reason. I am not your Creator. Not in the least. You owe the precious gift of life to my young friend here."

I waved my bleeding hand toward Frank. In their rapture he and Elizabeth were locked in a close embrace. That did it. Horrid, fiendish jealousy swept through the cat's whole being. All its twelve coats stood on end, the goat's eyes glared with fury, and its shovel tail lashed like that of a tiger. It sprang at Elizabeth, and with a single stroke of its powerful forepaws flung her to the ground.

I am proud to think that in that terrible moment I remembered what to do. I have always loved circuses, and I know that no trainer of tigers ever approaches his beasts without a chair in his hand. I seized up a chair and, in the approved manner drove the monstrous creature into a corner. But what I said was not in tune with my action, or the high drama of the moment. I admit it frankly; my words were inadequate.

"You mustn't harm Miss Lavenza," I said, primly; "she is Mr. Einstein's fiancée."

But Frank's words—or rather his single word—were even more inadequate than my own. "Scat!" he shouted, kneeling by the bleeding form of his fainting beloved.

Elizabeth was to blame for programming that cat with a vocabulary culled from the Gothic Novel. "Oh, Frankenstein," it yowled, in that tremendous voice, "be not equitable to every other and trample upon me alone, to whom thy justice and even thy clemency and affection is most due. Remember that I am thy creature; I ought to be thy Adam; dub me not rather the fallen angel, whom thou drivest hence only because I love—nay reverence thee. Jealousy of thy love makes me a fiend. Make me happy, and I shall once more be virtuous."

There is something about that kind of talk that influences everybody that hears it. I was astonished to hear Frank—who was generally contented with the utilitarian vocabulary of the scientific man—say—"Begone! I will not hear you. There can be no community between thee and me; we are enemies. Cursed be the day, abhorred devil, in which you first saw the light! You have left me no power to consider whether I am just to you or not. Begone! Relieve me of the sight of your detested form!"

Elizabeth was not the most gifted of my students, and the cat's next words lacked something of the true Gothic rhetoric. "You mean you don't love your own dear little Pussikins best," it whined. But Frank was true to the Gothic vein. "This lady is the mistress of my affections, and I acknowledge no Pussikins before her," he cried.

The cat was suddenly a picture of desolation, of rejection, of love denied. Its vocabulary moved back into high gear. "Thus I relieve thee, my creator. Thus I take from thee a sight which you abhor. Farewell!" And with one gigantic bound it leapt through the window into the quadrangle, and I heard the thunderous sound as the College gate was torn from its hinges.

I know where it went, and I felt deeply sorry for Trinity.

# The Afflictions of an English Cat

BY HONORÉ DE BALZAC

M ANY CAT STORIES are not really about cats, but about people, and this story is a case in point. Honoré de Balzac (1799–1850), a writer of wonderful fluency and imagination, has here chosen the person of Miss Beauty, a snow-white English cat of exceptional charm, to launch a splendid tirade against the hypocrisy, stuffiness, intolerance, gloominess, and general all-round unattractiveness of the inhabitants of Britain—at least from a French point of view. Poor Beauty is the victim, in spite (or to some degree because) of the efforts of a gallant young French cat named Brisquet, and ends up charged with criminal conversation. Balzac's main aim may be satire; however, his sly humor and story-telling genius make this a classic cat story, too.

★　★　★　★　★

WHEN THE REPORT of your first meeting arrived in London, O! French Animals, it caused the hearts of the friends of Animal Reform to beat faster. In my own humble experience, I have so many proofs of the superiority of Beasts over Man that in my character of an English Cat I see the occasion, long awaited, of publishing the story of my life, in order to show how my poor soul has been tortured by the hypocritical laws of England. On two occasions, already, some Mice, whom I have made a vow to respect since the bill passed by your august parliament, have taken me to Colburn's, where, observing old ladies, spinsters of uncertain years, and even young married women, correcting proofs, I have asked myself why, having claws, I should not make use of them in a similar manner. One never knows what women think, especially the women who write, while a Cat, victim of English perfidy, is interested to say more than she thinks, and her profuseness may serve to compensate for what these ladies do not say. I am ambitious to be the Mrs. Inchbald of Cats and I beg you to have consideration for my noble efforts, O! French Cats, among whom has risen the noblest house of our race, that of Puss in Boots, eternal type of Advertiser, whom so many men have imitated but to whom no one has erected a monument.

I was born at the home of a parson in Catshire, near the little town of Miaulbury. My mother's fecundity condemned nearly all her infants to a cruel fate, because, as you know, the cause of the maternal intemperance of English Cats, who threaten to populate the whole world, has not yet been decided. Toms and females each insist it is due to their own amiability and respective virtues. But impertinent observers have remarked that Cats in England are required to be so boringly proper that this is their only distraction. Others pretend that herein may lie concealed great questions of commerce and politics, having to do with the English rule of India, but these matters are not for my paws to write of and I leave them to the *Edinburgh-Review.* I was not drowned with the others on account of the whiteness of my robe. Also I was named Beauty. Alas! the parson, who had a wife and eleven daughters, was too poor to keep me. An elderly female noticed that I had an affection for the parson's Bible; I slept on it all the time, not because I was religious, but because it was the only clean spot I could find in the house. She believed, perhaps, that I belonged to the sect of sacred animals which had already furnished the she-ass of Balaam, and took me away with her. I was only two months old at this time. This old woman, who gave evenings for which she sent out cards inscribed *Tea and Bible,* tried to communicate to me the fatal science of the daughters of Eve. Her method, which consisted in delivering long lectures on personal dignity and on the obligations due the world, was a very successful one. In order to avoid these lectures one submitted to martyrdom.

One morning I, a poor little daughter of Nature, attracted by a bowl of cream, covered by a muffin, knocked the muffin off with my paw, and lapped the cream. Then in joy, and perhaps also on account of the weakness of my young organs, I delivered myself on the waxed floor to the imperious need which young Cats feel. Perceiving the proofs of what she called my intemperance and my faults of education, the old woman seized me and whipped me vigorously with a birchrod, protesting that she would make me a lady or she would abandon me.

"Permit me to give you a lesson in gentility," she said. "Understand, Miss Beauty, that English Cats veil natural acts, which are opposed to the laws of English respectability, in the most profound mystery, and banish all that is improper, applying to the creature, as you have heard the Reverend Doctor Simpson say, the laws made by God for the creation. Have you ever seen the Earth behave itself indecently? Learn to suffer a thousand deaths rather than reveal your desires; in this suppression consists the virtue of the saints. The greatest privilege of Cats is to depart with the grace that characterizes your actions, and let no one know where you are going to make your little toilets. Thus you expose yourself only when you are beautiful. Deceived by appearances, everybody will take you for an angel. In the future when such a desire seizes you, look out of the window, give the impression that you desire to go for a walk, then run to a copse or to the gutter."

As a simple Cat of good sense, I found much hypocrisy in this doctrine, but I was so young!

"And when I am in the gutter?" thought I, looking at the old woman.

"Once alone, and sure of not being seen by anybody, well, Beauty, you can sacrifice respectability with much more charm because you have been discreet in public. It is in the observance of this very precept that the perfection of the moral English shines the brightest: they occupy themselves exclusively with appearances, this world being, alas, only illusion and deception."

I admit that these disguises were revolting to all my animal good sense, but on account of the whipping, it seemed preferable to understand that exterior propriety was all that was demanded of an English Cat. From this moment I accustomed myself to conceal the titbits that I loved under the bed. Nobody ever saw me eat, or drink, or make my toilet. I was regarded as the pearl of Cats.

Now I had occasion to observe those stupid men who are called savants. Among the doctors and others who were friends of my mistress, there was this Simpson, a fool, a son of a rich landowner, who was waiting for a bequest, and who, to deserve it, explained all animal actions by religious theories. He saw me one evening lapping milk from a saucer and complimented the old woman on the manner in which I had been bred, seeing me lick first the edges of the saucer and gradually diminish the circle of fluid.

"See," he said, "how in saintly company all becomes perfection: Beauty understands eternity, because she describes the circle which is its emblem in lapping her milk."

Conscience obliges me to state that the aversion of Cats to wetting their fur was the only reason for my fashion of drinking, but we will always be badly understood by the savants who are much more preoccupied in showing their own wit, than in discovering ours.

When the ladies or the gentlemen lifted me to pass their hands over my snowy back to make the sparks fly from my hair, the old woman remarked with pride, "You can hold her without having any fear for your dress; she is admirably well-bred!" Everybody said I was an angel; I was loaded with delicacies, but I assure you that I was profoundly bored. I was well aware of the fact that a young female Cat of the neighbourhood had run away with a Tom. This word, Tom, caused my soul a suffering which nothing could alleviate, not even the compliments I received, or rather that my mistress lavished on herself.

"Beauty is entirely moral; she is a little angel," she said. "Although she is very beautiful she has the air of not knowing it. She never looks at anybody, which is the height of a fine aristocratic education. When she does look at anybody it is with that perfect indifference which we demand of our young girls, but which we obtain only with great difficulty. She never intrudes herself unless you call her; she never jumps on you with familiarity; nobody ever sees her eat, and certainly that monster of a Lord Byron would have adored her. Like a tried and true Englishwoman she loves tea, sits, gravely calm, while the Bible is being explained, and thinks badly of nobody, a fact which permits one to speak freely before her. She is simple, without affectation, and has no desire for jewels. Give her a ring and she will not keep it. Finally, she does not imitate the vulgarity of the hunter. She loves her home and remains there so perfectly tranquil that at times you would believe that she was a mechanical Cat made at Birmingham or Manchester, which is the *ne plus ultra* of the finest education."

What these men and old women call education is the custom of dissimulating natural manners, and when they have completely depraved us they say that we are well-bred. One evening my mistress begged one of the young ladies to sing. When this girl went to the piano and began to sing I recognized at once an Irish melody that I had heard in my youth, and I remembered that I also was a musician. So I merged my voice with hers, but I received some raps on the head while she received compliments. I was revolted by this sovereign injustice and ran away to the garret. Sacred love of country! What a delicious night! I at last knew what the roof was. I heard Toms sing hymns to their mates, and these adorable elegies made me feel ashamed of the hypocrisies my mistress had forced upon me. Soon some of the Cats observed me and appeared to take offence at my presence, when a Tom with shaggy hair, a magnificent beard, and a fine figure, came to look at me and said to the company, "It's only a child!" At these condescending words, I bounded about on the tiles, moving with that agility which distinguishes us; I fell on my paws in that flexible fashion which no other animal knows how to imitate in order to show that I was no child. But these calineries were a pure waste of time. "When will some one serenade me?" I asked myself. The aspect of these haughty Toms, their melodies, that the human voice could never hope to rival, had moved me profoundly, and were the cause of my inventing little lyrics that I sang on the stairs. But an event of tremendous importance was about to occur which tore me violently from this innocent life. I went to London with a niece of my mistress, a rich heiress who adored me, who kissed me, caressed me with a kind of madness, and who pleased me so much that I became attached to her, against all the habits of our race. We were never separated and I was able to observe the great world of London during the season. It was there that I studied the perversity of English manners, which have power even over the beasts, that I became acquainted with that cant which Byron cursed and of which I am the victim as well as he, but without having enjoyed my hours of leisure.

Arabella, my mistress, was a young person like many others in England; she was not sure whom she wanted for a husband. The absolute liberty that is permitted girls in choosing a husband drives them nearly crazy, especially when they recall that English custom does not sanction intimate conversation after marriage. I was far from dreaming that the London Cats had adopted this severity, that the English laws would be cruelly applied to me, and that I would be a victim of the court at the terrible Doctors' Commons. Arabella was charming to all the men she met, and every one of them believed that he was going to marry this beautiful girl, but when an affair threatened to terminate in wedlock, she would find some pretext for a break, conduct which did not seem very respectable to me. "Marry a bow-legged man! Never!" she said of one. "As to that little fellow he is snub-nosed." Men were all so much alike to me that I could not understand this uncertainty founded on purely physical differences.

Finally one day an old English Peer, seeing me, said to her:"You have a beautiful Cat. She resembles you. She is white, she is young, she should have a husband. Let me bring her a magnificent Angora that I have at home."

Three days later the Peer brought in the handsomest Tom of the Peerage. Puff, with a black coat, had the most magnificent eyes, green and yellow, but cold and proud. The long silky hair of his tail, remarkable for its yellow rings, swept the carpet. Perhaps he came from the imperial house of Austria, because, as you see, he wore the colours. His manners were those of a Cat who had seen the court and the great world. His severity, in the matter of carrying himself, was so great that he would not scratch his head were anybody present. Puff had travelled on the continent. To sum up, he was so remarkably handsome that he had been, it was said, caressed by the Queen of England. Simple and naïve as I was I leaped at his neck to engage him in play, but he refused under the pretext that we were being watched. I then perceived that this English Cat Peer owed this forced and fictitious gravity that in England is called respectability to age and to intemperance at table. His weight, that men admired, interfered with his movements. Such was the true reason for his not responding to my pleasant advances. Calm and cold he sat on his unnamable, agitating his beard, looking at me and at times closing his eyes. In the society world of English Cats, Puff was the richest kind of catch for a Cat born at a parson's. He had two valets in his service; he ate from Chinese porcelain, and he drank only black tea. He drove in a carriage in Hyde Park and had been to parliament.

My mistress kept him. Unknown to me, all the feline population of London learned that Miss Beauty from Catshire had married Puff, marked with the colours of Austria. During the night I heard a concert in the street. Accompanied by my lord, who, according to his taste, walked slowly, I descended. We found the Cats of the Peerage, who had come to congratulate me and to ask me to join their Ratophile Society. They explained that nothing was more common than running after Rats and Mice. The words, shocking, vulgar, were constantly on their lips. To conclude, they had formed, for the glory of the country, a Temperance Society. A few nights later my lord and I went on the roof of Almack's to hear a grey Cat speak on the subject. In his exhortation, which was constantly supported by cries of "Hear! Hear!" he proved that Saint Paul in writing about charity had the Cats of England in mind. It was then the special duty of the English, who could go from one end of the world to the other on their ships without fear of the sea, to spread the principles of the *morale ratophile*. As a matter of fact, English Cats were already preaching the doctrines of the Society, based on the hygienic discoveries of science. When Rats and Mice were dissected little distinction could be found between them and Cats; the oppression of one race by the other then was opposed to the Laws of Beasts, which are stronger even than the Laws of Men. "They are our brothers," he continued. And he painted such a vivid picture of the suffering of a Rat in the jaws of a Cat that I burst into tears.

Observing that I was deceived by this speech, Lord Puff confided to me that England expected to do an immense trade in Rats and Mice; that if the Cats would eat no more, Rats would be England's best product; that there was always a practical reason concealed behind English morality; and that the alliance between morality and trade was the only alliance on which England really counted.

Puff appeared to me to be too good a politician ever to make a satisfactory husband.

A country Cat made the observation that on the continent, especially at Paris, near the fortifications, Tom Cats were sacrificed daily by the Catholics. Somebody interrupted with the cry of "Question!" Added to these cruel executions was the frightful slander of passing the brave animals off for Rabbits, a lie and a barbarity which he attributed to an ignorance of the true Anglican religion which did not permit lying and cheating except in the government, foreign affairs, and the cabinet.

He was treated as a radical and a dreamer. "We are here in the interests of the Cats of England, not in those of continental Cats!" cried a fiery Tory Tom. Puff went to sleep. Just as the assembly was breaking up a young Cat from the French embassy, whose accent proclaimed his nationality, addressed me these delicious words:

"Dear Beauty, it will be an eternity before Nature forms another Cat as perfect as you. The cashmere of Persia and the Indies is like camel's hair when it is compared to your fine and brilliant silk. You exhale a perfume which is the concentrated essence of the felicity of the angels, an odour I have detected in the salon of the Prince de Talleyrand, which I left to come to this stupid meeting. The fire of your eyes illuminates the night! Your ears would be entirely perfect if they would listen to my supplications. There is not a rose in England as rose as the rose flesh which borders your little rose mouth. A fisherman would search in vain in the depths of Ormus for pearls of the quality of your teeth. Your dear face, fine and gracious, is the loveliest that England has produced. Near to your celestial robe the snow of the Alps would seem to be red. Ah! those coats which are only to be seen in your fogs! Softly and gracefully your paws bear your body which is the culmination of the miracles of creation, but your tail, the subtle interpreter of the beating of your heart, surpasses it. Yes! never was there such an exquisite curve, more correct roundness. No Cat ever moved more delicately. Come away from this old fool of a Puff, who sleeps like an English Peer in parliament, who besides is a scoundrel who has sold himself to the Whigs, and who, owing to a too long sojourn at Bengal, has lost everything that can please a Cat."

Then, without having the air of looking at him, I took in the appearance of this charming French Tom. He was a careless little rogue and not in any respect like an English Cat. His cavalier manner as well as his way of shaking his ear stamped him as a gay bachelor without a care. I avow that I was weary of the solemnity of English Cats, and of their purely practical propriety. Their respectability, especially, seemed ridiculous to me. The excessive naturalness of this badly groomed Cat surprised me in its violent contrast to all that I had seen in London. Besides my life was so strictly regulated, I knew so well what I had to count on for the rest of my days, that I welcomed the promise of the unexpected in the physiognomy of this French Cat. My whole life appeared insipid to me. I comprehended that I could live on the roofs with an amazing creature who came from that country where the inhabitants consoled themselves for the victories of the greatest English general by these words:

*Malbrouk s'en va-t-en guerre,*
*Mironton,* TON, TON, *MIRONTAINE!*

Nevertheless I awakened my lord, told him how late it was, and suggested that we ought to go in. I gave no sign of having listened to this declaration, and my apparent insensibility petrified Brisquet. He remained behind, more surprised than ever because he considered himself handsome. I learned later that it was an easy matter for him to seduce most Cats. I examined him through a corner of my eye: he ran away with little bounds, returned, leaping the width of the street, then jumped back again, like a French Cat in despair. A true Englishman would have been decent enough not to let me see how he felt.

Some days later my lord and I were stopping in the magnificent house of the old Peer; then I went in the carriage for a drive in Hyde Park. We ate only chicken bones, fishbones, cream, milk, and chocolate. However heating this diet might prove to others my so-called husband remained sober. He was respectable even in his treatment of me. Generally he slept from seven in the evening at the whist table on the knees of his Grace. On this account my soul received no satisfaction and I pined away. This condition was aggravated by a little affection of the intestines occasioned by pure herring oil (the Port Wine of English Cats), which Puff used, and which made me very ill. My mistress sent for a physician who had graduated at Edinburgh after having studied a long time in Paris. Having diagnosed my malady he promised my mistress that he would cure me the next day. He returned, as a matter of fact, and took an instrument of French manufacture out of his pocket. I felt a kind of fright on perceiving a barrel of white metal terminating in a slender tube. At the sight of this mechanism, which the doctor exhibited with satisfaction, Their Graces blushed, became irritable, and muttered several fine sentiments about the dignity of the English: for instance that the Catholics of old England were more distinguished for their opinions of this infamous instrument than for their opinions of the Bible. The Duke added that at Paris the French unblushingly made an exhibition of it in their national theatre in a comedy by Molière, but that in London a watchman would not dare pronounce its name.

"Give her some calomel."

"But Your Grace would kill her!" cried the doctor.

"The French can do as they like," replied His Grace. "I do not know, no more do you, what would happen if this degrading instrument were employed, but what I do know is that a true English physician should cure his patients only with the old English remedies."

This physician, who was beginning to make a big reputation, lost all his practice in the great world. Another doctor was called in, who asked me some improper questions about Puff, and who informed me that the real device of the English was: *Dieu et mon droit conjugal!*

One night I heard the voice of the French Cat in the street. Nobody could see us; I climbed up the chimney and, appearing on the housetop, cried, "In the raintrough!" This response gave him wings; he was at my side in the twinkling of an eye. Would you believe that this French Cat had the audacity to take advantage of my exclamation. He cried, "Come to my arms," daring to become familiar with me, a Cat of distinction, without knowing me better. I regarded him frigidly and, to give him a lesson, I told him that I belonged to the Temperance Society.

"I see, sir," I said to him, "by your accent and by the looseness of your conversation, that you, like all Catholic Cats, are inclined to laugh and make sport, believing that confession will purge you, but in England we have another standard of morality. We are always respectable, even in our pleasures."

This young Cat, struck by the majesty of English cant, listened to me with a kind of attention which made me hope I could convert him to Protestantism. He then told me in purple words that he would do anything I wished provided I would permit him to adore me. I looked at him without being able to reply because his very beautiful and splendid eyes sparkled like stars; they lighted the night. Made bold by my silence, he cried "Dear Minette!"

"What new indecency is this?" I demanded, being well aware that French Cats are very free in their references.

Brisquet assured me that on the continent everybody, even the King himself, said to his daughter, *Ma petite Minette,* to show his affection, that many of the prettiest and most aristocratic young wives called their husbands, *Mon petit chat,* even when they did not love them. If I wanted to please him I would call him, *Mon petit homme!* Then he raised his paws with infinite grace. Thoroughly frightened I ran away. Brisquet was so happy that he sang *Rule Britannia,* and the next day his dear voice hummed again in my ears.

"Ah! you also are in love, dear Beauty," my mistress said to me, observing me extended on the carpet, the paws flat, the body in soft abandon, bathing in the poetry of my memories.

I was astonished that a woman should show so much intelligence, and so, raising my dorsal spine, I began to rub up against her legs and to purr lovingly with the deepest chords of my contralto voice.

While my mistress was scratching my head and caressing me and while I was looking at her tenderly a scene occurred in Bond Street which had terrible results for me.

Puck, a nephew of Puff's, in line to succeed him and who, for the time being, lived in the barracks of the Life Guards, ran into my dear Brisquet. The sly Captain Puck complimented the *attaché* on his success with me, adding that I had resisted the most charming Toms in England. Brisquet, foolish, vain Frenchman that he was, responded that he would be happy to gain my attention, but that he had a horror of Cats who spoke to him of temperance, the Bible, etc.

"Oh!" said Puck, "she talks to you then?"

Dear French Brisquet thus became a victim of English diplomacy, but later he committed one of these impardonable faults which irritate all well-bred Cats in England. This little idiot was truly very inconsistent. Did he not bow to me in Hyde Park and try to talk with me familiarly as if we were well acquainted? I looked straight through him coldly and severely. The coachman seeing this Frenchman insult me slashed him with his whip. Brisquet was cut but not killed and he received the blow with such nonchalance, continuing to look at me, that I was absolutely fascinated. I loved him for the manner in which he took his punishment, seeing only me, feeling only the favour of my presence, conquering the natural inclination of Cats to flee at the slightest warning of hostility. He could not know that I came near dying, in spite of my apparent coldness. From that moment I made up my mind to elope. That evening, on the roof, I threw myself tremblingly into his arms.

"My dear," I asked him, "have you the capital necessary to pay damages to old Puff?"

"I have no other capital," replied the French Cat, laughing, "than the hairs of my moustache, my four paws, and this tail." Then he swept the gutter with a proud gesture.

"Not any capital," I cried, "but then you are only an adventurer, my dear!"

"I love adventures," he said to me tenderly. "In France it is the custom to fight a duel in the circumstances to which you allude. French Cats have recourse to their claws and not to their gold."

"Poor country," I said to him, "and why does it send beasts so denuded of capital to the foreign embassies?"

"That's simple enough," said Brisquet. "Our new government does not love money—at least it does not love its employees to have money. It only seeks intellectual capacity."

Dear Brisquet answered me so lightly that I began to fear he was conceited.

"Love without money is nonsense," I said. "While you were seeking food you would not occupy yourself with me, my dear."

By way of response this charming Frenchman assured me that he was a direct descendant of Puss in Boots. Besides he had ninety-nine ways of borrowing money and we would have, he said, only a single way of spending it. To conclude, he knew music and could give lessons. In fact, he sang to me, in poignant tones, a national romance of his country, *Au clair de la lune*. . . .

At this inopportune moment, when seduced by his reasoning, I had promised dear Brisquet to run away with him as soon as he could keep a wife comfortably, Puck appeared, followed by several other Cats.

"I am lost!" I cried.

The very next day, indeed, the bench of Doctors' Commons was occupied by a *procès-verbal* in criminal conversation. Puff was deaf; his nephews took advantage of his weakness. Questioned by them, Puff said that at night I had flattered him by calling him, *Mon petit homme!* This was one of the most terrible things against me, because I could not explain where I had learned these words of love. The judge, without knowing it, was prejudiced against me, and I noted that he was in his second childhood. His lordship never suspected the low intrigues of which I was the victim. Many little Cats, who should have defended me against public opinion, swore that Puff was always asking for his angel, the joy of his eyes, his sweet Beauty! My own mother, come to London, refused to see me or to speak to me, saying that an English Cat should always be above suspicion, and that I had embittered her old age. Finally the servants testified against me. I then saw perfectly clearly how everybody lost his head in England. When it is a matter of a criminal conversation, all sentiment is dead; a mother is no longer a mother, a nurse wants to take back her milk, and all the Cats howl in the streets. But the most infamous thing of all was that my old attorney who, in his time, would believe in the innocence of the Queen of England, to whom I had confessed everything to the last detail, who had assured me that there was no reason to whip a Cat, and to whom, to prove my innocence, I avowed that I did not even know the meaning of the words, "criminal conversation" (he told me that the crime was so called precisely because one spoke so little while committing it), this attorney, bribed by Captain Puck, defended me so badly that my case appeared to be lost. Under these circumstances I went on the stand myself.

"My Lords," I said, "I am an English Cat and I am innocent. What would be said of the justice of old England if . . ."

Hardly had I pronounced these words than I was interrupted by a murmur of voices, so strongly had the public been influenced by the *Cat-Chronicle* and by Puck's friends.

"She questions the justice of old England which has created the jury!" cried some one.

"She wishes to explain to you, My Lords," cried my adversary's abominable lawyer, "that she went on the rooftop with a French Cat in order to convert him to the Anglican faith, when, as a matter of fact, she went there to learn how to say, *Mon petit homme,* in French, to her husband, to listen to the abominable principles of papism, and to learn to disregard the laws and customs of old England!"

Such piffle always drives an English audience wild. Therefore the words of Puck's attorney were received with tumultuous applause. I was condemned at the age of twenty-six months, when I could prove that I still was ignorant of the very meaning of the word, Tom. But from all this I gathered that it was on account of such practices that Albion was called Old England.

I fell into a deep miscathropy which was caused less by my divorce than by the death of my dear Brisquet, whom Puck had had killed by a mob, fearing his vengeance. Also nothing made me more furious than to hear the loyalty of English Cats spoken of.

You see, O! French Animals, that in familiarizing ourselves with men, we borrow from them all their vices and bad institutions. Let us return to the wild life where we obey only our instincts, and where we do not find customs in conflict with the sacred wishes of Nature. At this moment I am writing a treatise on the abuse of the working classes of animals, in order to get them to pledge themselves to refrain from turning spits, to refuse to allow themselves to be harnessed to carriages, in order, to sum up, to teach them the means of protecting themselves against the oppression of the grand aristocracy. Although we are celebrated for our scribbling I believe that Miss Martineau would not repudiate me. You know that on the continent literature has become the haven of all Cats who protest against the immoral monopoly of marriage, who resist the tyranny of institutions, and who desire to encourage natural laws. I have omitted to tell you that, although Brisquet's body was slashed with a wound in the back, the coroner, by an infamous hypocrisy, declared that he had poisoned himself with arsenic, as if so gay, so light-headed a Cat could have reflected long enough on the subject of life to conceive so serious an idea, and as if a Cat whom I loved could have the least desire to quit this existence! But with Marsh's apparatus spots have been found on a plate.

# Quixote and the Cats

From *The Adventures of Don Quixote*

BY MIGUEL DE CERVANTES SAAVEDRA

HAVING PREVIOUSLY ATTACKED a windmill under the impression that it was a giant, in this famous passage Don Quixote, equally deluded and confused, takes on a large quantity of cats under the impression that they are evil sorcerers. Quixote's madness is the basic joke in *The Adventures of Don Quixote;* the amazing thing is that Miguel de Cervantes Saavedra (1547–1616) creates a satiric epic out of it, keeping the humor and adding to it great warmth and humanity.

So far as this episode is concerned, there is only one question: how did they ever manage to get all those cats into one bag?

★　★　★　★　★

DON QUIXOTE had come to this point in his song, which was heard by the Duke and Duchess, Altisidora and almost all the people in the castle, when suddenly, from a balcony which directly overhung his window, a rope was let down with more than a hundred sheep-bells fastened to it and, immediately afterwards, a great sack, full of cats with smaller bells tied to their tails, was flung after it. The jingling of the bells and the squawking of the cats made such a din that even the Duke and Duchess, who had contrived the joke, were aghast, while Don Quixote was dumbfounded with fear. Now two or three of the cats, as fate would have it, got through the window, and as they rushed about the room it was as if a legion of devils had broken in. They knocked over and put out the candles burning there, and ran about trying to find a way of escape. And all the while the rope with the great sheep-bells on it continued to rise and fall, and the majority of the people of the castle, not being in the secret, remained speechless with astonishment. Finally Don Quixote rose to his feet and, drawing his sword, began to make stabs through the window, crying loudly:

"Avaunt, evil enchanters! Avaunt, crew of sorcerers! For I am Don Quixote de la Mancha, against whom your wicked plots are powerless and of no avail."

Then, turning round upon the cats, who were running about the room, he dealt them many blows. And all of them rushed to the window and jumped out, except one which, finding itself hard pressed by Don Quixote's sword-thrusts, jumped at his face and dug its claws and teeth into his nose, whereupon Don Quixote began to roar his very loudest in pain. Now when the Duke and Duchess heard him, realizing the probable cause, they ran in great haste to his room and, opening the door with the master-key, found the poor knight struggling with all his might to tear the cat from his face. They went in with lights, and when he saw the unequal struggle the Duke ran up to disengage them, although Don Quixote cried out:

"Let no one pull him off! Leave me to deal with this devil, this wizard, this enchanter, hand to hand. For I will teach him myself what it is to deal with Don Quixote de la Mancha."

But the cat snarled and held on, heedless of his threats. At last, however, the Duke pulled it off and threw it out of the window, Don Quixote coming off with a scratched face and not too whole a nose. But he was much annoyed at not being left to finish the battle he was fighting so stoutly against that perverse enchanter. Then they sent for Oil of Hypericum, and that same

Altisidora with her whitest of hands put bandages on all his wounds, saying to him in a soft voice, as she bound them up:

"All these misfortunes befall you, flinty-hearted knight, for your sin of hardness and obstinacy. May it please God that your squire Sancho shall forget to whip himself, so that this beloved Dulcinea of yours may never emerge from her enchantment, and you may never enjoy her nor come to the bridal bed with her, at least while I, who adore you, am alive."

To all this Don Quixote gave no word of reply, but heaved a deep sigh, and presently lay down on his bed, after thanking the Duke and Duchess for their kindness, not because he had been in any fear of that cattish and bellish rabble of enchanters, but because he realized their good intentions in coming to his rescue. The noble pair left him to rest and went away concerned at the unfortunate result of their joke, for they had not thought the adventure would have proved so tiresome and costly to Don Quixote. But it kept him confined to his room for five days.

# Midshipman, the Cat

## BY JOHN COLEMAN ADAMS

A SEAGOING CAT may not be a novelty, but a seagoing cat that swims? In this warm account of Midshipman, a cat that adopted a yacht, John Coleman Adams (1849–1922) tells the story of a truly exceptional specimen of the feline kind. Adams was a clergyman in New York, author of a number of more or less unreadable works of theology and piety, along with some nature studies and a few poems on religious subjects. Reading this delightful tale, one could wish he had stuck to cats.

★　★　★　★　★

THIS IS A TRUE STORY about a real cat who, for aught I know, is still alive and following the sea for a living. I hope to be excused if I use the pronouns "who" and "he" instead of "which" and "it," in speaking of this particular cat; because although I know very well that the grammars all tell us that "he" and "who" apply to persons, while "it" and "which" apply to things, yet this cat of mine always seemed to us who knew him to be so much like a human being that I find it unsatisfactory to speak of him in any other way. There are some animals of whom you prefer to say "he," just as there are persons whom you sometimes feel like calling "it."

The way we met this cat was after this fashion: It was back somewhere in the seventies, and a party of us were cruising east from Boston in the little schooner-yacht *Eyvor.* We had dropped into Marblehead for a day and a night, and some of the boys had gone ashore in the tender. As they landed on the wharf, they found a group of small boys running sticks into a woodpile, evidently on a hunt for something inside.

"What have you in there?" asked one of the yachtsmen.

"Nothin' but a cat," said the boys.

"Well, what are you doing to him?"

"Oh, pokin' him up! When he comes out we'll rock him," was the answer, in good Marblehead dialect.

"Well, don't do it anymore. What's the use of tormenting a poor cat? Why don't you take somebody of your size?"

The boys slowly moved off, a little ashamed and a little afraid of the big yachtsman who spoke; and when they were well out of sight the yachtsmen went on, too, and thought no more about the cat they had befriended. But when they had wandered about the tangled streets of the town for a little while, and paid the visits which all good yachtsmen pay, to the grocery and the post office and the apothecary's soda fountain, they returned to the wharf and found their boat. And behold, there in the stern sheets sat the little gray-and-white cat of the woodpile! He had crawled out of his retreat and made straight for the boat of his champions. He seemed in no wise disturbed or disposed to move when they jumped on board, nor did he show anything but pleasure when they stroked and patted him. But when one of the boys started to put him ashore, the plucky little fellow showed his claws; and no sooner was he set on his feet at the edge of the wharf than he turned about and jumped straight back into the boat.

"He wants to go yachting," said one of the party, whom we called "the Bos'n."

"Ye might as wal take the cat," said a grizzly old fisherman standing on the wharf. "He doesn't belong to anybody, and ef he stays here the boys'll worry him t'death."

"Let's take him aboard," said the yachtsmen. "It's good luck to have a cat on board ship."

Whether it was good luck to the ship or not, it was very clear that pussy saw it meant good luck to him, and curled himself down in the bottom of the boat, with a look that meant business. Evidently he had thought the matter all over and made up his mind that this was the sort of people he wanted to live with; and, being a Marblehead cat, it made no difference to him whether they lived afloat or ashore; he was going where they went, whether they wanted him or not. He had heard the conversation from his place in the woodpile, and had decided to show his gratitude by going to sea with these protectors of his. By casting in his lot with theirs he was paying them the highest compliment of which a cat is capable. It would have been the height of impoliteness not to recognize his distinguished appreciation. So he was allowed to remain in the boat, and was taken off to the yacht.

Upon his arrival there, a council was held, and it was unanimously decided that the cat should be received as a member of the crew; and as we were a company of amateur sailors, sailing our own boat, each man having his particular duties, it was decided that the cat should be appointed midshipman, and should be named after his position. So he was at once and ever after known as "Middy." Everybody took a great interest in him, and he took an impartial interest in everybody—though there were two people on board to whom he made himself particularly agreeable. One was the quiet, kindly professor, the captain of the *Eyvor;* the other was Charlie, our cook and only hired hand. Middy, you see, had a seaman's true instinct as to the official persons with whom it was his interest to stand well.

It was surprising to see how quickly Middy made himself at home. He acted as if he had always been at sea. He was never seasick, no matter how rough it was or how uncomfortable any of the rest of us were. He roamed wherever he wanted to, all over the boat. At mealtimes he came to the table with the rest, sat up on a valise, and lapped his milk and took what bits of food were given him, as if he had eaten that way all his life. When the sails were hoisted it was his especial joke to jump upon the main gaff and be hoisted with it; and once he stayed on his perch till the sail was at the masthead. One of us had to go aloft and bring him down. When we had come to anchor and everything was snug for the night, he would come on deck and scamper out on the main boom, and race from there to the bowsprit end as fast as he could gallop, then climb, monkey-fashion, halfway up the masts, and drop back to the deck or dive down into the cabin and run riot among the berths.

One day, as we were jogging along, under a pleasant southwest wind, and everybody was lounging and dozing after dinner, we heard the Bos'n call out, "Stop that, you fellows!" and a moment after, "I tell you, quit! Or I'll come up and make you!"

We opened our lazy eyes to see what was the matter, and there sat the Bos'n, down in the cabin, close to the companionway, the tassel of his knitted cap coming nearly up to the combings of the hatch; and on the deck outside sat Middy, digging his claws into the tempting yarn, and occasionally going deep enough to scratch the Bos'n's scalp.

When night came and we were all settled down in bed, it was Middy's almost invariable custom to go the rounds of all the berths, to see if we were properly tucked in, and to end his inspection by jumping into the captain's bed, treading himself a comfortable nest there among the blankets, and curling himself down to sleep. It was his own idea to select the captain's berth as the only proper place in which to turn in.

But the most interesting trait in Middy's character did not appear until he had been a week or so on board. Then he gave us a surprise. It was when we were lying in Camden Harbor. Everybody was going ashore to take a tramp among the hills, and Charlie, the cook, was coming too, to row the boat back to the yacht.

Middy discovered that he was somehow "getting left." Being a prompt and very decided cat, it did not take him long to make up his mind what to do. He ran to the low rail of the yacht, put his forepaws on it, and gave us a long, anxious look. Then as the boat was shoved off he raised his voice in a plaintive mew. We waved him a good-bye, chaffed him pleasantly, and told him to mind the anchor, and have dinner ready when we got back.

That was too much for his temper. As quick as a flash he had dived overboard, and was swimming like a water spaniel, after the dinghy!

That was the strangest thing we had ever seen in all our lives! We were quite used to elephants that could play at seesaw, and horses that could fire cannon, to learned pigs and to educated dogs; but a cat that of his own accord would take to the water like a full-blooded Newfoundland was a little beyond anything we had ever heard of. Of course the boat was stopped, and Middy was taken aboard drenched and shivering, but perfectly happy to be once more with the crew. He had been ignored and slighted; but he had insisted on his rights, and as soon as they were recognized he was quite contented.

Of course, after that we were quite prepared for anything that Middy might do. And yet he always managed to surprise us by his bold and independent behavior. Perhaps his most brilliant performance was a visit he paid a few days after his swim in Camden Harbor.

We were lying becalmed in a lull of the wind off the entrance to Southwest Harbor. Near us, perhaps a cable's-length away, lay another small yacht, a schooner hailing from Lynn. As we drifted along on the tide, we noticed that Middy was growing very restless; and presently we found him running along the rail and looking eagerly toward the other yacht. What did he see—or smell—over there which interested him? It could not be the dinner, for they were not then cooking. Did he recognize any of his old chums from Marblehead? Perhaps there were some cat friends of his on the other craft. Ah, that was it! There they were on the deck, playing and frisking together—two kittens! Middy had spied them, and was longing to take a nearer look. He ran up and down the deck, mewing and snuffing the air. He stood up on his favorite position when on lookout, with his forepaws on the rail. Then, before we realized what he was doing, he had plunged overboard again, and was making for the other boat as fast as he could swim! He had attracted the attention of her company, and no sooner did he come up alongside than they prepared to welcome him. A fender was lowered, and when Middy saw it he swam toward it, caught it with his forepaws, clambered along it to the gunwale, and in a twinkling was over the side and on the deck scraping acquaintance with the strange kittens.

How they received him I hardly know, for by that time our boat was alongside to claim the runaway. And we were quite of the mind of the skipper of the *Winnie L.,* who said, as he handed our bold midshipman over the side, "Well, that beats all *my* going a-fishing!"

Only a day or two later Middy was very disobedient when we were washing decks one morning. He trotted about in the wet till his feet were drenched, and then retired to dry them on the white spreads of the berths below. That was quite too much for the captain's patience. Middy was summoned aft, and, after a sound rating, was hustled into the dinghy which was moored astern, and shoved off to the full length of her painter. The punishment was a severe one for Middy, who could bear anything better than exile from his beloved shipmates. So of course he began to exercise his ingenious little brain to see how he could escape. Well under the overhang of the yacht he spied, just about four inches out of water, a little shoulder of the rudder. That was enough for him. He did not stop to think whether he would be any better off there. It was a part of the yacht, and that was home. So overboard he went, swam for the rudder, scrambled on to it, and began howling piteously to be taken on deck again; and, being a spoiled and much-indulged cat, he was soon rescued from his uncomfortable roosting place and restored to favor.

I suppose I shall tax your powers of belief if I tell you many more of Middy's doings. But truly he was a strange cat, and you may as well be patient, for you will not soon hear of his equal. The captain was much given to rifle practice, and used to love to go ashore and shoot at a mark. On one of his trips he allowed Middy to accompany him, for the simple reason, I suppose, that Middy decided to go, and got on board the dinghy when the captain did. Once ashore, the marksman selected a fine large rock as a rest for his rifle, and opened fire upon his target. At the first shot or two Middy seemed a little surprised, but showed no disposition to run away. After the first few rounds, however, he seemed to have made up his mind that since the captain was making all that racket it must be entirely right and proper, and nothing about which a cat need bother his head in the least. So, as if to show how entirely he confided in the captain's judgment and good intentions, that imperturbable cat calmly lay down, curled up, and went to sleep in the shade of the rock over which the captain's rifle was blazing and cracking about once in two minutes. If anybody was ever acquainted with a cooler or more self-possessed cat I should be pleased to hear the particulars.

I wish that this chronicle could be confined to nothing but our shipmate's feats of daring and nerve. But, unfortunately, he was not always blameless in his conduct. When he got hungry he was apt to forget his position as midshipman, and to behave just like any cat with an empty stomach. Or perhaps he may have done just what any hungry midshipman does under the circumstances; I do not quite know what a midshipman does under all circumstances and so I cannot say. But here is one of this cat midshipman's exploits. One afternoon, on our way home, we were working along with a head wind and sea toward Wood Island, a haven for many of the small yachts between Portland and the Shoals. The wind was light and we were a little late in making port. But as we were all agreed that it would be pleasanter to postpone our dinner till we were at anchor, the cook was told to keep things warm and wait till we were inside the port before he set the table. Now, his main dish that day was to be a fine piece of baked fish; and, unfortunately, it was nearly done when we gave orders to hold back the dinner. So he had closed the drafts of his little stove, left the door of the oven open, and turned into his bunk for a quiet doze—a thing which every good sailor does on all possible occasions; for a seafaring life is very uncertain in the matter of sleep, and one never quite knows when he will lose some, nor how much he will lose. So it is well to lay in a good stock of it whenever you can.

It seems that Middy was on watch, and when he saw Charlie fast asleep he undertook to secure a little early dinner for himself. He evidently reasoned with himself that it was very uncertain when we should have dinner and he'd better get his while he could. He quietly slipped down to the stove, walked coolly up to the oven, and began to help himself to baked haddock.

He must have missed his aim or made some mistake in his management of the business, and, by some lucky chance for the rest of us, waked the cook. For, the first we knew, Middy came flying up the cabin companionway, followed by a volley of shoes and spoons and pieces of coal, while we could hear Charlie, who was rather given to unseemly language when he was excited, using the strongest words in his dictionary about "that thief of a cat!"

"What's the matter?" we all shouted at once.

"Matter enough, sir!" growled Charlie. "That little cat's eaten up half the fish! It's a chance if you get any dinner tonight, sir."

You may be very sure that Middy got a sound wigging for that trick, but I am afraid the captain forgot to deprive him of his rations as he threatened. He was much too kindhearted.

The very next evening Middy startled us again by a most remarkable display of coolness and courage. After a weary thrash to windward all day, under a provokingly light breeze, we found ourselves under the lee of the little promontory at Cape Neddick, where we cast anchor for the night. Our supply of water had run very low, and so, just after sunset, two of the party rowed ashore in the tender to replenish our water keg, and by special permission Middy went with them.

It took some time to find a well, and by the time the jugs were filled it had grown quite dark. In launching the boat for the return to the yacht, by some ill luck a breaker caught her and threw her back upon the beach. There she capsized and spilled out the boys, together with their precious cargo. In the confusion of the moment, and the hurry of setting matters to rights, Middy was entirely forgotten, and when the boat again was launched, nobody thought to look for the cat. This time everything went well, and in a few minutes the yacht was sighted through the dusk. Then somebody happened to think of

Middy! He was nowhere to be seen. Neither man remembered anything about him after the capsize. There was consternation in the hearts of those unlucky wights. To lose Middy was almost like losing one of the crew.

But it was too late and too dark to go back and risk another landing on the beach. There was nothing to be done but to leave poor Middy to his fate, or at least to wait until morning before searching for him.

But just as the prow of the boat bumped against the fender on the yacht's quarter, out from under the stern sheets came a wet, bedraggled, shivering cat, who leaped on board the yacht and hurried below into the warm cabin. In that moist adventure in the surf, Middy had taken care of himself, rescued himself from a watery grave, got on board the boat as soon as she was ready, and sheltered himself in the warmest corner. All this he had done without the least outcry, and without asking any help whatever. His self-reliance and courage were extraordinary.

Well, the pleasant month of cruising drew to a close, and it became a question what should be done with Middy. We could not think of turning him adrift in the cold world, although we had no fears but that so bright and plucky a cat would make a living anywhere. But we wanted to watch over his fortunes, and perhaps take him on the next cruise with us when he should have become a more settled and dignified Thomas. Finally, it was decided that he should be boarded for the winter with an artist, Miss Susan H——, a friend of one of our party. She wanted a studio cat, and would be particularly pleased to receive so accomplished and traveled a character as Middy. So when the yacht was moored to the little wharf at Annisquam, where she always ended her cruises, and we were packed and ready for our journey to Boston, Middy was tucked into a basket and taken to the train. He bore the confinement with the same good sense which had marked all his life with us, though I think his feelings were hurt at the lack of confidence we showed in him. And, in truth, we were a little ashamed of it ourselves, and when once we were on the cars somebody suggested that he be released from his prison just to see how he would behave. We might have known he would do himself credit. For when he had looked over his surroundings, peeped above the back of the seat at the passengers, taken a good look at the conductor, and counted the rest of the party to see that none of us was missing, Middy snuggled down upon the seat, laid his head upon the captain's knee, and slept all the way to Boston.

That was the last time I ever saw Middy. He was taken to his new boarding place in Boylston Street, where he lived very pleasantly for a few months, and made many friends by his pleasing manners and unruffled temper. But I suppose he found it a little dull in Boston. He was not quite at home in his aesthetic surroundings. I have always believed he sighed for the freedom of a sailor's life. He loved to sit by the open window when the wind was east, and seemed to be dreaming of faraway scenes. One day he disappeared. No trace of him was ever found. A great many things may have happened to him. But I never could get rid of the feeling that he went down to the wharves and the ships and the sailors, trying to find his old friends, looking everywhere for the stanch little *Eyvor;* and, not finding her, I am convinced that he shipped on some East Indiaman and is now a sailor cat on the high seas.

# Total Loss

BY SYLVIA TOWNSEND WARNER

T HE ENGLISH WRITER Sylvia Townsend Warner (1893–1978) had an odd relationship with cats, often remarking on how much she disliked them at the same time as she, with her longtime companion Valentine Acland, was contentedly keeping generations of cats at their home in Dorset. Cats often appear in her stories, and she was clearly fascinated by the way humans, young and old, become emotionally involved with them. The involvement, moreover, usually has consequences. In "Total Loss," Warner beautifully shows how a cat—even a dying cat—can function as a means of enlightenment, forcing a breakthrough into honest feelings.

★　★　★　★　★

WHEN CHARLOTTE WOKE, it was raining. Rain hid the view of the downs and blurred the neat row of trees and the neat row of houses opposite which the trees had been planted to screen. This was the third wet morning since her birthday a week ago. There would be rain all through the holidays, just like last year. On her birthday, Charlotte was ten. "Now you are in double figures," said Professor Bayer. "And you will stay in them till you are a hundred years old. Think of that, my Lottchen." "Yes, think of that," said Mother. Charlotte could see that Mother did not really wish to think of it. She was being polite, because Professor Bayer was a very important person at the Research Station, so it was a real honour that he should like Father and come to the house to borrow *The New Statesman*.

Charlotte's cat Moodie was awake already. He lay on the chair in the corner, on top of her clothes, and was staring at her with a thirsty expression. She jumped out of bed, went to the kitchen, breaking into its early morning tidiness and seclusion, and came back with a saucer of milk. "Look, Moodie! Nice milk." He would not drink, though he still had that thirsty expression. "You silly old Moodles, you don't know what you want," she said, kneeling before the chair with the saucer in her hand. Moodie had come as a wedding present to Mother. His birthday was unknown, but he was certainly two years older than Charlotte. Ever since she could remember, there had been Moodie, and Moodie had been hers—to be slept on, talked to, hauled about, wheeled in a doll's perambulator, read aloud to, confided in, wept on, trodden on, loved and taken for granted. He stared at her, ignoring the milk, and forgetting the milk she stared back, fascinated as ever by the way the fur grew on his nose, the mysterious smooth conflict between two currents of growth. At last she put down the saucer, seized him in her arms and got back into bed. "We understand each other, don't we?" she said, curling his tail round his flank. "Don't we, Moodie?" He trod with his front paws, purring under his breath, and relaxed, his head on her breast. But at the smell of his bad teeth she turned her face away, pretending it was to look out of the window. "It's raining, Moodie. It's going to be another horrible wet day. You mustn't be a silly cat, sitting in the garden and getting wet through, like you did on Tuesday." He was still purring when she fell asleep, though when her mother came to wake her he had gone. Sure enough, when she looked for him after breakfast he was sitting hunched and motionless on the lawn, his grey fur silvered with moisture and fluffed out like a coat of eiderdown. She picked him up, and the bloom vanished; the eiderdown coat, suddenly dark and lank, clung to his bony haunches. "Mother, I'm going to put Moodie in the airing cupboard."

"Yes, do, my pet. That's the best plan! But hurry, because Mr and Mrs Flaxman will be here to fetch you at any moment. They've just rung up. They want you to spend the day with them."

"And see the horses?"

The cat in the child's arms broke into a purr, as though her thrill of pleasure communicated itself to him. Though of course it was really the warmth of the kitchen, thought Meg.

"Yes, the horses. And the bantams. And the lovely old toy theatre that belonged to Mrs Flaxman's grandmother. You'll love it. It's an absolutely story-book house."

"Shall I wear my new mac?"

"Yes. But Hurry, Charlotte. Put Moodie in the airing cupboard, and wash your hands. I'll be up in a moment to brush your hair."

She had made one false step. The Flaxmans lived twenty miles away, and if they had just rung up they could not be arriving immediately. Luckily Charlotte, though brought up to use her reason, was not a very deductive child; the discrepancy between the prompt arriving of the Flaxmans and the long drive back to Hood House was not likely to catch her attention. But perhaps a private word to Adela Flaxman—just to be on the safe side.

"Mother! Mother!"

At the threatening woe of the cry, Meg left everything and ran.

"Mother! There's a button off."

The Flaxmans arrived, both talking at once, and saying what a horrible day it was, and Oh, the wretched farmers, who would be a farmer? in loud gay voices. Mrs Flaxman was Mother's particular friend, but today Mother didn't seem to like her so much, and was laughing obligingly, just as she did with Professor Bayer. As Charlotte stood on the outskirts of this conversation she began to feel less sure of a happy successful day out. She would be treated like a child and probably given milk, instead of tea. Moodie hadn't drunk that milk. "Mother! Don't forget to feed Moodie."

"Charlotte! As if I would—" At the same moment Mr Flaxman said, "Come on, Charlotte! Come on, Adela! The car will catch cold if you don't hurry," and swept them out of the house.

Meg went slowly upstairs, noticing that the sound of the rain was more insistent in the upper storey of the house. The airing cupboard was in the bathroom. She glanced in quickly and closed the door. She gave the room a rapid tidy, went down, and turned on the wireless.

Meg believed in method. Every morning of the week had its programme; and this was Thursday, when she defrosted the refrigerator, polished the silver and turned out her bedroom—a full morning's work. But today she did none of it, wandering about with a desultory, fidgeting tidiness, taking things up and putting them down again, straightening books on their shelves, nipping dead leaves off the houseplants, while the wireless went on with the Daily Service. There was bound to be a *mauvais quart d'heure*. In fact, everything was well in hand; Charlotte was safely disposed of with the Flaxmans, Moodie was asleep in the airing cupboard and the vet had promised to arrive before midday. It would be quite painless and over in a few minutes. But it was, for all that, a *mauvais quart d'heure*. There are some women, Meg was one of them, in whom conscience is so strongly developed that it leaves little room for anything else. Love is scarcely felt before duty rushes to encase it, anger is impossible because one must always be calm and see both sides, pity evaporates in expedients, even grief is felt as a sort of bruised sense of injury, a resentment that one should have grief forced upon one when one has always acted for the best. Meg's conscience told her that she was acting for the best: Moodie would be spared inevitable suffering, Charlotte protected from a possibly quite serious trauma, Alan undisturbed in his work. Her own distress—and she was fond of poor old Moodie, no other cat could quite replace him because of his associations—was a small price to pay for all these satisfactory arrangements, and she was ready to pay it, sacrificing her own feelings as duty bid, and as common sense also bid. Besides, it would soon be over. The trouble about an active, strongly developed conscience is that it requires to be constantly fed with good works, a routine shovelling of meritorious activities. And when you have done everything for the best, and are waiting about for the vet to come and kill your old cat and can't therefore begin to defrost a refrigerator or turn out a bedroom, a good conscience soon leaves off being a support and becomes a liability, demanding to be supported itself.

The bad quarter of an hour stretched into half an hour, into an hour, and into an hour and a quarter, while Meg, stiffening at the noise of every approaching car and fancying with every gust of a fitful rising wind that Moodie was demanding with yowls to be let out of the airing cupboard, tried to read but could not, looked for cobwebs but found none and wondered if for this once she would break her rule of not drinking spirits before lunchtime. She was in the kitchen, devouring lumps of sugar, when the vet arrived. She took him to the bathroom, opened the cupboard door, heard him say, "Well, old man?"

"Would you like me to stop? Is there anything I can do to help?"

"If you could let me have an old towel."

She produced the towel, and went to her bedroom where she opened the window and looked out on the rain and the tossing trees and remembered that everyone must die. At last she heard the basin tap turned on, the vet washing his hands, the water running away.

"Mrs Atwood. Have you got a box?"

"A box?"

He stood in the passage, a tall, red-faced young man, the picture of health.

"Any sort of carton. To take it away in. A sack would do."

She had not remembered that Moodie would require a coffin. In a flurry of guilt she began to search. There was a brown paper carrier; but this would not do, Moodie could not be borne away swinging from the vet's hand. There was the carton the groceries had come in; but it was too small, and had Pan Yan Pickles printed on it. At last she found a plain oblong carton, kept because it was solid and serviceable. Deciding that this would do, she glanced inside and realised that it would not do like that. Moodie could not be put straight into an empty box: there must be some sort of lining, of padding. She tore old newspaper into strips and crumpled the strips to form a mattress; and then, remembering that flowers are given to the dead, she snatched a couple of dahlias from a vase and scattered the petals on top of the newspaper. The vet was standing in the bathroom, averting his eyes from the bidet, the towel neatly folded was balanced on the edge of the basin, and on the bathroom stool was Moodie's unrecognisably shabby, degraded, dead body. Before she realised what she was saying, she had said, "If you'll hold the box, I'd like to put him in."

Yet what else could she say? She owed it to Moodie. She lifted him on her two hands, as she had lifted him so often. The unsupported head fell horribly to one side, lolling like the clapper of a bell. She got the body in somehow, and the vet closed the lid of the carton and carried it away. She knew she ought to have thanked him, but she could not speak. She had never seen a dead body before—except on food counters, of course.

She went downstairs and drank a stiffish whisky. Her sense of proportion reasserted itself. One cannot expect to be perfect in any first performance. She had not behaved at all as she had meant to when Charlotte was born. It was a pity about the makeshift box; it was a pity not to have thanked the vet; but the essentials had been secured, Charlotte was safe and happy at Hood House, Alan was happy and busy in his laboratory; neither of them need ever know what agony is involved in the process of rationally, mercifully, putting an end to an old pet. She would make a quick lunch of bread and cheese, and then be very busy. She heard a distant peal of thunder, and welcomed the thought of a good rousing thunderstorm. Something elemental would be releasing. After a few more long, grumbling reverberations the storm moved away, but when she went to defrost the refrigerator she found it darkened and cavernous, and the current off throughout the house. The power lines on Ram Down were always getting struck. She left the refrigerator to natural forces, and as she couldn't use the Hoover either, she polished the silver and sat down to do some mending. She was a bad needle-woman; mending kept her mind occupied till a burst of sunlight surprised her by its slant. She had no idea it was so late. Charlotte would be back at any moment.

Just as the current had gone off, leaving the refrigerator darkened and cavernous, the support of a good conscience now withdrew its aid. Charlotte would be back at any moment. Charlotte would have to be told. Time went on. Suppose there had been a car smash? Charlotte mangled and dying at the roadside, and all because she had been got out of the house while the vet was mercifully releasing Moodie? Meg's doing—how could one ever get over such a thing and lead a normal life again?

She was sitting motionless and frantic when Alan came in, switching on the light in the hall.

"Well, Meg—Why are you looking so wrought up? Didn't the vet come? Couldn't he do his stuff?"

"Oh, yes, that was all right. But Charlotte's not back."

"When did they say they'd bring her?"

"Adela didn't say exactly. She said, a good long day. But it's long over that—Adela knows how particular I am about bedtime."

"Why not ring up?"

"But I am sure they must have started by now."

"Well, someone would be about. They've got that cook. What's their number?"

She heard him in the hall, dialing. Then he came back saying the line seemed to be dead. Ten minutes later, a car drew up and Charlotte rushed into the house, followed by Mrs Flaxman.

"Mother, Mother! It's been so marvellous, it's been so thrilling. We were struck by lightning. There was a huge flash, bright blue, and the telephone shot across the room and broke ever so much china, and there was an awful noise of horses screaming their heads off and Mr Flaxman tore out to see if the stables had been struck too, and then ran back saying, 'They're all right but our bloody roof's on fire.' And there were great fids of burning thatch flying about everywhere, and Mr Flaxman went up a ladder and I and Mrs Flaxman got buckets and buckets of water and handed them up to him. And I was ever so useful, Adela said so, wasn't I, Mrs Flaxman?"

"I don't know what we'd have done without you, my pet," said Mrs Flaxman to Charlotte, and to Meg, "she got very wet, but we've dried her."

"And then people came rushing up from the village and trod on the bantams."

"No, nothing's insured except the portraits and the horses. Giles won't, on principle. Yes, calamitous—but it could have been worse. No, no, not at all, it's been a pleasure having her."

Adela was gone, leaving the impression of someone from a higher sphere in a hurry to return to its empyrean.

For the present, there was nothing to be done but listen to Charlotte and try not to blame the Flaxmans for having let her get so over-excited. Both parents lit cigarettes and prepared themselves for a spell of entering into their child's world; after all, fifteen minutes earlier, they had been fearing for her life. They smoked and smiled and made appropriate interjections. Suddenly her narrative ran out, and she said, "Where's Moodie?"

For by the time one is ten one knows when one's parents are only pretending to be interested. Back again in a home that had no horses, no bantams, no curly golden armchairs, no portraits of gentlemen in armour and low-necked ladies, was never struck by lightning and gave her no opportunities to be brave and indispensable, Charlotte concentrated on the one faithful satisfaction it afforded and said, "Where's Moodie?"

Mastering a feeling like stage-fright, Meg said with composure, "Darling. Moodie's not here."

"Why isn't he? Has he run away? Has anything happened to him?"

"Not exactly that. But he's dead."

"Why? Why is he dead? He was quite well this morning. Why is he dead?"

"You know, darling, poor Moodie hasn't really been feeling well for a long time. He was an old cat. He had an illness."

Charlotte saw Moodie's broad face, and his eyes staring at her with that thirsty expression. Moodie was dead. Mother had explained to her about death, making it seem very ordinary.

"You remember how horrid his breath smelled?"

"Yes. That was his teeth."

"It wasn't only his teeth. It was something inside that was bound to kill him sooner or later. And he would have suffered a great deal. So the vet came and gave him an injection and put him to sleep. It was all over in a minute."

Moodie had gone out and sat in the rain. The child's glance moved to the window and remained fixed on the lawn—so green in the sunset that it was almost golden. It was a french window. Without a word, she opened it and went out.

"Poor Charlotte!" said Alan. "She's taking it very well. I must say, I think you rubbed it in a bit too much. You needn't have said he stank."

Meg repressed the retort that if Alan could have done it so much better he might perfectly well have done so. In silence, they watched Charlotte walking about in the garden. It was a very small garden, and newly-planted, and the gardens on either side of it were small and newly-planted too, and only marked off by light railings. To Meg, whose childhood had known a garden with overgrown shrubs, laurel hedges, a disused greenhouse and a toad, it seemed an inadequate place to grieve in; but from the eighteenth century onwards people have turned for comfort to the bosom of nature, and Charlotte was doing so now, among the standard roses and the begonias. She walked up and down, round and round, pausing, walking on again. "Going round his old haunts," said Alan. Moodie, as Meg knew, shared her opinion of the garden; he used it to scratch in, but for any serious haunting went to Mopson's Garage where he and the neighbourhood cats clubbed among the derelict cars. A sense of loss pierced her; knowing Moodie's ways had been a kind of illicit Bohemianism in her exemplary, rather lonely life. But it was Charlotte's loss she must think of—and Charlotte's supper, which was long overdue.

"I wish she'd come in—but we mustn't hurry her."

Alan said, "She's coming now."

Charlotte was walking towards the house, walking with a firm tread. Her face was still pale with shock, but her expression was composed, resolved, even excited. I must give her a sedative, thought Meg. Charlotte entered, saying, "I've chosen the place for his grave."

After the bungled explanations that one couldn't, that the lawn would never be the same again, that it wasn't their garden, that the lease expressly forbade burying animals had broken down under the child's cross-examination into an admission that there was no body to bury, that the vet had taken it away, that it could not be got back, that it had been disposed of, that in all probability it had been burned to ashes as her parents' bodies would in due course be burned; after Charlotte, declaring she would never forgive them, never, that they were liars and murderers, that she hated them and hoped they would soon be burned to ashes themselves had somehow been got to bed, they sat down, exhausted, not looking at each other.

"That damned cat!"

As though Alan's words had unloosed it, a wailing cry came from overhead.

"O Moodie, Moodie, Moodie!

"O Moodie, Moodie, Moodie!"

Implacable, as the iteration of waves breaking on a beach, the wailing cries rang through the house. Twice Meg started to her feet, was told not to be weak-minded, and sat down again. Alan ought to be fed. Something ought to be done. The mere thought of food made her feel sick. Alan was filling his pipe. Staring in front of her, lost in a final imbecility of patience, she found she was looking at the two dahlia stalks whose petals she had torn away.

"O Moodie, Moodie, Moodie!"

The thought of something to be done emerged. "We must put off that new kitten," she said.

"Why?"

Completing her husband's exasperation, Meg buried her face in her hands and began to cry.

"O Moodie," she lamented. "Oh, my kind cat!"

# The Cat

BY MARY E. WILKINS FREEMAN

I T IS DIFFICULT to think of a more direct and powerful account than "The Cat" by Mary Freeman (1852–1930) of the relationship, unbridgeable yet somehow complete, that can exist between men and cats. It is written from the cat's point of view with obvious and heartfelt accuracy, and while severely avoiding sentimentality succeeds in being very moving.

Mary Freeman turned professional writer from necessity at a time when few women were able to make their living—much less support a family—that way. Now nearly forgotten except among students of late-nineteenth-century women's fiction, she wrote many realistic short stories about life in New England. "The Cat" is one of her very best.

★　★　★　★　★

THE SNOW WAS FALLING, and the Cat's fur was stiffly pointed with it, but he was imperturbable. He sat crouched, ready for the death-spring, as he had sat for hours. It was night—but that made no difference—all times were as one to the Cat when he was in wait for prey. Then too, he was under no constraint of human will, for he was living alone that winter. Nowhere in the world was any voice calling him; on no hearth was there a waiting dish. He was quite free except for his own desires, which tyrannized over him when unsatisfied as now. The Cat was very hungry—almost famished, in fact. For days the weather had been very bitter, and all the feebler wild things which were his prey by inheritance, the born serfs to his family, had kept, for the most part, in their burrows and nests, and the Cat's long hunt had availed him nothing. But he waited with the inconceivable patience and persistency of his race; besides, he was certain. The Cat was a creature of absolute convictions, and his faith in his deductions never wavered. The rabbit had gone in there between those low-hung pine boughs. Now her little doorway had before it a shaggy curtain of snow, but in there she was. The Cat had seen her enter, so like a swift grey shadow that even his sharp and practised eyes had glanced back for the substance following, and then she was gone. So he sat down and waited, and he waited still in the white night, listening angrily to the north wind starting in the upper heights of the mountains with distant screams, then swelling into an awful crescendo of rage, and swooping down with furious white wings of snow like a flock of fierce eagles into the valleys and ravines. The Cat was on the side of a mountain, on a wooded terrace. Above him a few feet away towered the rock ascent as steep as the wall of a cathedral. The Cat had never climbed it—trees were the ladders to his heights of life. He had often looked with wonder at the rock, and miauled bitterly and resentfully as man does in the face of a forbidding Providence. At his left was the sheer precipice. Behind him, with a short stretch of woody growth between, was the frozen perpendicular wall of a mountain stream. Before him was the way to his home. When the rabbit came out she was trapped; her little cloven feet could not scale such unbroken steeps. So the Cat waited. The place in which he was looked like a maelstrom of the wood. The tangle of trees and bushes clinging to the mountain-side with a stern clutch of roots, the prostrate trunks and branches, the vines embracing everything with strong knots and coils of growth, had a curious effect, as of things which had whirled for ages in a current of raging water, only it was not water, but wind, which had disposed everything in circling lines of yielding to its fiercest points of onset. And now over all this whirl of wood and rock and dead trunks and branches and vines descended the snow. It blew down like smoke over the rock-crest above; it stood in a gyrating column like some death-wraith of nature, on the level, then it broke over the edge of the precipice, and the Cat cowered before the fierce backward set of it. It was as if ice needles pricked his skin through his beautiful thick fur, but he never faltered and never once cried. He had nothing to gain from crying, and everything to lose; the rabbit would hear him cry and know he was waiting.

It grew darker and darker, with a strange white smother, instead of the natural blackness of night. It was a night of storm and death superadded to the night of nature. The mountains were all hidden, wrapped about, overawed, and tumultuously overborne by it, but in the midst of it waited, quite unconquered, this little, unswerving, living patience and power under a little coat of grey fur.

A fiercer blast swept over the rock, spun on one mighty foot of whirlwind athwart the level, then was over the precipice.

Then the Cat saw two eyes luminous with terror, frantic with the impulse of flight, he saw a little, quivering, dilating nose, he saw two pointing ears, and he kept still, with every one of his fine nerves and muscles strained like wires. Then the rabbit was out—there was one long line of incarnate flight and terror—and the Cat had her.

Then the Cat went home, trailing his prey through the snow.

The Cat lived in the house which his master had built, as rudely as a child's block-house, but stanchly enough. The snow was heavy on the low slant of its roof, but it would not settle under it. The two windows and the door were made fast, but the Cat knew a way in. Up a pine-tree behind the house he scuttled, though it was hard work with his heavy rabbit, and was in his little window under the eaves, then down through the trap to the room below, and on his master's bed with a spring and a great cry of triumph, rabbit and all. But his master was not there; he had been gone since early fall and it was now February. He would not return until spring, for he was an old man, and the cruel cold of the mountains clutched at his vitals like a panther, and he had gone to the village to winter. The Cat had known for a long time that his master was gone, but his reasoning was always sequential and circuitous; always for him what had been would be, and the more easily for his marvellous waiting powers so he always came home expecting to find his master.

When he saw that he was still gone, he dragged the rabbit off the rude couch which was the bed to the floor, put one little paw on the carcass to keep it steady, and began gnawing with head to one side to bring his strongest teeth to bear.

It was darker in the house than it had been in the wood, and the cold was as deadly, though not so fierce. If the Cat had not received his fur coat unquestioningly of Providence, he would have been thankful that he had it. It was a mottled grey, white on the face and breast, and thick as fur could grow.

The wind drove the snow on the windows with such force that it rattled like sleet, and the house trembled a little. Then all at once the Cat heard a noise, and stopped gnawing his rabbit and listened, his shining green eyes fixed upon a window. Then he heard a hoarse shout, a halloo of despair and entreaty; but he knew it was not his master come home, and he waited, one paw still on the rabbit. Then the halloo came again, and then the Cat answered. He said all that was essential quite plainly to his own comprehension. There was in his cry of response inquiry, information, warning, terror, and finally, the offer of comradeship; but the man outside did not hear him, because of the howling of the storm.

Then there was a great battering pound at the door, then another, and another. The Cat dragged his rabbit under the bed. The blows came thicker and faster. It was a weak arm which gave them, but it was nerved by desperation. Finally the lock yielded, and the stranger came in. Then the Cat, peering from under the bed, blinked with a sudden light, and his green eyes narrowed. The stranger struck a match and looked about. The Cat saw a face wild and blue with hunger and cold, and a man who looked poorer and older than his poor old master, who was an outcast among men for his poverty and lowly mystery of antecedents; and he heard a muttered, unintelligible voicing of distress from the harsh piteous mouth. There was in it both profanity and prayer, but the Cat knew nothing of that.

The stranger braced the door which he had forced, got some wood from the stock in the corner, and kindled a fire in the old stove as quickly as his half-frozen hands would allow. He shook so pitiably as he worked that the Cat under the bed felt the tremor of it. Then the man, who was small and feeble and marked with the scars of suffering which he had pulled down upon his own head, sat down in one of the old chairs and crouched over the fire as if it were the one love and desire of his soul, holding out his yellow hands like yellow claws, and he groaned. The Cat came out from under the bed and leaped up on his lap with the rabbit. The man gave a great shout and start of terror, and sprang, and the Cat slid clawing to the floor, and the rabbit fell inertly, and the man leaned, gasping with fright, and ghastly, against the wall. The Cat grabbed the rabbit by the slack of its neck and dragged it to the man's feet. Then he raised his shrill, insistent cry, he arched his back high, his tail was a splendid waving plume. He rubbed against the man's feet, which were bursting out of their torn shoes.

The man pushed the Cat away, gently enough, and began searching about the little cabin. He even climbed painfully the ladder to the loft, lit a match, and peered up in the darkness with straining eyes. He feared lest there might be a man, since there was a cat. His experience with men had not been pleasant, and neither had the experience of men been pleasant with him. He was an old wandering Ishmael among his kind; he had stumbled upon the house of a brother, and the brother was not at home, and he was glad.

He returned to the Cat, and stooped stiffly and stroked his back, which the animal arched like the spring of a bow.

Then he took up the rabbit and looked at it eagerly by the firelight. His jaws worked. He could almost have devoured it raw. He fumbled—the Cat close at his heels—around some rude shelves and a table, and found, with a grunt of self-gratulation, a lamp with oil in it. That he lighted; then he found a frying-pan and a knife, and skinned the rabbit, and prepared it for cooking, the Cat always at his feet.

When the odour of the cooking flesh filled the cabin, both the man and the Cat looked wolfish. The man turned the rabbit with one hand and stooped to pat the Cat with the other. The Cat thought him a fine man. He loved him with all his heart, though he had known him such a short time, and though the man had a face both pitiful and sharply set at variance with the best of things.

It was a face with the grimy grizzle of age upon it, with fever hollows in the cheeks, and the memories of wrong in the dim eyes, but the Cat accepted the man unquestioningly and loved him. When the rabbit was half cooked, neither the man nor the Cat would wait any longer. The man took it from the fire, divided it exactly in halves, gave the Cat one, and took the other himself. Then they ate.

Then the man blew out the light, called the Cat to him, got on the bed, drew up the ragged coverings, and fell asleep with the Cat in his bosom.

The man was the Cat's guest all the rest of the winter, and winter is long in the mountains. The rightful owner of the little hut did not return until May. All that time the Cat toiled hard, and he grew rather thin himself, for he shared everything except mice with his guest; and sometimes game was wary, and the fruit of patience of days was very little for two. The man was ill and weak, however, and unable to eat much, which was fortunate, since he could not hunt for himself. All day long he lay on the bed, or else sat crouched over the fire. It was a good thing that fire-wood was ready at hand for the picking up, not a stone's-throw from the door, for that he had to attend to himself.

The Cat foraged tirelessly. Sometimes he was gone for days together, and at first the man used to be terrified, thinking he would never return; then he would hear the familiar cry at the door, and stumble to his feet and let him in. Then the two would dine together, sharing equally; then the Cat would rest and purr, and finally sleep in the man's arms.

Towards spring the game grew plentiful; more wild little quarry were tempted out of their homes, in search of love as well as food. One day the Cat had luck—a rabbit, a partridge, and a mouse. He could not carry them all at once, but finally he had them together at the house door. Then he cried, but no one answered. All the mountain streams were loosened, and the air was full of the gurgle of many waters, occasionally pierced by a bird-whistle. The trees rustled with a new sound to the spring wind; there was a flush of rose and gold-green on the breasting surface of a distant mountain seen through an opening in the wood. The tips of the bushes were swollen and glistening red, and now and then there was a flower; but the Cat had nothing to do with flowers. He stood beside his booty at the house door, and cried and cried with his insistent triumph and complaint and pleading, but no one came to let him in. Then the cat left his little treasures at the door, and went around to the back of the house to the pine-tree, and was up the trunk with a wild scramble, and in through his little window, and down through the trap to the room, and the man was gone.

The Cat cried again—that cry of the animal for human companionship which is one of the sad notes of the world; he looked in all the corners; he sprang to the chair at the window and looked out; but no one came. The man was gone and he never came again.

The Cat ate his mouse out on the turf beside the house; the rabbit and the partridge he carried painfully into the house, but the man did not come to share them. Finally, in the course of a day or two, he ate them up himself; then he slept a long time on the bed, and when he waked the man was not there.

Then the Cat went forth to his hunting-grounds again, and came home at night with a plump bird, reasoning with his tireless persistency in expectancy that the man would be there; and there was a light in the window, and when he cried his old master opened the door and let him in.

His master had strong comradeship with the Cat, but not affection. He never patted him like that gentler outcast, but he had a pride in him and an anxiety for his welfare, though he had left him alone all winter without scruple. He feared lest some misfortune might have come to the Cat, though he was so large of his kind, and a mighty hunter. Therefore, when he saw him at the door in all the glory of his glossy winter coat, his white breast and face shining like snow in the sun, his own face lit up with welcome, and the Cat embraced his feet with his sinuous body vibrant with rejoicing purrs.

The Cat had his bird to himself, for his master had his own supper already cooking on the stove. After supper the Cat's master took his pipe, and sought a small store of tobacco which he had left in his hut over winter. He had thought often of it; that and the Cat seemed something to come home to in the spring. But the tobacco was gone; not a dust left. The man swore a little in a grim monotone, which made the profanity lose its customary effect. He had been, and was, a hard drinker; he had knocked about the world until the marks of its sharp corners were on his very soul, which was thereby calloused, until his very sensibility to loss was dulled. He was a very old man.

He searched for the tobacco with a sort of dull combativeness of persistency; then he stared with stupid wonder around the room. Suddenly many features struck him as being changed. Another stove-lid was broken; an old piece of carpet was tucked up over a window to keep out the cold; his firewood was gone. He looked and there was no oil left in his can. He looked at the covering on his bed; he took them up, and again he made that strange remonstrant noise in his throat. Then he looked again for his tobacco.

Finally he gave it up. He sat down beside the fire, for May in the mountains is cold; he held his empty pipe in his mouth, his rough forehead knitted, and he and the Cat looked at each other across that impassable barrier of silence which has been set between man and beast from the creation of the world.

# The Story of Webster

BY P. G. WODEHOUSE

T HE PLAYWRIGHT Sean O'Casey once described P. G. Wodehouse (1881–1975) as "English literature's performing flea." Wodehouse himself responded to this comment by saying that he assumed O'Casey had meant to be complimentary, because "all the performing fleas I have met impressed me with their sterling artistry and that indefinable something which makes a good trouper." Fleas apart (well apart), Wodehouse could also be very perceptive about cats. In "The Story of Webster," which first appeared in a collection called *Mulliner Nights* in 1933, Webster epitomizes the natural ability of any cat to look censorious, here to the point of terrorizing his human caretaker. Webster, however, has a flaw. But Wodehouse stories generally end happily—thank heavens and Webster's lapse—and this one is no exception.

★   ★   ★   ★   ★

"CATS ARE NOT DOGS!"

There is only one place where you can hear good things like that thrown off quite casually in the general run of conversation, and that is the bar-parlour of the Angler's Rest. It was there, as we sat grouped about the fire, that a thoughtful Pint of Bitter had made the statement just recorded.

Although the talk up to this point had been dealing with Einstein's Theory of Relativity, we readily adjusted our minds to cope with the new topic. Regular attendance at the nightly sessions over which Mr. Mulliner presides with such unfailing dignity and geniality tends to produce mental nimbleness. In our little circle I have known an argument on the Final Destination of the Soul to change inside forty seconds into one concerning the best method of preserving the juiciness of bacon fat.

"Cats," proceeded the Pint of Bitter, "are selfish. A man waits on a cat hand and foot for weeks, humouring its lightest whim, and then it goes and leaves him flat because it has found a place down the road where the fish is more frequent."

"What I've got against cats," said a Lemon Sour, speaking feelingly, as one brooding on a private grievance, "is their unreliability. They lack candour and are not square shooters. You get your cat and you call him Thomas or George, as the case may be. So far, so good. Then one morning you wake up and find six kittens in the hat-box and you have to reopen the whole matter, approaching it from an entirely different angle."

"If you want to know what's the trouble with cats," said a red-faced man with glassy eyes, who had been rapping on the table for his fourth whisky, "they've got no tact. That's what's the trouble with them. I remember a friend of mine had a cat. Made quite a pet of that cat, he did. And what occurred? What was the outcome? One night he came home rather late and was feeling for the keyhole with his corkscrew; and, believe me or not, his cat selected that precise moment to jump on the back of his neck out of a tree. No tact."

Mr. Mulliner shook his head.

"I grant you all this," he said, "but still, in my opinion, you have not got quite to the root of the matter. The real objection to the great majority of cats is their insufferable air of superiority. Cats, as a class, have never completely got over the snootiness caused by the fact that in Ancient Egypt they were worshipped as gods. This makes them too prone to set themselves up as critics and censors of the frail and erring human beings whose lot they share. They stare rebukingly. They view with concern. And on a sensitive man this often has the worst effects, inducing an inferiority complex of the gravest kind. It is odd that the conversation should have taken this turn," said Mr. Mulliner, sipping his hot Scotch and lemon, "for I was thinking only this afternoon of the rather strange case of my cousin Edward's son, Lancelot."

"I knew a cat—" began a Small Bass.

My cousin Edward's son, Lancelot (said Mr. Mulliner) was, at the time of which I speak, a comely youth of some twenty-five summers. Orphaned at an early age, he had been brought up in the home of his Uncle Theodore, the saintly Dean of Bolsover; and it was a great shock to that good man when Lancelot, on attaining his majority, wrote from London to inform him that he had taken a studio in Bott Street, Chelsea, and proposed to remain in the metropolis and become an artist.

The Dean's opinion of artists was low. As a prominent member of the Bolsover Watch Committee, it had recently been his distasteful duty to be present at a private showing of the super-super-film *Palettes of Passion;* and he replied to his nephew's communication with a vibrant letter in which he emphasized the grievous pain it gave him to think that one of his flesh and blood should deliberately be embarking on a career which must inevitably lead sooner or later to the painting of Russian princesses lying on divans in the semi-nude with their arms round tame jaguars. He urged Lancelot to return and become a curate while there was yet time.

But Lancelot was firm. He deplored the rift between himself and a relative whom he had always respected; but he was dashed if he meant to go back to an environment where his individuality had been stifled and his soul confined in chains. And for four years there was silence between uncle and nephew.

During these years Lancelot had made progress in his chosen profession. At the time at which this story opens, his prospects seemed bright. He was painting the portrait of Brenda, only daughter of Mr. and Mrs. B. B. Carberry-Pirbright, of 11 Maxton Square, South Kensington, which meant thirty pounds in his sock on delivery. He had learned to cook eggs and bacon. He had practically mastered the ukulele. And, in addition, he was engaged to be married to a fearless young *vers libre* poetess of the name of Gladys Bingley, better known as The Sweet Singer of Garbridge Mews, Fulham—a charming girl who looked like a pen-wiper.

It seemed to Lancelot that life was very full and beautiful. He lived joyously in the present, giving no thought to the past.

But how true it is that the past is inextricably mixed up with the present and that we can never tell when it may spring some delayed bomb beneath our feet. One afternoon, as he sat making a few small alterations to the portrait of Brenda Garberry-Pirbright, his fiancée entered.

He had been expecting her to call, for today she was going off for a three weeks' holiday to the South of France, and she had promised to look in on her way to the station. He laid down his brush and gazed at her with a yearning affection, thinking for the thousandth time how he worshipped every spot of ink on her nose. Standing there in the doorway with her bobbed hair sticking out in every direction like a golliwog's, she made a picture that seemed to speak to his very depths.

"Hullo, Reptile!" he said lovingly.

"What ho, Worm!" said Gladys, maidenly devotion shining through the monocle which she wore in her left eye. "I can stay just half an hour."

"Oh, well, half an hour soon passes," said Lancelot. "What's that you've got there?"

"A letter, ass. What did you think it was?"

"Where did you get it?"

"I found the postman outside."

Lancelot took the envelope from her and examined it.

"Gosh!" he said.

"What's the matter?"

"It's from my Uncle Theodore."

"I didn't know you had an Uncle Theodore."

"Of course I have. I've had him for years."

"What's he writing to you about?"

"If you'll kindly keep quiet for two seconds, if you know how," said Lancelot, "I'll tell you."

And in a clear voice which, like that of all the Mulliners, however distant from the main branch, was beautifully modulated, he read as follows:

"The Deanery,
"Bolsover,
"Wilts.

"My Dear Lancelot,
    "As you have, no doubt, already learned from your *Church Times*, I have been offered and have accepted the vacant Bishopric of Bongo-Bongo in West Africa. I sail immediately to take up my new duties, which I trust will be blessed.

"In these circumstances, it becomes necessary for me to find a good home for my cat Webster. It is, alas, out of the question that he should accompany me, as the rigours of the climate and the lack of essential comforts might well sap a constitution which has never been robust.

"I am dispatching him, therefore, to your address, my dear boy, in a straw-lined hamper, in the full confidence that you will prove a kindly and conscientious host.

"With cordial good wishes,

"Your affectionate uncle,

"Theodore Bongo-Bongo."

For some moments after he had finished reading this communication, a thoughtful silence prevailed in the studio. Finally Gladys spoke.

"Of all the nerve!" she said. "I wouldn't do it."

"Why not?"

"What do you want with a cat?"

Lancelot reflected.

"It is true," he said, "that, given a free hand, I would prefer not to have my studio turned into a cattery or cat-bin. But consider the special circumstances. Relations between Uncle Theodore and self have for the last few years been a bit strained. In fact, you might say we had definitely parted brass-rags. It looks to me as if he were coming round. I should describe this letter as more or less what you might call an olive-branch. If I lush this cat up satisfactorily, shall I not be in a position later on to make a swift touch?"

"He is rich, this bean?" said Gladys, interested.

"Extremely."

"Then," said Gladys, "consider my objections withdrawn. A good stout cheque from a grateful cat-fancier would undoubtedly come in very handy. We might be able to get married this year."

"Exactly," said Lancelot. "A pretty loathsome prospect, of course, but still, as we've arranged to do it, the sooner we get it over, the better, what?"

"Absolutely."

"Then that's settled. I accept custody of cat."

"It's the only thing to do," said Gladys. "Meanwhile, can you lend me a comb? Have you such a thing in your bedroom?"

"What do you want with a comb?"

"I got some soup in my hair at lunch. I won't be a minute."

She hurried out, and Lancelot, taking up the letter again, found that he had omitted to read a continuation of it on the back page.

It was to the following effect:

"P.S. In establishing Webster in your home, I am actuated by another motive than the simple desire to see to it that my faithful friend and companion is adequately provided for.

"From both a moral and an educative standpoint, I am convinced that Webster's society will prove of inestimable value to you. His advent, indeed, I venture to hope, will be a turning-point in your life. Thrown, as you must be, incessantly among loose and immoral Bohemians, you will find in this cat an example of upright conduct which cannot but act as an antidote to the poison cup of temptation which is, no doubt, hourly pressed to your lips.

"P.P.S. Cream only at midday, and fish not more than three times a week."

He was reading these words for the second time, when the front door-bell rang and he found a man on the steps with a hamper. A discreet mew from within revealed its contents, and Lancelot, carrying it into the studio, cut the strings.

"Hi!" he bellowed, going to the door.

"What's up?" shrieked his betrothed from above.

"The cat's come."

"All right. I'll be down in a jiffy."

Lancelot returned to the studio.

"What ho, Webster!" he said cheerily. "How's the boy?"

The cat did not reply. It was sitting with bent head, performing that wash and brush up which a journey by rail renders so necessary.

In order to facilitate these toilet operations, it had raised its left leg and was holding it rigidly in the air. And there flashed into Lancelot's mind an old superstition handed on to him, for what it was worth, by one of the nurses of his infancy. If, this woman had said, you creep up to a cat when its leg is in the air and give it a pull, then you make a wish and your wish comes true in thirty days.

It was a pretty fancy, and it seemed to Lancelot that the theory might as well be put to the test. He advanced warily, therefore, and was in the act of extending his fingers for the pull, when Webster, lowering the leg, turned and raised his eyes.

He looked at Lancelot. And suddenly with sickening force, there came to Lancelot the realization of the unpardonable liberty he had been about to take.

Until this moment, though the postscript to his uncle's letter should have warned him, Lancelot Mulliner had had no suspicion of what manner of cat this was that he had taken into his home. Now, for the first time, he saw him steadily and saw him whole.

Webster was very large and very black and very composed. He conveyed the impression of being a cat of deep reserves. Descendant of a long line of ecclesiastical ancestors who had conducted their decorous courtships beneath the shadow of cathedrals and on the back walls of bishops' palaces, he had that exquisite poise which one sees in high dignitaries of the church. His eyes were clear and steady, and seemed to pierce to the very roots of the young man's soul, filling him with a sense of guilt.

Once, long ago, in his hot childhood, Lancelot, spending his summer holidays at the deanery, had been so far carried away by ginger-beer and original sin as to plug a senior canon in the leg with his air-gun—only to discover, on turning, that a visiting archdeacon had been a spectator of the entire incident from his immediate rear. As he had felt then, when meeting the archdeacon's eye, so did he feel now as Webster's gaze played silently upon him.

Webster, it is true, had not actually raised his eyebrows. But this, Lancelot felt, was simply because he hadn't any.

He backed, blushing.

"Sorry!" he muttered.

There was a pause. Webster continued his steady scrutiny. Lancelot edged towards the door.

"Er—excuse me—just a moment . . ." he mumbled. And, sidling from the room, he ran distractedly upstairs.

"I say," said Lancelot.

"Now what?" asked Gladys.

"Have you finished with the mirror?"

"Why?"

"Well, I—er—I thought," said Lancelot, "that I might as well have a shave."

The girl looked at him, astonished.

"Shave? Why, you shaved only the day before yesterday."

"I know. But, all the same . . . I mean to say, it seems only respectful. That cat, I mean."

"What about him?"

"Well, he seems to expect it, somehow. Nothing actually said, don't you know, but you could tell by his manner. I thought a quick shave and perhaps change into my blue serge suit—"

"He's probably thirsty. Why don't you give him some milk?"

"Could one, do you think?" said Lancelot doubtfully. "I mean, I hardly seem to know him well enough." He paused. "I say, old girl," he went on, with a touch of hesitation.

"Hullo?"

"I know you won't mind my mentioning it, but you've got a few spots of ink on your nose."

"Of course I have. I always have spots of ink on my nose."

"Well . . . don't you think . . . a quick scrub with a bit of pumice-stone . . . I mean to say, you know how important first impressions are. . . ."

The girl stared.

"Lancelot Mulliner," she said, "if you think I'm going to skin my nose to the bone just to please a mangy cat—"

"Sh!" cried Lancelot, in agony.

"Here, let me go down and look at him," said Gladys petulantly.

As they re-entered the studio, Webster was gazing with an air of quiet distaste at an illustration from *La Vie Parisienne* which adorned one of the walls. Lancelot tore it down hastily.

Gladys looked at Webster in an unfriendly way.

"So that's the blighter!"

"Sh!"

"If you want to know what I think," said Gladys, "that cat's been living too high. Doing himself a dashed sight too well. You'd better cut his rations down a bit."

In substance, her criticism was not unjustified. Certainly, there was about Webster more than a suspicion of *embonpoint*. He had that air of portly well-being which we associate with those who dwell in cathedral closes. But Lancelot winced uncomfortably. He had so hoped that Gladys would make a good impression, and here she was, starting right off by saying the tactless thing.

Gladys, all unconscious, was making preparations for departure.

"Well, bung-oh," she said lightly. "See you in three weeks. I suppose you and that cat'll both be out on the tiles the moment my back's turned."

"Please! Please!" moaned Lancelot. "Please!"

He had caught sight of the tip of a black tail protruding from behind the chesterfield. It was twitching slightly, and Lancelot could read it like a book. With a sickening sense of dismay, he knew that Webster had formed a snap judgment of his fiancée and condemned her as frivolous and unworthy.

It was some ten days later that Bernard Worple, the neo-Vorticist sculptor, lunching at the Puce Ptarmigan, ran into Rodney Scollop, the powerful young sur-realist. And after talking for a while of their art—

"What's all this I hear about Lancelot Mulliner?" asked Worple. "There's a wild story going about that he was seen shaved in the middle of the week. Nothing in it, I suppose?"

Scollop looked grave. He had been on the point of mentioning Lancelot himself, for he loved the lad and was deeply exercised about him.

"It is perfectly true," he said.

"It sounds incredible."

Scollop leaned forward. His fine face was troubled.

"Shall I tell you something, Worple?"

"What?"

"I know for an absolute fact," said Scollop, "that Lancelot Mulliner now shaves every morning."

Worple pushed aside the spaghetti which he was wreathing about him and through the gap stared at his companion.

"Every morning?"

"Every single morning. I looked in on him myself the other day, and there he was, neatly dressed in blue serge and shaved to the core. And, what is more, I got the distinct impression that he had used talcum powder afterwards."

"You don't mean that!"

"I do. And shall I tell you something else? There was a book lying open on the table. He tried to hide it, but he wasn't quick enough. It was one of those etiquette books!"

"An etiquette book!"

" 'Polite Behaviour,' by Constance, Lady Bodbank."

Worple unwound a stray tendril of spaghetti from about his left ear. He was deeply agitated. Like Scollop, he loved Lancelot.

"He'll be dressing for dinner next!" he exclaimed.

"I have every reason to believe," said Scollop gravely, "that he does dress for dinner. At any rate, a man closely resembling him was seen furtively buying three stiff collars and a black tie at Hope Brothers in the King's Road last Tuesday."

Worple pushed his chair back, and rose. His manner was determined.

"Scollop," he said, "we are friends of Mulliner's, you and I. It is evident from what you tell me that subversive influences are at work and that never has he needed our friendship more. Shall we not go round and see him immediately?"

"It was what I was about to suggest myself," said Rodney Scollop.

Twenty minutes later they were in Lancelot's studio, and with a significant glance Scollop drew his companion's notice to their host's appearance. Lancelot Mulliner was neatly, even foppishly, dressed in blue serge with creases down the trouser-legs, and his chin, Worple saw with a pang, gleamed smoothly in the afternoon light.

At the sight of his friends' cigars, Lancelot exhibited unmistakable concern.

"You don't mind throwing those away, I'm sure," he said pleadingly.

Rodney Scollop drew himself up a little haughtily.

"And since when," he asked, "have the best fourpenny cigars in Chelsea not been good enough for you?"

Lancelot hastened to soothe him.

"It isn't me," he exclaimed. "It's Webster. My cat. I happen to know he objects to tobacco smoke. I had to give up my pipe in deference to his views."

Bernard Worple snorted.

"Are you trying to tell us," he sneered, "that Lancelot Mulliner allows himself to be dictated to by a blasted cat?"

"Hush!" cried Lancelot, trembling. "If you knew how he disapproves of strong language!"

"Where is this cat?" asked Rodney Scollop. "Is that the animal?" he said, pointing out of the window to where, in the yard, a tough-looking Tom with tattered ears stood mewing in a hard-boiled way out of the corner of its mouth.

"Good heavens, no!" said Lancelot. "That is an alley cat which comes round here from time to time to lunch at the dust-bin. Webster is quite different. Webster has a natural dignity and repose of manner. Webster is a cat who prides himself on always being well turned out and whose high principles and lofty ideals shine from his eyes like beacon-fires. . . ." And then suddenly, with an abrupt change of manner, Lancelot broke down and in a low voice added: "Curse him! Curse him! Curse him! Curse him!"

Worple looked at Scollop. Scollop looked at Worple.

"Come, old man," said Scollop, laying a gentle hand on Lancelot's bowed shoulder. "We are your friends. Confide in us."

"Tell us all," said Worple. "What's the matter?"

Lancelot uttered a bitter, mirthless laugh.

"You want to know what's the matter? Listen, then. I'm cat-pecked!"

"Cat-pecked?"

"You've heard of men being hen-pecked, haven't you?" said Lancelot with a touch of irritation. "Well, I'm cat-pecked."

And in broken accents he told his story. He sketched the history of his association with Webster from the letter's first entry into the studio. Confident now that the animal was not within earshot, he unbosomed himself without reserve.

"It's something in the beast's eye," he said in a shaking voice. "Something hypnotic. He casts a spell upon me. He gazes at me and disapproves. Little by little, bit by bit, I am degenerating under his influence from a wholesome, self-respecting artist into . . . well, I don't know what you would call it. Suffice it to say that I have given up smoking, that I have ceased to wear carpet slippers and go about without a collar, that I never dream of sitting down to my frugal evening meal without dressing, and"—he choked—"I have sold my ukulele."

"Not that!" said Worple, paling.

"Yes," said Lancelot. "I felt he considered it frivolous."

There was a long silence.

"Mulliner," said Scollop, "this is more serious than I had supposed. We must brood upon your case."

"It may be possible," said Worple, "to find a way out."

Lancelot shook his head hopelessly.

"There is no way out. I have explored every avenue. The only thing that could possibly free me from this intolerable bondage would be if once—just once—I could catch that cat unbending. If once—merely once—it would lapse in my presence from its austere dignity for but a single instant, I feel that the spell would be broken. But what hope is there of that?" cried Lancelot passionately. "You were pointing just now to that alley cat in the yard. There stands one who has strained every nerve and spared no effort to break down Webster's inhuman self-control. I have heard that animal say things to him which you would think no cat with red blood in its veins would suffer for an instant. And Webster merely looks at him like a Suffragan Bishop eyeing an erring choir-boy and turns his head and falls into a refreshing sleep."

He broke off with a dry sob. Worple, always an optimist, attempted in his kindly way to minimize the tragedy.

"Ah, well," he said. "It's bad, of course, but still, I suppose there is no actual harm in shaving and dressing for dinner and so on. Many great artists . . . Whistler, for example—"

"Wait!" cried Lancelot. "You have not heard the worst."

He rose feverishly, and, going to the easel, disclosed the portrait of Brenda Carberry-Pirbright.

"Take a look at that," he said, "and tell me what you think of her."

His two friends surveyed the face before them in silence. Miss Carberry-Pirbright was a young woman of prim and glacial aspect. One sought in vain for her reasons for wanting to have her portrait painted. It would be a most unpleasant thing to have about any house.

Scollop broke the silence.

"Friend of yours?"

"I can't stand the sight of her," said Lancelot vehemently.

"Then," said Scollop, "I may speak frankly. I think she's a pill."

"A blister," said Worple.

"A boil and a disease," said Scollop, summing up.

Lancelot laughed hackingly.

"You have described her to a nicety. She stands for everything most alien to my artist soul. She gives me a pain in the neck. I'm going to marry her."

"What!" cried Scollop.

"But you're going to marry Gladys Bingley," said Worple.

"Webster thinks not," said Lancelot bitterly. "At their first meeting he weighed Gladys in the balance and found her wanting. And the moment he saw Brenda Carberry-Pirbright he stuck his tail up at right angles, uttered a cordial gargle, and rubbed his head against her leg. Then, turning, he looked at me. I could read that glance. I knew what was in his mind. From that moment he has been doing everything in his power to arrange the match."

"But, Mulliner," said Worple, always eager to point out the bright side, "why should this girl want to marry a wretched, scrubby, hard-up footler like you? Have courage, Mulliner. It is simply a question of time before you repel and sicken her."

Lancelot shook his head. "No," he said. "You speak like a true friend, Worple, but you do not understand. Old Ma Carberry-Pirbright, this exhibit's mother, who chaperons her at the sittings, discovered at an early date my relationship to my Uncle Theodore, who, as you know, has got it in gobs. She knows well enough that some day I shall be a rich man. She used to know my Uncle Theodore when he was Vicar of St. Botolph's in Knightsbridge, and from the very first she assumed towards me the repellent chumminess of an old family friend. She was always trying to lure me to her. At Homes, her Sunday luncheons, her little dinners. Once she actually suggested that I should escort her and her beastly daughter to the Royal Academy."

He laughed bitterly. The mordant witticisms of Lancelot Mulliner at the expense of the Royal Academy were quoted from Tite Street in the south to Holland Park in the north and eastward as far as Bloomsbury.

"To all these overtures," resumed Lancelot, "I remained firmly unresponsive. My attitude was from the start one of frigid aloofness. I did not actually say in so many words that I would rather be dead in a ditch than at one of her At Homes, but my manner indicated it. And I was just beginning to think I had choked her off when in crashed Webster and upset everything. Do you know how many times I have been to that infernal house in the last week? Five. Webster seemed to wish it. I tell you, I am a lost man."

He buried his face in his hands. Scollop touched Worple on the arm, and together the two men stole silently out.

"Bad!" said Worple.

"Very bad," said Scollop.

"It seems incredible."

"Oh, no. Cases of this kind are, alas, by no means uncommon among those who, like Mulliner, possess to a marked degree the highly-strung, ultra-sensitive artistic temperament. A friend of mine, a rhythmical interior decorator, once rashly consented to put his aunt's parrot up at his studio while she was away visiting friends in the north of England. She was a woman of strong evangelical views, which the bird had imbibed from her. It had a way of putting its head on one side, making a noise like someone drawing a cork from a bottle, and asking my friend if he was saved. To cut a long story short, I happened to call on him a month later and he had installed a harmonium in his studio and was singing hymns, ancient and modern, in a rich tenor, while the parrot, standing on one leg on its perch, took the bass. A very sad affair. We were all much upset about it."

Worple shuddered.

"You appal me, Scollop! Is there nothing we can do?"

Rodney Scollop considered for a moment.

"We might wire Gladys Bingley to come home at once. She might possibly reason with the unhappy man. A woman's gentle influence . . . Yes, we could do that. Look in at the post office on your way home and send Gladys a telegram. I'll owe you for my half of it."

In the studio they had left, Lancelot Mulliner was staring dumbly at a black shape which had just entered the room. He had the appearance of a man with his back to the wall.

"No!" he was crying. "No! I'm dashed if I do!"

Webster continued to look at him.

"Why should I?" demanded Lancelot weakly.

Webster's gaze did not flicker.

"Oh, all right," said Lancelot sullenly.

He passed from the room with leaden feet, and, proceeding upstairs, changed into morning clothes and a top hat. Then, with a gardenia in his buttonhole, he made his way to 11, Maxton Square, where Mrs. Carberry-Pirbright was giving one of her intimate little teas ("just a few friends") to meet Clara Throckmorton Stooge, authoress of "A Strong Man's Kiss."

Gladys Bingley was lunching at her hotel in Antibes when Worple's telegram arrived. It occasioned her the gravest concern.

Exactly what it was all about, she was unable to gather, for emotion had made Bernard Worple rather incoherent. There were moments, reading it, when she fancied that Lancelot had met with a serious accident; others when the solution seemed to be that he had sprained his brain to such an extent that rival lunatic asylums were competing eagerly for his custom; others, again, when Worple appeared to be suggesting that he had gone into partnership with his cat to start a harem. But one fact emerged clearly. Her loved one was in serious trouble of some kind, and his best friends were agreed that only her immediate return could save him.

Gladys did not hesitate. Within half an hour of the receipt of the telegram she had packed her trunk, removed a piece of asparagus from her right eyebrow, and was negotiating for accommodation on the first train going north.

Arriving in London, her first impulse was to go straight to Lancelot. But a natural feminine curiosity urged her, before doing so, to call upon Bernard Worple and have light thrown on some of the more abstruse passages in the telegram.

Worple, in his capacity of author, may have tended towards obscurity, but, when confining himself to the spoken word, he told a plain story well and clearly. Five minutes of his society enabled Gladys to obtain a firm grasp on the salient facts, and there appeared on her face that grim, tight-lipped expression which is seen only on the faces of fiancées who have come back from a short holiday to discover that their dear one has been straying in their absence from the straight and narrow path.

"Brenda Carberry-Pirbright, eh?" said Gladys, with ominous calm. "I'll give him Brenda Carberry-Pirbright! My gosh, if one can't go off to Antibes for the merest breather without having one's betrothed getting it up his nose and starting to act like a Mormon Elder, it begins to look a pretty tough world for a girl."

Kind-hearted Bernard Worple did his best.

"I blame the cat," he said. "Lancelot, to my mind, is more sinned against than sinning. I consider him to be acting under undue influence or duress."

"How like a man!" said Gladys. "Shoving it all off on to an innocent cat!"

"Lancelot says it has a sort of something in its eye."

"Well, when I meet Lancelot," said Gladys, "he'll find that I have a sort of something in my eye."

She went out, breathing flame quietly through her nostrils. Worple, saddened, heaved a sigh and resumed his neo-Vorticist sculpting.

It was some five minutes later that Gladys, passing through Maxton Square on her way to Bott Street, stopped suddenly in her tracks. The sight she had seen was enough to make any fiancée do so.

Along the pavement leading to Number Eleven two figures were advancing. Or three, if you counted a morose-looking dog of a semi-Dachshund nature which preceded them, attached to a leash. One of the figures was that of Lancelot Mulliner, natty in grey herring-bone tweed and a new Homburg hat. It was he who held the leash. The other Gladys recognized from the portrait which she had seen on Lancelot's easel as that modern Du Barry, that notorious wrecker of homes and breaker-up of love-nests, Brenda Carberry-Pirbright.

The next moment they had mounted the steps of Number Eleven, and had gone in to tea, possibly with a little music.

It was perhaps an hour and a half later that Lancelot, having wrenched himself with difficulty from the lair of the Philistines, sped homeward in a swift taxi. As always after an extended *tête-à-tête* with Miss Carberry-Pirbright, he felt dazed and bewildered, as if he had been swimming in a sea of glue and had swallowed a good deal of it. All he could think of clearly was that he wanted a drink and that the materials for that drink were in the cupboard behind the chesterfield in his studio.

He paid the cab and charged in with his tongue rattling dryly against his front teeth. And there before him was Gladys Bingley, whom he had supposed far, far away.

"You!" exclaimed Lancelot.

"Yes, me!" said Gladys.

Her long vigil had not helped to restore the girl's equanimity. Since arriving at the studio she had had leisure to tap her foot three thousand, one hundred and forty-two times on the carpet, and the number of bitter smiles which had flitted across her face was nine hundred and eleven. She was about ready for the battle of the century.

She rose and faced him, all the woman in her flashing from her eyes.

"Well, you Casanova!" she said.

"You who?" said Lancelot.

"Don't say 'Yoo-hoo!' to me!" cried Gladys. "Keep that for your Brenda Carberry-Pirbrights. Yes, I know all about it, Lancelot Don Juan Henry the Eighth Mulliner! I saw you with her just now. I hear that you and she are inseparable. Bernard Worple says you said you were going to marry her."

"You mustn't believe everything a neo-Vorticist sculptor tells you," quavered Lancelot.

"I'll bet you're going back to dinner there to-night," said Gladys.

She had spoken at a venture, basing the charge purely on a possessive cock of the head which she had noticed in Brenda Carberry-Pirbright at their recent encounter. There, she had said to herself at the time, had gone a girl who was about to invite—or had just invited—Lancelot Mulliner to dine quietly and take her to the pictures afterwards. But the shot went home. Lancelot hung his head.

"There was some talk of it," he admitted.

"Ah!" exclaimed Gladys.

Lancelot's eyes were haggard.

"I don't want to go," he pleaded. "Honestly I don't. But Webster insists."

"Webster!"

"Yes, Webster. If I attempt to evade the appointment, he will sit in front of me and look at me."

"Tchah!"

"Well, he will. Ask him for yourself."

Gladys tapped her foot six times in rapid succession on the carpet, bringing the total to three thousand, one hundred and forty-eight. Her manner had changed and was now dangerously calm.

"Lancelot Mulliner," she said, "you have your choice. Me, on the one hand, Brenda Carberry-Pirbright on the other. I offer you a home where you will be able to smoke in bed, spill the ashes on the floor, wear pyjamas and carpet-slippers all day and shave only on Sunday mornings. From her, what have you to hope? A house in South Kensington—possibly the Brompton Road— probably with her mother living with you. A life that will be one long round of stiff collars and tight shoes, of morning-coats and top hats."

Lancelot quivered, but she went on remorselessly.

"You will be at home on alternate Thursdays, and will be expected to hand the cucumber sandwiches. Every day you will air the dog, till you become a confirmed dog-airer. You will dine out in Bayswater and go for the summer to Bournemouth or Dinard. Choose well, Lancelot Mulliner! I will leave you to think it over. But one last word. If by seven-thirty on the dot you have not presented yourself at 6A, Garbridge Mews ready to take me out to dinner at the Ham and Beef, I shall know what to think and shall act accordingly."

And brushing the cigarette ashes from her chin, the girl strode haughtily from the room.

"Gladys!" cried Lancelot.

But she had gone.

For some minutes Lancelot Mulliner remained where he was, stunned. Then, insistently, there came to him the recollection that he had not had that drink. He rushed to the cupboard and produced the bottle. He uncorked it, and was pouring out a lavish stream, when a movement on the floor below him attracted his attention.

Webster was standing there, looking up at him. And in his eyes was that familiar expression of quiet rebuke.

"Scarcely what I have been accustomed to at the Deanery," he seemed to be saying.

Lancelot stood paralysed. The feeling of being bound hand and foot, of being caught in a snare from which there was no escape, had become more poignant than ever. The bottle fell from his nerveless fingers and rolled across the floor, spilling its contents in an amber river, but he was too heavy in spirit to notice it. With a gesture such as Job might have made on discovering a new boil, he crossed to the window and stood looking moodily out.

Then, turning with a sigh, he looked at Webster again—and, looking, stood spellbound.

The spectacle which he beheld was of a kind to stun a stronger man than Lancelot Mulliner. At first, he shrank from believing his eyes. Then, slowly, came the realization that what he saw was no mere figment of a disordered imagination. This unbelievable thing was actually happening.

Webster sat crouched upon the floor beside the widening pool of whisky. But it was not horror and disgust that had caused him to crouch. He was crouched because, crouching, he could get nearer to the stuff and obtain crisper action. His tongue was moving in and out like a piston.

And then abruptly, for one fleeting instant, he stopped lapping and glanced up at Lancelot, and across his face there flitted a quick smile—so genial, so intimate, so full of jovial camaraderie, that the young man found himself automatically smiling back, and not only smiling but winking. And in answer to that wink Webster winked, too—a wholehearted, roguish wink that said as plainly as if he had spoken the words:

"How long has this been going on?"

Then with a slight hiccough he turned back to the task of getting his quick before it soaked into the floor.

Into the murky soul of Lancelot Mulliner there poured a sudden flood of sunshine. It was as if a great burden had been lifted from his shoulders. The intolerable obsession of the last two weeks had ceased to oppress him, and he felt a free man. At the eleventh hour the reprieve had come. Webster, that seeming pillar of austere virtue, was one of the boys, after all. Never again would Lancelot quail beneath his eye. He had the goods on him.

Webster, like the stag at eve, had now drunk his fill. He had left the pool of alcohol and was walking round in slow, meditative circles. From time to time he mewed tentatively, as if he were trying to say "British Constitution." His failure to articulate the syllables appeared to tickle him, for at the end of each attempt he would utter a slow, amused chuckle. It was at about this moment that he suddenly broke into a rhythmic dance, not unlike the old Saraband.

It was an interesting spectacle, and at any other time Lancelot would have watched it raptly. But now he was busy at his desk, writing a brief note to Mrs. Carberry-Pirbright, the burden of which was that if she thought he was coming within a mile of her foul house that night or any other night she had vastly underrated the dodging powers of Lancelot Mulliner.

And what of Webster? The Demon Rum now had him in an iron grip. A lifetime of abstinence had rendered him a ready victim to the fatal fluid. He had now reached the stage when geniality gives way to belligerence. The rather foolish smile had gone from his face, and in its stead there lowered a fighting frown. For a few moments he stood on his hind legs, looking about him for a suitable adversary: then, losing all vestiges of self-control, he ran five times round the room at a high rate of speed and, falling foul of a small foot-stool, attacked it with the utmost ferocity, sparing neither tooth nor claw.

But Lancelot did not see him. Lancelot was not there. Lancelot was out in Bott Street, hailing a cab.

"6A, Garbridge Mews, Fulham," said Lancelot to the driver.

# Permissions Acknowledgments

Honoré de Balzac, "The Afflictions of an English Cat," translated by Carl Van Vechten, from *Lords of the Housetops: Thirteen Cat Tales* compiled by Carl Van Vechten (New York: Alfred A. Knopf, 1930). Reprinted with the permission of the Van Vechten Trust.

Italo Calvino, "Autumn: The Garden of Stubborn Cats" from *Marcovaldo,* translated by William Weaver. Copyright © 1963 by Giulio Einuadi editore s.p.a. Torino. English translation copyright © 1983 by Harcourt Brace Jovanovich, Inc. and Martin Secker & Warburg Ltd. Reprinted with the permission of Harcourt, Inc. and The Wylie Agency, Inc.

Karel Čapek, "The Immortal Cat" from *If I Had a Dog and a Cat,* translated by M. & R. Weatherall. Copyright 1940. Reprinted with the permission of the estate of Maria and Robert Weatherall.

Angela Carter, "Puss-in-Boots" from *The Bloody Chamber and Other Adult Tales* (New York: HarperCollins Publishers, 1979). Copyright © 1979 by Angela Carter. Reprinted with the permission of the estate of the author c/o Rodgers, Coleridge & White, 20 Powis Mews, London W11 1JN.

Miguel de Cervantes Saavedra, excerpt from *The Adventures of Don Quixote,* translated by J. M. Cohen. Translation copyright 1950 by J. M. Cohen. Reprinted with the permission of Penguin Books, Ltd.

Eleanor Clark, "Piazza Vittorio" from *Rome and a Villa.* Copyright 1952 by Eleanor Clark. Reprinted with the permission of the William Morris Agency, Inc. on behalf of the author.